THE FIREBRANDS

THE FIREBRANDS

THE NORTHWEST UPRISING: BOOK THREE

NADYA SIAPIN

The Firebrands/Nadya Siapin – 1st Edition

The Travelling Storyteller Press

Cover art by MIBLArt https://miblart.com

Maps by @Saumyasvision/Inkarnate

To the women freedom fighters of the world

CONTENTS

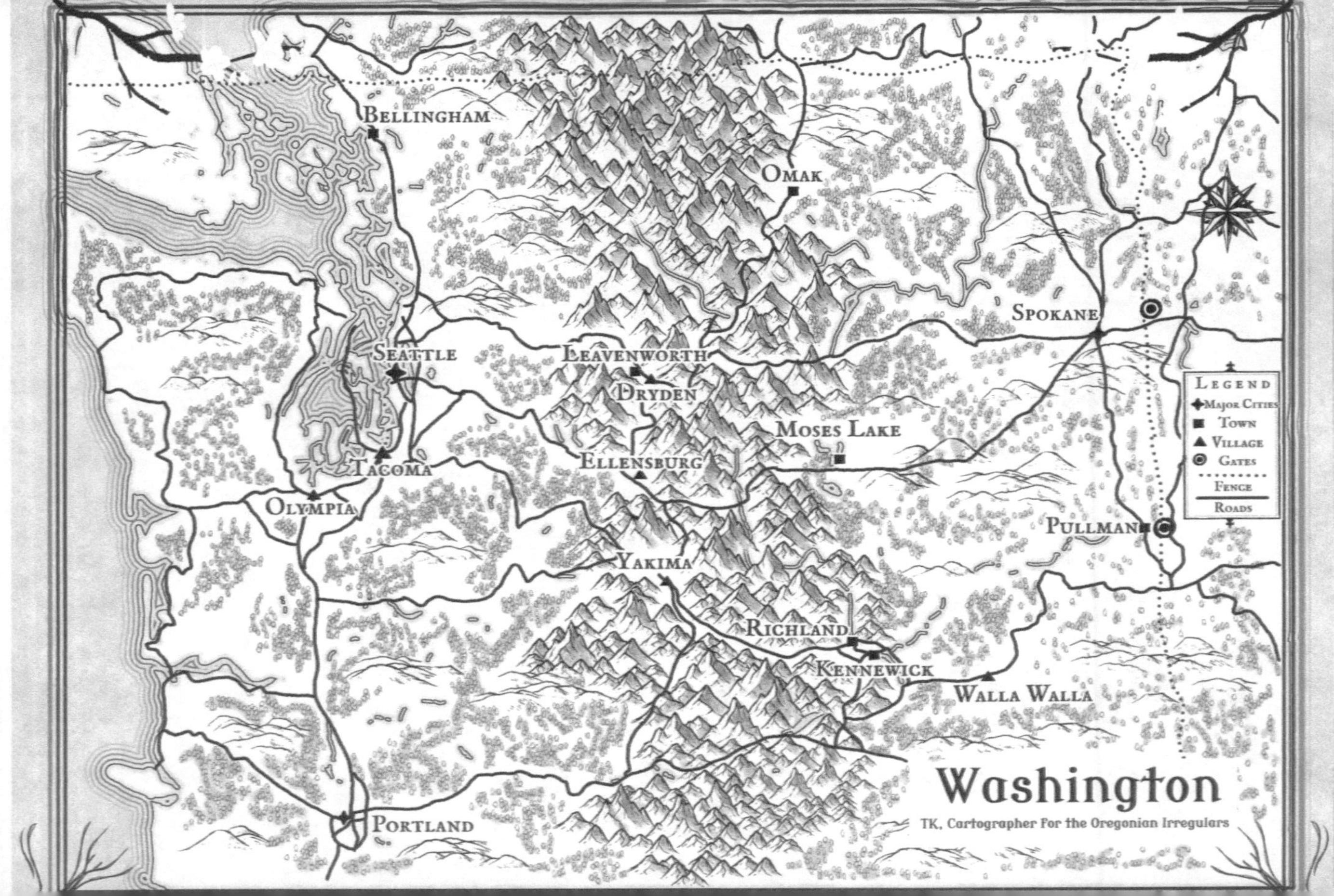

BELLINGHAM
OMAK
SPOKANE
SEATTLE
LEAVENWORTH
DRYDEN
MOSES LAKE
ELLENSBURG
TACOMA
OLYMPIA
PULLMAN
YAKIMA
RICHLAND
KENNEWICK
WALLA WALLA
PORTLAND
LEGEND
Major Cities
Town
Village
Gates
Fence
Roads
Washington
TK, Cartographer For the Oregonian Irregulars

California
TK, Cartographer of the Oregonian Irregulars
LEGEND
Major Cities
City
Gates
Camps
Fence
Roads
NEVADA
Salt Lake
Elko
Winnemucca
Redding
Reno
Cedar City
St. George
Las Vegas
Sacramento
Bridgeport
San Francisco
San Jose
Fresno
Bakersfield
Santa Barbara
Los Angeles
Anaheim
Long Beach
San Diego
Death Valley National Park
Sierra Nevada
Cascade Mountains

PROLOGUE - THE PRESENT

Hope Sanders, the newly revealed leader of the rebellion, paced slowly across the stage. Lights burst into life around the stadium, flooding it with light as the sun sank lower on the horizon, coloring the air golden.

Hope's right hand twitched slightly while she thought about Tom Carrington's odd request: Tell the whole truth.

It hadn't even been twenty years since the end of the war. Was it too soon? Looking over the masses of people barely illuminated by flashing cameras, she realized she didn't care anymore.

Tom was right.

It was time.

In the front row, her boys sat with two of her best friends. Gabriel slumped over in his chair, hand covering his eyes, while Michael quivered like a bowstring drawn too tightly until Tom grasped his knee, leaning over to whisper in his ear.

She so badly wanted to jump down there and beg their forgiveness, but she knew if she stopped now, she'd never be able to start again.

"Once Oregon was free, it didn't take a genius to figure out we had to help the other states. It was the right thing to do, and if we didn't, Steve had a staging ground to attempt to invade us again." Hope spoke absently, one hand caressing the pistol butt at her thigh. The move was from long habit. It was plain to the audience that she had no idea she was even doing it. "I had family in both states, provided my sister, Grace, still operated in Washington like Peter said. No matter how much I wanted, I couldn't be in both places at once.

"We now had a full army, thousands of men and women who'd joined the fight and passed basic training. I split our forces, sending half north to Washington under Seahorse's command. The rest went south with me, into California."

This simple summation never touched on the nights spent agonizing over seeing her sister while simultaneously never wanting to be seen by her.

The whispers and hissed questions from backstage barely registered and were immediately dismissed. This talk was only intended to be about Oregon. To this day, knowledge that she was both Captain and Ghost had never been common knowledge.

She relaxed infinitesimally when a louder voice shushed the questioners. She would not be interrupted.

Staring blindly as she paced, she slid back into the past. "Los Angeles was the worst of it. I don't..." Hope rubbed a hand over her mouth, pausing with her back to the crowd. "We've managed to tell them about Noah," she mumbled, the words barely caught by the mic at her collar. "How much worse could this be?"

They listened with bated breath to her inner debate.

"Tell the truth. Dammit, Tom. It's not as easy as it sounds." Sighing heavily, she turned smoothly on one heel. "So much happened so quickly. Hell, we never even knew how much help we'd had until we spread out."

CHAPTER 1

Wiretap on Marigold Hotel room #113. Booked under the name James Smith – December 10, 2060 at 10pm

Man 1: Breaking news, it's always 'Breaking News.' I don't need to hear anymore breaking news! That fucking bitch blocked us again! I want out.

Man 2: Pull yourself together, you pussy. You got into this to hide your affairs from the public, Bryce. So you better figure out a way to make it happen!

Northern California – Captain

A warm wind blew through my hair, sending my battle braids dancing over my shoulders. Beneath me, my pickup bumped over a road badly torn by tank treads. Even here, in the dry hills of northern California, we found plenty of evidence of Steve.

The scouts ranged well in advance of the convoy, racing over the hills on dirt bikes. Periodically, one would check in. More rarely, one would return requesting help dealing with a patrol.

The Irregulars' ranks had swelled to such an extent that we badly needed real-world experience for most of them. A quick word would send a group of veterans and rookies off to get the rookies blooded.

It was nice, having all of Steve's leftover toys and gas.

What did they call those? The spoils of war.

I'd rather have the people I'd lost, instead.

After the battle on the beaches where we'd finally won Oregon, we'd gone to ground to lick our wounds for months. The fight was won, but at a heavy cost. Over half my previous forces were dead or maimed beyond fighting again.

Those badly injured remained in Oregon, which I'd left under Amana's stewardship, to begin rebuilding and healing. I missed having Triskele's leadership skills here, but her wife, Kestrel, insisted she stay behind.

Now, she trained more troops with Goliath, who'd lost his left leg, guarded the borders, and prepared to take in more refugees.

I ran a finger over the jagged scar running over my left collarbone, disappearing under my shirt. Steve had gone for my heart and the knife bounced up, barely missing my throat.

So many close calls.

Most called it a miracle I still lived. I didn't know what to call it.

Disappointment?

Maybe.

Well, except for my sons. I'd already missed their first steps and first words. I didn't want to miss more of their young lives. They—and the other children—were the reason most of us fought on.

The last time I'd seen my babies, shortly before we left the greening Willamette Valley, everyone from Home had finally been brought down to the Valley. My kids hadn't recognized me, crying at the sight of this scarred stranger.

Olivia swept one up, Sam took the other, and I realized I couldn't tell my twins apart. Their hair was white-blond, as mine had been at their age, but their eyes were darker, more their father's color.

Olivia had given me a tortured look, but I'd shaken my head. It was better this way. This way, they couldn't miss me.

The pickup bounced, bringing me back to the present. The two rookies behind me flopped around in the bed, thrown off by the rough roads.

Sage—a cautious young woman who still had stars in her eyes—righted herself first. Moon Moon, barely competent enough to join the fighters, took longer. Absolutely no coordination to that one. I shook my head.

Anansi reached out his window, rapping on the cab. "We need gas," he shouted.

He'd taken over as Dereva's navigator after Hightide's death on the beaches. She was the only one we'd taken back to the Meadow next to the Lair. We'd buried her beside her beloved, Fox.

I hoped someone would do the same for me, if I fell far from home.

Since then, Anansi had stepped up to be his sister's navigator. Having him in the passenger's seat brought Dereva some comfort. It lightened my heart, seeing his kinky hair flying wildly in the wind. Sometimes, he pulled it back into a ponytail, like his sister, but he flat refused to cut it whenever some interfering idiot suggested it.

I held up a clenched fist as my pickup slowed to a stop on the side of the broken road. If we needed gas, everyone would. The tanker trucks made their way down, filling each vehicle as they passed.

We'd need to find Steve's gas stores down here soon, even with the modifications I'd made to the engines.

"I like seeing these back roads," Anansi said, sticking his head out the window. "I've never seen anything except the 99 or the I-5. This is pretty. And cool."

"Yes," I said dryly. "A close-up view of every inch of the ass end of California has also been my dream."

"Hey!" But he laughed. "The ass end of California is LA, not this gorgeousness."

I tipped my head, indicating the point, though the sequoias further north were my favorites. "What's your estimate?" I asked Dereva.

My driver didn't hesitate. "At our current rate, and if the number of patrols remain the same, Sacramento should be visible later tomorrow."

I looked south, as if glaring would make it happen sooner. "Aanisah!"

She appeared as if from thin air. The rifle over her shoulder, random weaponry, and belt pouches over fatigues, moccasins, and an earth-toned t-shirt were as close as we got to a uniform. The piece of clothing that set her apart was the hijab completely covering her hair.

"*Assalamu Alaikum,* Captain!" She threw me a salute.

Sighing, I looked heavenward. I hated those damn salutes. Since patience did not magically appear, I figured I'd get on with it. "*Wa Alaikum Assalam,* Aanisah. Take the saboteurs and soften the countryside, would you?"

Her eyes lit up. "Captain! Yes, Captain! *Alhamdulillah!*"

After being freed in the battle at the beach, Aanisah had found several other Muslim women and formed her own grouping within the Irregulars: the saboteurs.

They'd examine an area, find its weakness, then exploit it. Though we hadn't known it at the time, we had them to thank for several seasons of misplaced items, forgotten caches, and maps being mis-marked. Aanisah's second-in-command, Bakht, had been responsible for Steve's beach location that fateful day. I still don't know how she forged new markings on a map, but she did it.

What a fucking legend.

Aanisah blew a series of blasts on her whistle, then knelt at the side of the road. While the tanker truck finished its job, she redistributed her pack, placing some items into pockets, others into belt pouches. I didn't recognize everything, but after being around Sparrow for so long, I could recognize the basic components of a bomb.

Growing up, I never would've guessed so many women would have such an ability to make shit go boom. Now, they were organizing themselves. All I had to do was point them at a target.

Yay, me.

"Don't do anything I'd do," I said as they gathered off the side of the road. "I want you all back in one piece."

They all threw me loose salutes, damn them.

"We won't," they chorused.

"Liars."

"*Bismillah*!" They doubled up on dirt bikes, taking off cross country, leaving us trapped on the roads.

Lucky.

***

Fresno, CA – Faith

Faith examined her hair in the mirror, flipping through sections to make sure she hadn't missed any spots. Satisfied her ash-blonde hair was thoroughly coated in the walnut dye, she carefully ran her fingertips over each eyebrow, darkening those as well.

Biting her lip, she breathed through the panic that welled up every time she dyed her hair. When the Occupation first hit, girls disappeared at a rapid rate. Her mother, Abigail, didn't hesitate. Taking one look at the black-haired, black-eyed soldiers in the streets, she seized her daughter's arm, hauling her into the bathroom.

Faith protested her mother's rough treatment as she was shoved onto the toilet seat and her hair was dyed for the first time.

"To them, you're exotic," Abigail had said, pulling Faith's hair in her haste, making the young woman yelp. "But brown hair might be just enough to help you blend in."

And she had.

For the last several years, Faith dyed her hair twice a month and worked in the munitions factory, slowly working her way up. Finally, she'd been promoted to the offices, overseeing orders and meeting demand with adequate supply.

Leaning closer to the mirror, Faith carefully applied the homemade dye to her eyelashes. Sitting on the toilet seat, she drummed her fingers on her leg as she waited for the dye to set before beginning the onerous process of rinsing her hair.

Glancing out the window, she hissed. The sun was lower than she'd thought. Hurrying now, she hopped through the apartment, tying her shoelaces at the same time.

"Faith!" her father, Dan, called from the kitchen. "Dinner's almost ready!"

"I can't, I—shit!" Pausing, Faith re-tied her laces. She shouldn't skip a meal, food was scarce enough, but the thought of wheat mash with slivers of unidentified meat... Her stomach churned. "I'm meeting up with Lucas."

"Oooh, Lucas!" squealed Samantha from the living room. From one of the three families crammed into the tiny apartment, Samantha continually nosed into Faith's business, hinting that she'd be great at office work—or other types of work, wink, wink—and why wouldn't Faith recommend her? "Give loverboy a kiss from me! You're *so* lucky to have found a handsome man like that in this world. And at your age, too!"

Faith laughed, resisting the urge to rub her hands together. "I know." Patting her cheeks, she examined herself in the hall mirror. "Bathing in the tears of those I've disappointed has done *so* much to keep me looking younger than forty-six. But if you really want to feel younger, you've got to become a cougar."

Samantha opened her mouth, then frowned. "Wait. What? I thought you were twenty-nine?"

"And you're twenty-one going on idiot." Faith kissed her dad on the cheek. "Don't wait up for me!"

Her dad returned her kiss, forehead furrowed with worry. "Be careful," he murmured into her ear.

Waving, she sailed out the door. Once the door closed behind her, she slumped against it, head hanging. "This is ridiculous," she muttered.

"What's ridiculous?" asked a male voice behind her. Lucas.

She smiled. Turning slowly, she leaned her shoulder against the wall, copying the tall young man in front of her. "Samantha."

He grimaced. "Is she home?" Faith nodded. Grabbing her hand, he hauled her down the corridor, almost at a run. "Let's not wait around to say hi."

Giggling, she twined their fingers together. They ran past old Mrs. Jones, who had to be eighty if she was a day. "Have fun, dears!" She waved. "Practice safe sex!"

"We will," they called.

Once in the basement, Faith collapsed against Lucas, still giggling. "She's said that every time she's seen us for the last five years. Do you think she knows how to say anything else?"

"If she does, I've never heard her." Lucas held her tightly, his arms strong around her back, lips pressed to her hair. They waited, the darkness broken by the filthy, tiny windows set at ground level.

Lifting her head from Lucas's shoulder, Faith listened carefully. No giggles, no gasps, or moans. "I think we're alone," she finally said. "You know, I almost want to tell Mrs. Jones the truth, just to see her reaction."

Lucas led her deeper into the basement. "What? That we're faking it? She'd probably still encourage safe sex. Why? Do you think Samantha suspects anything?"

Faith stepped carefully over broken metal furniture. "No. But it's hard to tell. From all appearances, she's just so...dumb. Do you know what tonight's meeting is about?" she asked, changing the subject.

Lucas peered around, one final check. "Wait."

Gently, he shifted some furniture just enough to reveal a hole in the wall. After a last, few breaths of clean air and a short scramble, they stood inside the sewer system, thick sludge just inches from their feet. Nearly tiptoeing, they followed the sewer away from the building.

At the first corner, Faith relaxed. They knew from experience they were out of earshot of the guards set around their apartment complex. While residents were assigned apartments, as long as they didn't try to leave outside of curfew, they had the run of the building.

Standing so close his chest brushed her breasts, he whispered, "Meeting point E. Carter said they've had news from Sacramento. Something about the Ghost Captain."

Faith gasped. Some thought the rumors of the Ghost were just that, rumors, but Faith had seen messages from the north talking about the Ghost Captain. She knew this man was real and causing trouble to the North Koreans.

"He wouldn't tell me what," Lucas continued, "but it sounds like he's keeping them occupied up there."

"Well." Faith leaned back to see Lucas's face better in the dim light. "The more they look at him and his group, the less they notice us."

The green flecks in his hazel eyes glowed when a stray ray of light caught them. Her breath stopped and didn't start again until he took her hand and kept walking.

He led them unerringly through the sewer. They'd both memorized the systems years ago, but Faith preferred to let him lead. This way, he found any stray mounds of shit before she stepped in them.

They surfaced behind an old dumpster, a relic from the days when they had working vehicles, dump trucks, and freedom.

A stench hit Faith's nose and she covered it with her sleeve. "Is it just me, or has it gotten more aromatic around here?"

Lucas wiped his eyes. "I can't believe I'm saying this, but I think I preferred the sewer...Oh, shit!" He stumbled away from a pile of garbage.

"What? What?" Faith scrambled out of the manhole to his side. She gagged, accidentally kicking a pile of trash as she lurched away. A...something...person...had been here for a while.

Carefully, they made their way back, standing on either side of the desiccated body. "Do we know them?" Faith whispered.

"I can't even make out features, much less that." Unable to take the proximity any longer, Lucas walked away, breathing deeply of the slightly fresher air.

Faith quickly followed. She'd seen plenty of people die, but she'd never been quite so close, and not to one dead for as long as this. "Shit."

Finally remembering the manhole, he levered the cover back on it. Wouldn't do to have the NKs find one of their preferred exits. "Yeah. Shit. Come on. I'm in the mood to not be here anymore."

Hurrying deeper into the alley, Faith couldn't help looking over her shoulder frequently, as if the NKs would suddenly spring out of the shadows.

Which wasn't too crazy. There'd been a growing number of NKs and Corpsmen on the streets over the last several months.

Lucas rapped on a nondescript door deep in the shadows. A small piece of metal slid back. "Verification?" a husky male voice asked.

"Tango zero one kilo three India November."

The door opened. "Get in here. The NKs are busy tonight."

Faith smiled at the slender man holding the door. Barely an inch taller than her, he had dark brown hair and intelligent brown eyes filled with humor. "Jon. Who's left?"

"You're the last. We have a guest," he added. "Carter will fill you in," he said before she could ask questions.

Jon led the way through the derelict building, one of several they used, weaving around fallen walls and downed beams. Stars were visible through the broken roof, and Faith marveled that the walls stood at all.

At its center, an old panic room squatted, solid enough to block light and hide them from a cursory search.

Eleven other people already occupied the small room. Malva, an older woman, tapped her fingers restlessly, the fine lines around her eyes made deeper by the candlelight. Carter stood, still as a statue, at the far end of the room, his salt and pepper hair shining in the candlelight, while Jon shut the door, using his foot to keep it closed.

In the corner, a new man sat, fidgeting and jumping at the slightest sounds. When Faith and Lucas entered, he shot to his feet, looking wildly around the room.

Even with the warning of a new face at the meeting, Lucas stepped between Faith and the stranger. "There's a body in the alley."

Carter nodded grimly. "And it has to stay there, I'm afraid. Anything else would be suspicious. Now," he rubbed his hands together briskly, "let's get started."

"Hear ye, hear ye," Malva said, grinning wickedly. "This meeting of the North Fresno Chapter of the Resistance will begin."

"What is this news?" Abel asked. A younger man, he had only recently joined. He was barely old enough to know when to keep his mouth shut, Faith figured. She *did* have to give him credit for inventing a new way to make munitions look good while failing on impact.

"I heard it involved the Ghost?" Faith raised her eyebrows, peering over Lucas's shoulder.

"Not just yet," Carter said. "What's the news from the offices, Faith?"

Faith narrowed her eyes but answered readily enough. "The latest shipment due for Sacramento is three times the usual size. There hasn't been any communication out of Oregon in six months. The last we heard from Washington was five months ago. New troop ships landed at San Francisco, but rumors have it those troops aren't new to our shores. Inquiries into where those men are from are...discouraged."

"Excellent. Especially about Sacramento."

"Why?"

"What about Sheba?" Carter turned to an older man in the room, Gideon.

Gideon frowned at him, rubbing gray/blond stubble on his chin. It matched the thinning hair on his head. Carter's gaze remained firm, unwavering. Sighing, Gideon gave in. "She's passed through Oakhurst. With no setbacks, she should have them into the mountains within the next month."

Sheba, an experienced backpacker before the Occupation, took refugees out through her old stomping grounds, Yosemite National Park. One, sometimes two groups per summer, then she'd return to hiding in Fresno for the winter.

Faith still remembered stealing the stamp necessary to forge the documents that said her best friend had died. The first mission she'd ever worked on with Lucas.

"She'll be fine," Gideon continued, winking at Faith. "She's at her best the further she is from civilization."

"Enough!" Malva slammed her hand against the wall. Everyone jumped, no one higher than the stranger. "Carter! You've called us here for a reason, and I'm dying to hear it. If I don't in the next three minutes, I'm taking you down with me."

Carter nodded, the strands of gray in his black hair shining in the candlelight. "Friends, this is Nielsen," he gestured to the stranger, "from the Central Sacramento Chapter. It's been confirmed, the NKs have reported disappearing patrols and sighting a large convoy of vehicles that isn't theirs. We can only come to one conclusion."

He spread his arms. "The Ghost is in California!"

***

Pasadena, CA – Mercy

Mercy followed her Master down the hallway, head bent, eyes focused on her Master's heels. She stayed three paces behind and to his left, as was written in the Law. Her Master spoke casually with Master Leister, hands folded behind his back.

"The prophet Elias said that it is better to have a man's enmity than a woman's friendship," he lectured. "Their strict purpose is to produce the next generation of man, and to act as their husband's helpmate. It is ordained. But that also means that you are responsible for how you treat the women God has granted you.

"You are responsible for teaching women their places in your life. If you have strife, it is because you are not firm enough. If you wish to receive more, you must show God that you are obedient to His will. And teach them accordingly."

Fancy way to tell him to get his shit together, Mercy mused.

Master Leister nodded, hanging onto her Master's every word. He'd just acquired two new bondmaids, captured in a recent raid, and they were rebellious. She cataloged the herbs she had on hand to treat wounds, because as sure as her Master walked ahead of her, she'd see those women in her infirmary soon.

Walking languidly ahead of the Masters, the Mistresses kept an eye on their rambunctious children, their lovely gowns sweeping the floor. Each Mistress was accompanied by an older woman who nannied the children. Their behavior was the responsibility of both women, but only the nanny would be beaten for imagined crimes.

Such as the crime of dressing in a way that didn't please their Master. Mercy smoothed her hands over her plain, button-down men's shirt, ensuring it was tucked into her brown cotton skirt. This was the uniform of the bondmaid, as well as a kerchief to cover their hair.

The Mistresses wore...whatever pleased their husband. Her Master's wife wore blue today, to complement his eyes.

Wise decision, to stay on his good side.

Her eldest child, a boy, maybe six or seven years old—Mercy had long since lost track of how long it'd been since the airports were destroyed by suicide pilots, noting time only by the growth of the children—skipped ahead of the others. Little Samuel, the first baby she'd ever delivered.

Without moving her head, Mercy's eyes slid to her right, where Master Leister's current favorite, a bondmaid named Molly, struggled to keep pace, hampered by her large belly. Molly bent slightly, mouth open in a silent gasp, but she never slackened her pace.

Unless Mercy seriously miscalculated, she would deliver another baby soon.

But the Feast of the Tabernacles was tonight, and all were commanded to attend.

Entering the hall, formerly a huge conference room in a hotel, the Mistresses took their children to the women's tables while the Masters headed to the front, taking their seats on a raised dais.

The bondmaids lined up against the closest wall, leaving the far side for the kitchen slaves. All around, more tables were packed with men. These were the Warriors of Light—Mercy wanted to roll her eyes every time their title was mentioned—and the Sons of Judea, those either too young or too inexperienced to join the Warriors.

The Warriors of Light were the military the ten Masters had built to protect their compound and their interests, namely, the natural spring this hotel had once been famous for.

Folding her hands in front of her, head still bent, Mercy stood at the head of the line of her Master's bondmaids. She was the favorite, not because of his desire for her, but because of her unique skills.

Her Master raised his hands and the hall fell silent.

"Today is the Feast of the Tabernacles," he intoned, "in this sacred Kingdom Come to Earth. We are the fortunate ones who feel God's love, basking in the joy and plenty He has granted us. Outside these walls, the sinners face tribulations to cleanse them of their evil, perverted ways.

"But here, we follow God's Law. Women are given women's roles, men are men, as God intended. And I, your Shepherd, the pastor God has sent to show you the way to live, am here to guide you with God's own wisdom and love..."

Mercy tuned him out. You didn't have to read the Bible to know how much bullshit that man spewed.

She barely contained a snort of contempt. The young woman at her side, Natalie, shivered, her chains rattling softly. Captured in the same raid that had given Master Leister his two newest bondmaids, Natalie had been the prize, the youngest of the lot.

The girl was maybe seventeen, and in the month since her capture, she'd seen enough to be terrified but not enough to remain unseen. Perhaps she'd never manage invisibility, poor thing, not with her fine features and beauty.

"Hold still," Mercy whispered from the corner of her mouth. "Do not move, do *not* disturb the blessing. It's better for everyone that way."

A few curls of strawberry blonde hair escaped the child's bandana, and Mercy shifted slightly. As soon as their Master's blessing closed, she quickly tucked the strands back in.

"Haven't they told you to never let your hair show?" she murmured. "There are over twenty rules dictating how women must dress and behave. Step outside of those, and they'll use it as an excuse to hurt you worse."

If only she had five minutes alone with that kid… The corners of Mercy's mouth turned down, grief and anger warring within her.

Useless! Telling the girl all these stupid rules the Masters had made was only teaching Natalie to be a better victim, just like her. She'd been here too long, but there were so many who needed her…

A rustle at the far end of the bondmaid's line caught her attention. A full-figured woman just younger than Mercy herself approached the podium set directly opposite the Masters' dais. Susannah, one of Master Simpson's bondmaids, folded her hands in front of her, straightened her shoulders, and opened her mouth and sang.

Mercy closed her eyes, the line of her lips relaxing for the first time that day.

Susannah was gifted, without a doubt. Her rich, pure voice filled the hall, spiraling up on the wings of a hymn. The words didn't matter, a bunch of shit glorifying the Masters, but the tune... Oh, the music of it.

The quiet clatter of cutlery disappeared under the soaring melody, which then plummeted to depths that made her believe that maybe, just maybe, Hell held more mercy than Earth.

She'd rarely spoken to Susannah in all the years they'd been here, usually only when Susannah was pregnant and in the immediate aftermath. More pregnancies ended in miscarriage than birth in the Masters' compound, but either way, the women needed care.

When the song drew to a close, Mercy opened her eyes. Her Master rose to his feet, raising his hands. "Susannah's gifts were surely sent to us from God." Murmurs of assent ran through the room. Mercy's mouth twisted briefly, until she schooled her features. "We have long discussed the gifts of the Lord and how they came to be distributed, but tonight, let us hear from one such gifted, also called to serve us. Mercy, my bondmaid, speak. Tell us your thoughts on gifts and their distribution."

Singled out like this, the other bondmaids drew back slightly. Mercy stepped forward, kneeling and bowing her head. How to answer this? It was punishment, in a way. Master Hermann had captured an actual nurse two months ago. He didn't have access to the supplies Mercy had in her room and infirmary, but Rhia, the newest enslaved woman, likely had knowledge and skills Mercy didn't.

Her Master had been furious, calling her to his bed for the first time in ages. He'd pleased himself by humiliating her in other ways over the last while, preferring younger women and girls for his bed, but now...

Mercy was no longer unique. She didn't have the sole trade on this particular set of skills anymore, so now, she either performed well, or she died horribly.

"My Master." She bowed lower, sweating lightly under her shirt. Even when she straightened, she never met his eyes. To do so was dangerous. "There are many gifts of the spirit that any who are truly saved exhibit. Kindness, goodness, humility, and so many more. These gifts, anyone may attain."

She paused, licking dry lips. "Gifts such as Susannah shows are not immediately visible. They must be carefully nurtured through training and practice. Gifts such as hers are skills, like healing, carpentry, cooking, growing food, sewing, and weaving. Many people have them to a lesser degree, which makes a gifted one a blessing but not exceptional."

Oh, she wanted to hit herself for saying Susannah's singing was anything other than a joy, but she couldn't end it here. No, she had to bring it around to Master's favorite topic...

"There are other gifts that are truly from God and no amount of training may bestow them." Her voice remained steady and even. "The gift of leadership, or understanding God's Word, being a good shepherd to a flock of willful sheep..." Had she made it obvious enough? "Those blessed with such gifts are far beyond the puny skills and blessings that are occasionally shown to the multitudes.

"As to their distribution, gifts are scattered far and wide. It's up to us to nurture them or not. If we do not, we sin greatly before God for not caring for what He has given us. But those blessed with gifts that cannot be taught...they are rare, and I believe they are given only to those whom God has called his own."

Her Master smiled. "Ah! See, even someone as lowly as a bondmaid is occasionally given a small amount of wisdom."

Her lips tightened. She'd answered well and bought herself a bit more time. In his eyes, her answer set her above Rhia, the nurse, and he could still boast about having a uniquely skilled slave.

Behind her, Molly groaned. Water splashed on the floor. No, not water. Amniotic fluid.

Her Master's mouth tightened at the interruption. Mercy bowed deeply. "My Master! Forgive her, the child is upon her. She already loses control of herself."

Molly bowed awkwardly. "Forgive me." Her bow turned into a curl of pain around her rippling belly, and she moaned.

He nodded, turning away, and waving his hand for their dismissal.

"Ah, Master Kozlov." The man who stood and bowed to her Master from the far end of the table on the dais had graying hair and round, pleasant features. *Master Hermann will look like a jolly grandfather in about five years*, Mercy thought dispassionately. "Perhaps my bondmaid, Rhia, will be of some use to the healer. Rhia is, after all, a nurse."

Her Master's mouth tightened, but he nodded. *Can't lose face, can't look like he doesn't have everything.* Rising, Mercy backed towards the door, collecting Molly along the way. Rhia made her way over, the leg irons around her ankles jingling as she walked.

"We wish to hear good news, bondmaids," her Master said. "See to it."

Her lips compressed into a hard line, but Mercy bowed low once more. Oh, yes. Her Master was losing his patience with her. No longer unique, barely maintaining her position in his eyes.

And she'd never borne him a child, the ultimate sin in his eyes.

Mercy didn't turn around until they were through the door, taking one of Molly's arms to help her along. Rhia took the other one.

"Where are we going?"

"My room," Mercy replied.

Two Sons of Judea left the tables, following them out. In the courtyard, the spring water welled continually, pouring into wooden trenches that carted the water away. Some went to the bath house across the courtyard. Others carried it to the kitchens. Still more went to the fields.

Away from the trenches, on the east side, a smaller, three-story building rose. At its base, a small garden grew riotously. As they approached, Mercy sniffed. The rosemary needed to be harvested, and the calendula bloomed, also ready for harvest and processing.

At the base of the building, around the side, a small door was set at the bottom of wide, shallow stairs. Carefully, the women maneuvered Molly down the three steps.

"This is your room?" Rhia asked when they entered, her eyes wide.

Shelves lined three walls, full of books on the top, then small jars of dried herbs, tinctures, and salves. At the bottom were her tools. Bowls, mortars, pestles, pots, the complicated system she used to draw out essential oils. Closest to the door, she had extra blankets, sheets to turn into bandages, and three shelves of bandages carefully stored in bags.

Several small bags were tucked at the bottom with everything she might need if she were called to work as a medic during one of the many skirmishes that happened. People knew there was water here, and now, this resource was more precious than gold.

Against the free wall, a series of small windows were set, providing light. She had sinks, a hand pump connected directly to the spring, and a wooden stove. In the center of the room, two large tables stood. One was her work bench, where she chopped, mixed, and cooled. The other was a different type of work bench.

Their guards stayed outside the room, taking up positions with the sharpened wooden stakes they called 'spears.'

She unhooked a thick, knotted rope hanging from her ceiling, then pulled a birthing stool out of the corner. Well, a birthing stool she'd made by cutting up a wooden chair. While Rhia took care of Molly, Mercy lit two lamps, threw more wood on the coals in her stove, and began filling pots with water.

"I can't believe the guards," Rhia whispered when Mercy brought some cool water over. "Why are you still guarded?"

"Oh, they're not for me," Mercy replied.

"What is wrong with this place?"

Mercy snorted. "You mean besides the religious cult, slavery, and forced breeding? Gee, I don't know."

"What's the world like where you're from?" Molly whispered, gripping the rope tightly.

"Not like this. I was in Anaheim, and people die all the time, but from things like lack of water and starvation. Not being murdered by crazy men who gaslight you into thinking you're less than the dirt on their shoe and raped daily." Her voice shook on the last two words. "I've had sex with men to get supplies, sure, but it wasn't...it wasn't this."

Kneeling, Mercy checked Molly's dilation. "Well, you don't have too much to go. Rhia, would you grab us something to eat from that shelf, there?"

Against the far wall, rough bread, fresh and dried fruits, and dried meat occupied one shelf. She made trades with the kitchen, burn cream, extra bandages, and healing services in exchange for off the books food.

What her Master didn't know wouldn't hurt her.

"You live pretty well," Rhia said enviously. "But you called this your room. Where do you sleep?"

"There." Mercy nodded to the corner farthest from the door. A thin pillow and even thinner blanket were folded on the floor.

"Why doesn't anyone ever run away?" Rhia asked. *Why don't you run away,* hung in the air. "Because there's food and water here?"

"It's why they manage to recruit men," Mercy said. "But it's not why with women. You've already mentioned the gaslighting. The Masters prefer young women. Older ones go into labor positions, like in the fields. They don't last long."

Rhia shivered. "I can't decide what's worse, these people, or the crazy preppers we had to deal with at the beginning."

"I don't know about those," Mercy said neutrally. "I was the first captured, and it was barely three months after the airports were bombed."

For just a moment, she felt a strong hand, gentle on her waist, propelling her forward. Jonathan's dark eyes crinkled at the corners when he smiled.

"You've got this," he whispered into her memory.

"In this place," she continued, "you're either God's Wife or a Damned Whore, and heaven help you if you ever cross the invisible line."

Chapter 2

Central California – Captain

Looking west, my scope showed workers being loaded onto buses, finished with their field work for the day. The sun crept towards the horizon, the mountains a jagged black line.

What lay beyond that line?

"You say we're halfway between Sacramento and Fresno?" I asked Dereva.

"Pretty close," the driver replied. "That's Yosemite behind us."

"Yes, that clears it up so much," I said dryly. "It's only a massive park."

She laughed.

The mountainous park loomed at our backs, the crags thrown into stark relief by the lowering sun. The San Joaquin Valley stretched out in front of us, broken only by the ruins of towns and crops. It looked like these days the valley grew wheat and fruit, while cows and sheep grazed the rocky grounds.

"Shrike," I called.

After a while, slow, languid footsteps approached. "You bellowed, oh Captain?"

The former spy wandered over, sipping from a canteen. A wide-brimmed straw hat protected her face, red-framed sunglasses covering her eyes. She'd also found a loose, long-sleeved shirt, looking for all the world like a movie star about to head to the beach. Only the combat boots and gun strapped to her hip gave the lie to the rest of her clothing.

"What's the latest, please?" I leaned against my pickup, pulling a wide-brimmed hat of my own on.

Since leaving Salem, Shrike had taken on the shitty task of consolidating all the information brought in by scouts and saboteurs. She sifted through varying accounts of troop movements, numbers, and outposts to determine the most likely truth.

Working with River and TK, our artist turned mapmaker, they updated maps, giving the rest of us reprobates and high school dropouts an easy visual.

According to our information, the most populous centers were Sacramento, Fresno, and Bakersfield. The smaller outposts scattered over the state were slowly disappearing, marked off when they'd been confirmed as destroyed.

"Steve's dug in around Sacramento," Shrike continued. "They've got a good perimeter. An outer ditch filled with liquid—unconfirmed, but we suspect more oil like they used at the beach—and an inner fence. Outside the ditch, they've cleared the ground for five hundred feet."

I pursed my lips in a soundless whistle. More than twice what they'd done for Portland or Salem. "Do you think these guys have heard of us? Oh, and have you had any word from Aanisah?"

Shrike ignored the first question. "They're having fun. Delivered fifty more gallons of gas last night."

"Good."

"Now, per your request, I've been trying to find out more about LA. As far as California is concerned, it doesn't exist. But you said the soldiers," Dereva and I tensed, and I saw the same sadness I felt echoed in her eyes, "said that according to LA TV, Steve has no presence there."

I nodded, studying the toes of my moccasins. "Sounds like no one goes in, and nothing comes out."

"Well, we'll be able to find that border when we get there. It must be huge. Now," she brushed that aside, "the rumor of the birthing center was true. It took five patrols to get them out, but there were enough fighters to wipe out Steve with surprisingly little effort."

"Chaos?"

She nodded. "He is a bit...fond...of explosives, isn't he?"

Those women were on their way north. Amana and the border guard would welcome them. Once the buses dropped them off, they'd head back. We'd need every single vehicle before this was done.

I studied the vehicles and fighters chilling and stretching. Over half my forces were running around in pairs, causing general havoc, keeping Steve too busy to even think about Oregon. Shrike sent them to various locations, and whenever they saw groups of Steve too large, they sent back for more troops.

It was one of the things I appreciated about working with women. We didn't fuck around, pulling together when necessary.

"If you hear anything about LA, let me know," I said. Shrike inclined her head. "What about locals? Have they also formed some kind of resistance?"

Her eyes flickered, sorting through information stored only in her head. "We haven't had any direct contact, but there are rumors. Seems to be concentrated in the cities. Some of the farm workers have mentioned something very...obliquely before heading back."

"Headed back?" I asked. "Oh, wait. Families are hostages, huh?"

"You know it. Most of what the locals do is bombings, sending things to wrong locations. It's hard to determine what's them and what's an accident. Insurgency stuff."

"I like it. If Steve can't be sure, then these guys might actually be good. Steve's gotten a lot more conservative about wasting bullets over the years, so maybe..." I trailed off, then grinned at a thought. "We just need to get into a city."

Shrike folded her arms, her soft mouth firming. "You're not going into a city," she snapped.

"Of course I'm going in. Why the hell wouldn't I?"

"Because you're the leader of a big, fat army, that's why!"

I held my arms out, not moving my butt off my pickup. "Take a look at me. I'm a Basher. These people don't follow me because I lead from the back. They follow because I appoint decent leaders and let everyone get on with their shit. It's called 'delegation.'"

Her nostrils flared and she narrowed her eyes. "And what are we supposed to do if you die?"

Dereva cracked a laugh. "I'm not sure she knows how," she said to the air.

I snorted. "They'll find someone else to take over. We've got plenty of good people."

"Not like you," she said sharply. I rolled my eyes, but she grabbed my arm. I looked down at her. She hastily let go. "Listen, some of them are good, but they don't have your..." She waved a hand, encompassing all of me. "Whatever the hell this is. I don't know how you do it, but nobody else has this...this...controlled violence and general unflappability. Besides, losing the Ghost is bad for morale."

"Ghost? What...?"

"Oh, it's what they call you here."

Dereva looked up from her snack, a piece of jerky. "That's not bad," she said around a mouthful. "We should have thought of that. It's got pizzazz."

"Fuck off. And I'm still going in," I informed Shrike.

"River!" Shrike called, spotting her wife. "Will you please make your pig-headed Captain see sense?"

"Babe," River gave her wife a kiss, her hands full of tonight's dinner, "no one in the world can do that." Then, she continued on her way, a pair of rabbits in each hand, whistling.

"Hey," Dereva, finished with her snack, pulled my attention back, "scouts have had a good look at the roads higher up. Mostly paved, but they've found some gravel that will support two wheels. Too narrow for four."

"You're telling me the dirt bikes are important?"

"I'm telling you any and every bike is important. Storm's in Yosemite now, checking to see if Steve's back there. Really hoping not, since they had so many patrols down here."

Had. Just as I looked up, a commotion started at the edge of the group.

"I said to get your hands off me!" a female voice snarled. "What you doing, woman?"

The scouts, led by Storm, brought a short, stocky, *angry* woman and a ragged group of men, women, and children into camp. Roughly twenty, they all carried sizable packs.

Storm, ignoring the woman's fury, separated her from her people. Several of them cried out, the men squaring up to fight, but my fighters surrounded them.

"Take it easy," I called, straightening. "We just wanna talk. Shrike, wanna see what you can get from them?" I nodded to the civilians. Shrugging, she wandered over, taking a meandering route.

The short woman tried to shake Storm off, but the fighter seized her hand, spinning her until the stocky woman's arm was up between her shoulder blades. Storm looked sweet and delicate, but she didn't fuck around.

Phoenix and Gryph, drawn by the noise, made their way over. I tapped my chin, watching the short woman while Storm frog-marched her over. Something about the woman looked familiar...

Once she stood in front of me, she had to tip her head back. She looked me full in the face for a split second, arrested, as if she found me familiar, then her eyes flicked to the side. "What do you want?" she snarled.

"To help you." She snorted, clearly not believing a word of it. "Answer a few questions and we'll send you on your way."

"We had an exact amount of food," she snapped, shaking Storm off, and rubbing her shoulder. "Two days more than we needed to get to the next cache. You've put me off schedule."

"Where'd you pick them up?" I asked Storm.

"Entrance to Yosemite."

I nodded. "Where you going?" I asked her.

A long silence. I slouched against the side of the pickup. Gryph leaned against it, fascinated as if he was watching his favorite show. Phoenix wasted no time, pulling a pouch of pemmican off her belt, offering it around our little circle. Gryph and Storm accepted, but I shook my head, pulling my own pouch open.

It'd make Eleanor happy if I needed to refill mine.

"Just over the mountains," she said sullenly, after a long moment. "At least you're not the NKs," she muttered.

"NKs?" Phoenix asked around a mouthful of pemmican.

"The North Koreans?" The short woman's lip curled. "Maybe you noticed them?"

I grunted. "Whatever. I'll have the scouts give you a lift back in. Take you as far as they can."

Eleanor arrived where the civilians were clustered, immediately picking up a drooping child. Thank God. She could sort that lot out.

"Thank you," she said grudgingly. "You said all I had to do was answer some questions?"

It was the grudging expression that did it. If she'd smiled, I'd have recognized her sooner, but this one... She got this whenever an adult told her to do something she didn't want to do.

Sheba. My cousin Faith's best friend for her entire life.

I bit my lip to keep the smile off my face. "Just a few. Your militia. Who are they, where can we find them. What are your goals. Do you have weapons. Where's the fighting at?"

Settling onto the open tailgate of my pickup, I gestured for her to join me. Folding her arms, she glared blue murder at the air over my shoulder. Fine. She could stand where she wanted, as long as she talked.

"You're an asshole."

"True, but still not enough to get you that lift."

Phoenix shifted, showing her weapons. Storm tapped hers absentmindedly.

Phoenix spoke first. "You know, Captain, I'm..."

But I stopped listening, because the change that came over Sheba was immediate and awkward. She gasped, dropping her arms and rocking back on her heels, mouth opening and closing like a fish.

Apparently, she'd heard of me.

I frowned. How the fuck had... Oh, yeah. My people were running all over the countryside right now. I guess word travels when an army comes to town.

"You're...you're Captain?" Sheba choked. "As in...the Ghost Captain?"

"Am I?" I asked. "I thought it was just 'Ghost'?"

Phoenix nodded. "Ghost Captain is your full name."

"Oh."

"Then you people are...?" She looked from one to the other.

"Phoenix. Gryphon. Storm." I pointed to each in turn. "Will you talk?"

But her eyes darted from one face to another before focusing on the machete handle over my shoulder, the rifle at my side, all the weapons around her. Occasionally, she looked as if she couldn't decide between puking or passing out and still, she didn't say a word.

"Is this gonna happen a lot?" I asked the air. "Because this is taking up a hell of a lot of time and we've got places to be. As do you."

Her mouth worked for long seconds before she croaked, "I'm Sheba." Well, thankfully I got her name right. And she obviously didn't recognize me. Was that good or bad? "Um...Militia. No, we're not a militia. We are definitely a resistance, though. What else?"

"Goals," supplied Phoenix around the food in her mouth.

"Get rid of the NKs, protect as many people as possible."

We were on the same page about that, then. But... "How do you go about it? What are your methods?" I asked.

"Redirecting supplies. Forging orders. Occasionally, outright theft. Setting things up to look like accidental failure. Smuggling people over the border."

"Yosemite?"

Sheba shrugged. "I know that territory, it's far enough from the NKs usual routes, which makes it safer."

"Weapons?" I reminded her.

"Limited. Um... Some people have guns hidden away, but if you get caught..."

I frowned. "Do you all operate within Steve's territory? Like, do you have roaming patrols or fighters?"

"No. I'm the only one who regularly goes off grid, and that's strictly to smuggle people out. We have caches set up, but those are done by people who are trusted to return at the end of the day." She paused, her lips moving. "Who's Steve?"

"The North Koreans. Keep up." I ticked points off my fingers. "I take it there's no direct fighting."

"No."

"How do we make contact?"

She opened her mouth, stopped, thought about it, then tried again. "You don't. No one will trust you unless you're introduced by someone already known."

I looked around at our temporary resting place. Vehicles covered with camouflage, fighters sleeping, eating, cleaning weapons, or lurking nearby, attempting to look disinterested. And everywhere, weapons and signs of war.

Scars, limping people, worn and torn clothing. Our battle braids.

"You mean to tell me we don't look trustworthy on sight?" I asked dryly. "I'm almost hurt. No, seriously. Both my remaining feelings are slightly bruised right now."

"What about her reputation as the Ghost Captain?" Gryph wanted to know. "Won't that open some doors?"

"Who'd ever believe the Ghost is a woman?" Sheba replied automatically. Her forehead wrinkled. "How the hell are you a woman, anyway?"

I shrugged while Phoenix buried her face in Gryph's shoulder, sniggering. "I dunno. Got born with certain parts, grew up. That sort of thing."

"How the fuck did you lot end up adding the 'Ghost' part to her name?" Storm demanded.

Good question. Not overly important, but when... A distant memory surfaced. Salem, nighttime. Rain misting the air, Noah pressed up against me while Sung Ki raced past, laughing maniacally. The memory hit so strongly Noah's scent filled my senses. Leather, gun oil, and dirt.

Tears choked me, and I bowed my head.

Into the silence, Gryph spoke, bless him. "How often do you cross the mountains?"

"Two, maybe three times a season," Sheba said automatically. Then she really focused on him. The black hair, five o'clock shadow, the brilliant blue eyes. The scar bisecting his lean cheek that he'd gotten on the beach. "You look really familiar. Have we met?"

Gryphon shrugged, eyes wide in fake innocence. "We have never met before that I know of. Guess I have one of those faces?"

Phoenix snorted, choked, and bent over, coughing and laughing together. Her husband helpfully patted her back, all innocence and puzzlement over her condition. Sheba's awe slowly turned into confusion.

"Ignore them." I rubbed the space between my eyebrows and down, over the scar around my eye, trying to reduce the headache brought by holding back tears. "How many troops has Steve got around here, do you know? Or where the hell they prefer to go."

She nodded. "Knowing how to avoid them, huh?"

I snorted. If she wanted to think we were avoiding them, I'd let her.

Sheba continued. "If you've got any maps..."

She hadn't finished speaking before Dereva appeared, Anansi at her side, maps in hand.

***

Two hours later, Sheba and her lot left. Storm and the scouts carried them as deep into Yosemite as roads would allow.

Eleanor watched her daughter leave. "Is it just me, or did she have a little too much fun with this?"

Phoenix laughed. "We all had too much fun except Captain, and that's because people have heard of her."

I flipped her off. She laughed harder, but who cared? I kept turning over what she'd told us. She'd lead them over the mountains and release them just this side of the border, which was clearly marked by high fences.

Steve patrolled it sporadically, and she said she'd never had difficulty getting people to the fence. Once over, well, that was the mystery. The American military never crossed the border themselves, just opening the gate and immediately surrounding those who crossed with armed guards.

Almost exactly what Sirius had described when she crossed. Hopefully, these people didn't get the rest of it. Being used for experiments and having insecure men trying out torture techniques sounded like it sucked ass.

Around our tiny campfire that evening, we pulled the maps out again. Phoenix angled one so the setting sun lit it completely. "Sounds like all we have to do is park ourselves near a city and wait for these insurgents to find us."

I examined a map of Fresno. Kerman didn't exist as far as Steve was concerned. Maybe Faith, James, Uncle Dan, and Aunt Abi were there.

Downtown had numerous markers. Steve's government headquarters, a jail, their main barracks. More barracks were scattered through the city, each one close to a factory.

"Do we know if things have changed in LA?" Gryph asked. "Maybe Steve sent troops in there eventually."

"Guess we'll find out." I rolled my shoulders. "But hey, Shrike said there's an outpost near here, and I want a bit of fun. Do we still have people who need more field experience?"

***

The moon had just set but stars shone brightly overhead. I crouched behind a scraggly hedge, watching the gold lit windows of the large farmhouse. From inside, male laughter and women's cries.

It never changed.

An owl hooted.

Well. Loosening my muscles, I strode to the front door, machete in hand.

"Wait," Sage hissed. Turning, I saw her pale face barely peeking above the hedge. "Is it safe?"

I snickered. "It's not supposed to be." Standing to one side of the door, I knocked loudly.

***

Eastern Washington – Grace

Grace ran, bent low, a strung-out line of people following her like ducklings struggling to stay together in the dark. Stopping at a strange sound, she reached back, telling them to stop. They bumbled and thrashed, but nobody cried out.

At the bottom of the hill, a patrol drove slowly. Their man in the top flashed a little spotlight around, illuminating the brush on either side of the road.

Grace hissed silently. The Gophers—named after the college team Grace booed every season—didn't usually take patrolling this far from towns and the Oregon border too seriously. So, why were they looking so carefully now?

Full dark was the best time to start the run across eastern Washington. The Gophers watched the border between forest and plains, but the fifteen-day foot trek across the badlands was usually clearer.

They thought they could easily see people on foot. And, since they'd sent so many troops to Oregon to deal with whatever the hell was happening there, the Gophers had even more holes in their patrol routes.

Gaps she'd been more than happy to take advantage of.

Once they finished this run, she and her husband, Charlie, planned to take a several-month break. Partly to recover, and partly to contact Constance West, their only remaining friend in Washington, DC, in the hopes she had good news about government activity.

The other reason was to celebrate their anniversary. It'd be about two months late, but better late than not at all. Grace resisted the urge to pull out her notebook. She'd been planning their anniversary since this mission began. They'd barely celebrated since their wedding, which made sense, in a way, but it was time to begin making life happen for them again.

They'd been in Canada on their honeymoon when the invasion happened. Married less than a month, and they were refugees stranded in a foreign country.

They'd tried to go home. Charlie, an orphan already, had been fully adopted by her own family. He'd argued longer and louder than she had when their request to return to Oregon had been refused.

A soft smile curved her lips in the dark. At least they'd spent that night in jail together.

Like the others from the West Coast who'd been out of town when the invasion hit, they were shipped east. Abandoning the refugee camp they'd been stuck in, they'd made their way to Washington, DC. By the time they'd arrived, Atlanta and Portland, Maine, had already been destroyed.

Within weeks, a new border had been built, the maps had been reworked to show a new name—North Korean Liberated America—and Grace despaired of ever finding out what happened to her family. Until she'd met a junior aide to one of the many senators who'd voted to completely close the West Coast off from the rest of the United States.

In her last coded message, Constance suggested that she might finally be able to get her hands on information regarding the invasion. Information, or evidence.

Below her position, the Gophers had moved almost far enough to allow her and her ducklings to cross. She bared her teeth when the light flashed over ground they'd just covered.

They'd gotten so suspicious lately. What had changed? Nothing here, so it must be Oregon or California.

She and Charlie and been continually refused entry into Oregon. Something about hostiles and how the locals were all untrustworthy, and rumors that some had made it out but attempted to destroy the border outpost.

Her brother, Peter, had been sent in with a specially formed unit. Then, only a few men from the original unit came back with the people they were sent to rescue. None of those men had been her brother.

Sears's vague assurances were too old, too long ago, to still bring her comfort.

With all other avenues exhausted, they'd petitioned to go into Washington instead. With no mountain range to cross, it was by far the easiest route in and out. Once in...well, they could hardly refuse to help those who needed to escape, could they?

Then, three years ago, they'd found out that someone else was helping those in California. *They're led to the border by a woman,* Constance wrote. *She never crosses. She'd probably be detained if she tried. But no one comes from Oregon,* she'd finished.

So, for all these years, they'd operated only in Washington. Despite the fact that the entire region was controlled by the Gophers, the border between Washington and Oregon was too well patrolled for them to find a way through.

Instead, they'd built a network across Washington. Information on who needed to be taken out next, food caches that were regularly replenished, and a working relationship with Lieutenant John Sears, commander of one of the smaller outposts along the Washington border.

Ah! Grace perked up. Finally, the patrol rounded a corner, their lights disappearing. Listening intently, she heard nothing except her own group. Shouldering her rifle and rising to her feet, she waved them forward.

Charlie always took the rear guard, smudging tracks and ensuring they weren't followed. She didn't envy the times he had to push the slow ones to go faster. Too many people were wholly unused to walking for any length of time.

"Hurry," Grace whispered to the next in line, an older woman. "We need to cross as quickly as possible," she reminded them.

Their pace increased, but still Grace worried. This lot of ducklings were so malnourished, even after wiping out the contents of every food cache they passed.

Her head shot up, eyes wide in alarm. "Another patrol!" she cried, throwing caution to the winds. This was too soon! They never ran so close together... "Run!"

They'd barely taken two steps, most of the group still strung across the road, when the Gopher's lights rounded the corner, illuminating the ducklings.

Grace fumbled to unsling her rifle, but what was the use? What's two rifles against a machine gun?

She glanced back, hoping for one last look at Charlie. His own face, lit by the Gophers, echoed her regret. She'd always imagined that when she died, she'd be old, surrounded by their children and grandchildren, Charlie's hand gripping hers tightly.

Since the invasion, she'd just hoped she'd be close enough to hold him as they died.

I love you, she mouthed, bringing her rifle up for a futile attempt at life.

I know, he mouthed back, regret and sorrow pulling his face into sharp angles.

An explosion rocked the world, hurling her against the unforgiving ground.

CHAPTER 3

Wiretap on Marigold Hotel room #113. Booking name James Smith – December 10, 2060, 10pm

Man 1: Fine! Fine. Maybe if we...No, that'll never work. We need a way that doesn't involve passing trade legislation... Wait. (sound of papers being shuffled) Forget that. Look here, we need to ship plane parts to the South China Seas, right?

Man 2: So?

Washington, DC – Constance

Constance West walked quickly down the corridor, her heels clicking on the smooth floor of the Russell Building as she made her way to the cubicle she called an office. Tucked away next to Senator Bryce McKinney's, it was too easy for her boss to find his least-favorite aide.

She greeted the people she passed, struggling to maintain her composure. Against her thigh, her secret shifted. Walking with a slight hitch to her stride, she kept her thighs together, more concerned with keeping her secret than with who might see her.

Shutting and locking the door to her office, she slumped against it, wiping away a light sheen of sweat.

Finally. After *years* of searching. Years since she'd first learned of these documents, locked away in the Archives instead of destroyed as they should have been.

Maybe now, there'd be some answers for all the families of those who died, for those who'd been reduced to refugees in their own country. Something she could show to Grace and Charlie.

Ironic that despite knowing them a few short years, they were now some of the people closest to her. Certainly closer than her own father, now.

Her father. Kicking off her heels, she barely restrained a snort. She'd idolized the man. She'd grown up calling him a hero who helped shape the nation. He'd brought stability by bringing President Trembly in, eliminating the two-term laws. Given the nation a chance to make lasting change.

He'd even introduced her to her boss. She'd been a brand-new aide to a powerful man when the invasion happened. In awe of the man she worked for, one of her father's closest friends.

Then the West Coast went dark, bombs were dropped, and hell broke loose in DC.

Being an aide merely meant she had a front row seat to the backstabbing, blaming, and frantic attempts to cover up...what? Everyone ran around screaming "Not me!" when they weren't even accused of anything.

No. The veil lifted, and she'd seen behind the curtain. What she'd thought was unity, a strong front to protect the country, was nothing more than empty words and money changing hands.

How else to explain the slums inside DC where people slowly died from radiation poisoning, or worse, people who could recover, if only they had the help?

The day she'd met Grace and Charlie O'Connell was the day her life changed. She'd decided to be the change she wanted to see in the world.

How could she not, when Grace, two years her junior, showed such strength of conviction and willpower?

They'd come to beg for help, hope, or at least a chance to find their families. Instead, they'd been denied at every turn. Empty promises and 'thoughts and prayers' were thrown around when all they really wanted was *some* kind of action!

The more Constance advocated for them and the others like them, the more friends she lost. She continued until her own father sat her down and explained that if she didn't stop, at best she'd be out of a job. At worst, she'd disappear.

But now...now she had the flash drive. If it contained even a fraction of what she'd been promised, she might not have enough to take the perpetrators to court, but she might be able to sway her father away from his close friendship with Senator McKinney.

One final deep breath and she opened her eyes. Time to see. Lifting her snug skirt, she pulled the flash drive from her garter. Her breath quickened when she sat at her computer, waiting for it to boot up.

DC's official excuses for how North Korea had acquired U.S. bombs were worse than pathetic, dressed up as reasonable. It got lost in a complicated system, once you boiled it down to its most basic. Anyone who didn't know the intricacies of government would look at those reasons and think them entirely plausible, but the moment you dug a little bit...

Maybe that would be in here, too.

Her desktop lit up and she uncapped the flash drive, plugging it in. She ground her teeth and turned it over. Every damn time! Was there anyone in this world who could plug a flash drive in the right way up on the first try?

Constance bit her lip, waiting for the computer to accept the drive.

A knock sounded on her door, then the doorknob wiggled. It didn't go far, and a wash of gratitude washed through her, that she'd remembered to lock the door.

"Ms. West?" Constance started. Senator McKinney was back early? "Why is this door locked?" he demanded.

Snatching the flash drive from the computer, she tucked it into her bra, scrambling back into her shoes. "One moment," she called breathlessly.

Flipping the lock, it swung open before she had a chance to turn the knob. McKinney stood, framed by the doorway, showing him to his best advantage.

He was a handsome man, she had to admit. Hair going silver at the temples, the remaining still black, and both worked as the perfect frame for his brilliant blue eyes. Many a woman had been charmed into donating more than she'd planned by those eyes, and his deep, mellifluous voice.

Which had begun to sound irritated as he addressed her. "Ms. West. While I appreciate your privacy," this was news to her, "locking your door doesn't look right to security. It makes them think you have something to hide."

He pushed past her, shutting the door behind him.

Constance walked to the far side of her desk, hiding the trembling in her hands by straightening items, pulling out her tablet. Considering how much she now had to hide... "Of course, Senator. My apologies. One of..." She cast about frantically, searching for a name. "One of Senator Baser's aides has been...aggressively trying to get me to go on a date with him. I simply needed to get some work done in peace."

McKinney hummed in his throat, taking the chair opposite her, crossing his ankle over his knee. "Well, you are a very attractive woman. While I usually advise women to give men a chance, I have to say, sometimes, it's better to go a little older."

His fingers traced idly up his leg, and he sent her a charged glance from under half-closed eyes. Her stomach clenched. She'd seen that look before, but never directed at her.

And he'd closed the door!

"Did your proposal pass?" she asked, desperation too obvious. Her fingers were white where they twisted together in her lap as she struggled to remain calm.

The change from suave seducer to petulant man was instantaneous—and gratifying. So, it hadn't gone well. He'd been trying to take funds away from the disaster relief programs, arguing that since the invasion and bombings had happened so long ago, they hardly counted as disasters anymore.

After all, he frequently said, *shouldn't we be bolstering our military and police forces?*

His lip curled, making him look like a sulky child. "No," he said shortly. "That Baser woman is a menace! I don't know how she managed to bribe so many members of the Senate in such a short time, but..." He trailed off, stroking his chin. "You know what? That little crush you're dealing with couldn't have come at a better time."

"Sir?" Her heart sank. What now?

McKinney leaned forward, putting all his considerable charm into the blinding smile he turned her way. "Seduce him. Get dirt on the Baser woman so that I can shut her down for good." He ran his eyes up and down her body, licking his lips when they passed over her breasts. "Do whatever it takes. There's a promotion in it for you."

Constance's skin crawled and she sat back in her chair, as far from him as she could get. Her mind raced. Her first instinct, to scream "NO!" still hovered at the back of her throat, but...

She needed time with the flash drive. As an aide, she had a lot more freedom, and her internet usage wasn't as heavily policed. Plus, she needed to make sure that thing had good information on it. Corroborating any info would go much easier with the connections available to her here.

"Yes, sir," she said obediently. A satisfied smile stretched his full lips. She swallowed back vomit. He didn't have anything nearly as charming or subtle as he liked to think. "I'll need a bit of time, so he doesn't suspect anything, sir."

"Of course." He waved that away. "As long as you don't take *too* much time."

Don't take too much time? How annoyingly vague. Constance embraced the irritation. It overpowered her fear.

After a few more words, he left, self-satisfaction evident in every line of his body. At the door, he crooked his finger under her chin. "Once you're done with that man, we should have dinner to...discuss...your promotion."

Adding her to his little harem of women too eager or too terrified to tell him no? Hah! She'd known her time in this office was growing short.

Looks like it'd just gotten a lot shorter.

***

Fresno, CA – Faith

Faith grimaced at her parents over the breakfast table. She'd been avoiding them for two days now, an impressive feat in an apartment this small. Their eyes were full of questions they didn't dare ask in front of the others. She used that to her advantage, slipping out of the house to go to work.

Ever since Carter made his announcement that the Ghost Captain had finally arrived, she'd walked around in a fog. He was really here! Well, they assumed he was. There had yet to be a confirmed sighting of the Ghost simply because they didn't know what he looked like.

However, Nielsen had witnessed people completely wipe out a patrol of NKs. They'd even broken the vehicle down, taking some pieces, loading them into an ancient Jeep and van and hiding the rest.

This very event was why he'd been chosen to make the dangerous trek from Sacramento to Fresno.

She smiled, pulled from her thoughts. Lucas waited for her on the ground floor, as he did every day. He fell silently in beside her, walking her to the offices before heading to his factory.

Biting her tongue until they were alone, she blurted, "What do you think of the plan?"

He shook his head, looking up at the bright, brassy sky, summer's last hurrah. "Leaving the city seems risky. What if we're caught? It's a death sentence. But at the same time…" He exhaled. "The chance to meet the man behind the Oregon rebellion? The only *successful* rebellion? To help him?" He kissed his fingertips.

She agreed. Meeting a living legend? She'd take this over attending a normal concert any day of the week. "Ghost deserves to have the best intel, from the horse's mouth, as it were, and it's not like we're safe here, anymore." She fell silent as they passed another group.

Chapters had been falling like dominos, the members of each facing either public execution or quietly disappearing.

"It's not like we're leaving until we find out more about where Ghost is, anyway," she continued once they were past. "What are we going to do, sit in the countryside, hoping he stumbles across us?"

Their laughter cut off abruptly when they rounded the corner of a brick building. Ahead lay the gray metal door that Faith walked through daily. Faith gripped Lucas's hand. Every day, he brought her here, kissed her thoroughly, then left for his own job. And every day, she wondered if today would be the day he wasn't waiting for her when she finished work.

"Until next time." She smiled brightly, careful to avoid the words 'good-bye.' Her own, personal superstition, but it'd worked so far.

"*Au revoir.*" He kissed her then, turning her hand over, he pressed his lips to her palm, folding her fingers around the kiss. He left quickly, turning once at the corner to wave, then disappeared.

As she climbed the stairs to the office that acted as a hub for production, shipping, and troop movements, she prepared. In her mind, she'd created a little box, and into it she tucked Lucas, the Resistance, and everything she knew about the Ghost Captain.

All that remained by the time she reached the second floor was an efficient manager who processed information at breakneck speeds. Her masters required copies of everything.

Reopening paper factories had taken nearly as much time to set up as the munitions factories, but at least they were primarily recycling cardboard. If they'd dared touch the trees so painstakingly planted thirty years ago... Well.

She'd see red.

On the landing at the second floor, the guard sat at his little table, checking IDs and marking them off his list. Faith greeted him with a smile, identification card in hand.

He checked the card and Faith pulled a small cloth bag from her purse. "My mother sent you some apricots," she said, setting it on the table.

Bringing gifts had become a habit for her. The five-fruit tree on their balcony had a good harvest. Enough for them to trade with their neighbors. Their next-door neighbor had been growing potatoes in old laundry baskets for several years now and had gotten very good at it.

The guard checked the bag, then smiled, pulling one out and taking a bite. Juice ran down his chin. Faith laughed lightly, handing him a handkerchief. Waving her through, he gave the next man in line a hard look.

Her hair, pulled up in a simple ponytail, swung around her shoulders. The fresh-faced, innocent, girl-next-door look took some work, but it was worth it to be thought boring by the men around her.

Making her way to her desk, right in front of Colonel Han's office, she greeted her coworkers, the last one at the neighboring desk.

"Isn't it a beautiful day, Clara?" she asked.

"Yes, it is." Clara, an arresting black woman who looked in her mid-thirties but was really over fifty, smiled up at her. She kept her gray streaked hair in a crown braid, the rest left natural.

Once, she'd come in with cornrows. The fallout from that... Faith shuddered.

"What's on the menu today, honey?" Clara continued.

Faith pulled out her notebook, flipping through the pages. "Three orders of munitions to be sent to Sacramento that will need full paperwork, enough to leave one at every waypoint. Two for San Francisco, two for Bakersfield. We need to contact the northern command outpost—"

"We can't," Clara interrupted.

"What?"

Clara glanced around, then leaned in. "They sent a dispatch to Northern Command last week. We haven't heard back. I overheard them talking about it yesterday, just after you left."

Faith bit the inside of her lips, forcing them into a frown. Lost contact? The very next day after they had proof that fighters—that the *Ghost Captain*—had arrived? This must be more proof that the Ghost had come.

Hastily stuffing that thought into her mental box, she focused on the present. "If there's something we need to know, Colonel Han will inform us," she said primly. "Has there been any word from Oregon?"

She'd been asking this question every day for months. And every day, Clara shook her head and said, "No."

Just like yesterday, and the day before, Faith's heart jumped. Soon! Soon she'd know. In the meantime... "Let's get that paperwork typed up, please. We have a lot of work to do today."

As they settled into their day, runners came and went, carrying papers that needed to be checked and either handed to Colonel Han for signing, or filed away. Some brought sealed envelopes. Faith made a mental note of how many, and where they came from.

Anything from the south usually had to do with new orders or troop placements. Sometimes, she needed to find out what they said, but since Sheba's last known location was above Oakhurst, all was well on that front.

Occasionally, she'd take papers into Colonel Han's office and receive orders about where they should go next. In between, she typed busily away, preparing instructions to be relayed. Sometimes, she changed a word or two, replaced the original document, and went about her day as if nothing ever happened.

And even more rarely, she took up her pen, signing names she had no business signing. Names that would see her executed publicly as an example to all.

Just last year, Carter and Lucas stole an entire truck of guns and ammunition meant for the north in three simple steps: walking with confidence, wearing red armbands, and carrying papers that said 'Colonel Han' on them, none of which had ever been seen by the man.

Those guns were now hidden underneath Fresno, along with ammunition they'd carefully siphoned off over the years. The NKs still didn't know they'd been outright stolen, courtesy of the other papers Faith had filed.

As she worked, she typed up permission to travel papers in English, then writing up another set in Korean with the name Lucas Morales. Hiding it in the folder she'd taped underneath one of her desk drawers, she continued without pause.

As if she hadn't done something extremely illegal.

Just before lunch, she worked on papers for Carter. Before she could finish, a squad of NKs pushed into the office.

These men clashed sharply with the soldiers who normally frequented this building. Those ones wore standard camouflage with their country's flag on the shoulders.

These ones wore black, and even a Captain—such as the one who commanded this squad—outranked Colonel Han. She often thought it was the difference between a normal soldier and the German SS she'd read about in history.

In short, the Goon Squad.

"Step away from your desks!" the leader shouted in decent English.

Her lips tightening, Faith slid the paper off and under her loose sweater. Once safely inside the shifting mass of frightened office workers, she slowly worked it down, into her waistband, folding it twice more.

"Hands on the wall!"

A man bumped into Faith, knocking her to the floor. Swearing, she landed hard on her hip and left hand, slipping the paper further down her underwear. Scrabbling back, someone stepped on her leg, and she curled around it, crying out in pain.

"Honey, get your booty up here." Clara pulled Faith to her feet, hauling her bodily to the wall.

Faith found herself sandwiched between Clara and a young runner who trembled as the soldiers paraded up and down behind them.

"Spot checks," Faith mumbled. "Always the spot checks. I was on a roll!"

"Sshh!" Clara glared at her, barely turning her head. "Don't you rile them up."

One by one, soldiers patted each of the office workers down. These spot checks happened randomly, several times a year. It was impossible to know when it would happen. *The only orders that never passed through this office,* Faith thought darkly.

Faith breathed deeply through her nose at her own turn, shifting her feet when the soldier ran his hands around her waist. A corner of the paper dug into an unfortunate spot. Hopefully, the last time she hid incriminating documents in her underwear.

When it was the young runner's turn, she panicked. Faith closed her eyes. The girl was young, fresh, barely sixteen. Probably her first spot check.

The soldiers flung the girl to the floor, already grasping hands becoming rougher as they pulled at the girl's clothes. Faith closed her eyes, biting her lip. She hated this part. Where she had to choose to stay silent to protect her position.

She could speak up. Maybe she'd survive, but she'd never work here again. And as Carter and Malva so often reminded her, she was the only person they knew who'd managed to climb so high.

"What are you hiding?" the captain shouted at the girl.

"This girl is not part of my office," Han said in Korean.

"She may be passing information to one of the workers here," the captain replied in English.

"Leave her alone!"

Everyone froze, staring in astonishment. Clara pushed away from the wall, squaring off against the goons.

"She's not guilty of anything. She's just a terrified child."

"Clara," Faith hissed. "What are you doing?"

The older woman put a hand out, telling Faith to stay back. "No, honey, I think it's time I stop letting fear rule me."

Faith gaped at her. *Stop letting fear rule me.* The words bounced around in her head. One of the black-clad soldiers pushed Clara back, raising his baton.

I think it's time I stop letting fear rule me.

She had let fear win. Even as she worked to subvert the NKs weapons, every time she snuck out after curfew, fear roiled through her, so familiar she no longer noticed it.

The soldier brought his baton down.

Screaming, Faith lurched sideways, knocking Clara to the floor. Fire exploded through her back. Faith collapsed. She curled into a ball, arms over her head, shrieking with every blow.

She couldn't see, couldn't hear, could only feel pain. Through it all, one thought repeated itself, burning into her heart.

Oh, Lucas. I'm so sorry. I love you!

***

Eastern Washington – Grace

Awareness returned in a rush. An explosion from nowhere. What...?

"Charlie!" she croaked, scrambling on all fours across the road. Her ears rang, sound coming through as if she were under water. "Charlie!"

"Grace." Her name was muffled, but she knew the voice. Could recognize it in her sleep. Twisting, she rose to her knees just as Charlie snatched her up, pressing his lips into her hair.

Frantically, she ran her hands over him, checking for injuries even as he did the same for her. At his hip, her hand came away wet. Firelight washed over the scene, making the blood on her hands flicker between black and red.

"Charlie," she choked. "Oh, baby..."

Her chest tightened. He was injured, the Gophers were nearby. Why hadn't they been killed already? What would she do if he...he... She couldn't finish the thought.

"It's okay," he soothed. "It's not that bad."

He swayed.

"Yo!" An unfamiliar voice rang over the cries of their ducklings.

Squinting, Grace made out a woman, silhouetted by flames from...a burning truck? Beyond the woman, people sorted through those on the ground, helping some to their feet, stabbing (stabbing?!) others, and laying more out in a row. Another figure moved down the line, a strip of white in their hands.

"Everybody here okay?" the strange woman continued, as if this was a normal Tuesday. Grace clutched Charlie tighter. "My name's Seahorse—more on that later. I sincerely hope you were trying to avoid Steve over there." She jerked a thumb over her shoulder.

The woman—Seahorse—stopped a few feet away, thumbs hooked into the belts she wore at her waist. Dark haired, she moved with the confident grace of a dancer. Grace took another look at the aftermath of a battle that finished before she knew it started.

Or a fighter.

"Are you real?" The speaker was a middle-aged woman, one of their ducklings. She held her daughter close with one hand, the other outstretched to the newcomer. "Where did you come from?"

Seahorse bent down, clasping the woman's hand and drawing her to her feet. "I'm a commander in the Oregonian Irregulars. We're here to help."

"Oregon?" Grace and Charlie said together.

"What about Oregon?" Grace demanded.

Seahorse smiled briefly. "It's free."

Grace gasped. Her blood rushed in her ears. Free? Then maybe Papa...? And Peter, Hope, and Sean... Maybe they were free and safe?

"I'm sorry." Seahorse hadn't stopped speaking. "We need to get out of here ASAP. That fire is visible for miles, and we need to be gone sooner than later."

"There will be more patrols," Charlie said, struggling to rise. Silently, Grace got under his shoulder, lending her support.

The commander sniggered, the sound surprisingly unpleasant. "Oh, we're not worried about a patrol here and there. But eventually, Steve's gonna send a small army. Best we're gone before then." She scanned the group. "Who's in charge?"

Grace shared a sidelong glance with Charlie. He tilted his head. She nodded. This woman had good vibes. He shrugged, then nodded back. Biting her lip, Grace nodded and raised her hand. "We are."

Their chances of being shot seemed pretty low, considering the newcomers had done more damage to the Gophers in ten minutes than she and Charlie had ever managed.

"Why do you ask?" Charlie faced the commander head on. "What do you want with us?"

Seahorse studied them a moment. "Charlie and Grace, right?"

Grace froze, staring at the woman with wide eyes.

"How do you know that?" Charlie asked roughly. He stepped forward, but his leg wouldn't hold, and he buckled.

"Charlie!" Grace cried, staggering. His weight lifted suddenly. Grace raised her eyes to see Seahorse with Charlie's other arm slung around her shoulders.

"Got hit with shrapnel, huh? Sorry about that."

Grace didn't think she sounded very sorry.

Still, the commander called her medic over. "Squirrel!"

The small figure finished wrapping a bandage and quickly made their way over. Grace started in surprise. The medic was a girl, late teens, *maybe* early twenties. Kneeling, the medic tugged Charlie's shirt up, the small braids containing her long hair sliding over her shoulders.

"Hit with shrapnel, huh? That blows." Squirrel produced a flask from her belt. "Let's sit him down, this is gonna hit hard."

Grace helped Charlie stay on his side when the medic held the flask up, pouring a generous amount into his mouth. He coughed, spluttering and recoiling from the flask. The strong scent of alcohol hit Grace's nose and she flinched.

"What the hell is that?"

Squirrel grinned. "It's the best thing he could hope for. We call it Dirt Huggers."

Grace stared suspiciously at her. Under her hands, Charlie giggled. "Why?"

"Because it only takes a couple drinks and the next thing you know, the ground is your new best friend." Squirrel grinned, her teeth flashing in the fire-lit night. She poured more over her hands, rubbing the alcohol in while Seahorse undid her top belt, folding it and pressing it between Charlie's teeth.

"Bite down," the commander advised.

Charlie giggled again, clenching the leather tightly between his teeth. They'd barely closed when Squirrel poured more over his wound. He groaned, but didn't struggle, relaxing into Grace's arms. She stroked his hair back from his forehead, looking away when the medic probed the wound with her fingers, fishing out a chunk of shrapnel.

After a few more tense minutes and several tiny pieces, the medic sat back. "Well, it's enough he won't keep bleeding, but I'll need a clean workspace and plenty of light to finish it off. We've got several who'll need it. He'll also need watching because it's gonna get infected."

Seahorse nodded. "Hey, Grace, right?" Grace tore her attention away from her husband and Squirrel, who busily bandaged him. "You know of any spots Steve isn't likely to look too closely at around here?"

"What?" Grace looked to Squirrel for help, but she already gathered her things. "Who's Steve?"

"Ah. Yeah. That's the soldiers. You know?"

"No."

Charlie mumbled incoherently. Squirrel patted his hand. "That's right. You tell 'em."

"You understand that?" Seahorse asked.

Squirrel laughed. "He's had a couple solid drinks. Even he doesn't know what he's saying." With that, she left as quickly as she'd come, leaving Grace nearly alone with the commander.

"What happens to us?" Grace asked. "If you can take us to the border, there's medics and doctors there who can take care of him…" She trailed off. Seahorse was already shaking her head.

"It'll take us a couple days to get there, and his injury is bad enough it'll need to be seen to before then. Don't worry, Squirrel is better than what you'll find there in terms of care. Or we can drop him off, but you'll need to come with us."

"Oh, no." Grace tightened her arms. "You are *not* separating us."

"All right, then. Dionysius!" Seahorse folded her arms, watching a young man detach himself from the rest of the crew. The commander also sported a series of braids to contain her hair, Grace noted absently. But hers looked almost sewn down.

The young man, slender, with a medium build and wiry arms, arrived, tossing his braids back. "Seahorse."

"These two are coming with us. Help her get her husband to the trucks, will you?"

"Wait," Grace cried to the commander's back. "Why are you here? What do you want with us?"

Seahorse turned half back, revealing her laughing face. "I should've thought that was obvious. We're here to kick Steve's ass, and you're going to help us."

CHAPTER 4

Sacramento, CA – Captain

Phoenix handed me her scope. "Check it out," she said. "To the right, two buildings in. See it?"

Sacramento loomed in front of us, so much larger than the Salem or Portland compounds. Some of its skyscrapers had holes in them, damage from explosions. Others were untouched, dust covering their windows, turning everything brown and gray.

I focused on the spot she indicated. "Steve couldn't be that arrogant, could they?"

She shrugged. "Not completely. I mean, they know we're here."

Through the streets, Steve scurried like ants, lugging boxes closer to the perimeter. Some took two men to move. Too far away to see the writing on the boxes didn't mean we couldn't make a likely guess. Ammo boxes have a certain look to them.

The city's perimeter had the same fencing and guard towers of our northern cities, that was a given. Hell, Steve barely had to work to clear ground, the countryside was so flat and boring. But their cleared space was twice what we had in Salem.

"Wait." I zeroed in on a dark line about fifty feet outside the fence. "Is that a...moat? I mean, Shrike mentioned it, but hearing is different than seeing."

"Yep." Phoenix hooked her thumbs into her belt. "Original scout's reports confirmed, it's not water. We're thinking they're trying oil again."

Yes, because it worked so well last time, in our final battle in Oregon. Launching a burning car into it meant that while it made our lives more difficult getting in, it made Steve's a hell of a lot harder getting out.

"Good for them. I like an enemy who tries the same thing multiple times." I continued down the perimeter. "How many sites do we need to hit?"

"Scouts are counting now. Expecting them back sometime after dark."

The only thing we had that might reach were the mortars we'd stolen from Steve. Problem was, they'd fired a bunch that hadn't gone off. Sparrow and Chaos, working carefully and very far away from other people, had taken a whole bunch apart last winter.

The ones they'd put back together would definitely go boom.

"Cool. Let's figure on tomorrow night to fuck some shit up, yeah?"

***

The last vestiges of light silhouetted the coastal mountains while the rookies set up camp well over a mile away from Sacramento. I chewed on the last of my dried fruit and wished for a cup of tea. Dry camps suck, but better than an accidental spark setting off the whole fucking plains filled with drying grass.

Most of the Irregulars stayed in camp, resting and cleaning gear, ready to move if shit happened. The rest of us spread out around Sacramento. I rode in the back of my GMC with Anansi, Dereva at the wheel.

We were the last to leave camp as we had the shortest distance to travel. Scouts reported thirty ammo dumps around the perimeter, each carefully marked on the map. Ten teams left camp, some in Chimeras, the rest in random vehicles.

Earlier, I'd taken the mounted machine gun out of the pickup's bed to make room for our mortar and shells, each one carefully wrapped and stored so they didn't rattle.

"We're pretty sure they're stable," Chaos said, shrugging, "but honestly, who knows? These aren't the best made shells I've ever seen."

Which really ramps up confidence.

At our first target, Dereva let the truck idle while we watched the Big Dipper rotate. I leaned against the door next to her.

"Guess that's one good thing about Steve," she said. Dereva rested her hands lightly on the steering wheel, leaning forward. "We can actually see stars."

She'd been with me since day one, her and her brother. She'd been a beautiful teenager, and she'd only become more striking as an adult, her tightly curled dark hair shot through with blonde streaks and brilliant blue eyes, further offset by her dark skin.

While most of the fighters chose to braid our hair—generally called battle braids—she preferred to pull it back into a ponytail, letting it sit in a puff ball. Her brother Anansi took after their mother in looks and genius, had their father's deplorable sense of humor, and combined both to make him worthy of his namesake.

The boy was really too young for dad jokes, but he didn't let that stop him, unfortunately. He'd grown tall and lanky since the Invasion and now stood several inches taller than me. His tight cornrows, unlike the braids anyone else wore, made him easy to identify. With his dark skin, lucky little shit disappeared in the dark.

I looked ruefully down. Even with my deep tan, you could still see the shape of my arms in the dark. My bare legs were even worse, nearly glowing at night.

The Big Dipper finally reached its mark and I sighed. Sunrise was just around the bend, the air chill, perfect for lulling the night guards. Climbing into the back of the pickup, I threw a blanket over my head and lit a stub of a candle, checking the set angles one last time.

The blanket shifted and Anansi joined me. "You sure you've got it?" I asked quietly.

"Triple check, Captain. They're good."

Shrugging, I kissed my wedding ring for luck. "Let's go."

Tossing back the blanket, I rapped on the roof of the cab, picked up the first shell, and dropped it into the mortar.

Before it reached the apex of its arc, Dereva goosed the truck forward. I snatched up my scope, training it in the general direction of the target while Dereva took us cross country as fast as she dared.

The explosion lit up the night. "Bullseye!" I punched the air, watching the flames rise higher than I'd expected.

Several buildings around it caught fire as the sound of the explosion finally crossed the distance. Even further away, more explosions added light to the night sky all around Sacramento, punctuated with the staccato of gunfire.

In our wake, Steve fired, hitting where we had been. Dust formed tails that drifted with the breeze.

"Prep for two!" Dereva shouted.

Working quickly, Anansi adjusted the angles, checked our location, then made another adjustment. In the split second that Dereva paused, and my genius nodded, I dropped the next shell. Dereva hit the gas.

"Wait!" The truck slowed at my shout. "We missed."

"You missed? What do you mean you missed? We don't have time for you to *miss!*" Dereva shouted.

Anansi worked frantically over it, muttering to himself.

"Hurry up, kid." I unwrapped the next shell, resisting the urge to shift my weight.

"You could help," he snapped.

I half laughed. "Are you kidding me? When I add two and two, sometimes I get twenty-two and a half! And don't ask where the half came from. I have no fucking idea."

Bullets peppered the ground less than ten feet away, but Dereva held. That girl had nerves of steel.

As soon as Anansi pulled his hands away, I dropped the shell. Dereva hit the gas and we lurched forward. Catching myself on the tail box, I kept my eyes glued on the shell's target. We knew the moment it hit. My mouth dropped open, the explosion nearly twice the first one.

The pickup raced over uneven ground to our final spot, knocking us all over the bed. I laughed, watching the fires spread, and turned. "Babe, did you—" Anansi's black eyes met mine, and the laughter died in my throat. I smiled weakly, tears welling. "Did you see that, kid?"

He threw an arm over my shoulder. "Archangel would've loved this shit."

"Yeah. Language." Unable to get another word out around the tightness in my throat, I busied myself by unwrapping another shell.

He shot me a quick glance, nodded once, then nudged me playfully. "You afraid my mom's gonna kill you?"

My lips quirked. Little shit.

As I breathed, the tightness slowly receded. I knew it would. Being in the field was the only place to find real relief. Here, I had too much to think about, too much that needed to be dealt with *now.*

And out here, it was easier to forget he was gone.

The truck paused.

"Go." Anansi pulled his hands away.

My sleeve rode up when I dropped the shell. In the dark, the O+ tattooed on my right inner wrist showed as a dark blob against pale skin. We all had our blood types tattooed to help the medics and Doc treat injuries.

Anansi couldn't stop at just one tattoo, though, and is the original reason his mom wants to kill me. I thought Ink did a beautiful job. Which still doesn't cover the fact that his mom blames me for it.

As the pickup bounced over the grassy plains, the tightness in my throat slowly eased, helped along by the young man whooping at every new explosion. Little silhouettes raced around frantically, struggling to put out the fires cropping up everywhere.

Stray cinders drifted down, tiny glowing points of light. One touched the wrong spot and a wall of flames erupted, encasing the city within minutes.

"Welp." I shielded my eyes from the light. "Guess it's definitely not water."

***

As the first ones back to camp, I hopped out to walk the perimeter, waiting for the others. In ones and twos, the groups returned, laughing and jubilant.

Everyone loves a good bonfire except the poor bastards trying to deal with it.

Eleanor, Shrike, and River walked with me. "I want four battle partners out, two heading north, two south. Watch those fucking fires. That damn flaming moat could set this whole region on fire."

Fucking morons.

Okay, so we were the first ones to light the fires, but it was Steve's fault. *They* moved the ammo close enough for us to hit it. If they didn't want us to blow up their ammo, why would they make it so easy to hit?

Shrike sighed, rolling her eyes, but sent them out. Then, for good measure, River ordered the rest to pack the gear into the vehicles, just in case.

Once I loaded my things, I watched the last of the stars fade as dawn's first light rose in the east. The thick smoke rising above Sacramento couldn't conceal that. In the growing light, a small scavenging party returned with an entire butchered cow.

"I do like this part of California." River nodded to the scavengers. "Meat is so easy to come by."

Because the land had been put to use for grazing. Instead of hunting deer or elk, they just had to find a cow from one of the many herds dotting the countryside.

The soil was rich, but only if it got enough water. Since they no longer had access to water from other parts of the country, the usual crops were long dead. Most of what we'd seen was straight grazing, except near the rivers.

We still waited for mortar parties to return when the potential spark finally happened. The northern battle partners raced back to camp, dirt bikes flying, dust leaving a tail in the air. In the distance, a new, smaller plume of smoke rose into the air.

"Time to go," I bellowed, striding to my GMC.

Fighters scrambled for their vehicles, clearing the ground in minutes. Smoke from the grass fire mingled with the darker smoke from the moat, crawling across the sky.

"What about Phoenix and Gryphon?" Sage cried, one hand on the edge of the truck bed.

"They'll find us." I vaulted into the pickup.

Already, the burning section had grown large enough to be easily seen, and every second we waited, it expanded. If I remembered rightly, grass fires were a flash-in-the-pan, but that didn't mean we wanted to be in its path.

I squished the pang of fear that shot through my chest. I couldn't imagine how to deal with life if Phoenix and Gryph didn't find us.

***

Washington, DC – Constance

Constance shut the door to her tiny studio apartment, leaning her forehead against it. Locking it happened on autopilot. At least her curtains were already closed.

Kicking her heels across the floor, she stumbled to the fridge, pulling out a bottle of cider. Downing half the bottle in a rush, she savored the rest and turned on her laptop. Only being able to run the thing for the brief time she was home meant she'd almost make better time if she tried to decrypt it by hand.

She sighed as the alcohol did its work, loosening her muscles and relaxing her mind. Closing her eyes, she pressed the bottle to her forehead, hoping to forget McKinney. Temporarily, at least.

Wiggling her toes in the plush rug covering her living/bedroom—her biggest splurge—she sank to the floor, looking around her little apartment. Who cared if it was tiny? It was all hers. While she didn't mind roommates, after having people walking through her space all day, she needed something that was hers alone.

Reaching up, she pulled her laptop around. The bottle dropped from her nerveless fingers. She stared at the screen.

A file had been unlocked!

Hastily snatching up her bottle, she ran absentminded fingers over the carpet, checking to see if any cider spilled.

It'd be a waste of excellent cider if it did.

Clicking on the file, she scanned it quickly, her breath coming short.

She'd seen this file before, but every other time, it'd been so redacted she couldn't read more than three or four words in a paragraph. Now, she had every name of every soldier, and exactly what they'd done.

It was the debrief of one Sergeant James Perry, right after he'd returned from Oregon with only seven soldiers out of thirty. Even with the whole document visible, it still didn't make sense.

Phoenix. Sirius. Archangel. Gryphon. Were these places or people? By how they were used, most likely people, especially in conjunction with the one she *knew* was a name.

Captain.

Oh, my God. Her breath came short as she continued reading.

She needed to find James Perry.

***

Pasadena, CA – Mercy

Mercy rested a hand on Molly's shoulder, then brushed back her sweat-soaked hair. The young woman breathed softly, dark circles around her closed eyes as she slept the deep sleep of the terminally exhausted.

While this labor hadn't been as long as her first, the baby had refused to come out until near sunrise. Now, she lay on the thin mat Mercy kept for patients who had to stay longer.

While Molly rested, Mercy and Rhia cleaned. It wouldn't be long before Master Leister came to see his latest child. The nurse moved mechanically, stumbling through the directions Mercy gave.

"There are some things we need to talk about," Mercy said quietly, her arms full of dirty sheets. "These are important for your survival."

"What are you talking about?" Rhia asked without looking up from scrubbing the table.

Mercy leaned closer. "Listen," she said fiercely. Rhia glanced up, eyebrows raised. "You *must* learn the laws. Prove you know them, and those irons will come off."

Rhia's lip curled, a sign of defiance Mercy hadn't allowed herself in years. "Learn those horrible, misogynistic, stupid rules? I'd rather die."

Mercy's jaw tightened. "You idiot. There are opportunities available to people who aren't shackled. It's worth the humiliation of learning and reciting them. If you can please your Master, life can become...better."

Rhia was still so new. Dare she be more blunt? No. No. Hard-learned caution reasserted itself as she leaned back.

"Do you have tips to make rape more pleasant?" Rhia asked snidely. "Because that happens, too."

"That happens to every woman here, bondmaid, kitchen slave, and wife." Together, the women poured hot water into the tub on the floor. Then, Mercy dumped the sheets in, stirring them with a wooden paddle. "Be useful to your Master, speak softly, perform all the tasks he gives you."

Dumping in a little of her precious soap, she pumped cold water in, then continued stirring. The nurse curled her lip at Mercy's words but went back to scrubbing the table and floor. She moved on autopilot, with an economy of motion.

After a while, Rhia broke the silence. "I don't want to survive here. I want to get out! Even death would be better than this shit."

"That can be arranged." Mercy froze at the smooth, amused voice. Immediately, she turned to the door, dropping to her knees, head bowed before her Master. She watched through her eyelashes as he walked into the room, followed closely by Master Leister and Master Hermann.

"It seems your latest bondmaid doesn't know her place or appreciate the kindness you have done for her," Master said to Hermann, nearly purring. "What an affront to God. If you cannot keep peace in your house, how can you possibly receive more blessings?"

Hermann turned on Rhia, his chubby cheeks vibrating, his face slowly turning red. "You ungrateful whore!" he shouted, waving the Warriors forward.

Mercy closed her eyes when Rhia screamed at the men's grasping hands. Powerless, she listened to them drag Rhia from the room. They always preferred to punish bondmaids in the center of the plaza, in full view of everyone. Master Hermann followed them out, pouting.

Out of her sight, but that didn't matter. She'd seen this more than once. Men's laughter, a woman's screams...

The baby woke, a thin, wailing cry. Molly stirred but didn't wake. Mercy crawled to the infant when Master Leister, a noticeable bulge in his pants, snatched her kerchief from her head, exposing her light brown hair.

Mercy inhaled sharply, taking one long, crawling step to the side, but no sound escaped her throat. No fear could be shown around the other Masters, ever. When Master Leister reached for her again, her Master slapped his hand away.

"You would touch another Master's property not once, but twice?" he said, satisfaction curling through his words. Oh, yes. Her Master loved being able to show himself superior to the others. "She is not for you. Bondmaid. See to the infant, since its mother appears uncaring. Jesus said, 'Suffer the little children to come unto me,' and her lack speaks of sin."

Master Leister paled at those words. A woman's sin was her own, unless Master Kozlov said it could also spread to her Master.

"How shall you punish your bondmaid?" her Master purred.

Carefully crawling around Master Leister, Mercy scooped up the infant, rubbing Molly's arm. Molly shifted, moaning, but her eyes opened. "See Master," Mercy said softly. "She wakes. It's only exhaustion. The boy is large, and it took much effort—"

Master Leister shoved her aside with his foot. "Ignore my child, bond-maid?" Leister snarled. "A boy, no less? Let's see if you can ignore this!" His hand plunged into his pants as he climbed on top of Molly.

Molly squirmed, trying to buck him off. Mercy lunged to her feet. "No, Master Leister, you can't!"

She didn't even see it coming. Her Master's fist struck her face, knocking her to the ground. Only long habit and practice allowed her to protect the baby from the fall.

Her Master gripped her chin, squeezing brutally. When she opened her eyes, his face was inches from hers. "*Never* tell a Master that he cannot!" he hissed. "Know your place, bondmaid, or be named a whore! This is God's punishment on sinners, and as such, is holy. You will remain here to witness this and tell others to never speak against any man, ever."

He nodded to two more Warriors before striding to the door. He paused in front of it, one hand on the doorframe. "Beat her when it is done."

Those men took up position on either side of Mercy, holding her and forcing her to face the brutality in front of her, the screams of another woman still ringing in her ears.

***

Fresno, CA – Faith

Faith moaned, the sound faint to her ears. Everything hurt. Breathing hurt. Why did she feel like so much shit? She stirred, struggling to lift the giant weight that was her head, move a hand, or open her eyes.

Tears trickled miserably down her cheeks when nothing obeyed.

"She's waking up!"

"Come back to me, baby."

"Dan, come here!"

The words came too quickly, rushing through her head, nearly indecipherable. A hand slid under her head, cool metal pressed to her lips.

"Here, drink this." Her mother's voice.

"Mmm?"

"That's right, honey. I'm right here. Dad's here, too." Abigail's voice sounded choked.

Prying her eyelids up was the hardest thing she'd ever done, but once they were up, she smiled, the corner of her mouth twitching slightly. Mom and Dad on her left. Mom clutched her hand like she'd never let go. On her right...

She sighed. Lucas.

"Mm...kay?" Blearily, she rolled her head on the pillow. After another drink, she cleared her throat. "Wha...happened?"

Abigail closed her eyes, turning her face away. Dread opened in Faith's stomach, a black pit threatening to swallow her. What had happened? Had they...? She looked down, following the line of her body. Would she even know if the NKs had...had...

She shied away from that thought. Is it better to know? She looked to Lucas, pleading.

He gently lifted her hand, cradling it in both of his. "You were beaten. You defied the NKs to their faces, and you're alive to tell of it." He smiled, but his face remained pale, dark circles under his hazel eyes.

His beautiful hazel eyes. They'd always looked at her with so much gentleness, even when he was angry or she'd been reckless. So much patience in those striking eyes. Shards of green and gold...

He squeezed her hand, pulling her out of her reverie. "Faith." Gentle humor laced his tone. "You wandered there."

"Did I?"

"Do you want to hear the rest?"

Her situation crashed back. She must be in worse shape than she thought, if she'd gotten so distracted. The corners of her mouth turned down. "Tell me."

"Beaten, only. They intended for you to die in the street, a warning to anyone passing by. They put a sign on you. But the runner kid stayed nearby. When I got off work and found you..." He swallowed, his Adam's apple bobbing, and he shook his head.

"Does Carter know?" Faith whispered.

"He does," her dad answered.

Faith froze, eyes wide. "How did you know?"

They knew she was a part of the Resistance. She needed them to cover for her, but she'd never revealed any names. They knew Lucas was, but they were a part of his cover, too.

"You've been out for a while," Lucas interjected. "I brought you here, found the others. It took...it took a lot to take care of your injuries. I needed help."

"And it's a good thing you brought us into this," her mom said sternly.

Faith chewed her lip, drank more water when it was offered, and struggled to keep the tears at bay. Failing miserably, she turned her face towards

Lucas. He stroked her hair back from her face, leaning down until he could look her in the eyes.

"We'll be out of here soon," he whispered, his face tight, fierce. "Fresno will be in our rearview mirror and the next time we see Fresno, we'll be bringing the Ghost Captain with us."

Lucas's words sparked a rush of questions and excitement from her parents. In the babble of voices, Faith's eyelids slid closed with no prompting from her.

***

Her recovery blurred all sense of time. She woke, she slept, only the people sitting next to her changed in this windowless basement.

And no one sat with her as often as Lucas. They rarely spoke. He'd simply prop himself against the wall, their hands close enough to touch. She looked down at the space between their hands.

All she had to do was move her little finger.

Once, she woke to find him leaning against the wall, breathing deep and even, his face relaxed in sleep. Rolling slowly to her side, her eyes widened. A lock of her hair trailed across the narrow space between them, the end wrapped around his finger.

Taking the chance, she watched the candlelight play over his dark hair, bringing out the red highlights. His father's family were proud to call themselves *Californios*. The Morales family had been here since California was Mexico. His mother was from back East.

She'd never met them. They'd been visiting her family when the invasion happened, along with his siblings.

"It's not so bad," he'd said once, the day they met. "At least I know they're safe."

But you don't have safety here, she didn't say. *I'll be your safety.*

Because from the start, he'd been hers.

She'd been part of the only resistance in existence at the time, Central Fresno, and she'd intercepted news about a rebellion in the north. The first time she'd heard his name.

Captain.

Rushing home from work, full of new information about a rebel up north who worried the NKs, she didn't pay close attention to her surroundings.

"Where you going, girl?" The man appeared from the shadows less than five feet from her, grinning. A big man, over six feet tall, somewhere in his thirties, he blocked her way. On his right arm, the red armband of the North American Corps sat, prominently displayed.

He was one of the Americans who'd sided with the NKs when they arrived. She'd seen how they enjoyed the perks of their positions, turning in their neighbors, taking bribes, and hurting people indiscriminately under the banner of the law.

Faith frantically looked around. She'd gone down this street a hundred times by now, and it'd always been safe.

"Home," she said, raising her chin. She hitched her bag higher on her shoulder, resisting the urge to lick her lips and made to step around him.

He held out a hand. "Not so fast, girl. You have to pay the toll."

Her heart thundered in her chest, and she shifted. A pit of sick dread opened in her stomach. She already knew what he would say. His eyes roamed all over her, pausing at her breasts and thighs.

"Ten minutes," he continued, already reaching for her. "Then I'll let you go like nothing ever happened."

Rage sparked in her chest, drowning the hopelessness and dread. "What the fuck is wrong with you?" she screamed, even as things she'd overheard played through her head. If you stay still, he'll finish faster. If you don't fight, he won't hurt you as much. She grit her teeth. If he was going to hurt her, she'd damn well have a say in how much. "How would you feel if someone shoved their dick in your ass?"

He paused a moment. Maybe he wasn't used to being screamed at? In that split second, a blur slammed into the big man.

The blur turned out to be a slender young man, younger than herself. Almost as tall as his opponent, but much slimmer, Lucas had brought a brick to the fight, slamming it into the man's head again.

He'd grabbed her hand, whispered, "Run," and Faith had never looked back from that moment.

He'd changed little over the years. Determinedly cheerful, and he brought a brick to a few more fights, as she recalled. While she watched, his eyes opened. He started when he saw she was awake, but didn't release her hair, staying with her until she drifted off again.

CHAPTER 5

Eastern Washington – Grace

Grace dozed, curled next to Charlie. It'd been an exhausting few days. As the medic, Squirrel, predicted, Charlie had gotten an infection, but she'd doctored him competently, despite her carefree attitude. Now, Grace could understand why doctors normally acted so grave and important. It helped boost confidence in their abilities.

Next to her, Charlie's breathing changed. Grace lifted her head, peering at him in the early morning light coming through the broken window. "Baby?"

"Where...?" He coughed. "Water. Please."

She gently lifted his head, holding a water bottle to his lips. When he finished, he squinted up at her. "Where are we?"

Grace propped him higher on folded blankets and their bags, stroking his hair back from his face. "We're safe. Seahorse," the name still sat oddly on her tongue, but as a tool to make their users anonymous, it certainly did the trick, "took us to that old farmhouse just north of the 2. The one we saw last time."

Set back from any roads, the farmhouse was well hidden by thick trees and brush. A little ramshackle, it had two rooms that were still usable, and the barn itself only had a few leaks. They'd found it by following a deer track, avoiding the Gophers.

"It's been days." Her voice caught. "But you're on the mend, now."

"Our ducklings?"

Grace bit her lip, smiling through tear filled eyes. "They're fine. Seahorse sent half her forces to take them to the border."

"Why aren't we across the border?"

Grace bit her lip. "She, um, didn't give me a choice to leave. And since I wouldn't leave you, she kept us both. But she's got good vibes!" she hastily added.

Charlie's face darkened and he struggled to sit up. She held him down by simply putting more of her weight on him. A knock sounded at the door. Before Grace could respond, it opened.

"You all better be decent in here." Seahorse walked in without waiting for an answer.

"If we weren't," Grace muttered, "it'd be because you didn't give us time."

The commander surprised her by chuckling. "Yeah, I should know better, but I also know that a man in his condition isn't getting up to much. Oh, you're awake." Her smile grew, but it never quite reached her eyes.

Charlie's expression didn't lighten. "Nice of you to knock, I suppose."

"Yes." But the commander didn't leave. Instead, she fully entered the room, leaving the door open a few inches. "If you were awake, I thought it was time you got a few answers."

Jaw clenched, Charlie nodded. Taking her cue from him, Grace bit back the questions she'd been asking for days.

Soft vibrations ran through the weak floorboards, preceding a large man. His shoulders filled the doorway, and the rest of him was almost as wide. She'd had time to speak with the man, Sarge, a couple times. He avoided her questions, but always remained polite enough.

Now, he glanced at Seahorse. "Have you started yet?"

Seahorse shook her head, giving him the first real smile Grace had seen from the older woman. "You're just in time."

Sarge settled cross-legged onto the ground, a surprisingly graceful move. "Whenever you're ready, babe."

Babe? Grace's eyebrows shot to her hairline, and she exchanged a look with Charlie. So, the commander had a heart, after all.

Seahorse paced the small room, her fingers working restlessly. "A few months into the invasion, I was a captive in one of Steve's brothels. One evening—or maybe it was morning—I heard gunshots, screams, it was crazy. A man was in my room, when all of a sudden, an insane woman crashed through my door..."

It was an abbreviated version of events, but still... Who could believe gun fights, ambushes, homemade bombs, self-taught snipers and scouts? Yes, she and Charlie had made the switch, becoming guides, leading people out of Washington. Yes, they not only carried guns, but knew how to use them.

But still...

Through it all, a few names popped up, over and over. One, she'd heard before.

Captain.

When the story finished, ending with Oregon's liberation and the decision to split their forces, sending them north and south, Grace held up a hand.

"You mean to tell me that's only *half* your forces? There's several hundred of them!"

Seahorse shrugged. "Technically, I think there's a couple thousand. But yeah, this is only half."

"Holy shit."

Her reaction sparked another, sadder, genuine smile from the commander. "You look like him."

"Who?"

"I don't know his name," and though Grace knew why they didn't use names, it was still annoying, "but we all called him Hot Fuzz. That's how we knew about you. He told us."

"Who is he?"

"He *was*," Seahorse emphasized the past tense, her voice gentle, "a soldier. Tall, bit gangly. The younger girls thought he was handsome. A local to Oregon, from what I understood."

"Was?" Grace asked in a tiny voice.

Seahorse stopped at the opposite side of the small room, watching her sympathetically. "He died a few years ago."

Grace gasped, curling around the sudden pain in her chest. Tears spilled down her cheeks. Even though in her mind she didn't *know* it was Peter, her heart told her it was true.

Charlie struggled to sit up. "What did this soldier look like?" he rasped, finally giving up on getting upright and tugging her over to himself. Grace tucked her face into his chest, a thin, keening cry ripping from her throat.

"Brown hair, brown eyes. A sweet guy, but there were times when I'd have happily gagged him to shut him up."

Grace cried out against Charlie, pressing harder against him. *Peter's gone.* It echoed in her mind, as if by repeating itself, it could reduce the hurt.

"What's their relation?" Seahorse asked quietly. A gentle hand rested on her back.

"Her brother," Charlie said thickly. "How did he…?"

"Saving lives." She said the words matter-of-factly, as if it were an everyday occurrence for them. Perhaps it was. Grace didn't care.

Her baby brother was dead.

Eventually, worn out from her tears, Grace slumped against Charlie. The entire time she cried, the fighters stayed silent, present, but not intrusive, sharing her grief. Through her swollen eyelids, she watched Seahorse standing, head bowed.

"Hail the victorious dead," she whispered.

"Hail," the big man echoed. "Later, when we're done, we'll show you where he's buried with his brothers and sisters," Grace's heart seized again, but Sarge hadn't finished, "of the Irregulars. They are together, at last."

"Did you ever find more of our family?" Charlie asked. Grace cuddled against him. For now, he would be strong for her. Later, when he'd gotten herself together, she'd be strong for him.

Seahorse shrugged. "A little bit difficult to know, don't you think?"

More tears spilled from Grace's eyes. "It's not a No," Charlie whispered into her hair. "Maybe they were freed in the last push or something."

"You're not asking about your family," Sarge observed.

"Her family is the only one I have left." He tensed in Grace's arms. She wriggled, trying to get a little closer, even though a thread couldn't fit between them.

The door opened before anyone else could speak and Squirrel poked her head in. "I need to see to my… Oh, shit. They were related, weren't they?"

"Does everyone know everything?" Grace twisted to see the newcomer.

Seahorse shrugged. "Why keep information secret? No one knew for sure, but from how he spoke of you, we could guess."

"Yes, we share information." Squirrel shooed the fighters out. "Except whatever it is that rolls through our Captain's head, but no one can guess what goes on there. It's too scary to contemplate."

A new thought shot through Grace and she sat up. "Was Captain responsible for my brother's death?"

Seahorse paused, one hand on the door. "Only as much as any leader feels responsible. Could it have been avoided? He could have chosen not to rescue Captain and his in-laws, but he did. He could have chosen not to fight, but he did. And if he hadn't been there, a lot more people would have died.

"We honor him, as we honor all those who've fallen."

***

Fresno, CA – Faith

Lucas walked through her door. Faith smiled, her heart beating faster. "Lucas! How are things out there? When can I get out?"

He settled cross-legged onto the concrete floor next to her blanket mattress. His beautiful hazel eyes, the eyes she lived to see, were dark, shadowed. He took her hand, playing with her fingers.

"You're feisty this morning."

"I'm bored. Get me out of here. Please?" She fluttered her eyelashes outrageously.

He laughed quietly, leaning down to kiss her knuckles, holding her hand to his mouth for several long moments. Her heart twisted. Something wasn't right.

"Lucas?"

Barely lifting his lips, he whispered, "We have to move you today. Ready or not."

Faith cupped his cheek, unable to keep from stroking her thumb, savoring the texture of his skin, rough where he needed to shave, smooth higher up. "What happened?"

He turned his lips into her hand, kissing her palm. "I never did tell you what it did to me, seeing you in that alley. I didn't know if you were alive or..." His voice broke, and he closed his eyes. "I saw that kid first. She told me where you were, then booked it. It's a miracle she stayed as long as she did..."

"Lucas."

Noises came through the closed door, people moving and talking quietly. Lucas didn't move and just held her hand. She lay still, trusting him while the voices grew louder, breaking the silence in her room.

"They picked up Abel this morning," he finally said. "We don't know how they found him, but they did. Three days ago, two others in Central Chapter were taken in. The entire Fresno Resistance is bugging out over the next few days, all by different routes. It's beyond not safe anymore."

"They-they found...?" Faith choked, tears welling in her eyes. "It's because of me, isn't it? I drew attention to myself, and now—" She turned her face away, biting the blanket to stop her cries.

"*No!*" Lucas gripped her hand tight. "No, it's not your fault."

"I'm the go-between!" she cried. "I'm the one who sent messages, and I interfered. I made myself visible to an investigation."

She tried twisting away from him. How could he look at her with such compassion? She struggled when he slowly pulled her back, against his chest as he lay next to her on the pile of blankets.

"You weren't in contact with everyone who disappeared," he said. She finally noticed that he'd said this several times. She listened as he continued talking, but it wasn't the words that soothed her. His steady heartbeat and his low, rough voice, so familiar after these few years, yet new every time...

A knock on the door broke their tiny bubble.

"We need a minute," Lucas called.

Faith used the blanket to wipe away her tears, blowing her nose on a scrap of fabric Lucas gave her.

"You ready?" he asked. She nodded, and he carefully disentangled himself. The loss of his warmth and strength struck her immediately.

Carter and Jon quickly entered, followed by her dad. The men set a stretcher and body bag next to her while Lucas wrapped her in one of the blankets.

"It's the best way we could come up with to get you out," he explained when she tensed.

"Without you needing to stand or walk, too," her dad finished. He already wore the red armband of the Corps, the Americans who'd sided with the NKs.

Clenching her jaw, Faith looked from one man to the other, then nodded. Carefully, they picked her up in her blankets and laid her in the body bag. Zipping it partially shut, they left her face exposed while Carter and Jon—the only two remotely close to the same height—lifted the stretcher, carrying her through the door.

Upstairs, her mom stood ramrod straight next to Malva, both women wearing handcuffs. Women weren't allowed in the Corps, so prisoners and dead people is who the faux Corpsmen would be moving today.

The men set the stretcher down. Lucas peeked out the door, then grabbed an armband. Jon knelt next to her, smiling cheerfully.

"Ready to get out of this shithole?" he asked.

"Sure." Faith clenched her hands together, the trembling spreading through her whole body. Oh, convincing corpse she'd make, if she couldn't stop shaking. "So, Jon, what's Jon short for?"

She took several deep breaths, trying to calm herself. He gently set his hands on top of hers.

"Jondalev. It's okay. Everything will be fine. You'll see." He spoke with such assurance that she huffed a tiny laugh.

"Jondalev? I've never heard of that. Is it an old family name?"

"My mom got hit with that 'unique name' craze back in the day. Thank God I could shorten it to something normal."

"Poor guy."

Jon looked up, rising to his feet with alacrity. "Ah, Lucas. I'll give you two a moment."

She narrowed her eyes. Jon wasn't as calm as he let on. It was the only thing that made sense after his supreme confidence a moment ago.

Lucas took her hand and leaned close. "I love you. Just in case things go sideways, I wanted to say it at least once."

Faith stared up at him, her breath stolen by the declaration. He zipped the bag up before she got it back. Right before he covered her face, she closed her eyes so his expression would be what she took with her into the dark.

The road started rough, then smoothed out. She switched constantly from mentally charting their route to the expression of love, worry, and hope on Lucas's face right before the bag had been closed.

He said he loved her!

She'd fallen for him the moment he'd taken her hand and whispered, "Run!" They'd certainly become close over the years, but she wouldn't let herself hope. What if he was just an excellent actor and he only cared for her like a sister?

The truck stopped. Men's voices talking, but everything was too muffled. She tensed, clenching her hands until someone rested a hand on her leg.

"You're the best liar in the business," Lucas whispered. "So just...you're supposed to be dead, remember?" He stumbled over the word 'dead.'

Faith tried dredging up memories of yoga, and their tricks for relaxing, but this situation was about as far from zen as you could get. When the door latch clicked, the weight on her leg disappeared. Faith held her breath, closed her eyes, and flopped inside the body bag.

Someone kicked her feet, Lucas responded, her mom spat curses, and suddenly, they were rolling forward again.

"Just a bit longer," Lucas whispered. "Just to make sure we're safe."

In the darkness inside the bag, she went over Lucas's expression when he'd kissed her hand. They'd kissed so often over the years, to bring their lie to life. It'd been fun, passionate at times, but too often, they had to remember their job.

Today...oh, this was different. His expression had been pained, but she'd seen joy, too. Surety, but terror. What if she lost him? Or he lost her? Would it be easier or harder if she never spoke up about her feelings?

She thought of his declaration and sighed, joy bubbling to the surface. She bit her lip, holding back a laugh. Knowing Lucas loved her opened up so many thoughts of the future. For the first time, the future looked...good.

Fresh air brushed her skin when the zipper was drawn back. She opened her eyes, smiling up at Lucas as he leaned over her. He took her hand, lacing their fingers together. Abigail leaned over her other side, taking her free hand.

"We're out," she said, full of wonder. "I haven't been out of Fresno since...since they brought us in."

"Where are we going?" Faith asked.

"North." Lucas looked out the windshield. "We're going north, to find the Ghost Captain."

***

East of Sacramento, CA – Captain

Smoke choked the air, fires burning unchecked across the plains around Sacramento. Scorched earth and the seeds of new growth were left in its wake. We'd found higher ground across the river and watched the fires burn. The older members and several of the younger ones had been set to herding animals.

"I'm not leaving those poor creatures to burn," Shrike said flatly, folding her arms, blonde curls blowing in the wind.

I shook my head. "When have I ever said to leave the animals behind?"

"She reserves that for people," Dereva put in, looking up from the engine of my pickup.

I flipped her off.

"Notice that she's not denying anything," she continued, sniggering while she poured water into the radiator.

Shrike watched her, forehead wrinkled. "Doesn't that rust?"

"Yeah." I rubbed my forehead. "That's why we're on the fifty millionth fricking radiator. Honestly, I'm amazed she's still running."

"Bite your tongue!" Dereva shot up. "Don't you dare talk like that around her! She's very sensitive. You're such a good girl," she crooned to the truck, petting the engine.

Shaking my head, I wandered away. Outside the camp, the ground dropped away into a short, steep cliff, rocks jutting out along its top. I perched on the one sticking out the furthest, my feet dangling over empty air.

Brownish gray haze covered the sky, the smell of smoke sticking in my throat. Swinging my feet, I leaned out... Big rocks down there, too. If the earth loosened its grip just a little...

I flopped onto my back, shaking my head to clear it. No. Don't go there. I still had too much to do before I could see them again. Before I could see him.

A question that'd been brought up with nearly everyone I knew and lost crossed my mind: Who helped Steve?

Sitting up, I pushed my hair back, but my fingers came away wet. When had I started crying? Scrubbing my cheeks, I found a loosened tie on my shoulder. Twisting the hair back into its battle braid helped calm the raging emotions that I simply couldn't handle today.

"Yo, Captain!"

Ah. This particular knot finally relaxed. Phoenix and Gryph had arrived.

"We're back, and have I got news for you," she continued at the top of her lungs.

I waved and rolled backwards, ass over head to land on hands and knees. There really wasn't another way to get off that rock without falling off the edge. "How was the vacation?"

Phoenix strolled up, grinning, her face covered in soot. "I'm complaining to the travel agency. Way too hot. I specifically asked for a beachside resort. Hell, I'd take a lake. Seriously, though." She shook her head. "Steve didn't even *try* to stop the fires. They abandoned farm workers in little cages all over the place. They just needed someone to open the door."

Together, we walked back to camp. "Yeah, we found a lot of those, too." Taking a small sip of water, I let it trickle down my throat, clearing the taste of smoke. "Any sign of a resistance? Because I refuse to believe we're the only idiots on this entire coast."

Phoenix smiled, the smoke and orange glow lending her an evil air, her green eyes practically glowing. "As a matter of fact, we may have found something a little south of here."

***

The scouts reported lookouts ahead. Time to ditch the vehicles. We left them well hidden and guarded, along with our newest rescues who hadn't been evacuated to Oregon yet, up behind some casino.

The Irregulars spread out, each finding their own path. The land went either up or down, nothing in between. Small trees and thick scrub provided plenty of cover. I drifted past a man standing guard—so close I could have touched the back of his neck—a rifle clutched tightly in white fingers, resolutely watching the road instead of the forest.

I bared my teeth, continuing down the hill. The scent of wood smoke and cooking cut through the soot and wildfire that still filled my senses.

I waited in a copse of pine trees about fifty feet from this camp. Fighters slowly made their way to me while the scouts drifted with the wind, looking for the people in charge.

Crouching, I waited. Never let it be said I couldn't make an entrance.

CHAPTER 6

Coarsegold, CA – Faith

Faith opened her eyes to trees arching overhead, a mix of evergreens and beautiful orange and red foliage. She stretched, smiling, and reached up, tracing the air, following the branches with her fingertip.

No pain today. For the first time since she woke up after the beating, no pain. She rolled onto her side, facing the little fire. Two and a half walls enclosed their tiny camp, no roof except the trees, but once the sun rose, it hardly mattered anyway.

She even hoped for rain. It would help dampen the valley's fires and smoke.

Across the fire, Lucas's blankets were empty, but footsteps crunching through last year's leaves heralded his return. He carried a bucket in each hand, water sloshing over the sides with every step.

"We've had some more people arrive," he announced. "Malva's getting them settled."

"Excellent!" Carter rubbed his hands together. Morning sunlight picked out the silver strands in his black hair. "What are we up to now?"

Lucas set the buckets down, reaching his arms overhead. Faith bit her lip, eyes caught on the narrow band of skin showing at his waist, a thin trail of hair disappearing under the waistband of his jeans. "Almost two hundred."

"How are we going to feed all those people?" her mom asked.

Sitting up, Faith watched her parents lowering the bags of food. Everything had to be stored high, to keep the bears away. When people left, wildlife returned, and unfortunately, that meant bears and mountain lions, too.

"They're bringing food with them," Lucas said. "They're running away from the farms, carrying everything they can."

"The NKs?"

"They're more concerned with escaping the fires."

"They probably think they can round us all up again," Faith interjected. She touched her thumb to each fingertip in turn as she thought. "Trying to evacuate the workers would slow them down. Releasing the workers then rounding up the survivors is the safest way for them."

"I don't think that's quite it. A few have talked about a convoy," Lucas continued. "Armed people freeing them after they were left locked in cages."

"Is that the Resistance?" her dad asked. "Or...or is it the Ghost Captain?" He lowered his voice, as if someone might overhear.

Lucas shrugged. "No way of knowing for sure. Those people weren't really interested in talking."

"Hey!" Malva walked up the hill. "Can I get some help over here! We've got more people arriving and we need to set up more camps, guards..."

Faith held her hand out to Lucas, who pulled her to her feet. "You sure you're up for this?"

"Please!" She clutched his arm, laughing and glancing back at her parents. "Get me out of here."

***

They worked together through the day, taking a break once the sun got high overhead. Lucas took her to a little meadow near the water, producing a blanket from his backpack.

He spread it on the ground with a little flourish, holding his hand out to help her down. Taking it, she let him settle her onto the blanket, pulling another out to act as a pillow.

"Your mom threatened me if I didn't promise to make you rest," he said, grinning at her expression.

She patted the space next to her, sticking out her tongue and giggling. "Then you have to stay here, too. If you don't, I'm just going to wander around and find more work."

"Ah! I have orders to sit on you, if necessary." Laughing now, Lucas dropped down next to her, propping himself up on one elbow.

She gazed up at him, his lips curling at the corners, a dimple playing hide-and-seek in his left cheek. Reaching up, she gently ran her fingertip over it, then down to the corner of his mouth. He leaned over, gently pushing a lock of hair back from her face, suddenly serious.

Faith froze. "What is it?" she whispered, her eyes darting around the tiny clearing. "Did you hear something?"

He let out a breath she hadn't realized he'd been holding. "What? No! No, I just...I'm...shit." He flopped onto his back, groaning. "I'm an idiot," he said in a rush. "I'm trying to apologize if what I said the other week was out of line. After all, it's not like we've ever talked about...about...us. I mean, I get it! We had to pretend, and to you, it was probably all pretend.

You're intelligent, creative, clearly the best undercover agent we've got. The guys here are all asking about you to see if you're single..." He trailed off miserably.

Throughout his entire diatribe, Faith's mouth dropped open, her astonishment growing. "Why the hell are you talking about other men? Wait, you think I'm the best agent we've got? You think I'm beautiful?"

With every question, she got louder, until Lucas put a hand over her mouth. "You want to bring the NKs on us?" But his grin brought his dimple into full display.

Inside, Faith melted. There'd been so few occasions for that dimple to make an appearance, especially over the last few months. "Mmfmspebl!" Unable to get him to remove his hand, she twisted her head and bit the fleshy mound at the base of his thumb.

"Ow!" He snatched his hand back. "What was that for?"

"Oh, please. You knew I'd bite." Faith rolled her eyes. "Now, what I think I really need is for you to clear something up for me. Tell me again what it was you said that day. What you're now apologizing for." He hesitated. "Tell me!"

Sometime in all of this, they'd rolled towards each other. Now, they lay with their noses mere inches apart. His breath brushed over her mouth. Her lips unconsciously parted as she drowned in his hazel eyes.

Leaning closer, his eyes dropped to her mouth, then flicked back to her eyes. "I love you," he whispered. "In case something happens to us, I just wanted you to know that."

Tears filled her eyes, and she smiled. "I'd hoped for...so long. Why did you wait to say anything?"

He shrugged helplessly. "Every time I left you, I had to wonder if today was the day I'd never see you again. I didn't want...I didn't want you to miss me too much."

"You idiot!" She pushed his chest, too close to punch him like she wanted. "You bonehead! It wouldn't matter if you'd said the words or not! If you disappeared, I'd never have stopped looking for you. I don't have to say 'I love you' to feel the emotions. Idiot."

A slow smile spread across his handsome face. "You love me? I have to say, as much as I dreamed of you telling me you loved me, I didn't expect to hear it along with so many insults. Tell me again."

"I love you. Idiot."

When they wandered back into camp, the sun cast long shadows and a golden haze over the hills and mountains. The fires in the valley looked like they'd finally moved far enough away to allow them to breathe a little easier, another piece of good news.

Faith paused just outside of their camp, watching her parents and Malva moving around the fire, preparing dinner. In all their talk this afternoon, they'd forgotten something. "Are we planning to tell people that we're really together?"

Lucas laughed quietly. "Haven't they been assuming we were since about two weeks after I started walking you to work?"

"Only until I brought them into the fold. Mom said something about firebrands never living long and to hold onto every moment." She made a face. "Which I finally understand. How much better would the last few years have been if we'd really been together?"

"No. No regrets. We did what we had to, we made the choices we did. The end."

Sighing, she leaned against him, resting her cheek against his arm. "Easier said than done, but I'll try."

"Good enough." He wrapped his arm around her, holding her tightly against him. She smiled, hiding her face. How could she be so happy? How could she not? "Let's tell them," Lucas said. "Everyone could use some more good news."

They walked slowly into camp, arms wrapped around each other.

"Oh, good, you're back," Abigail said, without looking up. "It's not safe out there in the dark, and..." She looked up. A huge smile spread across her face. "You've finally figured it out, have you?"

"Mom!" She protested over Malva's laughter. "You don't have to make a big deal about it."

"Hah! I've been waiting for you two to figure out you loved each other for *ages*. How did I raise such a clueless daughter?" Abigail looked to the heavens, her hands raised.

"You raised a *busy* daughter," Faith grumbled.

Lucas shook her father's hand, grinning like...well, like an idiot.

"Now," Abigail continued, "sit down, eat, and you can tell us everything."

Color rose in Lucas's throat, a tide of deep red against his dark skin. "I'm not telling her *everything*," he mumbled against Faith's hair.

Remembering exactly where his hands and lips had roamed, she heartily agreed.

"Honestly," Malva interjected, pouring hot water into their teapot—a small metal bucket with a lid, "I thought the two of you were a couple already. I know," she held up a hand to stop their protests, "it was a cover, but those often turn very real very quickly."

"What turned real?" They turned to see Carter return with Jon, both carrying more firewood.

"Lucas and Faith," her dad said, beaming. "Though I'll be honest, with the way she waited for him to pick her up every morning..."

Carter shook his head. "Huh. I can't believe you've been faking it for over two years without actually..." He trailed off, realizing he was speaking in front of Faith's large father. He smiled weakly at the older man. "I met the Sheridans today," he said too heartily. Inside, Faith shook her head. How had he managed to fool the NKs for so long? The man was lousy at covering his own ass. "Their oldest son is nineteen. He wants to join the Resistance and become a real fighter."

As opposed to what? A fake fighter? There weren't any other groups *to* join. And could he even be trusted? There were too many people arriving. It wouldn't be difficult to hide a Corpsman in the incoming tide of refugees.

"Another reason to celebrate!" Dan said, clapping his hands. He turned to Abigail. "My dove, would you care to help me bring back something to help us celebrate?"

"Booze, dad?" Faith grinned. "Where did you get that?"

"Oh, it was already here." Dan leaned close, his dark blue eyes sparkling. "Your mother's cousin lived in this neighborhood, and he kept a little wine cellar. I checked it out the other day, and it's still intact."

Faith laughed as they picked up a lantern and headed out. Once they were gone, she seated herself against the wall on her folded blankets. Lucas took the spot next to her, their knees pressed together.

They chatted quietly, eating slowly. Faith couldn't resist brushing against Lucas every chance she could. And if she wasn't reaching for him, he touched her, a hand on her waist, brushing his hip against hers...She smiled, tipping her face to the still smoky sky.

"Hey," Jon spoke for the first time. "How long does it take to get wine? Do you think they need help?"

A branch cracked loudly. In the distance, an owl hooted. Faith shrank against Lucas. "I'm sure they'll be fine. But I stand with my mom. Forests at night are a little scary."

She could hear footsteps now and sat up. Wine! She hadn't had alcohol in literal years. She drained her mug, then the smile froze on her face.

Her parents walked slowly into the firelight. Abigail's white face visible first, her hands held stiffly at shoulder height. Dan walked tightly, furious, moving in small starts. Behind them—around them—dark figures moved silently through the bushes. A big man walked directly behind them, gun out, his black hair showing brown and red highlights.

Carter was the first to move, drawing his gun, ready to go down fighting, when a twig dropped onto his head. Then another. Faith's eyes widened.

A petite woman, sandy hair peeking out from under a dark cap, sat on top of the broken wall, grinning and shaking her head. She held a gun that seemed too large for her tiny hands pointed right at him.

Hardly daring to move, she took in the scene. More people entered the light, but she never heard them move. Most were women, only a few men scattered through the bunch. The women were beautiful, and completely incongruous out here.

Lucas tried to get his feet under him, only to find a young woman, strawberry blonde hair cascading around her shoulders in small braids, at his side, gun in hand. She looked like a movie star, with light blue eyes, high cheekbones, full lips, all of it marred by a thick scar twisting down the side of her face.

She caught Faith's eye and slowly shook her head. Meekly, she removed her hand from under her blankets, bringing out her knife, still in its sheath, and set it on the ground. Lucas put an arm in front of her, glaring at the blonde, who merely smiled, tapping a knife in her belt.

From the protection of Lucas's body, she had a better position to observe unnoticed. And there was a lot to notice. Particularly Jon, who looked just as fascinated as she.

A raven-haired, curvy woman held a pistol like an extension of her arm. A woman with mink brown hair and startling, blue-gray eyes bared her teeth in a fierce grin.

And every single one of them wore a motley collection of clothing. Jeans, cargo pants, and military fatigues were mixed with t-shirts, tank tops, and active wear. She noted moccasins, with a few pairs of hiking and combat boots.

Everyone with long hair used braids to contain it. Some wore a faux mohawk, others looked like their hair was sewn down. Some kept their hair short, but even they sported a braid or two.

Then, the elephant in the room. These people were armed to the teeth. Even the youngest, who looked still in her teens, carried an arsenal. Rifles, handguns, knives... Some carried long blades slung over their shoulders.

Barely turning her head, she counted. Twenty visible, and from their looks, they could take on everyone in the Resistance and barely break a sweat.

Strangest of all, everyone was silent. Perhaps, if they stayed quiet, no one else would get pulled into this. Hopefully, these strangers missed the rest of their camp.

This was her only hope. These people looked like they'd been through hell and back. They were good. They'd stopped any hope of a fight by simply...being there first. No one could make a move because they were already covered.

Then a new person entered the scene.

This woman was tall—nearly as tall as her father—her dark blonde hair done up in a mohawk braid, smaller side braids swinging around her shoulders, mingling with a bit of loose hair. Her eyes met Faith's and goosebumps rose on her arms.

This woman had the coldest eyes Faith had ever seen. Gray, with hints of blue, she saw no mercy in them. A series of thin scars around one larger one bisected her left eyebrow and part of her cheek, barely missing her eye.

As heavily armed as any in her crew, she carried a rifle, thigh guns, shoulder holsters just visible under a slightly large leather jacket, a machete over her shoulders... Faith was willing to bet she kept at least one knife tucked into the tops of her moccasins.

The other fighters maintained an awareness of this woman. No one turned to follow her, but there were small movements. The twitch of a head, a quick glance. She was their leader.

As she paced around the small camp, Faith grew increasingly uneasy. Something about this woman seemed so familiar, but what? Where could she have met her?

"Who are you?" Carter demanded, standing straight, chin up. He snarled when a girl relieved him of his weapon, handling it with more ease than he managed. "What do you want? Did the NKs send you?"

The woman cocked her head. "Steve?" She snorted, flicking her fingers, brushing the idea aside. "Not a snowball's chance in hell."

She continued pacing, a predator in a flock of sheep. *She was what the Corpsmen imagined themselves to be,* she dimly realized. A wolf, and the sheep couldn't escape, a fact of which she seemed to be aware. A smile flirted around her lips, but it never reached those cold, gray eyes.

"Why are you here?" Carter demanded, stepping forward, nearly pushing himself against the barrel of the gun aimed at him.

Faith clutched Lucas's arm, her fingers digging into firm muscle as she held her breath. The leader cast Carter a quick glance.

"We heard there was a resistance in town. Haven't found much yet. Are you supposed to be it?" She dismissed them even as she asked the question, but Faith sensed more. Was she playing with them? And there was still something about her...

Carter's lips tightened, but the leader hadn't finished. "We came here looking to help the local resistance. I see a lot of locals, not much resistance. Think we worked too hard to get here?"

There were sniggers, shaken heads, and their guard, the strawberry-blonde, laughed outright. The petite woman on the wall disappeared (*when had that happened?*), reappearing beside the leader.

"Stop playing with them, will you?" Faith's eyes widened. Speaking so disrespectfully to such an imposing figure was...terrifying. The tiny woman continued, "Aanisah is here with the saboteurs. Steve's in the area, on foot, heading this way. They already knew about this lot."

"Numbers?"

"Three hundred."

"Of course they fuckin' are." The large man spoke for the first time, startling Faith with his British accent. "Wankers never did have a sense of timing."

"Yes, they do," the tall woman said dryly. "Their timing sucks, as always."

"Who's Steve?" Carter asked.

"The soldiers."

Faith gasped, making the leader look her way. She froze, staring straight into those eyes for a second. Sorrow, rage, and sheer, implacable will stared back at her. She turned away, unable to look any longer.

The leader ignored the rest of the Resistance's sounds of surprise and shock, addressing her people. "We need to move fast. Raven, deploy the scouts. Find Chaos and the saboteurs. Booby traps, buy time, the lot."

A stocky woman in her mid-twenties materialized from the dark. Consulting briefly with the leader, she disappeared as quickly as she'd come.

"Dogwood found a spot for your civilians to hide," the leader announced. "Outside..."

"Wait!" Carter slashed his hand through the air. "Why the hell should we do anything you say? We've only your word about an attack. My people are watching the roads, and they haven't seen anyone."

"They didn't see us, either." The strawberry-blonde grinned nastily.

A cry came from the highway. "The NKs are coming!"

The leader rolled her eyes. "*As* I was saying, we found a safer spot for your people." A young woman entered the firelight, all brown hair and legs. "Legs will guide you there. We'll take care of Steve."

The sardonic expression, the way her lip curled... Goosebumps rose on Faith's arms, her heart pounding so loud it nearly drowned out all else.

"Please," Faith whispered, drawing their eyes again. "What is your name? Who are you?"

The leader turned slowly to face her. In a moment, the years lightened, and Faith saw a hint of the laughing cousin she once knew, hidden inside the lines and scars of the tall woman's face. She spoke carefully, as if she didn't want to leave any doubt as to her identity.

"I am Captain."

***

Washington, DC - Constance

It'd been two weeks since the first doc was unlocked and she learned of James Perry and his time in Oregon, and Constance still hadn't come any closer to finding him. Her modest network of informants hadn't heard anything about him.

Considering what she'd found on his men, that might make him the lucky one. Out of the seven soldiers who'd emerged from the Occupied Zone, six now rested in cemeteries, the most recent one passing eleven months ago under extremely suspicious circumstances.

Constance rested her chin in her hand, blindly staring at her screen. She hadn't had any luck with Senator Baser, either, not in digging up dirt for McKinney, nor in quietly getting close enough to voice her concerns.

And the second document that'd been unencrypted couldn't yet do her any good. Wire taps with hours of voice recordings, but the section with *where* those taps were placed still hadn't been opened.

Muffled shouting from Senator McKinney's office broke her reverie. She sat up, reluctantly booting up her tablet, striving to look busy.

"That Baser bitch blocked me again!"

Whoops. McKinney managed to yell at a level that breached his medium level soundproofing. Did soundproofing wear out?

And once he finished yelling at Albrecht, his personal investigator, he'd demand a progress report from Constance. One where she'd have to disappoint him yet again. She didn't mind disappointing him, but it was the way he looked at her while she stood in his office.

Like he was undressing her.

She still needed the resources available to her here, she reminded herself. She needed to find Sergeant Perry, she needed more information, she needed...so much.

Constance rubbed her eyebrows, applying pressure to the space between, hoping to stop the headache before it got any worse. Footsteps clicked down the corridor and she sat up straighter, typing out a document she didn't care about.

The only thing that mattered was the flash drive in her apartment.

Glancing at the clock, she nearly groaned. Still another hour. Maybe, by the time she made it home, her computer would have another document open. It seemed too much to hope for at this point.

McKinney's door opened and Albrecht, the Senator's lean, hatchet-faced aide, slid through. He paused outside her open door, leaning against the frame. She didn't look up, hoping he'd take the hint and keep moving.

"Oh, come on," he said, his raspy voice grating on her nerves. "Can't you give me a smile? You're so much prettier when you smile."

Constance pursed her lips, struggling to hold back a curse. McKinney didn't care for swearing, said it belonged strictly to the lower class, and she had no desire to get his attention so close to her weekend.

"It's Friday," she repeated softly to herself. Then, louder, "Thank you, but I don't need you to think I'm pretty. Have a good day, sir."

He walked into her office, hooking his thumbs into his belt. She hid her trembling hands behind her computer screen, continuing to write. Complete gibberish, but he didn't need to know that.

Albrecht sat on the end of her desk, one leg swinging as he leaned towards her. Instinctively, she slid back, giving him space. He shifted, sidling closer.

Maybe she should have taken those self-defense classes Nakia was always on about.

"Now, now. Don't be like that." He smiled, showing off his teeth. "I'd like us to be friends. After all, you can never have too many friends in a place like this." He smiled wider. "Pretty little thing like you should never be left on her own."

Panic made her breath come short. Then, the Senator's door opened again. Snatching up her tablet, she practically leaped to her feet. "Sir! Senator, I have some forms you need to sign, sir." Hurrying around her desk, clutching the device like a lifeline, she nearly ran.

McKinney stopped but didn't turn. "Unless you have that information I sent you for, forget it. I thought you wanted to move up in this world, but now…"

"Sir," Albrecht rasped from behind her, "maybe I can give Ms. West here some pointers or a bit of role playing," he leered, "to help her get that information."

McKinney waved without looking. "Thank you, Albrecht. See to it. Ms. West, you will offer him your full cooperation." He turned slightly. "Unless you wish to make it up to me in another way?"

Stunned, Constance could only stare at him, her eyes wide, nearly gasping for breath. Albrecht slid around her, grabbing the door. "Don't worry, Senator. I'm on it."

Shutting the door, he locked it. She'd never heard a sound so ominous. The lean man grinned again, surveying her.

"If you didn't notice, McKinney isn't too impressed with no results. But maybe I can teach you a thing or two about men..." He stalked her, head lowered slightly, hands held wide.

She backed up until she hit the wall. Albrecht removed his jacket, tossing it carelessly over a chair. Her breath coming in short pants, she looked wildly around the room for an escape. There, a window, but too small, and too high for her to reach.

The door, but Albrecht stood between her and it. Plus, she'd have to be incredibly coordinated to open it in the split second she'd have available to her.

"Get out," she whispered desperately. "I'm fine. I don't need your help. The worst comes to worst, I'll be fired."

He snorted. "I don't think you've noticed, but you don't get fired. Especially not from this position. Once you're in, you're in. But, since you've been failing your evaluations for so long, it's time to see if a little tough love can straighten you out."

She cut sideways, hoping to use her desk to get around him, but he dodged back. She froze, clutching the edge of her desk, ready to bolt in either direction.

"What do you want?" she asked, hating the tremble in her voice.

He licked his lips, undoing the top buttons of his shirt. "Does it matter? You have nowhere to run, and no one to help you. Even your daddy wouldn't stop this if he knew."

Feinting right, she ran left, making it to the door. Fumbling with the lock, she cried out when rough hands grabbed the back of her shirt, Albrecht flinging her back so hard she struck the desk with her side, lying half on it.

Albrecht smiled, pulling his shirt from his pants. "Now, now. If you promise not to scream, I won't hurt you."

Holding her side, she shrieked. "Get away from me! Help!"

Laughing and snarling, Albrecht lunged. Rolling, she barely evaded him, kicking off her heels in the process. She dived right, but Albrecht, quick as a snake, seized her arm. He grabbed her hair pulling her head up.

Screeching, she struggled to escape, scratching and pushing, but he twisted her arm up, behind her back. She cried out, her shoulder brutally wrenched. Spinning her around, he bent her over the desk, forcing her wrist up, between her shoulder blades.

Constance screamed.

He casually slammed her head against the desk. The world went dark. She lay, dazed, while his free hand wandered around her hips and legs, to the hem of her skirt. Tugging, he worked it higher, up her thighs. She wriggled, whimpering. Blood ran into her eyes, blinding her. His breathing grated harshly in her ear.

He grunted, settling his weight onto her. Her lips moved in a prayer she hadn't thought of in years. His fingers crawled up her leg, and she let out a strangled sob.

Sudden crashing, and the weight left her abruptly. Men shouting, more crashing, and Constance was pulled upright. Gentle hands pulled her skirt down, and soon she found herself looking into fierce hazel eyes.

The stranger was slender, shorter than Albrecht but taller than her. He gave her a quick, reassuring smile, taking her hand and leading her from the office.

"We need to leave, Ms. West." He spoke rapidly, head swiveling to look in all directions. She followed, her stocking feet silent on the cold marble floors, still dazed. "You're not safe anymore. McKinney is the type to suspect a molehill is a mountain, then panic and try to hide the evidence."

Soft grass under her feet. When did that…? She blinked. When had they gotten outside? Panic set in again. Digging in her heels, she leaned back. "Wait. Who are you? Where are you taking me?" Struggling, she mumbled, "I need to go to my apartment."

"Your apartment isn't safe, ma'am. It's being watched. I had a hell of a time finding a way to get to you without being seen."

"No!" She twisted, trying to free her hand. For such a slender man, he had a surprisingly strong grip. Panic roared through her. "I *need* to go home!"

The man seized her, hauling her off the path into the trees. He was going to murder her! She opened her mouth to scream and—

"I'm not going to hurt you," he hissed, his face inches from hers. "*Please* don't fight! I'm here to help, but you need to trust me."

"Why should I?"

"Because, Ms. West," he said, black hair mussed and falling across his eyes, "*you* have been searching for me. I'm James Perry."

CHAPTER 7

Pasadena, CA – Mercy

Mercy worked frantically, pressing a thick pad against a gushing wound, strapping it down quickly. Groans and cries filled the air. In the distance, the clacking of wood and clash of metal were sharp punctuations to the shouts of men.

Once, there'd been gunfire, but ammunition had run out within the first year or so. Now, men were reduced to killing each other with knives, staves, and clubs.

The fight raged just down the street, maybe two hundred feet away. She'd heard something about religious iconography. Baptists controlled this section, sworn enemies to the Masters and their fundamental teach-ings.

Holy wars, they called them.

Bloody stupid is what she wanted to shout to the skies.

Under her hands, her latest patient thrashed, cried out for his mother, then fell still, brown eyes fixed on the blazing sky. She moved immediately to the next man, yanking fresh bandages from her bag.

"Bleeders first," she called to her assistants, Susannah and Ruth. Both had undergone training, but this was their first time near a battlefield. "Stop the bleeding, then assess!"

Finished with her own task, she checked the rest of the man's limbs, putting bandages on cuts while assessing his bones. Damn clubs, she hated those things.

Barely done with that, she moved to Susannah. The singer, prized by her Master for the purity of her voice, grit her teeth, surrounded by injured and bleeding men. Her large hazel eyes barely blinked, focused and intent on the man in front of her even as tears rolled slowly down her cheeks.

"Why now?" Susannah whispered, over and over.

Mercy gently pushed her aside. She knew. Her Master, intent on making a point to Simpson, had called her name. His smile had been the barest crinkling around his eyes, but Mercy easily recognized it.

"'Time she served the Kingdom' my ass," Mercy muttered, finishing her examination. "Leave him."

"But...it's not that bad. I've seen worse."

"Before," Mercy said sternly. "Not now. Leave him. There are others we can save."

The man, in his thirties, cried out, one hand reaching for them. Mercy pulled her skirt aside before he could latch on.

"Why?" the man cried pitiably.

The small muscles in Mercy's jaw jumped. She bent over, whispering in his ear. "Rhia. Alice. Prudence. We both know what you did."

Sweeping around, she pushed Susannah to the next man, who'd already stopped breathing. No loss there. Next. She worked mindlessly over the men, mostly Warriors of Light. Useless and cruel, the lot of them.

Black eyes, intense and fierce, lived on in her mind's eye. The only man she'd met since the airports fell who'd shown kindness.

Pulling her from the rubble outside LAX after the planes hit, he'd held her, bandaged her wounds. Then, she'd done the same for him.

Jonathan.

The running and hiding as the residents of the Basin discovered all the exits blocked. Food and water growing increasingly scarce, yet despite that, he always brought something back for her until she could move more easily.

The people might have pulled together as a whole if it hadn't been for the preppers. Those men, crazed at being proved 'right,' shot anyone who even set foot near their homes. And every starving one of them knew they had stores of food.

Hungry people, driven by despair, raiding those bunkers, dying by the dozens but ultimately killing the original occupants. Those bunkers and homes traded hands a dozen times before bullets ran out.

And through it all, Jonathan protected her. In exchange, she bandaged him, struggling to find darker fabric so that it didn't stand out against his dark skin. Dog tags, shining silver against his chest when he gave her his shirt after hers tore.

Their first, hesitant, gentle touches when they were sure they were safe, those times of safety being too rare. His lips touching her eyelids, down her cheeks, to the hollow of her throat, warm, safe, there.

Jonathan's injury, shot in the shoulder after, blood gushing over her hands as she frantically tried to stop the bleeding.

Running across a heavily pregnant woman and her worried husband hiding in a building with their small church group. Delivering a baby—her first—and handing the squalling bundle to his father.

The father giving her a look of such avarice she physically recoiled. And three men jumping a still-weak Jonathan, holding him down while the new father drove a broken stake through his stomach.

Screaming—her screams—when she flung herself across him, struggling to stanch the wound.

His black eyes staring sightlessly at the sky as the men dragged her away.

Her own tears returned her to the present. Unconsciously, one hand went between her breasts. Beneath her blouse, metal chimed softly.

"Hurry up, whore!"

A short riding crop swished past her face. She glared up at the overseer, Macey. "If I go faster, I miss something and this man dies," she snapped. "And leave my assistants alone," she snarled before he could move on. "They're struggling enough without you. You tend to your work, leave me to mine."

If she saved enough men, this moment would become a good story for her Master, one he could use to show that she wouldn't obey just any man, but only him. If she didn't... Well. There were consequences for that, too.

"We're becoming overwhelmed with wounded, you stupid cunt," he barked, waving the crop towards the fighting.

"So, tell them to fight better!" Mercy finished wrapping a leg. "If you want things to hurry up here, give me more helpers. Once the bleeding's stopped, the wounded can be moved."

She could feel Macey glaring holes in her back, but she was right, and he knew it. Soon, several Sons of Judea—the third most pretentious name she'd ever heard—were also moving amongst the wounded.

During the work, Mercy made her way to Ruth. "How you holding up?" she murmured.

Ruth glanced furtively over her shoulder. "Are we still on for tomorrow?"

Mercy barely resisted shaking her head. The only way the woman could look more guilty of conspiring was if she'd begun whistling while looking around at nothing.

"Push it back until we're done with the wounded. I won't be free until then. At least two days. Your friends still in?"

"We'll all be there."

"Remember what I told you. Take the long route to my door and be there right before dark."

The tide of wounded pulled them apart. Her next patient had a crushed shoulder. She probed it gently. Absolutely pulped. Straightening, she waved one of the Sons over.

"He won't make it," she said quietly.

Nodding, the boy waved another over and they carried the injured man off to the side. Macey loomed over them, watching, while one took out a knife and set it against the injured man's throat. The man cried out, struggling feebly, but the other Son held him down, turning his face away.

"Get on with it!" Macey snarled.

Startled, the boy jerked, drawing the knife across the prone man's throat. Mercy shook her head. The Masters had no use for disabled people. This way, they also trained boys to become killers.

***

Ellensburg, WA - Grace

Grace huddled against Charlie in the back of a truck, the same kind she'd always seen the soldiers use. The fighters—the Irregulars—called it a Chimera. Her sister, Hope, would know exactly what kind of truck it was, and she'd've been itching to get her hands on the engine.

A tear trickled down her cheek and she buried her head against Charlie's chest, hiding from the others. Charlie held her close, stroking her hair while she cried. After learning about Peter's death, the slightest thing could set her off, even something as stupid as a truck.

The truck bounced over a rough patch, reminding her they were heading into dangerous territory. From the way the others behaved, it was just another Saturday night. Except they didn't know what year it was, and they certainly didn't know the day.

They apparently didn't believe in sleeping at night, either. While she and Charlie had grown used to night operations, this felt...different. Perhaps it was being in a vehicle. Or it could be the heavily armed people, chilled and relaxed around them.

Some of them were *teenagers*.

And knowing that her baby brother was gone...it changed everything, but at the same time, nothing. They had a job to do, and she wanted to...to what? Show them she could measure up to her brother? Not that, no. She wanted to contribute to them, to their cause, to help the people who'd meant so much to him that he'd laid down his life for them.

So, she and Charlie squished into the vehicle. Seahorse rode shotgun, and more fighters filled the back of the truck to bursting, all of them giving her quick glances. Were they wondering if she could hold up to the high standards Peter set?

"Sorry about the cramped quarters," Seahorse called. "Unfortunately, we don't have enough vehicles for everyone to ride comfortably."

"We'll find a few more, I bet." The young man they'd met the first night, Dionysius, leaned over her shoulder.

Grace stirred, lifting her head. A distraction from her loss was welcome. "After this many years, not likely."

"What do you mean?"

"I've got some family who are—were—mechanics. I learned a bit from them through sheer self-defense and osmosis—it's amazing what you learn when you can't get people to shut up. Anyway, according to them, cars that sit too long don't run anymore."

Seahorse laughed. "We're not looking to find older cars. The aim tonight is to not break all of *Steve's* cars. Then we'll steal the ones that are left."

"Oh."

"Who is this Captain?" Charlie asked suddenly. "You didn't answer the last time I asked. And what about the Ghost? We've heard a lot of rumors about him, too."

"That's a way cooler name than what you guys came up with," the driver, a woman named Wilder, muttered.

"Meaning?" Charlie's tone was hard. He didn't like not knowing, and he liked it even less when she was hurting. Maybe, if they finally gave him a straight answer, it'd be easier for him to trust these people.

A couple of the fighters shifted, muttering. Grace pressed closer to Charlie. Going from veterans to rookies in the space of a night didn't help her confidence or feelings of safety, either.

Seahorse patted the air. "Calm your tits, kids. I guess we can trust them a little. As for your question," she addressed them, now. "Captain and Ghost are one and the same. Steve calls them Ghost Captain, or something. Which *is* a pretty cool name, dammit."

Charlie settled back. "The same?" His eyes widened. "Holy fuck."

Grace glanced at him. "What?"

"Those rumors—you know, the mountain, Portland, all of it—it's all one person."

Her mouth dropped open, then she laughed, surprised at the sound, but pleased, too. "Why did I need to hear you say that for it to sink in?"

"Seahorse," the woman in the gun mount called. "Firelight ahead. We're nearly there."

"Thanks, Evenstar." Seahorse twisted around in her seat. "Time to gear up, children! And you two, stay in the truck, keep your heads down. I'd like you to be fine by the end of this. Captain'll want to meet Hot Fuzz's family."

"I don't know if I want to meet *him*," Grace muttered.

But there was no time for more, because they rolled past an old sign with a few stray bits of green and white paint on it. The name, Ellensburg, was more of an impression than actual paint anymore.

She and Charlie had first been through on their honeymoon. A cute town, known for its trees and museums, they'd spent a night here on their way to Canada.

Since the Invasion, they'd gone in twice to bring out a family or two, slipping through the fencing easily. Now, the Irregulars seemed quite sure they could put a dent into the town's occupiers.

Wilder spoke quietly with Seahorse. Grace caught the end of their conversation. "Did we ever get confirmation on what kind of half-assed shit this bridge is?"

"It's *very* half-assed shit," Charlie called up. "But I don't know exactly what. It's not like we ever used the front door."

"This is the main road," Grace reminded them. "There's gates ahead, which they keep very well guarded. That we already told you about. And they frequently send patrols through."

"We've got ways to deal with gates," Seahorse said absently. "Keep your heads down and hold onto your butts! Let's hope this shit bridge holds!"

This truck was the second in a small convoy of four mismatched vehicles. The two behind were minivans with rusty Oregon plates. Grace knew they had more cars than this, a lot more, but she had no idea where they were.

Seahorse kept things on a need-to-know basis, and apparently, they didn't need to know.

Light flared ahead and the ground shook. Charlie wrapped his arms firmly around her. Grace held onto him with one hand, the seat with the other. The truck dropped from under them, then bounced up, flying over some obstacle.

Grace cried out when they slammed back into their seat. Around them, fighters whooped and cheered while above their heads, Evenstar fired methodically, shells cascading around her feet. One ricocheted and grazed Grace's hand. She flinched, snatching her hand back, mouth open in shock.

It was hot.

The truck screeched to a halt. Peering out the window, Grace could see the sign for the Ellensburg Recreation Center. Steve used it for an armory.

Fighters poured out of the vehicles. Soon, it was empty except for them, the driver, and Evenstar. Wilder pulled into a tight U-turn and kept the engine running.

"I take it cars aren't the only things you're planning to steal tonight?" Charlie asked.

Wilder grinned. "You catch on fast."

"I don't think you brought enough people," Grace fretted, peering towards the building.

Overhead, Evenstar fired.

Wilder laughed. "Yeah, we did. Look over there." She pointed west.

Twisting, Grace crawled over Charlie to see where the driver pointed. Through the back windows, a huge fireball rose into the night sky.

"Busy night for them," Wilder said casually. "We've got another lot pulling civilians out. It's all good. We'll have a race for the border, that's for sure. It'll be your biggest rescue yet."

"And why couldn't Seahorse tell us this in advance?" Charlie demanded.

"Well…" Wilder fiddled with a dial. "It's like this. People tend to freak out the first time they really see what we do. If we don't tell you until it's too late, that's less time to freak out, right?"

Grace pressed her hands into the seat, striving for patience. "And you needed us because?"

Wilder twisted around in her seat. "We're taking this lot to Idaho, not Oregon. Steve won't expect that. You have the connections, you proved that the first night we met. We just want people who will care for them right, y'know? Plus, we're not going back to the farmhouse."

"This is how we work," Evenstar said from above. "We're always moving, making it hard for them to find us."

Grace exchanged a look with Charlie. He frowned, and she could see the thoughts crossing his mind. Where were the cautious meetings? The quiet exits? In and out before Steve even knew they were there?

And how had their nickname for the soldiers snuck into her own thoughts? Grace ground her teeth. These people were so frustrating!

Until Irregulars raced back to the vehicles, their arms loaded with bags and boxes, that is. They laughed, calling to each other. And were surprisingly organized. They stacked the stolen goods into the backs of the minivans and piled into the two trucks again.

Wilder gunned the engine before the last door closed.

"We don't wanna be here in five minutes," Seahorse shouted, laughing.

"How will the others know it's time to leave?" Grace called, holding onto the passenger headrest to keep from being thrown back.

Seahorse glanced back at her, eyes sparkling. "They won't be able to miss it. Don't worry, they're not remotely professional, but we've gotten pretty good at this."

"Probably better that we're not professional," Sarge rumbled from behind Grace.

"Why?"

He grinned. "The one time we had active-duty military members come in, they got captured before they ever managed to engage the enemy. We had to send four people in to break them out."

"What kind of crazy people only send in four?" Charlie asked. But his lips twitched, showing his dimple for just a moment.

Grace smiled. She knew he'd like these people eventually.

"Really crazy people," Seahorse said. "Captain was one of them. But it worked. Probably wouldn't have if we'd tried a more normal approach. I admit, they didn't like it, but it fucking worked."

Explosions behind them cut off any more talk and put the earlier fireball to shame. Grace's mouth dropped open, watching the flames. Was that...

"Did the roof just come off the building?" she asked.

"Hell yeah!" a young woman shouted, punching the air.

The truck rattled, the ground shook, and they all congratulated each other. "I think we've finally got the timing right!" Dionysius shouted.

"Even Sparrow's only right half the time," Sarge called back.

Big booms and maximum noise. Was this why her brother had died? Because they couldn't stay quiet?

"No," Sarge said quietly, nearly in her ear. "He died because he couldn't stand by and watch while others died. These explosions, they distract the enemy and let us move more freely."

"How would you know?" It did sound like him. It was why he'd enlisted in the first place, and why he hadn't fought it when he was sent into Oregon.

"Because I heard it straight from his fiancée."

"Fiancée?!"

"Later," Sarge promised.

Peter was the only reason she'd managed to convince Charlie to do this work. He'd argued that his sole job was to keep her safe. And the only way she'd be safe was if she stayed out of the Occupied Zone. But then they saw Peter, and just...

Everything snowballed from there. They'd been in and out a dozen times over the years, more than anyone else, but looking around, she could see they hadn't spent enough time taking the lunatics left here into account.

***

Coarsegold, CA – Captain

I listened with half an ear to the exodus of civilians towards the small depression in the hills Dogwood had recommended. The resistance moved slowly. Though its leaders had the right amount of urgency, these people had no experience working as a unit or quickly.

I bit my lip, still shocked at the sight of my aunt, uncle, and cousin, Faith. I hadn't seen them since Grace's wedding, and so much had happened since then... Part of me thought they were dead, and I'd not dared think more about them.

Instead, it turned out they were part of the resistance and hiding in the hills. Who knew? It must run in the family.

When Faith demanded my name, I hoped she'd take the hint and not spill the beans to anyone about me. So far, so good.

If Oregon had been dangerous, California could be described as a real shit-show. We couldn't take any chances on names leaking. The likelihood of someone being captured had risen about two hundred percent.

Yippee.

Considering the small army currently creeping towards our position, make it three hundred percent.

I loosened the machete over my right shoulder in its sheath. By reflex, I glanced to my left and right and the old, familiar grief rose in my chest, pouring into my throat. Neither of them were here. No Sonya. No Noah.

No Peter at my back, giggling at the thought of a good fight.

Tears clogged my throat, blocking my vision. Squeezing my eyes shut, I took one deep breath, then another. Rolled my shoulders, loosening the muscles, I took a firm grip on my rifle.

Too much at stake for me to lose my shit. My next breath ended in a snarl, teeth bared. Whether I could see them or not, I knew Peter, Sonya, and Noah stood with me.

Stalking through the trees to the front lines, I passed fighters hunkered down, gripping their weapons with anticipation. Those assholes thought they were dealing with a lightly armed resistance. If the resistance's reactions to our appearance was anything to go by, they operated more covertly than anything we'd ever managed. Which meant Steve was in for a surprise.

My step changed, as it always did before a fight. Pain, sore muscles, and age fell away. I moved lightly over the ground, feeling like a dancer must before a performance.

Phoenix glanced over her shoulder at my approach. She grinned wide enough to show the dimple in her cheek, green eyes dancing. At her side, Gryph hunkered down, trying to hide his bulk behind a scrubby bush.

"This is as far as you should go," Phoenix said. "At least until Steve walks through that section, there." She pointed downhill, to a relatively clear stretch of ground. Nothing more than very short bushes and green grass.

"Aanisah had fun, then?"

She giggled.

"Where are they at?"

She pointed to our right, slightly down. "They've got the flank. Plus, they're blocking the most direct route to the civilians." She bellied down, her huge sniper rifle already set up.

I nodded. Pressing a kiss to my wedding ring, I sighted down my rifle.

***

Pasadena, CA – Mercy

Two days after the battle, Mercy collapsed onto her little pallet in the corner of her room, rolling onto her back. Her eyes were gritty, like they were filled with sand, and every joint ached. She scrubbed her hands over her face, groaning.

There'd been catnaps in the corners of the conference room turned infirmary, but in the aftermath of a battle, there were some things only she could do. She had plenty of forced labor for mundane things like feedings, changing clothes, and bathing, but the more difficult things fell solely on her.

Damn her Master for killing Rhia. Even if he never physically touched her, he did it.

She tallied the dead. Over ten. Thirteen...fourteen, counting the boy who'd raped a kitchen maid just last week, out of one hundred and twenty men who'd gone to fight. Too bad there were so many more, so many bad ones, who never saw a battlefield.

Those ones she might never get her hands on.

Pity.

She stretched her arms above her head, arching her back. Hearing footsteps crunching in the gravel outside her door, she groaned upright, making her way to the door. Reaching up, she trailed her fingertips through the drying herbs hanging from the beams overhead, their strong scents filling the room.

Rosemary, lavender, mint, thyme, along with the previous season's persimmons. Her stocks of fresh plantain and marshmallow were completely gutted, used to treat the latest batch of injuries. Roots sat on the counter in bowls, waiting to be chopped and dried or boiled in decoctions.

When she opened the door, Ruth had her hand raised to knock. Two other women crowded behind her, glancing over their shoulders. Evening's last light cast long shadows, giving partial shelter to her doorstep when she ushered the women inside.

"It's okay," she said. "The garden hides my doorway."

As soon as the door shut, Ruth pulled her kerchief off, raking her fingers through her hair. "Those guards followed us all the way through the orchard." She sounded worried.

Mercy waved it off. "You know how it is after a fight. Everyone thinks there'll be an attack on the compound."

"How does this work?" A short woman with dark eyes, Allie, folded her arms. "Ruth said you can keep us from getting pregnant again? Do you have contraceptives? Is it surgery, like tying my tubes? My Master visits me every few days, so I don't think I could hide any sort of surgery."

"I think I could hide contraceptives." The other woman, Selena, clenched her hands. "I will not go through another pregnancy." Her mouth flattened, turning down at the corners.

"What did you come here for? What do you *really* want?" Mercy asked.

The final test.

"I want to ruin this hellhole forever," Ruth said. Despite her brave words, her hands shook.

"Most of all, I want to leave," Selena said. "Barring that, I never want to get pregnant again."

Alice nodded.

Mercy smiled slowly. "I can't guarantee you'll never get pregnant again." Despair filled their faces. "But I do have something that will ensure you never have to put up with your Masters again."

"What...?" Ruth trailed off when Mercy went to the corner, pulling her pallet aside. Using a small knife, she pried at a crack in the concrete floor. The women gasped when a section lifted, revealing a hole in the floor leading into darkness.

"I can get you out."

Ruth swayed, one hand to her mouth. Alice slumped to the floor, hands over her mouth, giggling. Selena took a step forward, then forced herself to stop.

"How long did this take you to do?" Ruth whispered.

Over a year, but they didn't need to know that. By the time she finished, her Master had lost interest in forcing her into his bed, so she found another use for it.

Mercy set aside the piece of plywood she'd carefully textured and painted until it resembled the rest of her floor. She could barely fit through the hole, which limited her on who she could offer freedom to.

"How many women have escaped?" Selena asked, never taking her eyes from the hole.

"Enough." Mercy refused to say more. If these women were captured, it was her life. If the Masters knew who had cheated them and escaped death, they'd never stop looking for them.

But it was good to be able to offer a genuine chance at freedom to the women who came to her door, begging for death. Others couldn't entertain the idea of leaving at all, so caught up were they in the lie the Masters created.

Tearing a page from her notebook, Mercy wrote careful instructions. "I don't know exactly what's outside the sewer exit, but there are places to hide."

"Wait." Ruth stopped short. "My daughter. The other children. We can't just leave them?"

"I told you before you ever came here, there's no turning back." Mercy glared at the woman. "Your daughter thinks Mistress Hermann is her mother. You really want to help her?"

Ruth nodded.

"Then get out there and find a group who can take on this bloody nuthouse!"

Footsteps on the gravel outside stopped her cold. Snatching supplies off her shelf, she shoved them into a sack and tossed it to Selena. The other woman caught it mid-air, slinging it over her shoulder and grabbing the directions off the counter.

"Wait," Mercy hissed. She pulled a candle out, lighting it from her lamp. "There's a short drop, then I'll pass the candle down. You're not in the sewers yet, so be quiet! You'll go past some vents that lead into the upper rooms. If you're caught…"

She didn't need to finish the thought with Rhia's murder a short time ago still fresh on everyone's mind. The person outside her door knocked. Not a Master, then.

Selena dropped down first. Mercy and Alice manhandled Ruth in, then Alice followed. Mercy passed the candle through, kicking the panel over the hole before they even got themselves together.

"Just a minute," she called. She didn't have to fake the exhaustion in her voice. That came all too naturally. Scrubbing her hands over her face, she knocked her kerchief slightly askew. When she opened the door, she still worked to straighten it.

"Oh, I should have thought you'd be asleep!" Mercy blinked to find Susannah on her doorstep. "I'm sorry, I can come back later."

"No, no." Mercy stepped back. "You're here now. What can I help you with?"

She'd have approached Susannah about escape a long time ago, were it not for the fact that with her curvy figure, she'd never fit through the hole. And Mercy dared not make it bigger in case the trap door extended beyond her small pallet.

"Well," Susannah held up a small packet, "my Master gave me some chocolates from a raid. I thought you might like one. And I thought we could talk. I've seen you here forever, yet we've never spoken. This battle was the first time—outside of birthings—that we've talked, and I thought...I thought I'd really like you for a friend."

"I'll never say no to chocolate." Mercy smiled, drooping as the adrenaline left. "Let me put the kettle on. We can have some tea."

"And...and friends?"

Mercy laughed quietly. Bitterly. "With my Master, that can be dangerous for you. But I think for one night, we might sit and talk."

CHAPTER 8

Coarsegold, CA – Faith

Huddling against Lucas, Faith held her breath, straining to hear the slightest noise beyond their hiding place. In the distance, gunfire rattled the night, punctuated by the occasional explosion, making her flinch every time.

Okay, it wasn't only the gunfire. Biting her lip, she pressed her face against Lucas's chest. Her *cousin* was *the Ghost Captain? When? How?* It was all too much. She'd just waltzed back into Faith's life, armed to the teeth, followed by a group of women who not only looked like they could take on the NKs and win, but were currently fighting with them!

She thought she could handle anything life threw at her, but Hope as the Ghost Captain was almost too much. *No, no. There must be a mistake. Rumors tended to be overblown. That was probably it.*

"You should go further down," Lucas whispered in her ear. "We'll warn you if anyone comes."

Yes. He, Carter, Jon, Malva, and a few others who'd taken direct action against the NKs over the years would warn the rest—then lay down their lives to give them time to escape.

"If you think I'm going to run and leave you here, you can go jump off a cliff, Lucas Morales," she whispered back. "If you cannot find a cliff, I'll give you directions."

The corners of his lips twitched, and he shrugged as if to say, *Can you blame me for trying?* But he wrapped an arm around her, resting his hand on her hip and his chin on her head, a position that had become all too familiar to them over the years of pretend.

Except... She nestled her head against his chest, listening to his heartbeat. She smiled, closing her eyes. It was different, now. The reassurance, knowing he loved her back...

An explosion rocked the earth. Automatically, she crouched, as if that would protect her. A woman cried out, the sound quickly muffled.

"I hope that Captain knows what she's doing," Carter muttered. He paced continually, his gun—returned to him by a grinning teenager—held low at his side. A few Resistance sported rifles, but on the whole, woefully inadequate protection if the NKs managed to break through the fighters' lines.

The fighters. Captain.

Faith shivered.

Scarred, graying at the edges of her hair, but with youthful skin, Hope was a walking contradiction. Fatigues and moccasins, a leather jacket over a gray t-shirt, a rifle, machete, and two guns visible strapped to her thighs... It was all too weird.

What happened to the mechanic who always had a book in her hand and cracked bad jokes? How did she end up not only leading soldiers, but looking like she belonged there?

The next rattle of gunfire sounded like it came from just over the hill. Screams and shouts carried more quietly, but still caused goosebumps to rise on her arms. Lucas released her to get a better grip on his rifle, holding it uncertainly in front of himself. Faith held onto the back of his sweatshirt, her breath coming too fast as she imagined what it would be like in the middle of a fight.

Carter set himself squarely in the center of the narrow trail, about ten paces in front of Lucas. The others disappeared into the bushes, ready to...to what? Die? Give their lives for strangers?

Not for the first time, Faith wished she had a watch. It wouldn't change anything, but for some reason, knowing how much time had passed might make her feel better.

Especially once all the noises stopped.

They waited, but no one came. The sky slowly lightened, turning from dark blue to the first hints of gold and pink.

"Don't worry," Jon said into the silence. "They're fine."

Lucas snorted. "You're so confident they're alive, Nostradamus?"

Jon snorted back. "Did you see how those people moved? I bet the Captain could take on all of us and win."

Faith shook her head, denial warring with disbelief. Jon was wrong. The NKs had proved too much for the fighters. All these years, all the hope held only because they knew of someone who actively fought and defied their oppressors, it all ended here?

After an eternity, her mom whispered, the sound loud in the dead silence, "Did they lose?"

"No, ma'am."

Faith squeaked, clutching Lucas more tightly. The words issued from ground she thought only had a few bushes covering it. Maybe the rumors about her were true.

Faith gaped. If she'd been the enemy, they'd already be dead. How had she arrived so quietly? Where were their own guards? Hope held her empty hands high, the corner of her mouth quirking. "Don't shoot. My lot react badly when I get hurt."

People cried out in shock when Hope—no. No, this bloodied woman, standing with her weight on one leg, as casual as if she was at a backyard barbecue, had little in common with the cousin she'd last seen at Grace's wedding.

It was Captain who stepped from the meager shelter of the bushes with barely a sound. The people who'd gone into the bushes to act as guards charged out, making almost as much noise as the just-finished battle.

Carter nearly leaped down the path to confront her. "How did you—?"

"My dude." She gave him a level look. "Don't insult me like that. I came to check on you as soon as I could, but our wounded and dead have priority."

He bristled. "Well, I think—"

"When I need your opinion, I'll ask." Captain dismissed him with barely a glance. "Are your people ready to move?"

"Move where?"

Faith shook her head. She could see the rebel leader didn't have much patience left. And when she walked, she favored her right side. Was she wounded? Faith doubted she'd tell them if she was.

"What can we do?" she asked, drawing gasps from those closest. She almost couldn't believe her own boldness in speaking to this frightening person who looked more at home in the dark.

"If you haven't already, gather your things. Do any of you have working vehicles?"

At the top of the hill, a twig snapped. Lucas jerked around, raising his rifle. Captain appeared at his side before she could blink, already pressing the barrel down.

"Whoa, there, tiger," she said. "That's public relations. If they don't like it when I get hurt, you *definitely* don't want to see what happens when she gets hurt."

'She' turned out to be an older woman, auburn hair liberally streaked with gray, walking carefully down the hill, accompanied by the beautiful, scarred, strawberry-blonde who'd held a gun on them earlier.

"Hello," the older woman called cheerfully, waving. "I'm Eleanor. I'm here to answer all your questions. Captain," she greeted her commander, reaching a hand out to her.

Captain took her hand, resting the other on her shoulder, drawing the woman close. Faith's eyebrows climbed to her hairline when the two women pressed their foreheads together, standing in silence.

"I'm glad to see you're okay," Eleanor said when they pulled apart.

Faith watched her cousin, mouth open. This unexpected gentleness gave her hope. Maybe traces of Hope were still there.

***

The sun traveled a quarter of the way across the sky before they were ready to leave the area. Faith couldn't believe how fast they were moving, between the injured, elderly, and the dead.

The Oregonian Irregulars refused to bury them in the valley, instead carefully loading them onto a monstrous bus and sending them first into the mountains. When Carter insisted that in order to move more quickly, they should bury the dead where they fell, he was met with stony glares and folded arms.

The tiny woman who'd made her first appearance on top of the wall only the night before (how long ago that seemed) watched Carter like a hawk.

Petite, with sandy-blonde hair pulled back in braids that almost looked sewn, she somehow managed to exude deadly intent.

Faith leaned closer to her mom. "Is it just me, or are most of the more experienced looking ones really beautiful?"

"Which one?" Abigail murmured, barely moving her lips.

Faith nodded to the petite fighter. With her high cheekbones, almond shaped eyes, full lips, she was even prettier than the big British man she'd just learned was the woman's husband.

"But all of them, really," she whispered.

Her mom nodded. It wasn't just her, then. Many of the women, especially those who surrounded her cousin, were beautiful. Some more exotic, especially the girl driving Hope's pickup truck. Eleanor hadn't covered that in her little talk.

She turned her attention to the truck, instead. She remembered it from the last time she'd seen Hope. It had more bullet holes, now. And some panels in random colors that didn't match the original blue and gray. Faith tipped her head. The pickup resembled her cousin in a lot of ways.

Movement from the corner of her eye heralded the action she'd been expecting from the gorgeous, petite fighter.

"Can it," she snapped, full lips curling. "Our people are laid to rest in the mountains. Now shut the fuck up and get your people together. We're not the ones slowing this shit-show down."

Carter's face darkened, but Malva put a calming hand on his shoulder, whispering into his ear. Nodding abruptly, he turned on his heel, marching away.

No, none of them liked the choices Captain gave them—stay and fight or go to Yosemite. And she made it very clear she wouldn't mind if the entire Resistance went to Yosemite.

The only ones who didn't get that choice were families with small children, the elderly, and those of her people too badly injured to continue.

Instead, the lightly wounded fighters helped the people in green armbands who cared for the badly injured and left with every load. Faith marveled at the number of medics they had.

Her own parents managed to join the non-combatants who traveled with the fighters. There were several, the most prominent among them the reassuring Eleanor, the woman who'd calmed the frightened and answered their questions in the early morning.

She watched with quiet pride at the number of Resistance members who chose to stay. Some, as they said goodbye to their spouses or children, were stopped. Captain murmured a quiet word to them. To a person, they nodded and joined the crowd waiting to leave.

One young man lightly brushed his hand over the spot where the Ghost Captain touched him, staring after her with wonder in his eyes.

The people continuing the fight followed the Irregulars into the trees, heading downhill. Her mouth dropped open, watching the Irregulars disappear into the brush as quietly as Captain had stepped from it this morning.

She grimaced. You could tell when the Resistance entered the forest. Branches breaking, whipping around, one person cried out when a branch slapped her across the face. It was terrible.

Faith sidled over to a young woman barely younger than herself with a friendly, relaxed face. This would be a good first target. Too many of the others were closed, with tight faces that brooked no welcome to new people.

"Hi." She smiled brightly. The young woman smiled back hesitantly. "I'm Faith. What's your name?"

"Sage."

Faith nodded. "Guess it's not your real name, either." Sage laughed. Faith drew her into a casual conversation, talking about the weather, making sure the woman was alright after the previous night's battle.

Sage relaxed more as they spoke. Satisfaction bloomed in Faith's chest. This was how she'd climbed so high in the office, how she'd managed to gather so much information for the Resistance. People liked to talk to her, and she liked to listen. Until it was the right time to start digging.

"Who is that?" Faith whispered, pointing to the tiny angry woman.

The fighter's smile grew. "That's Phoenix. She doesn't like most people."

"What's her story, do you know? Why is she so...so..."

"Bad-tempered?"

Faith laughed. "Yeah. Something like that."

Sage leaned closer, lowering her voice. "She's one of the Originals. She's been with Captain since Day One, along with Dereva, that pickup's driver," (*Ah, the woman with dark skin and bright blue eyes.*) "and Anansi." (*Tall, lithe, black, tattoos, hair done in cornrows. Gorgeous eyes.*) "He's our inventor. Anyone who lost a limb? All the original designs are his." She thought for a moment. "And Sirius. But Sirius died before I arrived."

Faith turned that information over. "Yeah, but...you're talking about them as if they had some big origin story."

Sage grinned. "They stormed Salem near the beginning. I was in Portland, but even there, we heard rumors. Captain, Phoenix, and Sirius broke thirty women out of a brothel, killed a hundred Steve, and completely demolished three gates on their way out. Then, twelve tanks and fifteen trucks chased them down. The stories say they destroyed ten of the tanks." Sage waved that off. "But you know how stories get exaggerated. I think it was only five tanks."

Faith's eyebrows climbed higher, but she held her tongue. There was more to the story, she could smell it.

"Afterwards, Steve sent out criers to announce they were all dead but, well, here we are." Sage grinned. "And that was only the first brothel. We've hit several pregnancy prisons, too."

"What's the Ghost Captain like? As a person, I mean."

Sage shivered. "She's stone cold. I went with her on a raid." The way the fighter said it, going with her was a huge honor. "And she walked right up to the door and knocked on it! Just knocked. And when they opened the door..."

She never got a chance to finish. The small fighter, Phoenix, glided over to them, giving Faith a sharp look. She didn't have to do more than that and Sage fled, muttering some excuse.

"It doesn't pay to know too much," Phoenix said, then left as abruptly as she'd come.

Faith watched her go, mouth open. *What the hell?*

"Is that why they say you should never meet your heroes?" Lucas asked behind her.

Faith just shook her head. "Oh, I don't know. They're more scary than in the stories."

***

The sun passed the halfway mark, slowly settling towards the west. The trees continued, interspersed with scrubby brush, the only thing that kept growing during the summer months.

Without paths, people made their own way over the rough ground, choosing the way easiest to them. They scattered, occasionally drawing closer together. The Irregulars stayed on the outer edges, ensuring nobody got lost or was left behind.

Faith mingled, mostly with the Resistance, surprised at how many names she already knew. People who'd helped divert supplies to the north, stole trucks, stashed supplies along Sheba's route.

Ahead, she spotted Captain, her braids mingling with the loose hair swaying across her back. She inclined her head, listening to something Phoenix said, then tossed her head back, laughing. Faith's mouth dropped open, then she hurriedly closed it when a fly tried to dive in, spitting and pawing at her mouth.

Laughing, Lucas wrapped an arm around her shoulders, pulling her against his side. Faith firmed her lips.

"I'm gonna talk to her," she said.

"That's a bad idea."

"Yeah." She couldn't deny that. "But I'm gonna do it anyway. And it has to be in private." Lucas's brow furrowed. She laid a hand on his arm. "Please? Trust me."

"With my life."

"Thanks." She sped up, gaining on Hope. The war leader didn't look pleased to see her, but didn't avoid her, either. After checking to make sure no one was close enough to hear, she lowered her voice. "Hope, what happened—"

Her cousin's eyes blazed. "My name is Captain." Her lips pulled back, baring her teeth, but in her eyes, Faith thought she saw a hint of grief overshadowed by rage.

Eyes wide, Faith fell back a step, though Captain never moved a muscle. "What?" she whispered.

Jerking her head, Captain cut across the shallow slope. "Walk with me."

She led the way to the edge of the large group, out of earshot, her pace faster than Faith could comfortably manage. Gasping, she slowed. "Can we take it a little easier? Sorry, I'm not in the best of shape right now."

A hint of her cousin reappeared, and Hope cocked her head, examining Faith. "You were injured recently." Not a question, an observation.

Faith shook her head. "Not recently, just badly."

Hope disappeared and Faith found herself looking into Captain's fierce gray-blue eyes. "Who?"

Faith involuntarily took a step back. "Soldiers. I..." Faith remembered what Sage said about the brothel. "I wasn't raped, but beaten and left for dead as a warning."

The fierceness didn't abate. "You ever see them, you point them out. I'll deal with them. What happened?"

"Luke found me." Briefly, she recounted the short story, ending with their arrival in the destroyed suburbs around Coarsegold. Struggling to remain detached, she spit the story out as quickly as possible. At the end, she paused, her mouth dropping open. Hope controlled this entire conversation, getting information without giving a thing.

Captain grunted. "So, not as useless as they look, then."

"What happened to you?" Faith whispered. "When did you get so harsh?"

Her cousin gave her a sardonic glance. "Me? Harsh? How are you still so sweet and innocent?"

Faith pulled herself up as tall as she could—still two inches shorter than Hope, dammit—before deflating. "Excuse you! I am the best liar you will *ever* meet."

The grim leader of the rough and ragged crew smiled slightly. "I'll keep that in mind if we can't shoot our way out."

Faith leaned closer. Her nostrils flared. Hope smelled like earth, leather, and oil. "Seriously, though. What happened? Where's Uncle Oliver? Sean, Grace, Charlie, and Peter? What about your other cousins?"

The corners of Hope's mouth turned down briefly and she shook her head. "No. I can't tell you anything, because you can't tell what you don't know."

"Except I know I'm related to the infamous Ghost Captain, now. Not that it matters. I held a high position in the offices. Once, they suspected one of us of being Resistance." Faith smiled slightly, holding up her left hand. Three of the nails were shorter than the rest. "They let me go."

Hope pursed her lips in a soundless whistle. Faith clenched her hand into a fist. Yes, Hope understood exactly what she said. She'd lied her way out while they were pulling her nails.

After a moment's consideration, Hope nodded. "Papa and Sean are safe in Oregon. Sickly, but alive. The last I heard, more seasons ago than I can remember, Grace and Charlie were operating in Washington, smuggling people out. Much like your friend, Sheba."

Faith's jaw dropped. "What? How do you know about Sheba?"

The corner of Hope's mouth twitched. "We get around. As for my cousins... They're all dead, except for Will. He's back in Oregon, helping with the reconstruction."

"Why isn't he down here?" Faith demanded. "He's huge. You could totally make a fighter out of him."

"Because he's blind as a bat without his glasses." Though the dry tone was all Hope, the strategy belonged to Captain. "He's a mechanic. I swear he's working on cars by braille, but it works." She flicked a braid over her shoulder. Something glinted on her finger.

Faith's mouth dropped open. Snatching Hope's hand, she held it just long enough to see the silver band on her finger. "You're married?"

"No."

Faith frowned. There was something there, but Hope's expression turned so forbidding she didn't dare ask. Did it mean she had been married? Or maybe it was a memento of someone who died? She nodded to herself. That made more sense.

When her breathing returning to normal, the two walked again in silence while Faith digested everything she'd been told. Until she found one glaring omission. Then she laughed.

"I almost asked if you knew where Peter was, but of course you wouldn't, would you?"

The rebel leader's lips turned down. "Peter stayed with us, for a while. He died a few seasons ago."

The bottom dropped out of Faith's stomach, freezing her in place. Tears spilled down her cheeks. "How..." She swallowed and tried again. "How do you know?"

"I was with him when he died," Hope said simply. "Soldiers were sent in. Peter was with them. Several of them decided to stay and help."

Hope stuffed her fists into her pockets, shoulders tight. She motioned with her head, and they began walking again. The main group had nearly passed them, but the Irregulars left their Captain alone.

"You can't tell anyone," Hope said.

Faith reached out to touch her, but the stern expression on her cousin's face changed her mind. "Mom and Dad didn't even recognize you," she said, wiping away tears. "And Lucas has never met you. But he'll notice I'm sad."

"Simple." Captain was back. "You asked about your family. I told you. It's the truth."

Faith glanced over her shoulder. Lucas stayed just out of earshot, talking with Resistance members as they passed. He caught her eye, smiled, and flashed her a thumbs up, then waggled his hand. *All good?*

She waggled her hand, unable to return his smile. She'd liked the Gatens. Didn't know them well, but Aunt Rose treated everyone she met like family.

A commotion from the rear caught her attention. Captain whipped around, spinning her rifle off her shoulder and into a firing position before Faith even turned fully.

An Asian woman—a Korean!—burst through the brush, running straight for Hope. Faith cried out a warning, but none of the fighters moved except Hope, lowering her rifle. The woman slid to a halt in front of Hope, panting and gasping.

Captain gave her a sharp look. "Report!"

The woman straightened. "I can't find...Dogwood...or Otter. I've looked...everywhere. Not in the dead or wounded. Last time seen was on the battlefield."

Captain's face hardened, her eyes turning colder. "You're positive?"

"Yes."

"All right!" Spinning to the few lingering fighters, she issued orders.

Faith glanced at the sun. Barely a finger above the horizon. Did they have time to rescue the fighters before dark? Apparently, that didn't concern them, because they disappeared, following orders.

The small, angry woman, Phoenix, appeared at a run, closely followed by the black-haired man, Gryphon. Lucas stood close to Faith, concern in his hazel eyes. Carter, seeing the crowd, also joined them.

Startled shouts came from the Resistance members when they finally noticed the Korean woman, several of them turning back, gathering others.

"Back off," Captain snarled, eyes blazing. She looked slowly around at the Resistance, staring them down. One by one, they dropped their gaze, unable to look at her for more than a couple seconds.

The Irregulars gathered around the woman, protecting her, though Faith didn't think she looked the least disturbed.

"This woman," Captain raised her voice, "is a valued member of the Oregonian Irregulars. You try to fuck with her, we will fuck with you. Spread the word. Sung Ki won't take any of your shit, and I will back her all the way."

Captain squared up against them, and Faith was suddenly aware of how tall she was. And broad. Her shoulders hadn't always been so bulky, had they?

A few of her fighters ignored the drama, talking with their compatriots, shifting things around in their packs, and accepting more magazines. No, even less than 'a few.'

Four. Four fighters.

Sung Ki began similar preparations. Five hardly seemed better.

"...keep those damn rookies from doing anything stupid," Captain finished, talking to a pair of women, one light, one dark.

"Who're you calling a rookie?" Faith demanded. One of the Resistance tripped over a downed branch, crashing into a bush. Faith winced. "Never mind."

"What, exactly, is happening?" Carter raised his voice to be heard over the noise. "Are you planning to leave us? You can't leave! We have a fight—"

"Two of ours have been captured," Captain said tersely. "We don't leave people behind."

"All in, all out," the fighters chanted.

The hairs raised on Faith's arms. Lucas glanced sharply around. Oh, yes, he'd noticed the almost ritual way they'd said the words, too.

"What about us?" Carter continued.

"Scouts say the area is clear. Hunker down. River," she nodded to the lovely, dark-haired woman, "will guide you on. We'll catch up."

Carter folded his arms. "Do you know where you're going?"

"No." For the first time, Captain looked troubled. "But we know what Steve likes to do, and we have maps."

Faith leaned forward, caught up in the moment. *Say it,* she urged silently. *Say it!*

"Take me with you," Carter said. *Yes!* Faith cheered silently, clenching her fist. "I know the area."

Captain stared at him levelly. He squared his shoulders but wouldn't meet her eyes. Finally, the rebel leader nodded. "Advisory role, only. Be prepared to run."

Carter nodded, lighting up. "Lucas, Faith. Tell Malva she's in charge. Help her keep our people organized and quiet."

"When should we tell her you'll be back?" Lucas asked.

Carter glanced at Captain, who shrugged. "We'll be back when we're back. You'll keep heading west."

The sun barely touched the horizon when they were ready to leave. Faith stood with her parents, who'd been among those who came to watch.

"Six people," Faith murmured. "They're mounting a rescue with only six people?"

But Abigail had other concerns. "Are you people crazy? In this world, monsters lurk in the dark."

Captain faced her, impassive, the scar around her left eye shining where the light hit it. "I *am* the monster in the dark."

CHAPTER 9

Central Washington – Grace

Grace buried her mouth against her arm to muffle her breathing. Three feet away, Steve—*they even had her calling them Steve!*—walked past, a noisy, boisterous group. Charlie tapped her shoulder, the signal that the last of their team had arrived.

One hand on the rough brick, she risked a quick glance at their target, the Eastonville Family Medical building. She and Charlie had had their eyes on this for a while as a maternity ward. Heavily guarded, they'd never dared try it before, but now...

Steve converted the entire town into a stronghold specifically to protect this one building, so Seahorse agreed to use Grace's preferred paths: the sewers. Emerging across the street from the building, it became a waiting game.

Grace tilted her head, eyes closed, listening. Behind her, an Irregular shifted and she held up a hand, putting a finger to her lips.

Seconds crawled by before the soft footfalls of a patrol reached them. More alert than their predecessors, this patrol carefully checked rooftops and looked down alleys. Grace held her breath, safely hidden amongst the trash and dumpsters filling the alley until they passed.

"Is it clear now?" Seahorse murmured.

She listened again, then nodded. "Good to go."

"Good ears," Seahorse whispered, touching Grace's shoulder as she passed. "Damn good."

Several more patted her shoulder or back as they went. She watched them go, a warm glow in her chest. Charlie shifted closer.

"You like them, don't you?"

She laughed silently. "Took a while, but...yeah. They're so...*real*."

Over the last month, they'd observed the fighters. An odd group, crazy to the last person, but loyal to a fault. After so long operating alone, she enjoyed having people to watch their backs.

And not having to live in fear anymore? Incredibly freeing. She and Charlie had seen their fair share of fighting over the years, but their best survival tip was 'You can't get caught if they don't know you're there.'

Stay small, be unobtrusive, don't get on their radar, and pray you never get seen. That was how they'd operated.

Charlie reached over, resting a hand on hers. Only then did she realize she'd been tapping them, trying to relieve her nervous tension. Leaning against him, she relaxed, then froze when another patrol walked boldly down the middle of the street.

"There's probably snipers up there," Grace whispered. "How do we warn Seahorse they shouldn't—"

"Sshh." Charlie stroked her arm. "They know what they're doing. They must," he muttered under his breath.

"But—"

"They've been at this for a while. We have to trust them."

Grace pouted, turning her face into his shoulder. "You've changed your tune." A strange noise caught her attention. She sat up, cocking her head. When Charlie opened his mouth, she held up a hand. "I think I heard...a baby? But that can't be right."

A dark figure appeared across the street, head turning both ways before racing across. In the dim moonlight, she could barely make out Dionysius's features, the young man grinning. "Oh, good. You're still here."

"Where else would we be?" Charlie asked.

The younger man shrugged. "Dunno. Got bored? Wandered off? Either way." Turning, he waved.

A small group of people hurried across the road, a mix of fighters and strangers, many of them clutching little bundles. No, Grace realized, not bundles. *Babies.* Children.

Her mouth dropped open. How did they take the place so quietly?

Dionysius sent the O'Connells with that first group back to the sewers. Babies and toddlers snuffled and whined, but a blonde fighter whispered that they'd given the little ones relaxing herbs to quiet them.

Grace supported a pregnant young woman climbing slowly down the ladder. Every splash echoed inside the tunnels, punctuated by quickly muffled squeals and noises of disgust. She glanced up and down the tunnel, barely illuminated by a single candle.

Above, Charlie guided another one down the manhole, passing her over to Grace. Every so often, a fighter descended the ladder, spreading slowly through the growing crowd of women and children.

At fifty adults, her breath caught. There were so many! How could they transport them all to safety? With no detours, it was a full day's drive to the Idaho/Washington border.

Finally, Charlie joined her in the sewers, closely followed by Seahorse and Sarge. The big man pulled the manhole cover back into place, grunting slightly with the effort.

"How did you manage this so quietly?" Grace asked the commander.

Seahorse grinned. "They can't raise the alarm if no one's left to raise it," she said.

Grace's stomach roiled. The only way they could've done it is if they'd ambushed the guards. In the rest of the country, that'd be called cold-blooded murder.

"We never told them to invade us, or to assault and imprison women," Seahorse said, reading her expression. "These are just the consequences of their actions."

Taking her hand, Charlie led the way back, raising a candle to his head height. Fighters scooped up children, ensuring no child was left behind. They kept to narrow margins where they could, occasionally stepping into muck Grace tried very hard not to think about.

A tiny girl wouldn't stop looking at Grace, her eyes huge. Eventually, she leaned away from the fighter carrying her, arms out to Grace. When the fighter pulled her back, the child's face scrunched up, tears threatening.

"Here," Grace whispered to the fighter, an older woman called Sparrow. "I'll take her. If we just..." Awkwardly, they shuffled the child between them, the fighter taking Grace's pack in exchange.

The little girl buried her head against Grace's throat, eyelashes fluttering against her skin. She cuddled the girl closer, resting her cheek lightly against the girl's hair as she followed Charlie.

***

The remaining Irregulars had been busy, Grace noted once they reached the surface. The rest of the fighters scrounged up two extra transports. No benches, so people piled in, sitting on the floor.

Grace stayed close to the child's mother, a heavily pregnant woman who needed three people to clamber into the transport.

"I'm sorry, sorry," she said repeatedly. "Thank you. I wish I could just…" The woman groaned when she finally sat down. "Oh, that feels good."

"You're all right," Grace whispered back. "I've got your daughter."

"You're good with her," the woman said, smiling. "Do you have kids?"

Grace shook her head, barely listening. The truck rumbled to life, and she sat up straighter, jostling the child. "Charlie?" she hissed, heart thumping in her chest.

Squirming around, she got to her knees, pulling aside a bit of canvas. Biting her lip, she peered out. No sign of him.

"Has anyone seen a tall man, lean, wearing a beanie and army jacket?" she asked, clutching the child too tightly.

Softly murmured "No's" echoed around her. Nearly gasping, she lurched to the cab when the canvas over the rear was yanked aside. The women closest to it cried out, leaning away, the noise quickly muffled. Grace relaxed, sitting down abruptly.

"It's okay," she whispered. "That's my husband."

He crawled carefully through the tangle of limbs and children, lurching when the truck started rolling. "Hi, babe," he said, kissing her quickly. "Sorry I'm late."

"Hey, handsome." She leaned against him, breathing easily again. "Come here often?"

Chuckling, he settled with his back to the cab, wrapping his arms around her and the child. She peeked up to see him studying her and the girl. "You look good like this," he murmured in her ear. "We should give it a go, someday."

She nodded against the little girl's hair, closing her eyes.

***

Charlie ran a hand down her thigh. She shifted against him, mumbling, not quite awake.

"Babe," he whispered. "We're slowing down."

"Mmmm?" Twisting, she turned her face up. He gave a deep-throated chuckle, dropping his head to kiss her. When he finally lifted his head, she bit his lip. Thoroughly awake now, including some parts of her that would—unfortunately—have to wait for them to have some alone time, she looked around.

Several women cooed or cheered quietly. "There you go." One woman, kinky black hair just showing in the faint light of dawn, grinned. "That's what I call some chemistry." She fanned herself, to general giggles.

Grace ducked her head, hiding her face in Charlie's jacket. He chuckled, stroking her hair.

"Oh, don't be like that, honey," the child's mom, Annie, said. "It's just been a while since we've seen mutual anything."

The truck slowed to a crawl. Grace frowned, pulled away from the banter. It was still hours until the border. She squirmed in place, but Charlie had already reached up, knocking on the window. It slid open and Dionysius poked his head out.

"Why are we...?" Charlie waved at the truck.

"We're at the border," he replied.

"How?" Charlie demanded. "It's still hours away."

The fighter grinned. "Oh, now, that depends on the border."

She and Charlie exchanged a look. Sighing and rolling her eyes, they clambered to their knees, peering through the windows. High bluffs dropped abruptly to a wide river. Across it, mountains rose, rocky to the east, covered in rich evergreens to the west.

Grace's mouth dropped. "You can't cross that," she whispered. "It's never been done."

Steve patrolled those waters in motorboats at all hours of the day and night. Even now, in the early dawn, she spied three different sets of V-shaped wakes cutting through the water.

Dionysius snickered. "How do you think we got here?"

"We did blow up a bridge to do it," the driver called over her shoulder. Her tiny braids flew when she turned her head. Small metal beads clacked against each other, dark against her pale blonde hair. "Oh, don't worry," she said in response to their looks. "We only blew it up *after* we crossed. And we have a backup plan. Captain insists on those."

"Not that they ever work as planned, do they?" Dionysius shook his head in mock dismay. He indicated the woman with his head. "The Celt is right. Captain does insist. Who knows? Maybe they have multiple backup plans going at once."

The convoy descended towards the river. They passed a beat-up sign informing them they were approaching the Good River Gorge when a thought struck Grace.

"How are we crossing?"

The fighters laughed. "You'll see."

***

Washington, DC – Constance

Constance sat across the table from Perry in a small, twenty-four hour diner, watching him intently. Whether he was as trustworthy as he looked remained to be seen. For now, he was right, she needed him.

But that didn't mean she had to like sharing a single seedy hotel room with him for the last few days. Okay, she hadn't minded at all. He didn't hog the towels, spoke politely to the cleaning staff, and kept things neat and tidy, unlike her last boyfriend.

And he'd been right, damn him. When they'd run from the mess left by the fight, he wouldn't let her return to her apartment. He'd taken her past it, showing her where the cops were hiding in plain sight. McKinney pressed charges against her for assaulting Albrecht—though how they thought she'd managed to so thoroughly hurt a man nearly twice her size, they hadn't explained.

Perry smiled up at the waitress, who set his plate of pancakes in front of him. She smiled back, giving him a quick wink before setting down Constance's omelet. She inhaled; the scent of pancakes fresh off the griddle filled her nose. The omelet looked good, but they didn't smell anywhere near as wonderful as the pancakes.

"You know," Perry said, drowning his pancakes in syrup, "this place also makes a mean gluten-free pancake, if that's your problem."

Constance smiled wryly, startled by his observation. "It's all grains that get me, but thanks."

Nodding, he returned to their earlier conversation. "Your things will be treated like a full crime scene, which means it's all been taken to the station for processing. If they've already broken into your laptop, what's the point of continuing?"

She shook her head. "Unless they've got some top-notch hackers, they won't. And even if they do, I didn't keep any information on there. It's all on two drives."

The unencrypted one she'd labeled *Christmas, 2064.* Long enough ago, no one would be interested in it. The encrypted one, she'd labeled *Birthday, 2064.* Why not keep them easy to identify?

"This drive better be as important as you say it is," he said, low voiced. "I don't much care to get arrested for useless information."

"It is," she insisted. "But if you're scared, let me go. I didn't ask for your help."

"You asked for it when you started throwing my name around." For the first time, a spark of temper lit his green-hazel eyes.

They had splashes of gold in them, too, she noted. Heat bloomed in her chest. Tamping it down, she shook her head.

"I need information from you. About the contents of your debrief. I need to find out who's behind this, because it sure as hell isn't North Korea. The government's claims on how they lost those bombs has more holes than a sieve."

"Why do you care so much?" Perry asked.

She looked away. He'd asked her several times, but after everything, it was hard to open up. "Trust has to be earned," she finally said.

"I'm breaking into a police station to get your drives back," he pointed out dryly, sitting back, looking satisfied, his plate empty.

Constance huffed, her nose scrunched. "Fine! You got me there." She fiddled with her omelet, then said in a rush, "I have friends who were displaced. And," she leaned forward, "I've thought for a long time that my old boss had a hand in it somewhere. He's made too much money since then for it to be an accident. And him and my dad are really tight. So..." She trailed off, unable to complete the thought.

My dad might be a traitor.

She swallowed, putting her fork down. The eggs didn't look so good anymore.

Perry leaned in, elbows on the table. "It's personal."

She nodded, throat tight. Would he condemn her now, for potentially having a traitor for a father? She looked up, startled, when his rough hand settled over hers. He squeezed.

"Our second-in-command on that last mission was a traitor," he said. "I'd served with him for one tour, then we were given that assignment. The betrayal..." He shook his head, eyes dark. Shaking it off, he gave her a smile. "This friend, I take it you trust her?"

"With my life." She and Nakia had been friends since Nakia was born, and she always stuck up for the underdog. "She's...good, in a way few people are." Constance sat up, a huge smile spreading across her face and waved. "She's here!"

Perry didn't turn, removing his hand from hers, but his eyes flicked to the windows. Watching reflections, she realized. Nakia slid onto the bench next to Constance, her wild, curling black hair tamed with a brightly colored headband.

"Girl, what the hell is going on?" she demanded. "I try calling you, your phone's off. I've got police officers on my doorstep asking me twenty questions. They say you beat up a man? Which is crazy. And now you're here with a white boy?"

"Hey!" Perry protested. "And what's crazy about self-defense?"

"White boy, self-defense isn't crazy. It's my girl here and self-defense. Despite my best efforts and weeks of work, the first time she actually hits a bag, she sprains a finger. And the second time, and the third."

Constance grimaced. The flip side of having a friend who'd known you your whole life. But Perry just laughed, giving Nakia a look of appreciation.

"That's what I'm here for." He gave her a winning smile.

Constance narrowed her eyes. Perry had smiled more in the last few minutes than he had over the previous days. A flush rose in Nakia's dark cheeks. Even she wasn't immune to the soldier's charm. *When he wanted to use it.*

Nakia shifted in her seat to face Constance fully. "You better tell me what's up, or so help you God."

She froze, panicked, until Perry's hand dropped below the table, his face turned from bantering to grim intent in a second. Constance shook her head, resisting the urge to melt in her seat.

He'd gone from relaxed to ready to fight because she'd become nervous?

"I can't tell you everything," she said. "It's for your safety," she added when Nakia started to speak. "But I'm being framed. He saved me…"

"Finally, a white boy good for something," muttered Nakia.

"…from Albrecht, the man I supposedly beat up. But I didn't just message to reassure you. We need your help."

Nakia glanced between the two of them. What did she see? Constance leaned an elbow on the table, resting her head on her hand, studying her friend. Her sharp brown eyes, one gold where the sunlight touched it, saw everything, but Nakia never told all she knew.

Finally, Nakia nodded. "What do you need?"

Perry rested his elbows on the table. "What? Just like that?"

Nakia snorted. "Listen, my girl doesn't ask for help often, so when she does, it's serious. And considering what I hear, the less I know, the better. But you better tell me everything as soon as you can," she warned.

Constance grinned. "Done. We need a distraction."

The black woman leaned forward. "Girl, why didn't you say so?" she purred. "When and where?"

***

Rolling Hills, CA – Captain

The sun finally set, until only the foothills still held onto the last wisps of light. Remnants of smoke from the Sacramento fires still clogged the hills, but down here, it had cleared enough to breathe comfortably.

A familiar engine rumbled somewhere to the north. Signaling the others, I walked to the road, thumb up, and stuck out a leg, pulling my pants up when a familiar, patched, gray and blue truck rolled to a stop, Dereva laughing in the driver's seat.

Arrow, a newer recruit, manned the gun in the back, leaning on it when I told them why we were out: two of our own, missing.

We rode in silence, hijacking Dereva's scouting mission and turning it into a rescue. We watched all sides, eyes peeled for signs of Steve.

Phoenix, Gryph, Sung Ki, Storm, and Chaos I could trust to watch my back. I didn't know Arrow too well, but if Dereva brought her along, she'd be solid. Which only left Carter. At least forty, his salt and pepper hair blended in with the night. He'd kept up with us well enough, but he didn't know when to ask questions and when to shut up.

At my feet, Chaos tinkered with some bits from his bag, twisting wires and using a pair of side cutters. I knelt, resting my rifle on the edge of the truck.

"You okay being away from Doc?" I asked quietly.

He flashed me a quick grin. "You know she'd have my ass if I let you go into this alone." He absentmindedly stuck his tongue out, concentrating on a connection, then, "*He'd* have my ass, too."

I brushed a sudden tear away with my shoulder. "I'll get you back to her." *In one piece. Alive. I promise.*

"I know. I wouldn't follow you otherwise."

"Hey, Resistance man," Phoenix said over our whispered conversation, "time to earn your keep. Steve likes to hole up. Where's shelter around here?"

Carter twisted around, trying to get his bearings. "There's several places. Madera—except it's a pain, especially if they're going back to Fresno after," he said to himself. "Uh, that way." He pointed east and south. "A small suburb, just north of Fresno. Mostly houses, a couple shops. It's pretty open, last time I saw it."

"How many roads in?" Phoenix asked.

"From here? Only one."

Nodding, I leaned around to the open driver's window and told Dereva what to watch for. We heard Steve long before we reached the road.

Shouting, loud music, and sporadic gunfire carried faintly over the still air. Celebrating. My lip curled. Those bastards were acting like they'd had a victory. Maybe that's what they told their bosses. Who knows?

Or maybe it's because they'd captured two women.

I clenched my teeth. I already knew what we'd find. All I could do was hope it wasn't another Lightning and Thunder. A slim hope. These days, I had so much less of it.

We stashed the truck in an ancient barn near the road. We'd go the last couple miles on foot. Finding their exact location was too easy. Between the bonfire and the noise, it was like a beacon, guiding us between the houses, straight to them.

"You think it's a trap?" Chaos whispered when we were close enough to see the firelight around the edges of the buildings.

I shook my head, unsure. A drunken man stumbled down the road, falling to his knees and heaving, right in the middle of the street.

"What the hell?" Carter muttered. "I've never seen them act like this. Normally, they're incredibly disciplined."

I considered that. "Do you guys have recreational outposts?"

"What?"

"Brothels."

He shook his head slowly. "There are women who are more like courtesans in the city, but it's pretty exclusive. One of the local higher ups doesn't go for that sort of thing. At least, that's what Faith says."

"It appears the cat's out of town," Phoenix said, the moonlight giving her face harsh angles.

"Grab one we can interrogate," I said. "Please."

Gryphon moved to the corner of the building, leaning his head against it. Abruptly, he stuck his arm out. A squeak and a brief scuffle later and he returned, hauling a squirming soldier.

"Got one." He shoved Steve to the ground.

Sung Ki dragged him through a broken wall, into the house. We kept an eye out for patrols. No one turned when the soldier squealed in fear. Interrogations were, by and large, boring, but Sung Ki had a knack for it. She never hit them. She didn't have to. Fear and intimidation worked wonders.

Eventually, she called us back. Steve snored in a corner, Sung Ki sucked a knuckle. Removing it, she reported on her findings.

"They are here. Close." She consulted her notes. "Two streets over, there are stores. We look for Sleetha, turn right. At the next street, left. They are down there. Patrols keep those houses in good shape for their use," she finished.

I nodded, turning over what she'd said. The Irregulars waited, but Carter immediately spoke.

"We need to stay quiet," he said, straightening to his full height, barely taller than Storm. "You and you," he pointed to Gryph and Chaos, "should take point, and..." He trailed off.

Chaos turned his back, Gryph kept looking right at me, and Phoenix laughed. I sighed, scrubbing my hands over my face. God save me from rookies. Sudden warmth at my back made me straighten, and a familiar scent filled my senses.

Noah.

I closed my eyes, breathing his scent. The guys moved to stand on either side of me, close enough their shoulders brushed mine. Shaking my head to come back to the present, I handled Carter in my usual way.

With panache, stupidity, and a good bit of force.

"What the fuck do you think you're doing?" I snapped. "What did I tell you about tagging along?"

Phoenix subsided into sniggers.

His mouth tightened. "Advisory role only," he ground out.

"Yeah, so shut the fuck up and let the professionals talk. Listen up, children." They gathered close, grinning. "Chaos, take Sung Ki, Storm, and Arrow. Make distractions. Have fun. Go nuts." Chaos's grin widened and he pumped his fist once.

"Phoenix. The water tower is your best choice." She nodded. "Gryph." I tipped my head, indicating his wife.

He nodded. He had her back, the Basher who guarded his Sniper.

"Carter." My lip curled. "I'm going to grant your wish and give you a role in all this. You're with me. Final instruction: don't die." I nodded around the circle. "All in, all out."

"One shot, one kill. No luck, all skill," they finished.

"What?" Carter demanded. "That's it? That's your grand plan?"

Folding my arms, I glared. "Yeah. Don't make me regret bringing you. You're way prissier than I'd expected from the local resistance."

"We work behind the scenes," he snapped. "We make deliveries disappear and convince distribution it got delivered. We tell the destination nothing was sent. We put bad gunpowder into bullets and leave the explosives out of mortars. This...this is all new. And weird."

"And *yet*," Phoenix put in, shaking her head, "your first move is to try to give us orders? Bold move. Stupid, but bold."

Without wasting any more time, Phoenix and Gryph peeled off, heading straight for the water tower. Chaos and his gang followed me until we caught a glimpse of the Sleetha building. From there, they took off, heading towards the light. Then, it was just me and Carter, who bumped into me the first time I stopped.

"How can you see?" he hissed.

"It's clear skies and a half moon," I murmured. "How can you not?"

For me, it was damn near daylight. In Oregon, we might have a grand total of two months of nights like this. The rest of the time, we contended with not enough moonlight or too many clouds. Mostly clouds.

The fourth time Carter ran into me, I grabbed his hand and placed it on my shoulder.

"Follow."

Soon, we spent as much time hiding as moving, waiting for Steve to get out of our way. When we turned the corner onto the street with houses, a sick pit opened in my stomach. Too many men on this street. Most had mussed clothes, some lay passed out, others were too drunk to care when we walked by.

I clenched my teeth, over and over. Were they even alive? Did they even want to be alive?

I stepped over another prone man, but this one caught my ankle. I jerked my foot away, but he held on with surprising strength. He mumbled, desperation in his tone. Curious, I leaned down.

"Don't do it," he whispered in Korean. "Leave them...leave them alone. Remember your mothers, your sisters."

I checked him over briefly, stepping to the side so moonlight shone directly on his face. Definitely been in a fight, that one.

Interesting. Beaten, yet he pleaded for the women. How many had there been like him over the years? Ones who actively protested? Ones who didn't participate?

How many of those men had I killed? I swallowed. How many? Leaning down, I whispered, "I will find them. They will be safe." He relaxed slightly. "Thank you," I added. Maybe they weren't all bastards.

Grunting led us to the right house. The yawning pit in my stomach burned, fire spreading through my chest when I stood near the open window, listening to exhausted whimpers and a man's grunts. When Carter caught on, he gagged silently, mouth open like he was about to puke.

I grabbed his collar, dragging him close. "Keep your shit together," I breathed.

"How are we going to get them out?" he whispered. "There's at least two men in there."

I shook my head. "It's not even a fair fight."

CHAPTER 10

White Salmon, WA - Grace

Grace walked, crouching, along a narrow path leading down to the water. They'd waited several days for the searching to die down, and for the patrols to lose some of their alertness, before getting the women out.

One pregnant woman gave birth while they waited. Grace closed her eyes, haunted by the woman's screams that slowly died to wails and eventually to a pitiful mewling. The medic, Squirrel, had closed the woman's eyes, her own dark and tormented.

"Over a quarter of the pregnant women die," she said softly. "Another third can't bring themselves to accept the result. It never gets easier," she said, even as she cradled the body of the baby. "Forced birth is...it's fucking hell."

While she wanted children someday, she couldn't help but think that having one in these circumstances was practically a death sentence.

Grace shook herself, coming back to the present. Ahead, the Celt walked confidently, her light hair covered by a dark cap, followed by a line of women and children. Fighters, interspersed with the civilians, acted as guides and protectors. Charlie followed closely behind her, one hand on her waist, the other holding a child's hand.

Downstream, nearly a mile away, the ongoing battle filled the night with gunshots and shouting. Flames shot up, the sound of the explosion reaching them long seconds later.

To the side, a bush thrashed. "Motherfucking, sonofabitching, piece of shit *bush*!" emanated from the shrub.

Grace's lips twitched. How often had she heard her sister swear just like that? But it was obviously not Hope's voice. This woman was too high-pitched to be her sister.

Slowly, they emerged onto the riverbank. Fighters headed back to the brush lining it, returning with canoes, kayaks, and two rafts. The Celt lowered the kayak she carried, tucking her battle braids back under her cap, and surveyed the scene.

"Load 'em up," she said softly. "It's at least two trips, so make it fast. We want our people out of that fight ASAP, but you know Seahorse and Sarge won't leave until we're all clear."

She and Charlie volunteered on the raft. They gave her a paddle and directed her to the front. As soon as they launched onto the water, the air turned colder. Shivering, she wished she had a cap like the Celt's to keep her ears warm.

"Slow down a little," Charlie murmured behind her. "You want to keep time with the other front person."

She pouted. The only good thing about paddling was keeping warm, and now she had to slow down? Soon enough, the distance began to wear on her, and she realized: they were in it for the long haul, not a sprint like the canoes.

Those things cut through the water like a hot knife through butter compared to the raft. *They have fewer people*, she grumped to herself, glancing at the women packing the raft.

Downstream, a huge explosion lit the night. Ducking from habit, she stared, wide-eyed at the flames slowly dying down.

"Direct hit on a gas tank," the other fighter, Anarchy, called, grinning. "Keep paddling. Let's make the most of it."

As if they'd planned it, all the patrol boats hovered around the bridge. Ahead, a light flashed on the bank. Slowly they made their way to it.

The light gradually revealed a woman in her mid-thirties, rifle slung over her shoulder. She wore a mix of clothing styles, hiking clothes mixed with fatigues, her hair braided close to her head. Beside her, a huge, handsome black man hauled canoes to shore.

They offloaded in less than a minute before the man gave them a shove to send them quickly on their way. He greeted their raft, moving awkwardly when he pulled them closer, one leg held stiffly when he bent.

People wearing the grab-bag of clothing that marked them as members of the Irregulars swarmed the shore, moving silently and without lights. People with green armbands checked through the rescued, converging on anyone who moved poorly.

Doctors, Grace realized. Lots of them.

"How does it, Bear?" A man, Gummy, seated directly behind Anarchy, hailed the woman carrying the lantern.

"All quiet on the southern front, Gum. You're lucky your scout found a patrol as fast as they did."

"Hah," the huge black man rumbled. "You're lucky we've got this area covered in patrols. Steve's staying out, minding their manners," he replied to Gummy's unspoken question.

"Yo, Goliath!" The huge black man turned back. "Word on Captain?" Anarchy asked. "Seahorse'll be wanting to know."

Goliath. The name suited him.

Goliath grinned, teeth white against his dark skin. "Hella busy. Buses are always coming in from the south."

By this point, the people had been offloaded.

"Back up!" came the harsh whisper from the stern of the raft.

Obediently, Grace dug her oar in, pushing against shifting gravel and mud. Goliath gave them a push, raising one hand in farewell.

And just like that, it was done. They paddled back, the last canoes going in the opposite direction for a drop off. The fighting on the bridge continually drew her attention.

A truck burned in the center of the bridge, illuminating everything around it. Some of that light fell on the water below, silhouetting the patrol boats sitting there. The fighting itself appeared to be dying down, each side hiding and only taking potshots at each other.

Grace closed her eyes briefly, offering up a silent, but heartfelt *Thank you* to the universe. Hopefully, they hadn't lost anybody tonight.

The raft grated on gravel, jarring her. A grinning fighter offered her a hand up, pulling so enthusiastically she nearly flew off the raft. The rest were given the same treatment, then many hands hauled the raft back into the bushes, where the rest of the boats were stored.

The fighters clasped each other's arms, some pressing their foreheads together, all grinning and pointing at the bridge.

The Celt, leading the way back to the vehicles, chuckled.

"What's so funny?" Grace whispered.

"Not so much funny," she replied. "Just, blowing up the truck. I remember the first one I set off. Some of the best fun I'd had in years."

Grace sucked in a breath. "Aren't you worried for your friends in the fight?"

The Celt stopped abruptly, causing Grace to crash into her back. It seemed more like running into a brick wall than another human.

When she spoke, her voice was as tight as her shoulders. "Do *not* assume shit about me. They're my family. I would die for them, just like they would for me. Like your brother did for us. We do what we have to, and we face the consequences every fucking day."

Without turning, she continued. Back at the vehicles, Grace paused next to her. "I'm sorry," she said softly. "I didn't think..."

The Celt relaxed, her shoulders dropping. "I know. We mourn them all, every time another falls. We remember them. You need to learn to use their sacrifice to fuel what you do. Live more, laugh louder, fight harder."

Grace watched the sky lighten in the east. "I'm not sure I can," she whispered.

***

Outside Madera, CA - Faith

"She didn't even hesitate!" Carter exclaimed, shaking his head, falling silent for several long moments.

The setting sun created long shadows stretching over the ground, the tall eucalyptus surrounding them no longer providing shade. Clouds formed in the east, burnished gold against a deep blue sky.

Carter and the others returned on foot three days after they left. The driver and her navigator took the survivor, Otter, and the dead woman back to Yosemite. The demolitions man, Chaos, escorted them. Something about acting as a bodyguard for the doctor, she heard.

Faith stood in the small crowd surrounding Carter where he sat on a tree stump, listening to his story of the rescue. The crowd remained spellbound, mouths agape at the things he described. And who could really believe it?

Nine people taking on an army and not only surviving but escaping with the prisoners.

Faith glanced to the other side of the camp, where the Irregulars had their own gathering, this one about the woman whose injuries were too severe. She didn't survive.

Finally, Carter continued. "She goes in alone—*alone*—quiet as a mouse. Then, a couple of thuds, a grunt, and the next thing I know, she's passing a woman out to me. I took a peek in. There were three NKs down on the ground." Unable to sit still, Carter rose, pacing in the small clearing left for him. "This sounds ludicrous," he said, almost to himself. "She walks into a room, fights with three men, and makes it out without even a bruise?"

"So, you're telling us that she's definitely the Ghost Captain?" her dad, also listening, asked.

"I'm telling you I've never seen anything like it. I'm starting to think that rumor about her blowing up a mountain is true. We hadn't even gotten the second woman out of the room when things started exploding all over the place. It was complete chaos..."

"Well," Abigail murmured in Faith's ear, "I guess we know how that one got his name."

"...and she acted like it was just another weekday." Carter sank back onto the stump. "Cool as a cucumber, walking down the street with a person slung over her shoulders. A soldier came running, pulling his gun out, and then he just...fell down. The second time it happened, I saw why Captain stuck to the middle of the bigger roads.

"It was so her sniper could see her."

He leaned forward, elbows on his knees, covering his mouth with shaking hands. "Her sniper! She has a sniper! We don't...I've never been in the middle of a firefight like that. She kept turning around to make sure I was there. And we just...walked out. How the hell do you do that? No papers, no passes, nothing.

"When we got to the truck, her driver was cleaning off a knife. I didn't see a body, but that sweet girl had a bit of blood on her hands. What the fuck?" He giggled, then clapped his hands over his mouth. "And the biggest thing? It was her face. She just…" He shuddered. "I can see why they call her the Ghost Captain. It's not because there's no sign of her when she leaves. It's because they never see her coming."

Faith left after that, unable to hear more. Walking, head down, she ended up on the edge of camp, which itself was an old campground outside of the town. She couldn't reconcile her cousin with the person Carter described.

But at the same time, she was definitely the Ghost Captain. She believed everything she'd heard about him. Except *he* was a *she*, and… And so her mind went around and around.

"Faith. Faith. Babe."

She started out of her daze, looking into Lucas's eyes. They crinkled at the corners, and he smiled down at her. Over his shoulder he carried rolled up blankets. In his other hand, a large hiking backpack she'd never seen before.

"Where were you?" he asked. Taking her hand, he led her back towards the eucalyptus trees dotting the campground.

"A million miles away," she said ruefully. "Did you end up listening to the rest of Carter's story?"

"Yeah."

Kneeling, he spread their blankets on a grassy patch while she familiarized herself with the pack. A first aid kit, water bottles, pouches of dried food, socks (socks!), knives, and moccasins, along with a few other things it was now too dark to identify.

They laid down, pulling the thin wool blanket over the top. She rested her head against his shoulder, running her hand over his chest until it rested over his heart.

Sleeping together was still so new. Only their third night, and she wasn't accustomed to it. And they still hadn't gotten up to anything that could raise your heart rate. They didn't have the privacy for it.

Close—closer than she would have thought—someone coughed. And that was why.

Since they weren't getting up to anything fun tonight... "What did you think of his story? Any of it true?"

They all knew how inaccurate people's memories could be after a mission. This one being completely out of the ordinary for them made it more likely that Carter had gotten details wrong.

"Honestly," he said after a while, "it all sounds ridiculous. But we've been hearing rumors about him—her—for years, and this tracks with what we've heard."

"So now we have to wonder how much of that's been exaggerated?"

He shifted under her. "You said it, not me."

"Except..." She shifted to better see his face. "That first night. They appeared out of nowhere. They made it past our guards and we never saw them coming."

On those words, she drifted to sleep, lulled by Lucas's deep breathing. She woke to an evil chuckle and a toe in her side.

"Wakey, wakey, children." She cracked her eyes open to see Phoenix looming over her. "Sun's almost up and it's time you were, too."

Groaning, they rolled apart. They'd learned the hard way that these people didn't mind getting a little rough to get people moving.

***

Pasadena, CA – Mercy

Her Master paced through Mercy's infirmary while she knelt, hands folded meekly in front of her. He huffed, muttering and slapping his leg.

His current favorite, Mary, lay on the table, struggling to breathe. She'd been hauled in by two Sons of Judea at her Master's orders just this morning, with instructions to "Fix her."

The Master himself entered once Mercy managed to stabilize the poor girl and make her more comfortable. As long as she didn't move too much, none of her broken ribs should be problematic.

Finally, Master Kozlov huffed to a stop. If she turned her head, she could see his face more clearly. Hah! And be beaten for her effort? No, she'd long since learned to bide her time and wait. Men couldn't stop themselves from talking, and they liked punishing any woman who spoke too soon. Even Mistresses.

"Has it not been enough that we protected you?" he burst out. "Given you shelter, purpose, and brought meaning and order into your lives? Speak!"

Mercy took a long moment before answering. "You have been very generous in your ministrations, Master. But I feel you're speaking of something specific?"

His lip curled, a manic light entering his eyes. "Three bondmaids have disappeared."

Whoops. Maybe getting out three at once hadn't been such a great idea, but all three had felt in more danger than usual.

"Where were they last seen?" she asked, keeping her head down.

"In the orchard." His eyes bored holes into the top of her head, fury vibrating through every word. "They have not been seen since."

Mercy concentrated on a memory right after the last battle, when Ruth had been cleaning and bandaging a man's arm. "What do you wish to know, Master?"

"The bondmaids. Ruth, Selena, and Alice. When did you last see them? Answer well and I will reward you." He patted her head so hard it bobbed.

She grit her teeth, keeping her voice neutral only through years of terror and training. "I don't know Selena or Alice. Perhaps I've seen them, but I couldn't pick them out even if I had a photo. Ruth had been with me during the Holy Battle against the Baptists, and in the aftermath. I remember seeing her bandage a Warrior's arm, but after I dismissed her from the hospital to rest?" She shook her head.

"But my Master," she lifted her head now. Oh yes, time to plant this seed. "You said they were in the orchard, yes?"

"Yes," he said tersely.

She hesitated, found the emotions. It had to be sincere. "Is it possible...? Sometimes, the dogs bark at things outside the fence, and with so many men injured... They are godless men outside," she finished.

"Yes. Yes!" He slapped his leg. "Of course. Those heathens have stolen our chattel, the women God has granted us as a reward for our righteousness and piety to His will!"

Mercy repressed the urge to roll her eyes, instead looking down once more. He stood in silence, then spun on his heel, storming from her room, leaving the results of his temper tantrum struggling to breathe on her table.

After readjusting the girl, making her more comfortable, Mercy sat with her back against a bookshelf, clutching the dog tags hidden beneath her shirt, the metal digging into her fingers, and closed her eyes.

Black eyes watched her warmly in her memories.

"Bondmaid!" A harsh voice pulled her out of her only refuge. Two Warriors of Light stood just outside her door. "We've been sent by your Master. You will be guarded continuously for your safety, in the event the heathens try to take you."

Mercy nodded, cursing herself inwardly. Now, she would be even more useless than usual. She'd also have to postpone her own escape.

Damn it.

***

Washington, DC – Constance

Constance chafed at being sidelined, even if her face was plastered across every screen east of the Mississippi. And she didn't have any particular skill in sneaking, anyway, so going with Perry into the police station was out.

Instead, Perry set her up on overwatch from the flat roof of the building across the street. A quiet library, they'd strolled in and set up in a corner until they could be sure they weren't watched, then he took her through the door to the stairs.

Someone spent time up here. A small, potted garden surrounded her, along with a bench, umbrella, and side tables, all mismatched. Even with all that, she got to sit in a patch of sunlight, taking in the view.

She pointed an infrared at the building, tracking Perry's progress. Blueprints, weighed down by rocks, lay next to her. The backpack Perry gave her leaned against the wall, the zipper undone for a fast getaway.

She held a walkie-talkie in her other hand, its range barely far enough to encompass the police station, according to the label. She kept one finger lightly resting on the button in case she needed to push it in a hurry.

Using the walkie's antenna, she scratched the black wig covering her long, brown hair. The bobby pins holding her hair back pulled uncomfortably. The second thing she'd do once she got to safety would be to remove them, she promised herself. The first would be to have a minor panic attack.

When he'd handed the walkie to her, she thought it was an old phone. It looked exactly like the first car phones from old movies, and she had to wonder how he'd even thought of using ancient tech like this.

"I learned a lot in Oregon," he'd said, as if reading her mind. "High-tech isn't always the best way, especially when your opponents aren't expecting something like this."

He'd grinned, and a small part of her heart melted. He looked so severe after he'd rescued her from Albrecht, but the more time she spent around him, the more he loosened.

Another red oblong appeared on her infrared. Biting her lip, she pressed the button. "Perry," she whispered loudly. "Can you hear me? There's a person in the hallway ahead of you, to your left. Hello? Are you there?"

"I can hear you." His low voice, distorted by the tech, was easy enough to understand. "I won't always respond. Just tell me what you see and trust I can hear you."

"Sorry! Sorry. Yeah, okay."

Perry's red oblong turned into a blobby circle, but the other one walked right past him. She waited, counting, then clicked the button three times. *All clear.*

Occasionally, she glanced at the front of the police station. Through the large glass windows, she could make out a crush of bodies, all facing a clear space in the middle. When the door opened, Nakia's strident tones reached her.

From other parts of the building, more red blips moved to the front. She didn't know what Nakia had chosen to complain about, but it certainly got their attention. She had to tell Perry to hide only twice more, and again on his way out.

As soon as Perry stepped out into the watery sunlight, she dialed Nakia's number from memory, let it ring twice, then hung up. Quickly packing the blueprints, she made her way down the stairs, slipping quietly out of the library.

Perry met her in the parking lot, casually dropping a kiss on her cheek. "Go with it," he whispered when she started.

Right. Right. She had to pretend they were together. All the notices about her said to look for a lone woman. After all, she hadn't dated in nearly two years. No one on Capitol Hill wanted anything to do with the junior aide constantly in the doghouse.

Nakia joined them when they entered the park next to the library. As soon as she saw them, her scowl disappeared, and she broke into giggles. "You think if I hug you, people will assume I'm with two white people?" She flung her arms out. "I haven't had this much fun since the last time we went out. We should go out more, girl."

Constance threw one arm around her, hugging her tightly. "All this excitement will do me in, so no, thanks."

"You should go on a vacation," Perry added. "I'm hoping they don't notice anything is missing, but you might not want to be too easy to find."

Nakia squeezed her hand, pulling her a few steps away from Perry. "Take care," she whispered in Constance's ear, her breath puffing against the wig. "But you don't have to worry, none. That boy is solid. I can tell. Trust him."

Constance smiled wryly. Nakia always saw too much. "Oh, good. I was going to ask if it's crazy that I already do. See you."

Nakia tossed her head, waving as she sashayed away.

***

Constance buried her face in her hands. Midnight had just passed, and the gaming laptop Perry used to decrypt the hard drive had just handed them a single file. Just enough for her to prove the drive's importance to Perry.

The dingy motel room hadn't changed, but her entire world had shifted on its axis, and she didn't know if it could ever be put right again. When she finally lowered her hands, Perry still stared blankly into the distance.

Worse than the words on the screen was his reaction. It wasn't final proof, not enough for the courts, but a wiretap on the Secretary of State's house was damning.

The contents of the audio file were even worse. They had no names, so a good lawyer could claim that two nearly random people were speaking, but a woman speaking to a man like she was his mother? And that was only the first file. There were dozens, still waiting to be decrypted.

"I spent years trying to learn why the fuck they sent a unit of inexperienced boys into a war zone like Oregon," he finally whispered. He turned his head slightly, the first time he'd acknowledged her in several minutes. "Did you know there were only eight of us who had more than basic training? Six, not counting Hendricks and French. Out of the thirty they sent in."

Constance sat carefully next to him. Unable to watch him suffer, she reached out, laying a hand cautiously on his arm, ready to snatch it back. He sat quietly, and she squeezed gently.

"Thirty," he repeated. "By the time Captain got us out, there were only seventeen left. Fifteen by the time we made it to safety. We never see casualty rates that high anymore." He snorted softly, closing his eyes, his face drawn. "And they sent us in to die. French, that son of a bitch, led us right to them.

"I've given my life to this country. I've obeyed orders I didn't always agree with because I trusted the people giving those orders. And now...I watched good soldiers die, be butchered, and for what?" He turned to her with sudden intensity. "I *need* to know why. How do we find out?"

Constance bit her lip—too hard—and winced, licking to soothe the spot. "It won't be easy. These files are huge. Too many are audio. We need an internet connection for it to decrypt, but it can't be traceable. I don't have any contacts like that.

"Then, we'll need to sort through it all. From that one file—and my own conversations—people are rarely named, which means finding out *exactly* who is a part of this will take time. And as important as who is named is who isn't." Just how her father taught her to play Clue.

Perry turned his hand over, lacing their fingers together. She didn't think it had anything to do with flirtation and everything to do with comfort. She couldn't imagine being alone when she discovered this.

Wait! Grace and Charlie! Maybe they couldn't do anything, but if something happened to her, at least they'd know who to look at.

"I need to write a letter," she said, right as Perry looked at her.

"I've got an internet connection we can use," he said.

"Where this is going, the internet won't work."

CHAPTER 11

Wiretap, Keller Residence – June 20, 2062, 8:30pm
Woman: We just need them to become a little more desperate, sweetheart.

San Joaquin Valley, CA - Captain

I shook my head, watching the Resistance gather. Farmers were easy to tell from the city dwellers by how they dressed and moved. The laborers wore sturdy clothing, walking comfortably on soft, uneven ground.

The rest rubbed their eyes, yawning and stumbling, many shivering in insufficient clothing. Not that I could do anything about that. Our stores were nowhere near enough to clothe this lot. Shaking my head over their sorry state, I rubbed two fingers over the scars around my eye.

How was I supposed to turn this lot into fighters?

A small group stayed together. Faith, her parents, boyfriend, and a few other people high up in the Resistance. I pursed my lips. No, I didn't have to change them. They were insurgents. They should know how to walk around in broad daylight and blend right in.

"Don't hurt yourself thinking too hard," Phoenix murmured at my shoulder. "I can see those gears turning."

"Just thinking that we have a whole new skill set to work with. We've got people who can walk in, take what they want, and walk right back out again..."

"Within reason," she pointed out. "But yeah, they've got a few things in common with the saboteurs."

I nodded. "Yeah, but backed by snipers and bashers?" I grinned. "I feel like being a menace to society."

She shrugged. "So? Pick a city. Better yet, let Shrike pick a city. She's had her eye on a few things for a while, waiting for us to get centralized. Now's as good a time as any."

Carter approached, followed by a small cluster of people, my cousin at the back, craning her head to listen in.

"Captain," he said, quieter than he had been before our little jaunt. "I wanted to introduce you to some Chapter leaders."

He went through the names, which went in one ear and out the other. I was far more interested in where they were from. Four were from Fresno, one from Sacramento, two from Bakersfield, one from San Francisco.

I nodded to the San Franciscan, a Latino man. Varro. I could remember that name. He was the only one to hold a hand out. In the way we'd been doing, I clasped his forearm, surprising him.

"It's an honor to meet the Ghost Captain." He smiled briefly. "Though you're not exactly what we expected."

I grunted. If I had a candy bar for every time I'd heard that, I could have a sugar high for the first time in donkey's ages.

"We've been very surprised and impressed at all the mayhem you've managed to cause," another one, a gray-haired woman, added.

"Yo!" One of my fighters, passing by, stopped. "I hear my name?"

I watched their confusion, snickering. "Her name is Mayhem."

She grinned. "That's me!" Her brown eyes still had their sparkle, and she fully enjoyed their dismay.

"*Fucking* nicknames," one man muttered, glaring at her.

Yeah, this wasn't the first time they'd said that, I was sure. Still, couldn't stay here all day. I clapped my hands. "Okay, children. Time to go. Less talkie, more walkie!"

While we walked, the Resistance leaders stayed in a group, talking in low voices.

"Let them," Eleanor said. "And!" She held up one finger. "Don't interrupt them. You scare nearly all of them, and they really need to focus. Being a complete agent of chaos has its downsides, and they need to talk. Most of them have never met before. They need to figure themselves out as resistance people, because we don't have time to train them to fit in with us."

I grinned down at her. "Look at you! All full of strategy and psychology! Okay." I held one hand up, palm out. "I promise I'll leave them to their little meetings."

And I did. But that doesn't mean I didn't have my people nearby, listening in. We headed towards a river. These people weren't used to walking day in, day out, and they'd need a bit of time to acclimate if we wanted to avoid tendonitis and bad blisters.

"Boring!" Phoenix groaned, joining me at the side of the group, where I could keep an eye on everyone. "I'm so bored!"

Gryph laughed. "Luv." He yanked her close. "If you jinx us, I will...I will..."

Phoenix brightened. "Yes? Do tell me it'll be something naughty."

I groaned, flinging a hand up. "No! No, I don't need or want to hear any more of this. You're bored, great. Go find a good spot at the river where we can camp for at least two nights. Yes, you can take your husband. No,

I don't want to know what you'll get up to. I've suffered enough brain damage already."

Giggling, they ran ahead, carrying their rifles. As soon as they left, my smile faded. Once upon a time, they were Noah and I. Would I ever get used to this empty space around my heart?

Maybe sensing my mood, Eleanor joined me, walking silently, lending me her presence. I relaxed slightly.

"Are you ready to talk about it?" she asked.

"What?"

"What got you so sad."

I squinted up at the blue sky, slowly darkening as the sun crept towards the horizon. A wispy cloud arched overhead, lit gold by the setting sun, looking like nothing so much as an outstretched, feathery wing.

"No."

We found Phoenix and Gryph shortly before sundown, the two of them happy with themselves. Another reason for that may have been the three Chimeras and my little pickup, all of them covered with camouflage tarps.

"Looks like you're getting *all* your wishes today," I said by way of greeting. She bounced on her toes, grinning.

"Dereva said soldiers are all over the main roads. They're moving troops. Think they know we're here?"

"Yeah, somewhere. Grab the rookies that still need experience."

Her face fell. "Including the idiot?"

"Moon Moon needs all the experience he can get. And I prefer to keep him where I can see him."

***

Which is how I found myself hanging onto the sides of the pickup while Dereva weaved over bad roads sometime after midnight, chasing a Chimera full of Steve.

"I'm *sorry!*" Moon Moon wailed, huddled into a little ball in the corner.

Bullets peppered the ground around us, some of them pinging on the front of my poor truck. Cold wind blew my battle braids back, chilling my ears. I bared my teeth.

"Listen, kid," I glanced down briefly. "Apologies are all well and good, but I expect improvement! All the words in the world don't mean shit when you make the same stupid mistakes *repeatedly.*"

He'd gotten antsy, firing too soon instead of waiting for the signal, springing the ambush early. This one hadn't been inside the firing range, and now those bastards were racing for Sacramento. Last thing we needed was Steve having an inkling of our location, not with all those raw resistance people at camp.

If this was Moon Moon's first mistake, I could forgive him. But not the fifth. Nope, as soon as we made it back, I'd have Eleanor give him every shitty job we had, including digging trenches for latrines. We didn't use latrines, but just for this, I'd make an exception.

"Give me another chance, Captain!" he cried.

"Get your shit together, boy," I snarled. "You're acting like it's all over. It's not until I say it is."

Dereva took a corner like she was on rails, gaining a few extra feet. Slipping around the machine gun, bouncing with every step, I unlatched it, taking aim, teeth bared.

"My turn."

***

Spokane, WA – Grace

Seahorse folded her arms. "I'm not crossing over, and I'm *definitely* not ordering any of my people to, either."

Grace looked from the rebel commander to the border fence and back, her face screwed up in confusion. "Why not? The lieutenant in charge of this post has been really helpful to us. We've crossed tons of times. It's how we get out to take a break."

After using the river to evacuate another group of residents, the Irregulars decided to mix it up and bring a group to the Idaho border. A longer drive, yes, but they'd been steadily clearing Steve from these parts. For the first time in years, Grace stood in the open, the morning sun cresting the horizon. The whole thing was surreal.

No hiding, not hunting for the deepest shadows to disappear into. Out in the open, grasslands dotted with trees and a few houses. So exposed, and yet…

A fresh breeze whipped her hair around her cheeks, making her glad for her jacket. The fighter wore a lightweight sweatshirt in dark colors that looked suspiciously like active wear.

"Isn't polyester flammable?" she asked suddenly.

Seahorse paused, looking down at her shirt, then back at Grace. "Don't judge me."

Charlie, however, wasn't ready to let go of their previous topic. "Why won't you just tell us why you won't cross the border and meet with Lieutenant Sears?"

"No. You go. That's part of why we kept you."

"We don't have to come back," Charlie said stubbornly.

Seahorse smirked. "You don't. But you will."

Charlie's jaw set, and he glared at her. "Why?"

"Curiosity."

Grace burst out laughing. The commander had her husband figured. And he knew it. It was the same argument she'd used to get him over the border the first time. After that, well, he wasn't heartless. He couldn't leave people in there any more than she could.

"Dammit," he muttered.

"Just..." Seahorse waved vaguely at the fence in the distance, "lead them across, talk to your lieutenant, see what's what, give as little as you can get away with in return, then come back. Maybe see if they'd you know..." She hesitated. Sarge, off to one side, gave her two thumbs up and an encouraging smile. She finished in a muttered rush. "Come over to help out."

Charlie choked. "What?!"

"See if they'd like to do a little invading. Captain told me if we found you, and you really had the contacts Fuzz said you did, to ask them. You know, do their job. Be a good neighbor. Whatever."

Grace opened her mouth. Closed it. Frowned. "This really sounds like something you should ask them yourself."

Sarge covered his mouth, but his eyes crinkled. "Go ahead," he said. "They're Fuzz's family. I reckon it's okay."

"The last time some of ours crossed the border, they were tortured," Seahorse said in a rush.

"...Oh."

"Do I want to know?" Charlie asked.

"Definitely not."

"But you should ask them," Sarge put in. "I, for one, would love to know what version of events is the official one. Take your ducklings and ask."

Well, now she had to know, too. Which is how she found herself crossing the border once more. This time, there were no furtive glances over their shoulders, no dodging patrols and crossing in the dead of night.

The Irregulars, staying well away from the fence, let them take their group of fifty or so civilians and walk boldly up to the fence. Soldiers waited on the other side, grouped around the slowly opening gate. Lieutenant John Sears stood at their head, arms folded, shaking his head.

"What the fuck, O'Connell," he said when Charlie crossed. "I want to ask, but a large part of me is afraid to know."

Charlie hesitated, and Grace knew he was thinking of Seahorse's comments about torture. She bit her lip. Charlie knew Sears better than she did, so she'd leave the choice to him. In the growing light, she saw the precise moment he decided to throw caution to the wind.

"We need to talk. Privately."

Medics and corpsmen ushered the ducklings into tents, throwing curious looks over their shoulders as they went. So many had never crossed the border at one time. Not here, not anywhere. Rumor had it that bands of up to twenty would come out of California, and once, there were several celebrities to come out of Oregon.

No one had crossed that border since.

Sears said something, and Charlie caught her hand, pulling her from her thoughts. Sears led them into the trees, away from the outpost. Along the way, he passed a letter to Grace.

"This came from your cousin."

It had obviously been opened and resealed, which was to be expected.

"I didn't know you had family back east." At her glance, he shrugged. "You know they check everything that comes here, digital or otherwise."

Grace turned the letter over in her hands. Constance had news, but did she dare open it here? She looked up at Charlie, eyebrows furrowed. He nodded slightly. He trusted Sears, anyway.

Tearing the envelope open, she listened with half an ear while Charlie mentioned help without saying where they came from—giving the impression that some folks from Washington had turned firebrand.

Holding the letter higher, Grace frowned, then turned the letter. "Babe," she interrupted, "get the book."

"Now?"

"Now. I'm not exactly sure what she's saying, but it's important, I can tell that much."

Turning, she gave him access to her pack while Sears watched them, confusion giving way to understanding. Constance rarely used code, but when she did... It was a cypher whose code was an old book, *The Dragon Court*. It required a specific edition, published in a certain year, in order to decipher it.

She only had four pairs of numbers, less than the usual. Charlie noted down the four words, then turned pale, swaying slightly. Grace grabbed his arm, holding him steady.

"What is it, Charlie?"

Mute, he handed her the paper. Her eyes widened. This, alone, wouldn't be enough for the courts, but Constance wouldn't write unless she was *very* sure. And the contents of her letter gave more clues. She passed Charlie the letter, his lips moving as he read it silently.

"Would you like some privacy?" Sears asked irritably. "This seems like a lot for a letter from your cousin."

Grace leaned against a tree, swallowing repeatedly, afraid that at any moment, her last meal would crawl up her throat.

"Do you trust him this much?" she asked.

"What?" Sears asked.

"If we're out of earshot, yes," Charlie replied.

"No one can hear us," Sears groused. "Will you tell me already? I hate being out of the loop."

Charlie straightened, firming his jaw. "*Listen.*" Sears shut up. "If I tell you this and anyone finds out, you're dead and we can't ever return to the

States until it's cleared up. Even if it's only a suspicion, it could ruin a career, and I don't think this person would take that lying down."

"There's only one place we can safely talk about this," Grace said.

Sears looked from one to the other. Grace could practically see the gears turning in his head. Should he trust them? Did he want to upend his life by hearing this secret?

Apparently, he did, because he nodded. "I'm game."

Charlie snorted. "Then you'll have to come with us. There." He nodded to the Occupied Zone.

"Are you crazy?"

"You have no idea," Charlie muttered. But Sears followed when Charlie took Grace's hand, lacing their fingers together, leading them towards the gate.

***

Pasadena, CA - Mercy

Mercy worked frantically over the young woman on her table, pressing cloths between her legs in a fruitless effort to stem the bleeding. The bondmaid, Patience, didn't even respond when Mercy knew she pressed too hard.

"No. No," she whispered over and over, mindful of the guards at her door.

Throwing away the blood-soaked fabric, she snatched more from Susannah, sent in to assist in the 'premature' birth. Only the most naive idiot would believe this to be anything other than the result of a beating, but the first person to suggest it out loud would lose their tongue.

She'd seen it happen.

Susannah held the infant, rubbing her chest and patting her cheeks with two fingers, but it didn't even have the wherewithal to cry. Glancing over, Mercy shook her head. The baby was pale, thin, and too small.

Hadn't Patience been allowed to eat enough?

"How is the baby?" Mercy asked, stepping away from Patience, her shoulders slumped.

This was the third woman Master Simpson had named Patience, and the second who'd died at his hands. Each time he introduced another confused young woman as 'Patience,' the poor thing never protested long.

She couldn't.

Simpson, overly fond of the ball-gag, would use it at the slightest provocation. To Mercy's knowledge, the only woman in his circle—including the Mistress—that she'd never treated for injuries from the ball-gag had been Susannah. He wouldn't risk damaging her voice. Susannah made Simpson unique, gave him value.

Not so the poor young woman on the table behind her.

"I don't...I'm not sure." Susannah handed the baby over, tears running down her face. "I don't think she's breathing."

Quickly, Mercy flipped the infant over to lie face-down over her forearm, tilting the baby to raise her bum, and lightly tapped her back with two fingers. Some liquid drained, but she still didn't cry.

Flipping her back, she stuck one finger into the baby's mouth, making a scooping motion. There! Working carefully, she scraped out something thick, jelly-like.

With the piece out, Mercy rubbed the baby's chest again, not stopping until the tiny baby let out a thin wail. She didn't have the strength for more and soon fell silent. Shaking her head, Mercy settled onto the floor with some breast milk donated by two of the nursing mothers in a bottle.

These first few hours were critical.

"What was that?" Susannah asked, examining the substance.

"My best guess?" Mercy shrugged one shoulder, opening her blouse to press the baby to her skin, holding the bottle to the infant's mouth, her lips still pressed in a thin line. "Uterine lining. Going by the bruises, she'd taken a good one to the stomach." All things considered, would survival really be in the baby's best interest?

"Hey!" At the door, a Warrior pounded roughly on the wall. "The Master requires an update. Immediately."

Her Master. Shit. Mercy didn't look up. "The mother is dead. The babe needs constant attention if she is to survive. That is the update."

The Warrior entered her room. "He requires your presence upstairs. He and Master Simpson demand both of you attend. Give the child to her." He nodded to Susannah, who immediately stepped forward, hands held out for the baby. Her eyes warned Mercy not to protest. There was only so much delay or disobedience her Master would allow, even from as valued a bondmaid as she. Susannah was right, she shouldn't say anything, but...

She bit her tongue on the words that wanted to spill from her lips, bowing her head to hide her expression. Turning her back to the Warrior, one who'd lived long enough to get a sprinkling of gray hairs, she buttoned her blouse.

"Keep her against your skin," Mercy whispered to Susannah. "Try to get her to drink. If she doesn't..." She shook her head. "She might not. She's too small." It was too soon.

"Now, bondmaids," the Warrior snapped.

Her head still bowed, Mercy rose smoothly to her feet, shaking out her skirt before following the man. He led the way, grumbling about lazy slaves, women having it 'too good,' how women should be grateful for what their betters gave them.

All drivel Mercy had heard before, a million times. Her lip curled involuntarily. All she needed was her scalpel, three seconds, and no witnesses... Immediately, she schooled her expression.

It'd become so much harder, staying silent these last few weeks.

Just a little longer.

On the third floor, the Warrior led them through a door held open by two Sons of Judea and halted just inside, standing to attention. Susannah stayed behind Mercy, who now felt the weight of eyes cataloging and judging her.

Never meeting anyone's eyes, she walked straight to the far end of the room, where her Master stood with his hands clasped behind his back, Master Simpson at his side. Susannah stopped when her Master shook his head, leaving Mercy to continue alone.

As soon as she reached her Master, Mercy dropped to her knees, bowing her head. To her left, Mistress Simpson looked down her nose. Mistress Kozlov turned her head away. The few other bondmaids blanched, and she knew none of them envied her right now.

To her right, Master Hermann sat against the wall, glaring balefully at her. Apparently, he still blamed her for Rhia. Around the room, Warriors of Light stood, armed with the sharpened sticks they called spears, chests puffed out.

"Tell me of the babe," Simpson demanded, leaning down.

"It is a girl child," Mercy said, careful to keep all inflection from her tone. "The mother is dead, the child weak."

"Bah!" Simpson flung a hand up, barely missing Mercy. Her Master shifted, giving Simpson a cutting glare, and Simpson subsided. "Another useless girl," he whined.

Because most of his children were girls. Mercy pitied the children. If older children of the Masters that survived the starvation and destruction were anything to go by, this next generation would also go to serve their fathers' ambitions.

They called it marriage, but every woman knew the truth. Still, better to service one man instead of many.

"Now, now," her Master said, smiling. "Every child is a gift from God. If she survives, we must do our best to ensure she learns correct obedience and subservience, as commanded by God."

Mercy bowed her head, hands folded in front of her, waiting. How much of her life had been spent waiting? Waiting to be struck, waiting to be humiliated, waiting to be condemned, waiting to be hurt. Now, waiting to escape.

"Do you not believe that children are gifts from God, bondmaid?" Her Master seated himself, slouching in his chair, lightly running his fingers over his lips to hide his smile.

"Children are a gift and reward from the Lord," Mercy said dutifully. "May your children bring you great joy."

Master Simpson gave up pacing and plopped into his own chair. "And how many such children have you given your Master?" he asked, gently tipping her face up.

She stared sightlessly over his left temple, face blank. "The Lord has never blessed me thus," she said, the words automatic. "But my mother had great difficulty conceiving, and I was born to my parents late in life. None of her other pregnancies made it past the first trimester."

He frowned at her composed answer, gripping her chin, and turning her face to examine it. When her Master coughed, he dropped his hand, dismissing her. Mercy crawled back a few steps, then rose to her feet, bowing and backing away, not turning until she was halfway across the room.

Silently, she collected Susannah and they left. None of the Warriors followed, leaving them to go alone to the infirmary. She remained straight-backed until she closed her door, pushing to make sure it latched.

Only then did she collapse against the door, pressing her face to the warm wood, taking deep, shuddering breaths.

"Oh, thank goodness," Susannah whispered. "I honestly thought you had ice in your veins. Even though you have more freedoms than we do, none of us have ever envied you because of how often you're called in front of them like that."

The infant fussed slightly, and she bounced her gently, walking slowly around the room. "How do you stay so calm? One wrong move and..." She shivered.

"Hush." Mercy glanced swiftly at the door. "Don't think about it. You just have to concentrate on your story."

"I'm so sorry," Susannah added.

"For what?"

"Your mother's trouble conceiving. That you're an only child. I couldn't imagine life without my siblings..."

"Oh, that." The words spilled recklessly from her lip. "I have seven siblings. My mum's never had a pregnancy or conception issue in her life."

Susannah's eyes widened and Mercy cursed herself. Susannah now had dirt on Mercy. One word to her Master...

"You...you lied? To their faces?" She shuddered, then laughed shortly. Mercy saw the next thought cross her gentle features. "How have you kept from getting pregnant?"

Mercy shook her head, unwilling to put herself in more danger. With this admission, she was already slated to die in several unpleasant ways. "That'll take too long. Pass me the baby."

When Susannah held the infant out, the baby's hand dropped limply. Susannah gasped. "Is she...?"

"Not yet," Mercy said grimly, setting the baby on her table. But no matter what she did, the baby continued to fade. Finally, she began chest compressions using two fingers and gave the tiniest puffs of air.

After three sixty counts, nothing changed. Shaking her head, she wrapped the tiny body in a blanket, carefully covering her face. Only twenty-eight weeks. Even with a hospital, it would have been difficult, considering the mother's injuries.

Susannah cried out, hand over her mouth, tears in her eyes. Mercy gently touched her shoulder before going outside. Sure enough, the gray-haired Warrior had taken up his position at the entrance to her garden.

"The babe is dead," she informed him dully. "Please send someone to bury the child." He gripped her arm when she turned back. She looked down at his hand, then up at him. "You have not been given the right to touch me."

Though he released her, he moved to block the way back. "How did it die?"

"*She*," Mercy stressed the pronoun, "was born prematurely. Even in the best of conditions, babies often wouldn't survive that."

"It is God's Will, then."

"If you like." She left then, too tired and heartsick to care about her reckless words. Her time here was already limited, her Master testing her nearly every time she saw him to see if she still mouthed their bullshit.

"Send the other bondmaid back then," the Warrior called. "I will send a slave to bury the body."

Opening her door, Susannah's rich voice filled the space. Mercy's breath caught in her throat. Low, husky, before soaring high, Susannah leaned over the tiny bundle, stroking her head, crooning a lullaby. Leaning against the door jam, eyes closed against the tears, she let Susannah's voice wash over her.

When the song—about a mother's hopes and dreams for her baby—finished, Mercy sighed, slowly coming back to herself. She straightened, going to the other woman.

"That was beautiful." She laid a hand on Susannah's arm, shocking herself. When was the last time she'd touched anyone when it wasn't medically necessary?

"Thank you." Susannah straightened, her eyes oddly blank. "If you'll excuse me, I must return to my Master."

She left abruptly, leaving Mercy staring after her, frowning. Something was off with the singer, but she didn't have time to think about it. Men had arrived to collect the small body.

***

Washington, DC – Constance

"Stop scratching," Perry muttered, moving to stand between her and the security guard.

"Wigs itch," she hissed. "Have you ever worn one?"

They walked down familiar hallways. Her old office was just three turns away, across the building from them. She shivered. Perry had been adamant she stay in the hotel room, but she'd refused.

How could she explain her fear that something would happen to one or the other of them while they were separated? She knew she didn't have the resources or skills to survive alone with police looking for her.

Instead, she accompanied Perry to the Russell Building. Carrying a tablet, they walked from one office to another. The building's closed internet meant that if you wanted information regarding the senators, you had to be in the building with the appropriate codes.

"How are those codes still working?" he muttered, stepping aside, putting one hand in the small of her back to guide her through the doorway, into the waiting room beyond. "They should've been changed the moment a warrant was taken out against you."

Constance smirked, stopping just out of sight of the doorway. Perry joined her there, shielding her from view. The most difficult part of this was never lingering in one spot long enough to look suspicious, forcing them to constantly move.

She scanned the tablet, stylus moving quickly. "Do you know how many people work here? And how many devices one person can use? Each device would have to be recoded."

"You knew this?"

She looked up, biting her lip to keep from grinning. He pursed his lips in a soundless whistle, so close she could see gold flecks hidden in his hazel eyes. She breathed out softly, swaying towards him.

"Are you okay?" he asked. "You look...flushed."

She started, looking hastily down at the device in her hands. "Yeah," she mumbled. "I'm just...waiting for the schedule to load."

"Excuse me?" a strange man said from behind Perry. "Can I help you?"

Perry spun, one hand behind his back. Constance could see his fingers wrapping around the EM tucked into his belt, underneath his dress uniform.

Constance stepped around him, holding her tablet behind his back. She smiled. "I'm sorry." She tucked a lock of the blonde wig behind her ear. She didn't recognize this guard. "We came here to...to..."

"Have a quiet...conversation," Perry jumped in, releasing the EM and wrapping his arm around Constance's waist. He tugged. Taking the cue, she leaned against him, resting her head on his shoulder, looking down, avoiding the guard's gaze.

The guard laughed. "You know you should save that for home." He shook his head. "I'll give you a warning this time, but if you fraternize at work, you know I'll have to report it."

"Of course!" Constance smiled up at Perry. "Sorry, we've just been so busy, and we're working different hours…"

The guard snorted. "Yeah, ever since that secretary attacked one of Senator McKinney's aides, it's been crazy, hasn't it? Still," he gave them a once over, "straighten up. Remember what I said."

"Sure. Thanks." Perry gave him a nod as the guard turned away. Hidden behind his back, the tablet in her hand chimed.

Constance closed her eyes briefly. When she opened them, the guard faced them again. "What are you doing?" He put one hand on the holstered EM at his waist. "Show me your hands!"

Perry surged forward, snatching the man's hand off his weapon and spinning him into the room, kicking the door shut behind them. Constance fell back against the wall, squeezing herself into the corner, watching, one hand over her mouth.

When he'd rescued her, she hadn't seen Perry move. Now, all she could do was stare as he struck using hands and feet, nearly too fast for her to follow. One final blow dropped the guard to his knees. Whipping out the guard's own EM, Perry fired once. He toppled slowly to the side, twitching.

Perry grabbed her hand, pulling her from her stupor and out the door, shutting it gently behind them.

"I sincerely hope you got what we need," he muttered, holding her elbow and escorting her to the nearest exit.

"Me, too."

Her heels clicked on the hard floors, barely able to keep up with his rapid pace. They stepped outside just ahead of an alarm sounding behind them.

Without looking back, Perry hustled her down the stairs and into the crowd around the building.

"Where are we going?" she asked.

"Home."

CHAPTER 12

Sacramento, CA – Faith

The way the Irregulars operated left Faith breathless. They never stopped moving. After only two nights at the river, more vehicles arrived, and Captain gave the order: Move out.

They spread out in small groups, a few Resistance members in each one, though they acted more like guides than the insurgents they were.

"When we get to a city, then we'll use you," Captain said, but Faith could hear the *maybe* in her voice.

The days were warm, but the nights stayed cold, and she huddled against Lucas every night to warm up enough to sleep. Each night, she fell into an exhausted slumber, never knowing what the next day would bring.

Once Sacramento was in sight, by some unheard order they all gathered in an abandoned vineyard outside the city. She still hadn't gotten used to how they spread out, hunkered down, and disappeared in what should be open ground.

No tents, tiny fires, minimal speech, and this lightly scorched vineyard looked...normal. If you walked through, you could see packs scattered over the ground, some with people lounging or sleeping nearby, others looking abandoned, markers for their owners to find later.

Captain pulled the Resistance leaders into a meeting with her lieutenants. There was the only thing she did differently than her fighters. Captain had a low tent created from a couple of small tarps. They sat and scrunched inside, listening to the rebel leader.

"Now that Steve's worried, it's time to make some moves. That's where you come in." She looked at Hackett, the leader from Sacramento. "I've got people working on how to get in. We'll need you to guide us to prime targets."

Hackett, an older woman with iron gray hair and hooded black eyes, nodded. "What are the targets you want?"

"We can see where they store munitions on the perimeter," she replied. "I want to know where the factories are, the armory, and any government offices are located."

"I can help with that," Faith volunteered.

"What are you doing?" Lucas demanded.

She put a calming hand on his arm. "I've received and sent messages to Sacramento, so I know the addresses of our counterparts here. I can guide you."

"You're not going anywhere without me," Lucas stated, folding his arms over his chest.

A knot she hadn't realized she had released in her chest. She smiled up at him. "I wouldn't want to." Then she looked back at Captain, wilting slightly under that cold look. Even with all their discussions, she still had so many moments where she didn't recognize her cousin.

Like right now.

"I'll allow it," Captain eventually said. "We'll take as many as are willing. Fair warning, we aren't used to operating quietly in cities."

"Usually, we leave behind a boom and some fire," Phoenix said cheerfully.

"Now, luv, you know that's not right," the large Brit said. "Sometimes, the explosion doesn't end in flames."

Phoenix pouted. "It's so disappointing when it doesn't."

As weird as they were, Faith couldn't help but like the fighters. They had a strange sense of humor, but they seemed...well, honorable. They had a code and kept to it.

Or so she thought until late the following day, when a patrol brought back three NKs. Snarling, one lunged. She started back so violently she rammed into Lucas, who caught and swung her behind him in one smooth move.

Grabbing his jacket with shaking hands, she pressed her face against his shoulder, images flashing through her mind. *Rough hands pulling her upright. A foot drawn back. Bared teeth, black eyes hard when the guard's boot crashed into her stomach. Vomit coating the front of her shirt. Her collar choking her. Someone dragging her downstairs, her feet kicking uselessly...*

Gradually, she became aware of hands stroking her hair back from her face, a gentle voice crooning soothing nonsense.

When she came fully back to herself, Faith opened her eyes to find herself sitting on the ground, Lucas at her back and Eleanor watching her with concern in her hazel eyes. Beyond Eleanor, the fighters surrounded them, most smiling when she met their eyes.

Faith flushed, leaning against Lucas. "I'm sorry, I don't know what happened."

Eleanor smiled gently. "You were triggered, dear. It's a PTSD flashback."

A large person stepped up, casting a shadow. Faith looked up, into Captain's pale eyes. She looked away. Would her cousin regret bringing her along now?

To her surprise, Captain knelt so they were eye to eye. Faith found it easier to look at her, the differences, and similarities to the person she used to be, even the scars around her eye, when she didn't have to tilt her head back.

"I'm sorry," Faith said again.

"There's no need to be sorry," Captain said quietly. "We've all been there. But I want to ask you. Those men, do you recognize any of them?"

The ring of fighters parted and the NKs were dragged forward. Keeping her distance, Faith examined them, then finally shook her head. "I don't. But so many people were always in and out of the offices."

Nearly unnoticed, Sung Ki slipped through the crowd, coming to stand at Captain's right. One of the NKs noticed her, snarling something and spitting at her feet.

Captain knocked him back. "That's not polite," she said, resting her foot against his chest. "Just because you don't like her life choices is no reason to be a shit about it. After all, *we* really disagree with many of your choices, but we're not bringing *your* ancestors into it."

Sung Ki laughed. "Your Korean is getting very good!"

The soldier bit out some words. Captain cocked her head. "Okay, I didn't follow that. I'm better with cussing."

Sung Ki shook her head. "He called her," she indicated Faith, who shrank back, "a traitor."

"Oh!" Captain turned on the soldier, a predatory look in her eyes. Faith's heart sank. "So you *do* know her! And tell me this." she asked something in Korean. Sung Ki shook her head and the soldier screamed.

"You just called his mother a frog with a dog's butt."

"Dammit!" But Captain smiled slightly. "I told you I'm better at swearing."

Looking around the circle, Faith was relieved to see she wasn't the only one bewildered by this exchange. Even a few of the Irregulars stared at their leader in shock.

"Fine," Captain said. "Ask him what he thinks we should do with them."

Sung Ki raised her eyebrows.

"While I know he knows Faith, we don't know if he was part of the lot that beat her." Captain folded her arms.

Even Lucas looked shocked at the amount of muscle bunching and sliding under her scarred skin. Faith examined her cousin. How had they never noticed...? Ah! She wasn't wearing her leather jacket. Even on the days when the other Oregonians wore t-shirts, Captain still wore her soft leather jacket.

Sung Ki and the NK had a rapid conversation in Korean. Eventually, she turned to Captain. "He said that he will never become like me and betray his country. He said he would die for his Beloved Leader. And he said he would fight you for their freedom."

Captain contemplated it for a moment. "Yeah, I'm good with that. I like fighting people who are willing to die for their country, leader, whatever. It means we both have the same goal. I take it he's suggesting a fight to the death?"

Sung Ki nodded.

The fighters immediately gathered into small groups. No, she realized. They went in small groups to the driver, Dereva, who had a pen and paper out, taking notes.

"Oh, my God," Lucas muttered. "I can't believe they're taking bets."

"Who?" He nodded to the driver. "That's what they're doing?"

"Yeah."

"But what'll happen if the NK wins?"

Apparently, she wasn't the only one with that concern. Carter and Varro approached her while she shed her weapons—creating a substantial pile—and chatted with Sung Ki.

They had a low-voiced conversation that ended when Captain picked up two knives. "If you don't like this," she said, "I can just shoot them now."

"Some of ours would want you to," Carter admitted. "But we have to be better than them."

"Which is why I'm fighting him to the death." Captain shook her head as if this was obvious. They opened their mouths, but Captain stepped past them, into the ring. She threw one knife down, so it landed blade first in front of her opponent. "Relax, guys. Either I'll die or I won't."

One of the fighters cut the soldier's hands free, and the fight began. Faith tried to act like an observer only, tried to stay impartial, but soon, she hid her face against Lucas's chest, clutching his sweatshirt in a white-knuckled death grip.

As far as the fighters were concerned, the fight was a foregone conclusion. They cheered, jeered (frequently at their own leader), and whooped. Sung Ki watched it all with her arms folded, completely impassive.

When it ended and Faith could look at the combatants, Captain had a thin cut on her arm and another, even finer, on her cheek, below her left eye. The NK...Faith forced herself to examine him. He had remarkably few cuts, which meant...

"She didn't play with him," Lucas said softly. "It was obvious she could have, but she didn't. She made it fast, at least."

"Fast and what?" she asked. "I can tell there's a 'but'."

"Brutal," he said, his lips compressed into a thin line. "It was brutal."

Intermingled with the fighters, Resistance members—including several Chapter leaders—turned away. Even those she knew were constantly pushing for mass annihilation looked gray.

"Nobody ever expects it to be like this," Faith whispered. "Where's all the glory you hear about in songs?"

***

No Man's Land, WA – Grace

"Don't worry," Charlie said. "Steve's got bigger problems than us right now."

Grace smothered a smile. The Irregulars even had Charlie calling the soldiers by their name.

"But *why* do we have to come over here?" Sears asked again. "Do you know how hard it'll be for me to do the paperwork?"

Sears looked unhappily around the peaceful grass and scrubby pine trees, Spokane's skyline in the distance. A few ruined houses dotted the land, their gardens overgrown and wild. The road crossing the border lay a short way to the south, weeds growing between asphalt broken by tank treads years ago. The new dirt road created by the North Korean's border patrol crossed it, completely empty for the first time in years.

"Because these," Grace waved to his comms, phone, and biometrically locked handgun, "won't work."

"And you think disarming me is a good idea because why?"

She understood his reluctance. She and Charlie had been the only people crazy enough to continually cross the border, and he'd been so willing and eager to help save people that now, the entire operation worked through his base.

Volunteers helping get the rescued resettled were called in by his personnel. Medical supplies raised through donations were brought straight here instead of distributed along the border camps.

But sometimes, he was still a member of the U.S. military, and he felt things had to be done through certain channels.

"Dude." Charlie punched him lightly on the shoulder. "It's not about disarming you. This area is the safest it's been since the Invasion. It's about ensuring little ears can't hear."

Grace turned her back to the sun, warmth finally seeping through. Winter came a little earlier this year.

"Besides," Charlie continued, "there's someone else who really needs to hear this news."

As if his words conjured her from the air—and Grace wouldn't be surprised if they had—Seahorse materialized from the empty countryside, Sarge at her side.

Okay, I get her showing up from nowhere, but how does a man as big as Sarge do that?

"What the fuck?" Sears scrambled backwards, snatching a gun that couldn't work from its holster, swinging back and forth between them before settling on Sarge.

The fighters just watched him, Sarge with his arms folded over his massive chest. "We know that won't work here, genius," he rumbled.

"What part of 'give as little information as you can' escaped you?" Seahorse rounded on the O'Connells.

When Sears shouted for them to put their hands up, Sarge laughed more, Charlie tried to calm it, and...

Grace stormed into the middle. "Enough!" she bellowed. "You can all calm *the fuck* down! John Sears!" He flinched away from her wrath. "We brought you here, promising your safety. Trust us! And you two," she rounded on the fighters, "need to hear what we've just learned. This is the only safe place to talk about it, so please, *listen*."

Surprised, they fell silent. Sears and Sarge mumbled little 'sorry's,' but Seahorse folded her arms, eyeing Grace. "You wouldn't happen to have cousins living in Oregon, would you?" she asked. "Because you pissed off looks really familiar."

Tears rushed in, and she blinked them back. "I don't know," she said thickly. "How do I find out if they're still alive?" *Because my brother isn't.*

She burst into tears, all the ones she'd been smothering since first hearing about Peter's death pouring out.

As quickly as that, the men settled. Charlie went to her, wrapping her tightly in his arms. Sarge patted her back, pulling a small flask from one of his many pockets, offering the eyewatering contents to her, while Sears anxiously hovered behind, all animosity towards the fighters temporarily forgotten.

When she calmed, Sears offered her a handkerchief. "My mother's always sending me them," he mumbled in response to Sarge's raised eyebrows.

"Good man," he said. "Respecting your mother."

When Charlie loosened his grip enough, Grace found herself eye to eye with Seahorse, close enough to see gold flecks in her dark brown eyes. "I'm sorry for your losses," she said clearly. "And I hope, when this is over, we manage to find more of your family. When you're ready to talk, any one of us," meaning the Irregulars, Grace gathered, "is here to listen. Including me. And when it's safe, we'll get horrifically drunk and tell stories. They don't make the pain go away, but it helps to share the love and grief."

Grace nodded, mopping her eyes, and blowing her nose on the borrowed handkerchief. When she held it up, eyeing it dubiously, Sears waved it away.

"Keep it. I've got tons more. My mother will be thrilled I could be a gentleman."

"For once," Charlie said under his breath.

Sears glared. Seahorse smiled slowly. "You know what?" she said. "You're all right, Sears. So, I'll do you a solid and not shoot you yet, you jumpy, gun-happy bastard. But keep your useless gun holstered, will you? Not all my people will know your gun doesn't work and they'll shoot first, then think about it afterwards."

"Hey!"

"My love," Sarge said, laying a hand on her hip. "We used to *be* those jumpy, gun-happy bastards."

"Yes, but I've learned differently." She folded her arms, the fabric pulling tight across muscled arms and shoulders. "Captain is a cynical asshole and I feel I've become a better person for knowing them. Now." She turned to Grace. "Why did you bring a soldier into our territory? Especially when I asked you not to tell them about us? And why do I recall asking these questions earlier and never getting an answer?" She glared around at the men, who looked up or stared at their toes.

Giggling, wiping away the last of the tears, Grace shook her head. "We received a letter from our contact in DC..."

Seahorse snapped to attention. "You have a contact in DC? When were you going to mention that?"

"I don't know," Grace snapped, setting her mouth in a stubborn line. "It's not like it's something that comes up in casual conversation."

"Sweet baby Jesus." Seahorse flung her hands up. "That's what volunteering random bits of information is for! Feel free to drop shit like that down in the middle of a conversation! Unless, after everything, you don't trust us?"

Charlie made a strangled sound, and Grace wrapped her arms around him.

"Let's not answer that," Sarge interrupted. "How about you just tell us what was so important?"

Grace pulled the nearly forgotten letter from her pocket. "Our contact put a cypher in here. The letter itself talks about responsibility for tragedies, so we know she's talking about who's been backing North Korea."

"And the cypher?" Seahorse made a rolling motion with her hand.

"Secretary of State Keller."

Grace didn't often get the chance to make people speechless. Turned out, she enjoyed the sensation.

Probably more than she should. She came back to the present at Seahorse's first words after the announcement.

"Captain needs to hear about this."

***

"You know Captain?" Sears asked again.

Seahorse frowned at the soldier, then looked at Charlie. "Are you sure he's alright? I mean, I have answered this question already, correct?"

"Yeah." Charlie rubbed a hand over his face.

Seahorse sent the blonde woman, the Celt, south yesterday. Sears returned to the outpost just long enough to reassure his men. It was only on his return to the Occupied Zone that he'd begun asking about Captain.

Grace chewed her lip. "Lieutenant," she said, waving a hand to get his attention. "What did you read? About Captain, I mean?"

"Who says I read anything about him?"

"All your sudden questions," she said dryly.

He shrugged uncomfortably. "Let's just say that if I ever get the chance to meet the man, I'm not sure whether I should shake his hand or shoot him."

"Oh, don't shoot him," Seahorse said, grinning wickedly. "Captain doesn't take being shot at very well. Now." She surveyed her fighters, who slowly gathered in Spokane's eastern suburbs.

Grace tipped her head, trying to see what Seahorse saw. Despite their varied clothing, the motley collection of weapons, and the fact that they couldn't seem to decide on footwear—she saw combat boots, hiking boots, and moccasins, as well as the occasional pair of sneakers—they were identical in their expressions.

Fierce, determined, and wild. Somehow, they fit well into the ruined cityscape. Crumbling skyscrapers, broken roads, and rusting abandoned cars were a fitting backdrop to this feral militia.

"Courtesy of that letter from your friend," Seahorse continued, "I think it's time we took the fight to Steve."

Grace stared at her, confused. "Isn't that what we've been doing?"

"No. That was softening the enemy. Now, it's time to really get down to it. Sears," she barked.

"Yes, ma'am!" He saluted, then froze. His eyes rolled up, then looked wildly around. Grace bit her lip to keep from laughing.

"Don't call me ma'am," Seahorse said gruffly. She couldn't hide her smile for shit, but she tried, Grace had to give her that. "You border boys want to finally see a bit of fighting?"

He didn't even have to think about it. "Yes, ma'am! My boys are sick to death of sitting on the sidelines."

"Take it easy, Tiger," Sarge rumbled. Sears glared at the big man. "You still have to find weapons that'll work here."

"What's the plan?" Charlie asked. "And what will you need us to do?"

Seahorse nodded, leading them to one of the pickup trucks. After a quick word, a series of maps were produced. "We need to know Steve's most likely route of retreat, every single outpost you know of. Some of them we've already taken care of, but I need to know them all."

"The plan, ma'am?" Sears had apparently decided his superiors could jump off a cliff, because Grace had never seen this level of deference in him.

"We'll start here and sweep east, pushing Steve in front of us. There'll be a lot of hit and run fighting, them testing the edges. From now on, we don't give up an inch of ground. Once we've got them on the coast, we'll use some of the toys we took from them last year and blow them to hell."

Charlie leaned over the state map, following her finger. "What makes you think this'll work?"

"This is basically what we did to get Oregon back. And since we don't have a set in stone strategy, we can be flexible."

"Didn't you do this with Captain, last time?" he asked. Sears perked up, all ears.

Seahorse smirked. "Be glad Captain *isn't* here. Then you'd have some *really* dumb shit going down."

Sarge laughed. "My wife is the soul of reason. Comparatively speaking."

Grace leaned over to the older woman next to her, Sparrow. "What did Captain do last time?" she whispered.

"She had us throw burning cars at their position," Sparrow whispered back. "It was *amazing*."

Grace edged slowly away from the other woman, eyeing her. Slender, with a beauty that aged gracefully, Grace thought she might have been a former model. Or tennis player. Not talk about burning cars with such...glee.

"Yeah," whispered Wilder, one of the drivers. "Don't worry. We've got a decent idea what we're doing."

"Only *decent?!*"

Wilder sniggered. "And we're *really* good at improvising. We've got this."

***

Pasadena, CA – Mercy

Mercy sighed, wringing cloth out over the dirty water bucket before dipping it into the clean water, continuing to wash. Dirt came off reluctantly, smearing over her skin. The sandy soil hated parting from anything it touched, including skin.

She'd removed her sweat-soaked blouse, discarding it onto the floor. Running the cloth over her neck, then down, she wiped sweat from between her breasts and belly, then more awkwardly from her back. With every swipe of the cool cloth, she deliberately relaxed.

Another terrible day, finally done.

Outside her door, in her garden courtyard, sounds of a scuffle drew closer. Snatching up a fresh blouse, Mercy barely had time to hold it in front of herself before the door flew open. Master Simpson stood, silhouetted in the doorframe, face white with fury.

Mercy scrambled back, clutching the cotton blouse to her chest, brought up short by the bookshelves. Behind Master Simpson, Susannah struggled wildly in the overseer's grip. Macey had one hand clamped over her mouth, fingers digging brutally into her cheeks. Her large hazel eyes were wide, filled with tears.

Master Simpson held up a slender scalpel, the blade trembling in his hand. "Did you give her this, bondmaid?" he hissed. "Did you aid this whore in her attempt to rebel against her Master?"

"You're no master of mine!" Susannah, freeing her mouth with a well-timed bite, took full advantage. "You're a pathetic excuse..." She gurgled, mouth gaping, when Macey gripped her throat.

"*Did you help her?*" Master Simpson screamed.

Mercy looked from Susannah to Simpson and back, unsure for the first time in years what the best next step would be. Taking her wildly moving head as a *No*, Simpson snatched up a handful of Susannah's long, black hair, flinging her to the ground.

Kicking her viciously, he glanced at Mercy to see her reaction. He continued raining kicks over her, stomping on her stomach, causing Susannah to curl into a ball, gasping and retching. Mercy looked frantically around the room, hoping that someone would intervene, but the room only contained herself, Susannah, Master Simpson, and Macey.

Gritting her teeth, she launched herself forward when Master Simpson drew his foot back, scrambling to cover as much of Susannah as she could.

"Please, Master," she screamed, but his only response was to deliver two hefty kicks to her bare back. "She doesn't know what she's doing," Mercy croaked. "It's the child's death that's driven her insane. Please, show her mercy, Master."

Master Simpson wrenched her head back, his fingers tangled in her kerchief. "Whore!" he hissed, his face mere inches from hers, his breath hot on her skin. "Slut. Look at you, exposing yourself like this."

Beneath the pain of her neck being unnaturally twisted, her scalp on fire, the thought dimly crossed her mind that she wouldn't be half-naked if he hadn't burst uninvited into her room. Her exposure wouldn't be an issue if they'd just leave her in peace...

She screeched, arms flailing. Simpson dragged her backwards, flinging her into the center of the room. Striking her head against the table, her mind exploded, her vision bursting with colors. Susannah shrieked once and suddenly, Master Simpson's blurry face filled Mercy's view.

He had clean, even features, a straight, narrow nose, and dark brown eyes. His thick hair, shot through with silver, was cut short. If he weren't so reprehensible, he'd be handsome. Mercy's forehead furrowed with the effort of thinking.

These men acted as if women had denied them constantly before the compound was formed, which seemed stupid. All they had to do was be kind and women would be falling over themselves for him.

She squinted, struggling to focus. In the background, Susannah sobbed, and he continued talking to her.

"Ensure she lives, bondmaid," he snarled. "She has more to answer for. As for you, I will be telling your Master what an immoral slut he has for a bondmaid, exposing yourself to another. Your lewd behavior will not go unpunished."

A chill ran down Mercy's spine, pulling her from the fog clouding her mind. Lewd behavior was whatever the Masters decided. Being accused of such was a death sentence.

When Susannah's cries roused her, the men had left. She crawled forward, every motion pounding through her head. She stopped, stomach revolting, and vomited, barely turning her head to the side in time. Gasping, she raised a trembling hand to her mouth, wiping the remainder away.

"Susannah?" she whispered, feeling blindly, closing one eye in an effort to make the world stop spinning, following the sounds of Susannah's pain. "What did he do?"

"You mean besides the beatings, the rapes, and losing my babies?" Susannah half sobbed, half laughed. "I think...he broke my legs."

"Oh, sweet Jesus."

Her head finally clearing, Mercy examined Susannah's legs. Thankful she'd just emptied her stomach, Mercy repeatedly swallowed back bile. Simpson hadn't just broken each leg, he'd shattered them. Without surgery and extensive care, she wouldn't walk again.

But she'd live, if she didn't get an infection. However, Mercy had no way to straighten her legs correctly. Not that Simpson intended for her to walk. He wanted Susannah well enough to suffer more, that was it.

"How bad is it?"

Mercy stroked her hair back from her face. Finally remembering her nakedness, she pulled on the clean blouse, buttoning it haphazardly.

"I'm sorry. You'll live. You'll never walk again, not with the care I can give you, and you'll live."

Tears welled in Susannah's eyes, though she tried to blink them back. "Please, no," she whispered, her voice trembling. "You know what he'll do to me. Is there no escape?"

Mercy clenched her jaw, holding back tears. "I can give you mercy."

"Will my Master—No!" Susannah dashed a hand across her eyes. "No, I won't call him that anymore. Simpson. Will he know you helped me?"

Mercy bared her teeth in a parody of a smile. "Yes. Not that it will matter. I've already been accused of lewd and immoral behavior."

Susannah paled. "What will *he* do?"

"He'll likely hand me over to the Warriors of Light." Mercy kept her tone even, adjusting Susannah to make her more comfortable. "If I survive that, then I'll be sent to the Sons. And if I'm still alive after that, he'll give me to the dogs."

"So sure?" The singer clenched her hands against a wave of pain.

"I've seen it happen before. Then again, I've been with him the longest, so he might view this as a greater betrayal. But my Master has never had a very good imagination, so he's likely to stick to what's familiar." His lack of imagination was how she'd been able to send so many to safety. "But I've known for a while that his patience was running out," she continued, sitting back on her heels, rubbing a hand over her mouth.

The door slammed open, bouncing off the concrete wall. "Bondmaid!" A young man wearing the white armband of a Warrior blocked the light of the setting sun. "Master Simpson wishes to hear of your progress with the slave."

Mercy pursed her lips, considering. "Her wounds are extensive," she said carefully. "If she is to live, I must treat her carefully. It will be some time."

"Very well." He dragged a chair from her little table and set it in the doorway, seating himself with finality. "Carry on."

Her lips thinned. Bloody Warriors, always around when you least wanted them.

"Perhaps," the Warrior said pleasantly, "when your Master punishes you, healer, I will be the first." He smiled. A beautiful smile, full of charm, but his eyes were cold, calculating, when he examined her. "I don't care for sloppy seconds."

Mercy broke out in a cold sweat, only years of lying keeping her face still and her hands steady. "Perhaps," she said neutrally. Going to the shelves, she pulled a dark, glass bottle off the shelf. "May I offer you refreshment, Warrior?"

He laughed, the sound ringing joyfully through the room. "Seeking to lessen your punishment? Very well, but we all know what whores deserve. You may serve me." When Mercy made to bring him a glass, his voice hardened. "On your knees, cunt."

Immediately, Mercy dropped to her knees, crawling awkwardly to the younger man. Bowing her head, she raised the glass with both hands, the deep red of the wine catching the last bits of light, spilling like blood over the shelves.

"You truly do know your place, don't you?" He raised the glass, gulping noisily. "It's a pity you've been denounced as a whore. You would have made a good broodmare for me." As he spoke, his breathing became more labored.

Her back to him, Mercy smiled. Trailing her fingers through the dried herbs overhead, she pulled down a bundle of mint, then went to the shelves covered in small glass bottles, each one meticulously labeled. Occasionally, she checked on Susannah, who lay still on the thin mattress, her long eyelashes standing out against her white skin.

The Warrior continued talking, almost to himself. "I hope I get to feel your lips wrapped around my..." Choking, he slumped sideways, the glass shattering when it hit the floor. "What...?" he wheezed, his fingers clumsily working around his throat.

Susannah gasped, struggling onto her elbow, staring at the man. Mercy hurriedly dragged him away from the door and shut it carefully, wedging the chair under the handle. Stepping over him, she kicked his grasping fingers away from her ankle, watching him die.

In the end, he couldn't even lift his hands to his throat.

"What...did you give him?" Susannah asked faintly.

Mercy shrugged. "When my Master first brought me here, there was a hospital. I was allowed to go through it, taking anything I might need. Not everything was as harmless as he thought."

Though it'd taken her a long time to discover this particular drug and its effects.

"Is that..." Susannah swallowed heavily. "Is that how you'll take care of me?"

Mercy knelt at her side, stroking her hair back from her face. "No. For you, it will be more like falling asleep. It will be peaceful. Painless. I promise."

"You've done this...many times?"

"More than I care to remember." But she couldn't forget a single face. Susannah, she knew, she would never forget. This woman had almost been a friend. If only...

Sighing, she went back to the table. 'If only' could be written on her headstone. If only she'd never stopped to help a woman in labor. If only she'd murdered her Master years ago. If only she'd had access to all the Masters... If only.

Pouring clear liquid from a bottle innocently labeled *Pure* into a glass of apple vodka, she added the mint leaves, giving it a minute to soak.

"It's ready," she said softly. "Is there…anyone you want to leave a message for?"

Susannah shook her head. "I only have one living child, and I've never been allowed to hold her. She's only two." Mercy gently raised Susannah's head. Before she could put the glass to her mouth, the singer seized her hand. "Wait! Promise me you'll get my daughter out."

"I can't—"

"You're the only one here who might. You look meek, but you're the only one I've met who's actually defied them, lied to their faces. You have to!"

Mercy bowed her head before the other woman's desperation. "All right," she said softly. "I promise I'll do my best to get your daughter out."

This time, Susannah dutifully drank, licking her lips to catch the last drops. "So, you're the one who makes the vodka, huh? I always wondered. Good stuff. I like the mint."

Mercy laughed quietly, tears starting in her eyes. "Now? You're making jokes now?"

"Well, my legs don't hurt anymore. Nothing does." She sighed dreamily, staring at things only she could see. "What will you do now? I can't see you sticking around for punishment."

"No," she whispered, still stroking Susannah's hair. "I have a way out."

"See? I knew you were the right person for the job."

Tears spilled down her cheeks, splashing onto Susannah's face, but the other woman didn't notice. "Why don't you rest now? You've done your work. Close your eyes and sleep."

She hummed, breaking out into a rough, low song, her voice rusty from lack of use, the tune barely above a whisper.

Rest my angel

Sleep my precious one

I will hold you

Until the night is done

Susannah smiled, her eyes sliding shut.

She continued singing long after she knew Susannah was gone, long after the sun had set. Gently, she laid the singer down, folding her hands over her chest. She stayed that way for a long time, tears falling freely.

"Watch over her, Jonathan," she whispered thickly. "She's good people."

Finally, her tears spent, she crawled to her feet.

She had work to do.

CHAPTER 13

Wiretap, Lowes Hotel Room #113. Booking name James Smith – September 12, 2066, 6:24pm

Man: This is ridiculous! How long are we supposed to wait? Do you know how much money I'm losing?

Woman: Don't be such a little girl. Money isn't being torn from your pocket. Once we have approval to send troops in, the payoff will be astronomical.

Washington, DC – Constance

Constance's eyebrows rose when she saw the noisy street in Chinatown. Perry had taken her on a winding route, hopping from subway to bus to tram to Uber and back to the tram, ditching her wig in the process while he stuffed his dress jacket into the backpack he'd dropped in the bushes. On the second tram, he put his arm around her, drawing her close.

"Time to change how we look to other people," he whispered. "Can't make ourselves too easy to follow."

"Do you think someone is?" Immediately, she examined every person in the car with them, her eyebrows drawn.

They'd just been in the Russell Building. Who knew what kind of hidden security they might have?

"Relax," he murmured. "We lost them in the subway. And even if there is another tail, good luck to them."

Surveying Chinatown, she could see why. Shop-lined streets were packed with people, some hustling, others browsing the windows. The windows above the shops, with their curtains and decorations, showed that many of those below lived above.

The homeless lingered in alleyways, hands out. Some showed signs of sickness. Others were scarred from their brush with radiation. The survivors of Maine and Georgia.

"You live here?" Twisting, she leaned away slightly to see his face better. He looked out on the crush of humanity with surprising calm.

"Yeah." He put his arm around her. To keep from getting pulled away, she wrapped hers around him, holding tightly.

They walked past shops selling everything from food to groceries to trinkets. At one restaurant, she leaned back, her nose leading her towards some delicious scents.

He laughed. "Later. They deliver."

Three doors down from the tantalizing scents, he stopped, keying a code, then pressing his thumb to the pad. The door swung inward, and they nearly fell inside, shutting it behind them.

Inside, the walls were painted brown and cream. At the end of a short, narrow hall, stairs led up.

"No elevator?" Puzzled, she looked around. Just little letterboxes, each one numbered, the remains of a bygone era. "This is seriously where we're hiding out?"

"Of course. What did you expect?"

Walking down the hall, she continued examining it. Maybe there was something she'd missed. "I don't know. One of those warehouse deals like you always see in the movies, tricked out with the latest gadgets?"

He laughed, stopping on the first small landing. "And stand out as the only people in an area that should be abandoned? No. Plus, I prefer a little more comfort than that."

At the second landing, she followed him down a hallway, the walls painted the same brown and cream, every door painted red. His had a small green symbol at his eye level.

She peered over his shoulder while he entered another code and pressed his thumb to the pad. "So why didn't we come here sooner?"

He shrugged one shoulder. "We needed to get off the street fast. Hotel rooms that rent by the hour don't ask questions and are generally in neighborhoods where government people stand out."

"They could have sent someone covert after us."

"You weren't labeled a threat, yet. Here." He opened the door, standing aside to let her precede him into the apartment.

She surveyed the room, walking slowly through it. A small studio apartment, it only had a twin bed against the wall to her left, its blankets and sheets tucked with military precision. Next to the single window, a series of hooks held clothing. A small chest of drawers rested beneath it, neatly closed.

Resting one hand against the wall, she looked out the window onto a narrow alley, the fire escape creating a tiny balcony and partially blocking the dismal view of the building next door. A desk sat in the right-hand corner, the bathroom door near that, opposite the bed.

Perry stood in the tiny kitchenette, hands in his pockets, watching her examine his room. "Can I get you a drink?"

"Water. Please."

He had two chairs at the counter, a desk chair, and a tiny couch. The kitchenette consisted of a convection oven, half fridge, a couple cupboards, and a single sink. Other than his clothing, there was nothing in the place to say someone lived here.

"How long have you been here?" she asked, accepting the glass of water.

He perched on one of the kitchen chairs, turning his own glass on the counter. "A year. After that report you mentioned, they dishonorably discharged me. Us. Those of us who returned. We went our separate ways until I heard about the first death.

"I've been trying to figure out why they sent in so many green boys." The corner of his mouth quirked in a half smile. "Guess I should have tracked you down sooner. You've gotten farther than I ever managed."

Constance sank onto the desk chair. "Speaking of your report..." She licked her lips. "Thirty went in, seven came out. How did that many men die?"

He broke into a full grin. "Did I say they died?"

Her breath caught. "Are you saying...some just didn't come out?"

That smile was his only response.

***

Sacramento, CA – Faith

Two nights after Captain made an example of the NK, Faith lay under a bland, olive-green blanket, her head pillowed on Lucas's arm, waiting for sunset. Lucas, a warm weight at her back, breathed steadily. Twisting around carefully, she examined his face. He really was asleep.

How could he sleep?

Peeking out from under the blanket, a wash of cold air made her huddle more tightly against Lucas, Sacramento's silhouette slowly disappearing as the sun sank below the horizon. Around the camp, no one moved. At this point, she'd rather be forging papers in the office, terrified that at any moment she'd be caught than stuck in this endless round of waiting.

A hand touched her leg and she started. "Time to get up," Captain murmured.

How the hell had she come upon them so quietly? On throwing the blanket back, Faith saw many vague forms walking around camp. Gently, she shook Lucas awake. The fighters had been moving around the whole time, when she'd seen nothing. How did they do it?

While they quietly packed away their blankets and took them to a truck, she kept her ears peeled for any sound of Captain. There!

Placing a hand on Lucas's arm to hush him, she turned towards the sound.

"...should stay back," Carter said. "What if something happens to you?"

Captain snorted. "Dying isn't the worst thing that can happen to you out here. And if you ever suggest I stay behind and send my people into danger, you and I will have a chat much like the one I had the other day, understand?"

Carter remained silent. And what else could he do? If it were daylight, she'd give him a cold stare that would silence him anyway. It was like she didn't care what happened to her. Faith shivered. What had happened to her over the past years to make her like this?

She and Lucas made their way to Captain's pickup truck. Once upon a time, it'd been blue with a gray stripe around its middle. Now, it had several new panels along it, all of them dented. Bullet holes peppered most of the rest. The glass was gone from the windows, but somehow, it still had those running boards.

Slowly, the other members of Faith's group materialized from the dark. Sung Ki, Chaos, the company's first doctor, Doc, herself, Lucas, and last of all, Captain.

Being around Captain still made her a little uncomfortable. She'd killed a man with nothing but a *knife*. Being on par with trained soldiers when the weapon was firearms somehow made sense. Taking a soldier on one to one with a knife just seemed like a new level that Faith couldn't be comfortable with yet.

Most of the groups had already left by the time Captain moved out. Some of them had Sacramento Chapter members as guides, but most were made up entirely of Irregulars. Faith privately wished them luck. How were they going to accomplish their objective without a guide?

Eleanor met them halfway across camp, pressing her forehead to Captain's, her head tilted back at a sharp angle. "Stay safe. Cause trouble."

Captain grinned wickedly. "You know me so well." At the edge of the camp, Captain stopped Lucas with an arm across his chest, her earlier levity gone. "She's your responsibility. You have *her* back, understand? We handle everything else, you watch her."

Because Faith knew where they were going. She knew the location of reams of files and orders. And she'd seen a document with a seal that definitely didn't belong to the NKs.

Unless she was gravely mistaken, it had an official U.S. seal on it, and she knew what it looked like and how the NKs filing system worked.

For this mission, she was, unfortunately, the most important person here, right after Captain.

***

Following the Irregulars was its own unique exercise. She panted, belly down in the ashy dirt, Captain's heels bare inches from her forehead. When they moved, she moved. When they crawled, she crawled. When they ran, she panted and puffed in their wake.

During one of their pauses, Faith shivered. Chaos only wore a t-shirt, making it easy for Doc to stay close behind him, her left hand gripping his belt. Didn't these lunatics realize winter was nearly here? She and Lucas were bundled in long sleeve shirts, sweatshirts, jackets, and knit caps, but these idiots dressed like it was late summer.

Captain wore her too big leather jacket, but underneath, Faith could plainly see a black t-shirt. Sung Ki and Doc opted for long sleeves, but they were still t-shirts!

Even the damn ditch didn't slow them down. One of the previous groups left their ropes behind. Faith reeled at their speed.

Inside, Chaos took the lead, Doc still in his shadow, she and Lucas right on their heels. Sung Ki and Captain occasionally disappeared into the dark. Once, she swore she heard a fight, but when she went to investigate, Lucas blocked her way and Chaos tugged her back into place, shaking his head.

Captain quickly reappeared, sucking her knuckle and grinning.

Faith directed them through the streets, relying on maps she'd seen to find the address. Across the city, an orange glow lit the sky, barely visible around the skyscrapers. Soon, more fires grew, scattered across the city.

Her breath came short, the instincts she'd built over the last few years telling her to get underground and find cover. Lucas took her hand, lacing their fingers together. Biting her lip, looked for roads signs to see where they needed to go next.

"Left," she whispered, inclining her head towards a major road.

The fighters proceeded with caution, staying close to the edges. Halfway down the block, the fighters shoved them into an alley, crouching at the mouth, weapons ready.

A patrol of NKs raced past, engines roaring.

Faith exhaled slowly, then tentatively touched Chaos's shoulder. "The building we're looking for is on this street. Number 10566."

"You ever seen it?" he asked.

"Once. Looks like most everything here. Concrete and glass, but it's shorter, maybe ten stories."

Continuing down the road, Chaos suddenly stopped, reaching back. Faith followed his pointing finger to check out the building. She nodded. Right building. Putting a hand to his mouth, he hooted softly, then led them across the road at a run.

Captain and Sung Ki joined them in the alley next to the main doors. Faith bent over, putting her hands on her knees, struggling to catch her breath. She glared at the others, who all seemed perfectly fine. Including Lucas, that rat.

"Lights on the second floor," Chaos said softly.

"Guards on the ground floor, going past in patrols," Captain replied.

"I thought this place was just storage?" Doc raised one eyebrow, looking at Faith.

Faith shrugged. "As far as I know, it is. I don't know why they'd have guards. Can you guys...handle them?"

Chaos, Sung Ki, and Doc dissolved in nearly silent laughter, broken only when Doc snorted a giggle. Captain tapped her foot, rolling her eyes and sighing, and as suddenly as that, her cousin was back.

"Are you idiots done?" she asked eventually.

Doc sank to the ground, wheezing, her hands not quite enough to muffle her laughter. Scooping her up, Chaos held her to his chest, shaking his head at her muffled snickers.

"Sorry, Captain," he said, his teeth white in the dark. "While she's getting her shit together, is there another entrance that's not the front door?"

Faith closed her eyes, tapping her fingers on her thigh, scrunching her face with the effort of thinking. Her eyes popped open. "Yes! There's a large service entrance at the back, so it's probably guarded too, but on the far side there's a smaller entrance on the blueprints. I don't know if it's still there, but..."

The Irregulars shared an unreadable look, then Chaos shrugged. Captain nodded, and they were off.

***

Dryden, WA – Grace

Two weeks later, Grace had to admit they were right. They hadn't been truly fighting. The Irregulars spread out, on foot, in cars, bikes, and quads, riding roughshod over everything they found. Their speed left Grace breathless. Seahorse remained at the center, rolling forward with the implacability of the ocean, sending smaller groups to support, stop, harass, and harry.

But always, always, they drove Steve west.

She rode with Charlie, who drove an ancient car, held together with what looked like wire and baling twine, pulling one of their 'toys.' She wasn't quite sure what it was called. It looked like a giant gun, and the shells it used were *huge*.

And every night, they pored over maps with the commander and a few others in her core group, making suggestions on routes that Steve might use, pointing to the farm camps, and talking about the conditions in the cities.

"I need your knowledge," she explained. "We need to be prepared before we hit the cities."

"Hey!" Anarchy, one of the fighters, jogged up, pulling Grace from her thoughts. "Seahorse needs you two. Steve finally got creative."

Her battle partner, Gummy—short for Gummy Bear, a family name, he'd said, laughing—ran over to Charlie's side. "We've got the gun. Seahorse is directly ahead. Just follow the road."

Grace's thoughts raced ahead but slowed down with running. "I just can't...think and *breathe*...at the same time," she gasped. "I hate running!"

"My love." Charlie ran easier than her, slowing down to allow her to keep up. "No one likes running. It's just that it's a great way to stay alive."

Turned out, they needn't have run. Seahorse stopped less than a mile ahead, drumming her fingers against the truck, glaring down the road where...Grace's eyes widened.

Steve set up a barricade across the highway and into the trees on either side of the road on the east side of a bridge spanning a river running high from the recent rains. The trees themselves were sparse enough to make sneaking up on Steve difficult, thick enough to prevent them from driving through.

To the north, barely visible from their position, a railroad paralleled the road, but it ended right before the river. To the south, on the far bank of the river, a low bluff provided an extra wall for Steve.

"Here." Sarge handed her a scope. Searching, she finally found the faded green sign.

Dryden.

"We showed you this place," she said. "It's got some civilians. Field hands."

"We don't know if the civilians are still here," Seahorse said grimly. "And either way, that's not important. What I need to know is if there's another bridge nearby."

"That's the Wenatchee," she said slowly, thinking furiously. "Not for several miles, and then those roads are north-south, not east-west. And one of them, the closer one, is down."

The area behind them, Washington's Badlands, was dry grass and canyons broken by small farms. Grace thought of Dryden as part of the curving border where Washington changed from Badlands back into green and rainy, the way the Pacific Northwest should be.

Seahorse continued to study the roadblock while they talked, relaying everything they knew about the area. A fighter, dripping wet, made her way over.

"Seahorse," she called, shaking herself off.

"Deerskin. S'up?"

"River's blocked." Deerskin accepted a cloth, wrapping it around her dripping hair. "It's fast running, but too shallow to let anyone slip through. Plus, they've got a secondary roadblock on the other side of the bridge."

Seahorse snarled. "I *knew* this was too easy. They were keeping us busy while they built this."

"Easy?" Grace looked from one woman to the other. "The fighting has been crazy."

Deerskin shook her head, braids swinging. "They've been melting away like snow in the rain."

"And now we know why." Seahorse folded muscled arms across her chest. "Fine. Get the saboteurs."

***

"We don't need that bridge," Grace said stubbornly. "There's a section here," she pointed above a patch of suburbs to the north, "where the river is fordable on foot. Most of your vehicles can probably make it."

"I don't have enough cars as it is," Seahorse said. "So I want that bridge. But..." She leaned closer. "It does give a woman some ideas. What else can you tell me about this area?"

"There are some landmines," Grace said slowly. "I know it's not great, but if you go over the ridge, then use a rope to climb down, you can do it."

"You and Charlie did?"

"Yeah, and we've brought people back that way a couple times. They don't watch it because of the landmines, so it's perfect for us."

"Did I hear landmines?" The new person, wearing a dark hijab over a green, long-sleeve shirt, and black cargo pants, walked silently over, moccasins on her feet. "*Assalamu Alaikum,* Seahorse. Do you want me to do something about those?"

"Ah, Kinette. *Wa Alaikum Assalam.*" Seahorse turned to the newcomer. "You haven't met Grace yet, have you? Kinette heads the saboteurs."

The woman inclined her head to Grace, assessing her through dark eyes. "So, you're the guide."

"Um...yes?" Grace leaned closer. "Where did you get eyeliner? I lost mine the last trip in, and I haven't had time to get more."

Kinette laughed. "It's kohl. We make it. After all, we use the ingredients in other things, so we thought we would bring a bit of civilization to the barbarians."

"She means us," Seahorse said dryly.

"I will get you some kohl later, if you like," Kinette said, then turned to Seahorse. "What do you need us for?"

"You're good with architecture, right?" The saboteur nodded. "Okay. How far from the bridge do we have to be when we detonate a bomb if we send it down the river? I don't want to blow the bridge up," Seahorse hastily added. "I just want to create some confusion down there while we get troops into position."

"It's the detonator that's the problem, though." Kinette stroked her lower lip while she contemplated the bridge. "We need Sparrow, but you know we can't get an accurate time on it."

"Sparrow!" Seahorse bellowed. "Please! And Grace," Grace started at being addressed calmly on the heels of a yell like that, "what about our new friends? Would they have anything accurate?"

Grace opened her mouth, but Kinette made a moue of distaste. "They're mostly using our things. They're bodies on the ground, yes, and I know we were hauling a lot of weapons that no one was using, but those...men...are still trying to adjust to life here."

Sparrow arrived on the tail end of Kinette's diatribe, wiping her hands with a greasy cloth that she stuffed into her back pocket. "What can I help you with?"

"I need a floating bomb and a way to detonate it. It needs to be precise so we don't damage the bridge but big because it's a distraction."

Sparrow studied it, going into a huddle to mutter with Kinette. When they broke apart, Sparrow nodded. "I've got a little toy boat. We can put the explosives in there. As for a detonator..."

"Who's our best sniper?" Kinette asked. "We think it will be best to shoot it when it gets to the right location, though I need a better look at the bridge to determine where that will be."

"Excellent." Seahorse clapped her hands. "We need Kmart. When the boys get back from checking out that ford, we'll have a working plan."

Grace choked, then doubled over coughing. Sparrow patted her back until she straightened. "That's your plan? Shoot a bomb that you send under the bridge?"

"Don't be ridiculous," Seahorse said. "That's the distraction. You'll guide a good bunch of fighters north, take them along that route you mentioned. If the southern ford is any good, we'll send more along there."

She spoke matter-of-factly, as if the rest of the plan were completely obvious. And since the other two found a spot off to the side where they immediately opened belt pouches and began pulling out tools wrapped in cloth, perhaps it was, to them.

The saboteur and the demolitions woman muttered to each other, fiddling with tiny wires and a piece of cream-colored clay. Negative charge, positive charge, ease of combustion... All things Grace felt she was better off not knowing.

"Babe!" Turning, she smiled, relief melting her muscles. Charlie waved at her, walking up the road with Sarge and a scout. Running to him, she leaped into his arms. "Did you miss me?"

In answer to that, she kissed him soundly. In the background, Irregulars wolf-whistled or cheered. When they broke apart, she unwrapped her legs from around his waist and he slowly lowered her to the ground.

"The southern ford will work for people," he said. "They'll be able to get onto the bluffs."

"Seahorse also wants to use that northern route," she told him. "You know, the one past the minefield?"

"Why are we using two routes?" Charlie asked.

"Three-pronged attack," Seahorse said cheerfully. "We'll go once it gets dark. The saboteurs decided they want some of those mines for other things, so they need a couple hours."

"What, exactly, is the plan?" Charlie looked from one woman to the other, and Grace shook her head.

"You really don't want to know." Seahorse grinned evilly. "Knowing won't make you feel any better. Trust me."

***

Sacramento, CA – Faith

Faith squeaked, swiping with her knife at an NK reaching for her, making him shout. Lucas spun away from his fight, punching the soldier she'd injured, knocking him to the ground.

And when Faith looked up, the other five men were down, Captain, Chaos, and Sung Ki rifling through their pockets. When they finished, Sung Ki slid into deeper shadows, disappearing.

Chaos nodded to Lucas. "Nice. You've got a hell of a right."

Faith blinked. That was the closest to a compliment she'd heard from any Irregular so far. Lucas straightened and Faith could practically see his glow of pride. Until Captain ruined the moment by appearing in front of them, making her squeak and Lucas start.

"Don't you make any noise?" she snapped sotto voce.

"Yes." Reaching out, Captain bumped fists with Chaos. "Time to move. We've found the other door and cleared another patrol."

Doc readjusted her pack. "Why did I have to come here, again?"

"Because you can read fast, read a bit of Korean, and I needed Chaos to come and he wouldn't leave you." She answered shortly, but Faith heard a note of humor in her tone.

"Ah. Right."

At the side door, Captain tested the knob carefully. It didn't move. Kneeling, she reached into a pouch, removing...Faith squinted.

"Are those lock picks?"

"Yep." She worked on the door while other fighters kept watch.

"If those don't work, I have a couple of specially made ones that definitely will." All four of the Irregulars twisted around to look at her. "What? Did you think those locked file drawers opened themselves?"

"You know what?" Captain clambered to her feet. "You unlock the damn door. Just don't open it. I go first."

Faith quickly took her place, her own picks already in her hands.

"Why?" Lucas asked behind her. "Is it because you're the leader? Don't get me wrong," he said quickly. "Leading from the front is admirable."

Doc snorted. "No. It's because she's the battering ram."

CHAPTER 14

Pasadena, CA - Mercy

Mercy dropped lightly into the tunnel, casting one last glance up at the gray shadow of the infirmary she'd occupied for so long. Tugging gently on the rope hanging next to her, she frowned when it didn't move.

Clenching her jaw, she pulled harder. This was proving to be more difficult than she'd thought. She spent long minutes wiggling and jiggling the rope, trying to pull her false floor and folded bedding back over the entrance. Finally, the panel settled over it, and she was left with nothing but her lantern and small pack.

Taking up the lantern, she headed down the tunnel, towards the sewers. At every side tunnel, small breezes sent her hair fluttering, causing her to flinch. At the third one, she squatted, arms wrapped around her head, her hair coming out of its bun.

Her heart pounding, Mercy squeezed her eyes shut, shaking. *It's okay, it's okay. I'm in the tunnels. They can't see me. They can't hurt me.*

Leaving her kerchief off seemed so defiant at the time. She hunched down tighter when a door slammed overhead. Wiping her eyes on the hem of her shirt, she yanked a bandana from the side pocket of her pack, tying it over her hair.

Fine. If she couldn't focus because old beatings continually came to mind, she'd cover her hair and try again later. Shouldering her pack once more, she set off down the tunnel, counting her intersections.

Hours later, Mercy stood at the base of a tunnel cave-in, broken concrete and bricks forming a rough ramp to the surface. Blowing out the lantern, she stared up, looking for...what? Firelight? Signs of people?

She didn't know how long she stared at the gaping hole in the ceiling, watching the light change, slowly brightening into an LA fall, which wasn't much different from an LA winter or spring. Shaking herself, she scrambled up the ramp, cautiously testing each step as she went.

Poking her head above the surface, she examined her surroundings. An abandoned warehouse, only two and a half walls still standing. Rubble littered the floor. Leaves drifted through the huge missing sections, piling up against one of the remaining walls, and a few, sad weeds struggled to live.

But no signs of people.

Biting her lip to hold back tears, she lunged out, heading for the road, her pack bouncing around her shoulders. Stepping out of the warehouse, she put a hand over her mouth, holding back sobs as she stared at the open sky.

No walls, no fences. No people. No Masters, commanding her obedience.

Spinning, her arms wide, Mercy cried. Relief, sorrow, joy...

"I made it, Jonathan. I made it."

In her mind's eye, Jonathan smiled, his black eyes crinkling at the corners. She could almost feel his hand on her cheek.

"I knew you would. You're strong, woman. Always told you you were stronger than you knew."

Shouting in the distance brought her back. Stuffing the lantern into her backpack, she set the mountains at her back, walking west.

***

Mercy lifted her head, peering over the dead leaves and low mound of the old, dry flower bed she'd made her nest for the night. She'd thought she might be tired enough to sleep yesterday, but fear kept her going until long past sundown.

Then, fear of her light being seen in the dark made her stop, finding a hiding place behind a crumbling house.

Today, all she could wonder was if she'd left her Master far enough behind. She didn't even know where she was. Well, suburbia, obviously, but which bloody one?

She stayed huddled in the dead remains of the backyard until the sun rose high overhead. Which way to go? Was anywhere safe? Pulling out her first water bottle, she drained the last few drops. Shaking the second one, she cursed under her breath.

One full liter.

Shit.

Gathering her things, she crawled out of her shelter. Peeking around the corner of the house, she checked the street. Abandoned homes, many of them burnt in the frequent fires, and an empty street.

Squaring her shoulders, she set out, staying close to the sides, heading towards the westering sun. At sunset, she found herself near stores. Deciding one of those might be safer—since they looked a lot less comfortable than the houses—she chose one with a back door and curled in the corner.

Raucous male laughter woke her. Bolting upright, she strained to hear where it came from. A woman's laugh pealed above the rest, joyful, free. Mercy crept to the broken window, peering cautiously around the corner.

"Dudes! There's a chick over here!"

The call made her heart clench into a fist. The man she'd inadvertently come face to face with stared back at her, his surprise changing as he slowly looked her up and down.

Not again.

***

Dryden, WA – Grace

Grace scrambled carefully down the ridge, holding onto the rope for dear life. She and Charlie had left it here sometime last year. They had such a large group and the soldiers had been so close on their heels, they didn't feel safe sticking around to reel it in.

Now, that accident allowed them to bring the Irregulars and American soldiers down to the water's edge more quickly. Barely a finger of the sun showed above the horizon, and Seahorse said they had until the stars were bright overhead to get into position.

Then, they were to wait for the explosion.

Charlie waited for her at the bottom, already holding the rope that crossed the river. Water dripped from it, and further out, small branches and weeds still clung to it.

"Good idea to leave it in the water, huh?" he murmured in her ear.

Shaking her head and smiling, she smacked his hip lightly. She'd given him hell for leaving it in the water, but it looked like it held up pretty well.

Pulling it tight, he secured it to a tree with a bowline knot, tugging to make sure it was secured.

Before the last person in their group made it down, Thorin, the young man leading this arm of the attack, began sending fighters across the river. In twos and threes, they crossed, holding onto the rope for stability.

Grace watched the sky, tapping her fingers on her leg. "Are we going fast enough?" she whispered to Thorin and Charlie.

"We have close to two hundred people," Thorin murmured. "Seahorse knows how long it takes, and my mom is taking the ones who've crossed south. Our people know what's what."

The soldiers who crossed disappeared into the bushes. She only knew they were there because she'd heard Sears give the orders. When over half their forces were over, Thorin sent her and Charlie across.

She sucked in a breath when the cold water reached her knees, lifting her rifle overhead with her free hand and grimacing when it slowly climbed higher. Focusing on the far side, she carefully stepped from rock to rock, relaxing when the water slowly receded. Every so often, the rope trembled.

At the far side, a soldier appeared. Taking his proffered hand, she let him pull her up onto the bank. Charlie emerged next, water running off him. Bundled into the trees, they found an Irregular waiting for them.

"Nice evening, isn't it?" She recognized Dionysius's voice. "I'll be your guide tonight. Brought your rifles, huh?"

"We're not beginners," Charlie murmured, a hint of humor in his tone.

He shrugged. "Reassuring to have them, yeah?"

"Yeah."

"Good. Hold onto them like they're your favorite blankie."

Grace stuck her tongue out, sure he couldn't see it in the dark. Charlie, drat him, laughed silently. Taking her hand, Dionysius put it on his jacket.

"Hold on."

Charlie hooked his fingertips into her waistband, and they were off. She kept one eye on the tallest hills, using them as landmarks, and the other on the stars. The last of the sunlight was nearly gone when Dionysius stopped.

They stood at the top of a steep hill. Below them, lights illuminated the soldiers swarming the eastern side of the bridge. More fires lit up the barricades. From this angle, she couldn't see Seahorse's group. An arm of land blocked her view, but it did allow them to see the bridge.

Pressing a hand to her shoulder, he had them kneel with him. "Stay here," he whispered. "We've got our less experienced staying between you and the fight."

With one last reassuring pat, he slipped down the hill, only the barest rustle telling them where he'd gone.

"What if they lose?" Grace whispered once he was out of earshot.

"I don't know if they can," Charlie murmured.

"You think they're that good at fighting?" She gave him a sideways glance. After all his grumbling when they first met the fighters, now this?

"Not like that." He nudged her, then wrapped his arm around her waist. She leaned against him, resting her head on his shoulder. "I mean that they don't have long supply lines Steve can cut. They live off the land and what they steal from Steve. They don't have a base, they're not protecting towns. They're like...the ultimate guerilla fighters."

She muffled her laugh in his sweatshirt. "You sound like Hope."

"We do like the same kinds of books."

Before she could respond, an explosion lit the sky. The smoke from the bomb rose in a tall column, obscuring their view of the bridge.

One hand to her mouth, they watched the scene unfold below. The smoke hadn't even begun to dissipate when a volley of shots hit Steve from two sides. Soldiers fell, their screams a terrifying counterpoint to the gunfire.

Eventually, Grace found herself caught up in it. Not in the fighting and dying, but in watching the Irregulars. They were constantly moving, slipping from tree to bush to rock, never giving Steve a set target. If one were pinned down, the others would provide withering cover fire.

"Look!" she whispered, pointing.

Gray shapes made their way up the bridge's supports, barely visible through the smoke. Definitely two on the side nearest them. Then she lost her view when they disappeared underneath the bridge itself.

"What are they doing?" Charlie murmured.

"The bombs!" Grace gasped.

"What?"

"The bridge is booby-trapped. I bet those are the saboteurs."

"Wait." He held up a hand. "They have another group? I thought it was just scouts, bashers, snipers, demolitions, healers, scavengers... Actually, they have a lot of groups within the whole, don't they?"

"While you were scouting the southern ford, I met the leader of the saboteurs. A Muslim woman named Kinette."

Several minutes after they disappeared below the bridge, a red flare landed on it. Across the river, a clamor rose above the sounds of fighting.

"All in, all out! One shot, one kill! No luck, all skill!"

Chills rose on Grace's arms and the first truck appeared on the road, swiftly followed by more. Fighters stood in the gun nests. More ran alongside, using the trucks for cover, but no one shot at them. They were already busy here.

Then, Charlie nudged her. Startled from her scrutiny, she followed his pointing finger. A small group of soldiers crept along the back of the Irregular's fluid lines.

"Ambush from the rear," Charlie breathed.

"How do we warn them?"

Grinning, he adjusted his rifle. "We do know how to use these, right?"

"Oh. Right." Abashed, biting her lip, she shifted, kneeling, making sure to stay behind a tree and some shrubs. "You know I've never knowingly shot anyone before, right?"

Charlie took aim. Fires sprang up, some of them accompanied by booms (Grace wondered, in an abstract way, whether those booms came from Sparrow or the saboteurs), causing their targets to occasionally vanish into shadows before reappearing when the flames found new tinder.

"Well, babe, right now, I'm imagining that the only thing standing between us and home—our *real* home—is those bastards down there."

"But they're people, too," she said in a small voice.

"Yeah, but for better or worse, they're aiming to kill people we know and like. And yeah, they're only following orders"—the fact that he knew her next protest before she said it made her smile—"but those orders are *wrong*. I wish we could take a moment to talk to them, but they're loaded for bear, and I won't risk losing you.

"So, don't shoot them if you can't, but for the love of all that's holy, *shoot*."

Suiting action to words, he opened fire. Their targets ducked, then fired back. Bullets peppered the trees around Charlie. Snuggling her cheek against the stock, she grit her teeth and opened fire, shooting the ground around their feet.

They yelled, one fell when her shot accidentally hit him, but he thrashed, reassuring her he wasn't dead yet.

"That's my wife!" Charlie yelled.

On the slope below, the fighters finally noticed the enemy group. Some fired too, others charged.

"Charlie!" Grace crawled away from her position. "Let's find a better spot!"

Together, they moved up, seeking sheltered viewpoints.

***

"...fucking reckless idiots!" Seahorse shouted, storming back and forth, her breath white plumes trailing behind her.

The sun's first rays lit her dark brown hair and turned her eyes to honey, but the fact that she'd been shouting at them for five minutes really reduced any sense of romanticism the dawn light lent her, Grace thought.

"Captain asked me to keep Fuzz's family safe, and here you are, about to make me break an almost promise because you're as fucking reckless and brave as your dumbass brother!" she finished at the top of her lungs.

Various fighters lurked nearby, and the O'Connells received many sympathetic glances, but no one dared deflect Seahorse's wrath.

Until she opened her mouth again, then Sarge stepped in. "I'm sure they've got the picture, my love," he rumbled. "Don't you?"

They nodded, but secretly, Grace glowed. She'd never been considered reckless before, much less brave. Even when she and Charlie decided to enter Washington, they'd worked through numerous scenarios, cultivated friendships and contacts amongst the military, and made sure they were up to date on their first aid and weapons proficiency.

To others, it may have looked spontaneous, but Grace ensured they were prepared.

Seahorse stopped pacing and faced them, her shoulders slumped. "And thank you for saving my fighters," she finished quietly.

Finally freed from Seahorse's fury, all attention quickly turned back to the cleanup. Steve had retreated in the face of overwhelming bombs, and now the Irregulars combed through the debris, looking for the wounded and dead.

Together, they walked the battlefield, incongruously lit with a warm, golden glow that illuminated the spatters of red. For all this looked like the perfect autumn dawn, clouds roiled up from the south.

Sometimes they found a wounded fighter or Steve. More often, they followed a blood trail to find a body lying too still on the ground.

The call went out. Only two people still missing: Thorin and Kmart.

The cry of a wounded animal rent the morning air, jolting Grace to her feet. Emerging from behind a thick bush, Thorin carried a body. It only took one look for her to know the fighter was dead. Her sightless eyes stared at the sky, hands hanging limp, bumping against his legs with every step. Thorin cried out again, his face drawn with grief, staring at Kmart's face.

Charlie reached her, catching her around the waist when she moved forward. "Leave them," he murmured against her hair, his voice thick. Twisting, she saw tears in his eyes. "His friends will help him."

"I didn't know he had a girlfriend. Or wife."

"Me neither, but right now, I just want to go somewhere quiet and hold you for a while."

Turning completely, she cupped his cheek, his skin warm and rough under her palm. "We really made it through a full battle, didn't we?"

"Together."

A reminder that not everyone had. Unwillingly, her eyes were drawn again to the young man walking across the rough ground and the woman he carried in his arms. More fighters reached them, and he collapsed, unable to stand but still holding her close.

"Thank God she had someone to miss her."

***

Sacramento, CA – Captain

The lock *snicked* and Faith sat back on her heels. I wet my lips, my right hand twitching at my side. Lucas quickly pulled Faith away from the door and I hissed, calling back the sentries.

Sung Ki gripped the doorknob, a gun in her other hand. Chaos put a hand on my shoulder. Ready there, too. Now all I had to do was feel ready. Rolling my shoulders, I took a firm grip on the machete in my left hand, hunting knife in my right.

Nodding to Sung Ki, I lowered my shoulder. The door swung open. I shot through, weapons ready, Chaos hot on my heels.

I made it three steps in when my foot connected with something that squeaked and scuttled away, rustling through debris on the floor. Pausing another second to make sure I didn't have some Steve hiding deeper inside, I tapped my foot in the Morse code for *all clear.*

Another explosion rocked the earth, sounds muffled when the door closed, blocking the light from the fires. Sheathing the machete, I trailed the fingers of my left hand over the wall. Faith said we needed to go upstairs, and that the stairs were somewhere towards the middle of the building.

We took the first left, moving in single file, Chaos keeping one hand on my shoulder. Up two flights of stairs and we paused at a door, light glowing around its edges. Through it, I could make out the sounds of two men talking with their mouths full, chewing loudly.

I flinched at a particularly loud slurp. Chaos made as if to open the door, but I stayed his hand, baring my teeth. I know it's cultural, we had a hell of a time breaking Sung Ki of the habit, but goddammit. Time to face the wrath of a person with misophonia.

Faith's nails dug into my arm for a bare second before I shook her off. Taking the machete again, I sheathed the hunting knife, two fingers on the latch. One deep breath later, I flung it open, going through in a forward roll. Popping to my feet right in front of them, they barely had time to stand, their chairs clattering to the floor in their haste.

My heartbeat stayed calm, even, and in seconds the men were down, blood pooling. I stepped back before it reached my moccasins, using my sleeve to wipe away a trickle on my cheek. The others followed Chaos inside while I picked up one of the fallen candles, exploring the room further.

Shelves loaded with boxes extended back twenty feet. I counted six rows. Shit. This could take a while. Circling the room, I didn't find any other exits. One way in and out. I bared my teeth. Fuck.

"This is the room, right?" I asked Faith over my shoulder.

She examined the shelving, occasionally giving me uneasy glances. "Yes."

I sidled over to Doc. "Do I have more blood on my face?"

Shaking her head, she pulled a small square of cloth from a pouch at her belt, wetting it with her canteen. "Just a little."

Then, she proceeded to wipe my entire face. Puffing against the wet cloth, I let her get on with it. If I didn't, she'd just get Chaos to sit on me.

Slowly, people dug out candles and wandered through the stacks. Labeled in a mix of Korean and English, I couldn't make heads or tails of any of them.

"Look at dates," Faith called. "It was June, 2061."

I shared a look with Chaos and Doc. What year was it now? In the end, we found three boxes, a mix of languages. Sung Ki and Doc settled down on the floor with the Korean boxes, pulling sheaves of papers out.

"I don't know how much use I'll be," Doc muttered, holding one closer to the light. "It's been a while since college."

"Here." Sung Ki pulled a pencil out, drawing a few symbols. "Look for these."

"What do they mean?"

"These ones are 'American,' this is 'foreigner,' and this," she pointed to the last sequence, "is 'informant.'"

Faith joined them with another box. "This one sounds familiar," she said, "but I'm not sure why."

The rest of us settled with the English box, dividing it up amongst the four of us.

***

I'd lost track of time when Faith broke the almost complete silence in the room.

"I think I've got it!" she shouted, straightening.

There was a momentary pause, then I dropped my papers. This coincided with a flurry of movement from everyone else, paper flying through the air as we all scrambled to her. She'd moved over to the wall, leaning against it with two boxes next to her.

She passed a paper over to me and continued checking over another. Groaning, I slowly laid on my back, muscles screaming.

"I think I'm too old to sit like this," I moaned.

Doc, also on her back, scooted closer to read with me. "If it makes you feel any better, my butt is numb."

"I haven't been able to feel mine for the last hour." I shifted my hips, trying to ease the tightness in my lower back.

Chaos slid over, massaging Doc's legs while we read. Part of my attention stayed on them. How could it not when I could clearly remember my own physical therapy? Noah had given me the massages necessary to get me into better shape.

Closing my eyes, I breathed, letting the pain wash over me until Doc's tiny gasp caught my attention. Welcoming the distraction, I followed the direction of her pointing finger.

"Fuck me," I whispered.

"What?" Chaos demanded, his hands pausing on Doc's thigh. "What is it?"

"It's an evacuation order. I don't know these names, but they mention regions, including Bull of the Woods." The Lair lay deep inside Bull of the Woods Wilderness.

"May I?" Chaos held out his hand.

I passed it to him, rolling my shoulders around to loosen them while I waited.

"Fuck." He drew the word out. "I recognize these names from our debrief when we came here. These are the bunkers up and down the West Coast."

"Check out the date and signature," Doc said.

I squirmed around to see her better. "What?"

The paper rustled when Chaos's hand shook. The others crowded behind him, leaning in, attempting to read it themselves.

"It's dated three months before the Invasion," Chaos whispered, "and signed by President Trembly himself."

"Any chance Trembly planned this?" I asked. My voice sounded like I was underwater.

"No," Chaos said immediately. "Not because he wouldn't, he's just too stupid. The man can't keep anything to himself."

"There's more," Faith said faintly, holding up another sheet. "Look at the seal."

This document didn't have a signature, but it did have a seal. A lovely stamp of an eagle with a shield in front of it. Around the edges, the words SECRETARY OF STATE.

I let the document rest on my chest, staring sightlessly at the ceiling. "Does this mean the Secretary of State is involved?"

Faith chewed on her lip. "From what I understand, this is an agreement of cooperation. There's no signature, but because of the seal, I think whoever wrote this would have to, at the very *least*, be in the Secretary's office."

"You know what?" I said dreamily, back to staring at the ceiling. "I'm gonna go to DC and ask some motherfuckers."

There was a long pause. "Can you do that?" Faith asked eventually.

"If I worried about what I *could* do, I'd never get anything done." I sat up abruptly. "All right, children, I think it's about time to ditch this joint. This neighborhood's gone to hell."

As soon as the words left my mouth, an explosion rocked the building.

"Right." Faith scooped papers into her bag. "Might need these," she muttered to herself. "Might not, but..." She shrugged.

Chaos watched the door while we finished grabbing anything that looked interesting. Once, I heard a squeak, and when I looked over, the large man dragged another body into the corner with the others.

"All good?" I asked.

"We're good," he said, tossing his hair back as he stood.

Doc sighed, one hand fluttering to her chest. I nudged her. "Keep it in your pants," I muttered, smirking. She shot me a murderous look. "You'll have time once we get out of here to jump him."

She relaxed slightly at that. "I know."

Noah's body, flying through the air, landing in an untidy heap. My heart contracted painfully, and I stopped, pressing my palm to my chest. When it finally released, I straightened, swiping a sleeve over my eyes.

I hadn't gotten another day, but I'd damn well make sure they did, even if I had to jump between him and a bullet. Doc watched me, sympathetic, but knowing I couldn't handle it right now.

Chaos stuck his head into the room. "I can see orange," he called.

"Copy." Shaking off my grief, I scanned the room. "Time to bug out!"

CHAPTER 15

Wiretap, Lowes Hotel Room #113. Booking name James Smith – September 12, 2066, 6:24pm

Woman: The moment that little rebellion is squashed and it's obvious the people over there can't do this themselves, we'll finally be able to introduce Military Mobilization Act.

Man: Then tell that Colonel to get moving! Why is it so hard to kill one man?

Washington DC – Constance

Constance flopped onto her back, the hard floor a welcome relief. "This is impossible," she moaned. "It's been weeks, and all we know for certain is that Bryce McKinney is a coward and a traitor."

"You're forgetting that NRA lobbyist, Whatshisname," James Perry said. He sat with his back against the bed, holding a sheet from the schedule, checking it against a list of wiretaps. "Dammit," he muttered.

"What?" Constance rubbed her eyes before letting her arms sag to the floor.

"You know that guy who said no guns could be good in the long term?"

"Yeah."

"It's not Petersen."

"Shit. Where?"

"He was in Pennsylvania, apparently."

"Alright. I'll mark him off that one." Rolling over, Constance crawled across the floor to the whiteboard tacked to the wall. Finding the empty square corresponding to *Petersen* and *No Guns Good,* she put an X in it.

"I still think he's one of these. Have we gotten anything from the bank accounts list yet?"

"Computer's still trying to crunch the encryption on that."

Slumping back onto the floor, she squirmed around. They'd been locked in here almost constantly for at least three, maybe four weeks. Snuggling deeper into his sweatshirt, she watched his forehead wrinkle as he tried to focus.

"All right," she said, sitting up. "That's it."

"What?" He glanced up, over the papers.

"We need to get out of here for an hour. See the sky. Maybe have a little fun."

"You do realize your face is all over the news? Especially since that guard we stuffed in a closet?"

"Fine. No parks. Can we go downstairs and eat *inside* the restaurant instead of having them deliver?"

His eyes crinkled at the corners, but the paper still blocked her view of his mouth. "What? Are you planning to go wearing my sweats, too?"

She frowned down at the baggy clothes she wore. She only had the basics, what they'd managed to pick up in the days immediately after they'd met. They hadn't even dared to buy anything online for her in case it set off alarms. Trying to decrypt the files was the most they were connected to the internet for.

"Wait!" She grinned at him. "We just did laundry yesterday, right?" Twisting, she caught a glimpse of the laundry bag where they'd left it in the kitchen. "I have leggings!"

She smirked. Sighing, he got to his feet, tugging his shirt down and hiding the intriguing sliver of visible skin before giving her a hand off the floor. "Downstairs only," he said sternly, but she laughed.

She'd grown to recognize his hidden smiles. "And drinks," she coaxed.

"One," he grumbled.

"Four."

"Two."

"Three."

"Deal."

Dancing ahead of him, she fished through the laundry, tossing him his clothes as she found them. Grabbing her leggings, she sailed into the bathroom. "Get presentable!"

"I'm always presentable." But he smiled, his hazel eyes lighting up.

Dressed in leggings and still wearing his sweatshirt, she pulled on ballet flats and met him at the door. She smiled. Jeans, boots, and a t-shirt that clung to his lean frame was what he considered 'presentable.' Good enough.

He opened the door, checked the hallway, then held out his arm. "Shall we?"

Laughing, she took it. "Let's."

***

Monroe, WA – Grace

Grace woke with a start, jerking upright. Her quick, panting gasps filled the small room.

"Grace?" Charlie mumbled, fumbling around in their blankets to find her.

"I'm...I'm okay," she whispered, curling against him, her head on his chest. The thump of his heart under her ear brought her fully out of the dream.

"Was it those feelings again?" Charlie asked.

She nodded. Over the years, she'd woken like this many times, adrenaline coursing through her. Once, she'd begun sobbing in her sleep, though she never knew the reason why.

She'd always found reality better than those adrenaline-inducing dreams, even this reality: A room in one of the few houses left in Monroe that didn't stink of too many people and years of mold. Though she couldn't hear them, Irregulars filled the house to the brim, all of them enjoying sleeping out of the rain.

Charlie pulled the blanket up to her ears, rubbing her arms to warm her. She'd just begun to settle back into sleep when a knock sounded at the door.

"Wakey, wakey, children!" Sarge boomed. "It's D-Day."

D-Day. The day of reckoning. Seahorse said that one way or another, after this fight, it would be over. They'd managed to push Steve back, into Seattle. The Army was camped to the south, they were in the north, and Seahorse had pulled troops in from Oregon to camp on the islets across the sound from the city.

"I am *not* combing through fifty million islands to find every last one of them," she said with finality.

"What about the civilians still in the city?"

"They'll have to fend for themselves."

Grace's teeth chattered as she and Charlie dressed, packed, and joined the Irregulars heading to the park in this suburb. Those who could cook had stew over massive campfires they'd built in the middle of the park. They'd scrounged pots, and now the smell drifted through the house.

She cast one last glance back at the house. The room was bare, cold, and the furnishings were disgusting, but it wasn't the upcoming battle.

Through the broken glass in the living room, weak sunlight filtered through the dirt filming the remaining glass. The sun had nearly set, the top barely visible over the horizon. Grace shivered again, and Charlie wrapped his arm around her waist. She leaned into him gratefully, clutching his jacket.

"Still no sign of ships," Seahorse called cheerfully to the fighters. A few of them, more weathered than the rest, perked up at that piece of news.

"Ships?" she and Charlie asked simultaneously.

Seahorse pressed her lips together. "They suck so bad."

In the park, they ate their fill, the fighters laughing too loudly at bad jokes and touching more than usual. People surrounded them, but Grace couldn't focus. Too many people, their forced jocularity drained her. Charlie, noticing her unease, led her out of the thick of it.

There, she saw the ones who preferred to mentally prepare alone. To the side, Thorin did a last weapons check, reassembling his weapons, his expression hard. The medic, Squirrel, sat cross-legged, her hands resting palm up on her knees, meditating. Another did yoga, stretching back in Downward Dog.

Pulling Charlie along, she went to that fighter. "May I join you?" she asked. The woman nodded, sinking into Upward Dog. Grace smiled. "Sparrow. Thank you."

"I'm not doing yoga," Charlie murmured.

"I'm okay now." She waved him off, twisting to loosen up. "I know you like being in there." She nodded to the crowd.

Dropping a quick kiss into the middle of her forehead, he headed back. Probably for more stew, she thought, amused. Following Sparrow, she relaxed into the familiar rhythms of yoga. Breathe in, breathe out. Closing her eyes, she stretched.

Some minutes later, at an unseen signal, Sparrow straightened, raising her arms to the sky. "It's time," she said, lowering them slowly.

Seahorse climbed onto a steel picnic table, towering over the gathering fighters.

"All in, all out," she called, the fighters chanting with her. "One shot, one kill. No luck, all skill!"

Roaring, the fighters streamed out, heading for their vehicles.

Seahorse, spotting them from her position, waved them over. "Remember what I said. Stay high. Shoot if you have to, but if things look like they're going sideways, if it looks like we're not doing well, take any car and head south as fast as you can. Oregon is preparing to defend the border. She'll take you in."

Her blood humming through her veins, Grace took heart from the fierce, wild fighters. If anyone could do this, they could.

***

LA County, CA - Mercy

Mercy scrambled backwards, swinging her pack. "Get away!" she screamed.

The men laughed, nudging each other. How many were there? Too many... One man grabbed her pack, pulling it from her grip. He said something lost to the rushing in her ears. Panicked, she pulled the scalpel from her pocket, flicking off the cork she'd used as a sheath.

"Back!" she shouted.

"It's okay," one said, his voice floating through the clamor filling her head. "We're not gonna hurt you."

"I'm not going to hurt you." Her Master's voice, the very first time.

He twisted her arm up, behind her back, gripping her chin with harsh fingers, holding her firmly against his chest. She wriggled frantically, hardly recognizing the muffled squeals as coming from her own throat. She looked from the man's lascivious smile down to Jonathan, lying too still on the ground, his black eyes gazing sightlessly into the sun.

Jonathan, *she tried to scream,* Jonathan, help! Get up!

The man whom she would call Master dragged her past a woman—his wife!—lying on the floor of the small house, propped up on blankets and pillows, a tiny bundle in her arms.

"My dear," she protested softly. "She delivered your son and saved us both..."

Reaching down, he patted her head, much like you would a dog's, Faith thought muzzily. "You know the Bible states that women must obey and serve men. I did not wish to impose upon you so soon."

She bowed her head. "Of course. Thank you for your consideration."

Mercy squealed louder, twisting and jerking, finally freeing her mouth. "What the fuckin' 'ell is wrong with you, you bloody bastard!" He continued inexorably dragging her to the other room. "Jonathan! Jonathan, please wake up! Help!"

But no one answered her cries. Not then, not through all the days and years since.

"Oh, my God, you assholes!" A woman's voice broke through Mercy's waking nightmare. "You're scaring her! Can you be any more idiotic? Back the fuck off."

A small woman pushed her way through the men, fearlessly shoving them back until she stood alone in front of Mercy. Mercy bared her teeth, one hand on the wall behind her, the other brandishing her scalpel.

"Take another step," she snarled in a shaky voice, "and you'll find out just how fast the human body can bleed out."

The woman held her hands up, showing she was unarmed. "It's okay. They won't hurt you. They're just really stupid."

Stepping carefully, she circled around Mercy. To stay away from her, Mercy moved slowly back, stumbling over broken bricks until the lowering sun struck her full in the face.

The woman gasped. "Oh, my God. It's *you*," she breathed.

Some of the men, staying within hearing, muttered to the rest of them. Their soft babble filled the air, closer than she'd thought. Freezing, she hoped she could wait until the sun sank enough for her to see and move.

"Who are you?" Mercy asked, squinting into the sun.

"Mercy," the woman said. Mercy jerked at hearing her name from a stranger's mouth. "You knew me as Prudence. You saved me from that horrible place."

"P-Prudence?" Mercy's knees went weak. One of the women she'd sent out through the tunnels? They hadn't gone to their deaths after all?

"That was the name Hermann gave me. But my real name is Emery. You're safe with us."

Safe. She was...free?

CHAPTER 16

Fresno, CA – Faith

Faith stared into space, lost in the recent past. Their escape from Sacramento had been both the second most terrifying event of her life, and strangely easy.

They ran out the front door of the building, the fighters spreading out to take on what soldiers were left. Once outside, when she made for the narrow side streets again, Captain pulled her back, shouting that Steve had more to worry about than them.

And all around, the city burned.

Small fights were everywhere. Sometimes, the fighters would jump in. Watching her cousin smash through brawling groups like a wrecking ball, she finally understood *why* they called her type Bashers.

They hadn't run far when a transport truck pulled to a stop near them and a woman leaned out, her braids swinging around her face, inviting her and Lucas on board. Then, it was a mad ride across the city. At the fence, they paused to tie ropes from the truck to the fence and drove away. She'd leaned out the back, watching posts fall, the driver going in a huge loop around the city, occasionally stopping to pull a different section down.

It was just…

"Move out," Captain whispered harshly, pulling Faith back into the present.

She jolted into motion with the other members of the team before the words fully registered. Ever since Captain came into their lives, things moved at a breakneck pace.

Which is what she'd wanted, but somehow, she hadn't imagined it being so much like trying to ride a hurricane.

Even the aftermath of Sacramento was insane. There'd been sporadic fighting for a week, all of the Sacramento Chapters leaping into action the moment the Irregulars 'started the party,' as they put it.

The Resistance led the efforts to find random pockets of NKs, and with the NK leadership either dead or escaped, Captain turned her eyes south, to the next big city: Fresno.

She crashed into something hard, bouncing off it to rebound against a wall. She looked up, into Captain's fierce eyes mere inches from her own. This close, it was easier to see the smaller scars around the single larger one. Several of them barely missed her eye, and the largest one bisected her eyebrow. When she blinked, Faith thought she could see a hint of a line on her eyelid.

"Get your head in the game, Wilkins," Captain growled. "Or I'll bench your ass before you know what hit you."

"You're on my turf now," Carter said quietly from behind her. "And we need people like her that can blend in."

After one more fierce frown, Captain turned back to Carter. The moment those gray-blue eyes left her, Faith relaxed, giving Lucas a small, reassuring nod. She was okay.

Yes, Carter needed her, and Lucas, and everyone else who could walk around in Fresno without raising the alarm. They were currently under the city's streets, walking through the sewers to one of the munitions factories.

They had four new Resistance members, Celina, Matthew, Roger, and Eli, as well as an Irregular, Moon Moon. Captain gave Carter a disgusted look when he chose the younger man, but he insisted, on the grounds that "we need everyone who doesn't look like they could commit murder with just their pinky."

Captain grinned insolently. "I could blend in."

"No, you can't, and we need to. I'd rather not have another Sacramento, thanks."

"What?" Faith could swear she heard a laugh lurking in Captain's tone. "You didn't like what we did with the place?"

"You brought down half the city!"

"Only the half Steve was in."

Carter continued leading them through the sewers, dripping water breaking the fresh silence. Finally, Carter stopped at a ladder. Cautiously, he moved the manhole cover back before peeking over the edge. Faith held her breath.

"Clear," he said quietly, the words almost echoing in the tunnel, and Faith exhaled in a rush, relaxing.

Captain was the second one up the ladder, guarding the entrance to the narrow alley by the time Faith surfaced, followed by Lucas and Moon Moon. Faith stepped carefully around the litter piled against the long-abandoned dumpster, blown in by the wind.

"Hide your weapons better," Carter muttered to Captain.

Her lips flattened, but she shrugged her jacket off, revealing the shoulder holsters, and adjusted the machete, flipping it over so the handle sat in the small of her back. With her jacket back on and two of the antler buttons done up, Faith couldn't see anything odd.

Other than everything.

"Are you sure you should leave your hair like that?" Faith asked, nodding to the leader's braids.

She'd gotten Eleanor to tie the hair on both sides back, leaving it loose on top. She'd woven cords and hair together, occasionally knotting it. The results were just as feral as their battle braids, although she'd foregone the faux mohawk.

It didn't help.

"If you wore your hair loose, you'd look more like a woman," Moon Moon offered.

"Nah," Roger said, giving Captain a quick once-over. "You definitely look good with this."

Captain's face stilled and she focused on the young men with an unblinking stare. Moon Moon shifted away, ducking his head and paling. Roger gulped, turning gray under that cold look.

"No," she said.

"Yes, ma'am."

"Never again, ma'am."

"Hey, get your heads out of your asses." Carter snapped his fingers. "We've got work to do."

Faith quickly surveyed the scene. She didn't recognize the building, not from this angle. The munitions factory sat at the end of the alley, but there were no doors opening onto the alley itself. The buildings on either side did, but...

"These are used as a barracks," Carter said, nodding to each in turn. "We really don't want to make too much noise, okay?"

"Then what's your plan to enter?" Captain asked.

Carter smiled, showing all his teeth, pulling baseball caps from his bag. "Through the front door, of course."

Around the front, Carter, Lucas, Captain, and Faith tugged their caps lower, mingling with the younger members of their group. They all chatted and laughed, creating a jumble in front of the door guard, handing over their IDs.

The guards took them, peering at faces while they barely held still. When Carter arrived at the front of the line, he gave the guards a sympathetic look.

"Kids, right?"

Nodding, the guard waved him through. Faith held her breath when it was her turn. The guard looked, looked again, leaning closer, and Faith's stomach plummeted.

Reaching out, he picked up one of her pigtails, stroking the ash blonde hair he held between his fingers. She'd been so happy when she'd gotten that haircut and could look at her own hair for the first time in years. Now...

Captain jostled her forward, breaking the guard's view, handing over her ID. Lucas grabbed her hand, pulling her into the building, lacing their fingers together, grinning down at her. Glancing over her shoulder, Captain stood with her weight on one leg, cocking her head so the guard could only see the right side of her face, smirking.

When he waved her through, Captain reached out to take her ID back, but the guard held it away. "You new? We give back when you leave."

Carter hurried over. "Sorry! Sorry, she's new to the factories." Grabbing Captain's arm, he hustled her away. "We can't do anything without IDs, so workers are effectively imprisoned while they're inside," he said in a low voice.

"I know, you said," Captain replied. "But they needed something else to think about than a pretty woman with crazy light hair."

Faith leaned against Lucas, closing her eyes. "I can't believe that worked."

"Why?" he whispered. "We've done it often enough."

Shaking her head, she tugged him around the corner. The moment they were out of sight, she turned into him. Being the object of the guard's unblinking stare had unnerved her more than she could admit.

This close to the entrance, they had to stay quiet. If they took a left at the end of the hall, they'd end up on the factory floor. The sharp scent of gunpowder overrode everything else. Clanks, mechanical groans, and chatter drifted in from that direction, but their target lay here, behind the doors halfway down this hall—the munitions storage room.

They were here to raid it, which is why Carter had reluctantly agreed to bring one of the Irregular's Bashers in the first place. They'd need someone to take care of any guards quickly and quietly. Everyone had been slightly unnerved when Captain appointed herself to go with them.

The younger members high-fived each other, barely smothering their laughter, whispering triumphantly. Lucas turned a grim eye on them. He'd been on so many of these missions over the years.

Reaching up, she touched his cheek gently, wanting to reassure him. Not all of those missions had gone smoothly, and she knew the memory of it plagued him some nights.

"Hey." Turning, she saw the guard who'd stared at her so intently. "You have a sister?" he demanded, shoving her ID card in her face.

"No, of course she doesn't," Carter said loudly, but the guard ignored him.

Lucas stepped between Faith and the guard, who whipped up his rifle. Faith cried out, clutching Lucas's jacket, and peering over his shoulder.

"She is a *traitor*," the guard snarled.

Faith gasped, finally recognizing him. He was one of the many revolving guards on her office's doors. She'd given him peaches once. Her heart pounding, the rifle in front of them seemed to expand, filling her view until Captain appeared behind him, wrapping her arm around his neck, the other clamping over the trigger.

She snarled, jerking her arm, shaking him like a terrier with a rat, forcing him to his knees, her left hand still gripping the rifle. A quick jerk, and a quiet, wet *crack* filled the air. The whole thing was over in seconds, happening in near silence.

Faith's stomach heaved. Rushing to the wall, she retched, tossing up everything she'd eaten recently. That sound...her bones had sounded like that the day she'd been beaten.

When the NK slumped to the floor, the Resistance members were freed from their stupor, the hallway filling with a babble of voices. They talked over each other, but all Faith recognized were the gentle hands pulling her hair away from her face while she vomited.

When Lucas helped her to her feet, she heard Celina. "I didn't...I thought you were exaggerating, Carter. About...about her."

Faith didn't detect any horror in the younger woman's voice, just fascination. Captain stood off to the side, examining her hand.

"How did you keep the rifle from going off?" Moon Moon asked.

She showed him the middle finger of her left hand, the area around her nail already turning purple. "Shoved my finger behind the trigger. Hurts like a mother, but..." She shrugged.

"Well." Carter rubbed his hands together while Roger knelt in front of the door, lockpicks already out. "I'm ready to steal some munitions. What about you?"

"Borrow," Captain corrected him. "We're only borrowing them. After all, we do intend to give them back." She smiled, one of the few, full smiles Faith had seen from her recently. It constantly surprised her how nasty a smile could be.

"Either way." Carter gave Captain a nervous smile, then turned back to the door. "Let's get some bullets and..."

The storeroom doors swung open. A group of NKs waited on the other side, weapons at the ready.

She gasped.

How were they already here?

***

Faith looked desperately around the tiny room, sobs shaking her shoulders, knocking on the walls as if a secret door would magically appear, but the bricks didn't budge. Carter kicked the closed door, swearing loudly. Lucas slumped to the floor, a hand over his eyes.

"They killed them," he mumbled again, still in a daze. "They're dead. They're all dead."

Captain shook her head, a hint of tears in her gray-blue eyes. Surprise temporarily numbed Faith's grief. She hadn't thought the rebel leader was fond of her fighter. "Moon Moon, you stupid bastard," she muttered.

Faith replayed it over again, trying to see if there was anything she could have done differently. The NKs had been waiting when the doors opened. The other four Resistance members had fallen in the first volley, along with the Irregular, Moon Moon.

Celina...Celina, her first girl friend in forever... She squeezed her eyes shut, but blood pooled around Celina's small, still hand. The engagement ring she'd never taken off gleaming silver on her finger...

"How did they know where we were?" Carter rounded on Captain. "It's impossible!"

"Murphy's Law," Captain snapped. "Nothing is impossible. Right now, we need a way out."

The door crashed open, three NKs spilling into the small room. Faith shrieked, fumbling for the knife she still carried, her heart in her throat. Lucas leaped to his feet, pushing her behind himself. She stepped to the side, swearing and crying as she struggled with the weapon.

Captain surged forward, lips twisted into a feral snarl. Faith froze, the knife hanging from numb fingers. The basher bulled into the three men, scattering them like bowling pins, stomping the one who fell, then slamming her elbow into another. Carter danced around the outer edges of the fight, looking for a way to help, but Captain didn't need it.

It was over in moments, Captain climbing off the body of the last man, wiping her knife clean on his clothes. Faith gaped at her. The only times she'd actually *seen* Captain fight had been one to one. This had been...so much worse.

"A way out sooner than later would be good," Captain said, as if nothing had happened.

Faith stumbled when Lucas shifted her. "This might work," he mumbled.

Captain dragged one man away from the door, shutting it quickly, more voices already echoing up the stairway. Bricks crashed together at the back of the room. Captain dropped to one knee, drawing her gun, but in the dust knelt Lucas, holding a brick in front of a hole in the wall.

"I thought those bricks didn't look even," he said, grinning.

Carter punched the air. "Yes, Lucas!"

Running to him, Faith flung herself into his arms, raining kisses on his dusty face. "You noticed that even in your shock?"

"They were the bricks behind you," he said. "And I notice everything around you."

***

"No," Lucas moaned. "I really thought we'd made it."

"Not your fault," Carter said, putting a hand on his shoulder. "The NKs just...got here first."

They clustered at the end of a hallway on the second floor of the near-empty apartment building, their escape stymied once more. At the other end of the hallway, someone hammered on the door. Its hinges shook with every pound.

Captain tested doorknobs. Flinging a door open, she shoved them all into a tiny apartment, slamming the door shut and putting a chair under the doorknob. An empty studio apartment, with nowhere to hide. The only window looked out onto the square, the grass showing the barest hints of green.

More NKs poured into the square, taking orders from an older soldier who directed them around.

"We can't use the window," Faith said, her voice trembling, looking at each of them in turn.

Carter, her leader these past few years, and the one who'd always taken the biggest risks.

Captain, her cousin, a stranger, looking wild with her hair braided and tied back on the sides, her gray-blue eyes feral, teeth bared in a grin.

Lucas. Her anchor in this insane world. His dark brown hair mussed and sticking up in places, a bruise on his right cheekbone, yet he'd never looked more beautiful to her than in that moment.

"We could go up," Lucas said. Faith admired his calm tone, especially since she could see his pulse pounding in his neck. "If we go up, we might be able to cut past them and get back to the ground."

Carter peeked out the window and winced. "How's your climbing, Captain?"

"I'm not a fucking lizard, Carter."

"We can't climb anywhere with that many NKs outside," Faith pointed out. "They'll see us. We need a diversion."

Captain nodded. "We do." She immediately shed her jacket and un-buckled her machete. "Here." She handed the weapon to Faith. "Don't lose this. It was a gift."

"What are you doing?" Faith cried.

In the hallway, something crashed.

"I'm a diversion," Captain said patiently, removing her shoulder guns next. "Seriously, don't lose this shit. I happen to like them."

"Let me get captured," Carter said desperately. Lucas and Faith jerked instinctively. Lucas opened his mouth to protest, quickly silenced when Captain handed him another set of guns. "I'm valuable—"

"Not as valuable as Captain."

"I can pretend to be you!"

"You go out there, you'll die in less than a minute," Captain said harshly, donning her jacket once more. "Unless you've magically become a fighter and can buy us time?"

Silence.

Captain moved to the window, shoulders squared, an evil glint in her eye. Faith looked from the machete in her hands to her cousin. From her knotted hair and bloodied face to the knee-high moccasins, Captain looked every inch the rebel war leader.

"The moment they begin pulling back, get the fuck out of here," Captain said. "Find Phoenix. Tell her exactly what happened. Then tell her to come rescue me, got it?"

More soldiers ran into the square, splitting up and searching individual buildings, leaving thirty in the square. They surrounded the old soldier giving orders.

Faith swallowed, sick to her stomach. If anyone could survive, it would be Captain, but at what cost? They all knew what soldiers did to captured women. And how would they find her to rescue her?

Too many things caught in her throat, silencing her. In the end, she could only whisper, "Be careful."

"As careful as I ever am," Captain replied, giving Faith the first genuine smile she'd seen.

"You're never careful!"

"Exactly."

Faith hissed in frustration, but by that time, it was too late. Captain hopped onto the windowsill, their protests falling on deaf ears.

"Oh, come on," she said. "It'll be fun."

And then she leaped.

The last view Faith had of Captain was burned into her memory. The NKs hadn't expected someone to drop from a building, and she was amongst them before they knew what happened. She went in with two knives—"Where the hell was she hiding two more knives?" Carter complained—spinning and cutting her way through the soldiers, the NKs shouting in surprise and pain.

Captain had her arm wrapped around the old soldier's neck when Lucas dragged Faith away from the window.

"We can't just leave her here," she whispered, struggling against him.

He held her tighter. "We can't do anything else," he said softly. "Otherwise, it's all for nothing."

Carter, his ear pressed to the door, hissed, waving them over. "They're leaving."

Faith risked one more glance out the window. One blonde head marched away, surrounded by a sea of black and green.

***

Seattle, WA – Grace

Despite Seahorse telling them they could sharpshoot and help the fighters if necessary, Grace found herself completely unable to track the mess below them.

Flames stretched high, people surged back and forth, and for some reason, some lunatic kept throwing flaming cars down steep hills. She and Charlie remained above it in a two-story bookstore at the top of Capitol Hill Road.

The remains of a bookstore, anyway. Below them, only metal shelves remained. She assumed the rest had been burned to keep the residents warm in winters past.

"How are we supposed to tell if the fight's going badly?" Grace whispered, though even the screams were quiet at this distance.

Charlie shrugged. "I guess we'll see more Steve?" He continued watching the fight through his scope. "I think I'm starting to make some sense of this."

"Oh, good. Tell me."

"Okay, way down south, you can barely see those cars—that's regular army. They had a hard time finding enough vehicles to work in here, but Sears did get some. I recognize that tank. It's the Irregulars who keep throwing the damn burning cars. Though how they're getting all four wheels off the ground, I have no clue."

He switched to the center, right in front of them, talking occasionally. The moon rose high while they waited. Occasionally, Charlie fired. Once, someone fired back.

The moon had crossed its zenith when Charlie commented on the fighting again. "I can see Thorin and his mom on this lot in the middle. It's hand to hand now. Wait! There's way more Steve here than there should be... Get your rifle, Grace."

Hastily, Grace shouldered her rifle, aiming where Charlie directed. Between the fires and moonlight, she was just able to differentiate between the two sides.

"Pick your shots," Charlie said, only the slightest quaver to his voice. "But don't stop shooting. Our side isn't doing too great in that section."

Suiting action to words, Charlie fired, slow and methodical. Grace's first three shots were too quick, but Charlie's steady presence helped calm her.

Until, when looking for a new target, she passed over something odd. Going back to it, she studied the thing, finally lowering her rifle to see if that helped her get the big picture.

"What is it, babe?" he asked.

"One o'clock, behind that brick and concrete building. I can't tell..."

It rolled forward a little more. Grace suddenly found herself staring down the barrel of its forward gun, trained right at her.

"Tank!" Charlie shouted. "Down, down, down."

Flinging their rifles into the bookstore, she grabbed the rope ladder they'd used to get up here, swinging awkwardly down. Charlie leaned over the side, holding the ropes to steady her, the whites of his eyes showing, his mouth moving when the world exploded.

CHAPTER 17

Fresno, CA – Captain

Blackness.

Water hit my face and I jerked, snorting and sputtering, struggling to wipe it away. My hands were brought up short, metal clanking. I shifted my feet and they barely budged, cold metal around my bare ankles. More water. Snorting, I shook my head, wincing at the pounding headache.

Oh, yeah. Now I remembered that hit to the head. Bastards left me to sit overnight in a cell, then sucker punched me and chain me to a chair? Assholes.

"What the fuck, man," I mumbled around a split lip.

Various aches and pains spoke up, but nothing screamed. Shaking my head again, I looked around a room that looked like it came straight out of an American cop drama. Taupe colored walls, dust gathering in the corners. Boring linoleum with a couple tears in it. One-way glass window, metal chairs. No table. Huh.

Two men sat across the room from me, one young, one old, both in fancy uniforms. Off to the side, a soldier in fatigues stood, hands folded behind his back.

I touched my lip with my tongue, feeling the extent of the split while watching the two men sitting across from me. They studied my every limited move.

"Who are you?" the younger one asked. I dubbed him Larry.

I smirked, causing a warm trickle down my chin. "They call me Captain." They'd asked me this yesterday, too. Guess they didn't quite believe it.

The two talked too rapidly for me to follow, but one word kept repeating. I think it was the one that Sung Ki said loosely translated to 'bullshit.' The younger one watched me even more carefully, his eyes flicking from my face to my hands and back.

What else would they ask? I had no idea, and without knowing, I couldn't get a lie sorted in time. Well, they'd probably ask where my people were. Easy. I had no idea. Probably some names. Not like it would do them much good.

"Prove that you are the Ghost Captain," Larry challenged me suddenly.

What?

I snorted, dissolving into laughter. How the fuck was I supposed to prove who I am?

"Yesterday wasn't proof enough? Fine. Unchain me, gimme a knife, and I'll show you."

His lip curled. "Do you think I am stupid?"

"Well...yeah. I mean, you came here, didn't you?"

Reaching out, he slapped me. My head rocked a little, but after years of fighting, it didn't sting as much as I'd thought.

"Prove you are Captain," he demanded again.

I shifted in the uncomfortable chair. At least the room is cool. California is too fucking hot, even in winter. Wait. Where was my jacket? The moccasins would be easy to replace, but not Noah's jacket. What else had they taken? Frantically tapping my fingers, I heard my ring chime on metal before I focused enough to see it.

My shoulders dropped, relief flooding me. I still had my ring. A tiny piece from Noah, reassuring me that no matter where I was, I wasn't alone. Pressing my ring finger against the chair until the band pressed hard against my flesh, I grinned insolently.

"All right, Larry," I said.

"My name is not Larry," he snapped. "It's Kam Jeong Gwon."

I flicked my fingers, turning my head away. "Whatever, Larry. Listen, you want me to prove who I am? Fine."

I recounted the final battle in Oregon, how Steve set up their camp and what we'd done to them. I went into detail about the explosions and the acid, especially the effects the acid had on human flesh.

The older Steve's face turned red, mottling with rage. I dubbed him Curly.

"Enough!" he shouted, slamming his fist on the table. "How dare you—" He broke off, speaking in rapid Korean.

I slouched in my chair, grinning at the two men. "You asked. Shouldn't ask if you don't want an answer."

Larry slapped me again, rocking me back in the chair. I laughed.

He sat back, fingers working, uncertainty showing in the tightening around his eyes and mouth. He shouted and outside, a guard answered. While we waited, he drummed his fingers on his leg while Curly refused to look at me.

Long minutes later, footsteps sounded in the hallway and the door swung open, guards pouring in. Gritting my teeth, I waited to see what would happen next. Torture? Rape?

Then, Moon Moon stepped into the room.

***

Fresno, CA – Faith

"What do we have to do to get people moving around here?" Faith muttered, storming through the Irregulars' base, an abandoned farmhouse outside the Fresno boundary fence.

She, Lucas, and Carter hadn't needed to find the Irregulars. Instead, the rebel group found *them* while they were still running through Fresno's streets. They'd been hustled underground to a half-burned hulk of a house in the middle of an almond orchard.

Then, they'd been left to wait until what passed for a command structure arrived. Fighters trickled in, the vehicles left hidden in the orchard. When the sun sank halfway below the horizon, Phoenix and Gryphon showed up, the small sniper agitated.

"What the fuck do you mean, '*you left her there*'?" Phoenix exploded without preamble. Only her husband stopped her from trying to punch Lucas.

Faith curled her lip. Why was this woman so concerned? It was *her* cousin who'd been captured! Not that these people knew that, but still...

Gryphon, spotting someone, hauled his wife outside, and Faith dismissed them. Apparently, they were only as good as their leader, otherwise relying on violence to get anything done.

"We need to figure out where she's been taken," she said to Lucas, grabbing his hand.

His fingers curled around hers, warm and reassuring. "We will."

"Faith?" Turning, her mom and dad entered the room. "We heard about your brush. Are you alright?"

Faith nodded, tears gathering in her eyes. "We're fine, but Captain...Captain gave herself up so we could escape."

Abigail relaxed slightly, wrapping her daughter in a warm hug. Dan stroked her hair, and for a moment, Faith believed everything would be okay.

"Are you," Abigail lowered her voice, glancing around, making sure they were alone, "are you sure Captain being gone is a bad thing? That woman is unpredictable and dangerous."

"The NKs are gone from here all the way to Oregon," Faith reminded her sharply.

"Yes, but...her methods," her mom whispered.

Faith paused in agonized indecision. Captain told her not to tell anyone who she was, but this was her family! Surely, she could tell them? Shouldn't she tell them the woman they were glad was captured was their beloved niece?

Carter appeared in the doorway, taking the choice from her, looking dazed. "Captain's being held in the downtown jail, the Fresno County Plaza building."

Faith stared at him, mouth open.

"How the hell...?" Lucas demanded.

Carter shrugged, waving outside. "That woman, Shrike, she's... Well, come talk to her for yourself."

All four of them piled out the door after him, tumbling down the creaky steps. Fighters were everywhere. Some had the contents of their small packs spread around them, others cleaned weapons. Still more slept on thin blankets on the ground. Those ones stayed to the edges, where they could have something at their backs.

"I've had people in there gathering information for weeks," Shrike said, in answer to their barrage of questions.

"How could you have people in there already?" Carter demanded. "We've kept the Chapters so separate, I don't even know all the members!"

Shrike snorted, pushing her hat back so it framed her heart-shaped face. "How do you think we found you so quickly?"

"Do us a favor," River said shortly. "Don't question how we do things every five seconds. It'll go faster that way."

Phoenix arrived, a young woman wearing a hijab in tow. "Aanisah has more information," she announced, nodding to the woman.

Aanisah pulled a map from her pack, spreading it on the ground. The Irregulars knelt around it. Realizing if she wanted to know what was happening, she'd have to join them, Faith made a space for herself between River and Aanisah. Lucas leaned over her, resting a hand on her shoulder.

"I couldn't get too close," Aanisah began, "there's soldiers everywhere. I don't know which building they're holding Captain in, but it's one of these two." She pointed to the central building, and another one behind it.

"Most likely that one," Faith said, putting her finger on the rear building. "Those are the cell blocks. Most prisoners end up there."

River glanced up sharply, her blue eyes intense. "You've been there?"

"Only twice." Faith shook her head. "I don't know it well, just that the front building is their government. We tried breaking prisoners out once. It didn't go well."

"We'll need help," Lucas said grimly. "A lot more help."

Phoenix smiled, showing her teeth. "Gryph sent Storm and Sweetpea to get reinforcements."

"Good," Aanisah said, "because word on the street is that Captain is due to be executed tomorrow."

"What the hell?" Phoenix's shout woke several of the sleeping fighters, who started out of their bedrolls and came up, weapons in hand. "Sorry," she called. "Sorry, it's just…" Lowering her voice, she turned back to their circle. "*Lead* with that next time!" She paused, considering. "Actually, that makes this easier."

"How?" Faith asked.

But before she could answer, a commotion at the far end of camp had everyone on their feet, weapons raised. Until a blonde woman tumbled into camp, sunlight glinting on the silver beads threaded onto her braids.

"Celt!" Phoenix cried.

***

Los Angeles, CA – Mercy

Mercy followed Emery—the woman she'd once known as Prudence—down dark, narrow streets, the setting sun casting long shadows, and into a side alley, always staying close to the buildings. More people trailed after Mercy. Two streets over, a fight raged, filling the air with shouts and screams.

This is what she'd stumbled across, a group out on a raid. The men were absolute wankers for that first scare, but as Emery repeatedly told her, they didn't mean her harm. That didn't stop her from watching them as warily as she did the Masters. She'd only met one man who could be trusted, and he was gone.

Emery ducked through a broken window, already pulling her backpack off. Glancing up at the red sky, Mercy took one last, deep breath, and followed her in.

"Quick, take everything," Emery whispered. "Quietly!" she snapped when one of the group whistled.

And well he should, Mercy thought. The room was filled with boxes and barrels. Inside, they found food, water, medical supplies, and basic weapons. Everything people were desperate for in this city.

Mercy loaded her backpack with medical supplies, keeping a surreptitious eye on the others. "How did you know about this?" she whispered, holding a small tub of ointment, her own handwriting labeling it as an antibacterial ointment.

This was where all her extra stock had gone. There were times when her Master—no, Kozlov, she corrected herself sternly. There were times when Kozlov had ordered her to make more of certain things, and now she loaded them back into her pack.

His face filled her mind. Panic threatened to overwhelm her. Desperately, she sniffed the air, identifying three scents. Then, she looked for three objects with corners. Finally, she touched three surfaces, bringing herself back to the present.

"Are you okay?" Emery asked.

"No. But I'm getting there."

After watching her for another second, Emery shrugged. "I used to work in supply for a large corporation. Hermann ordered me to set these up all over the city. Everything a patrol needs to restock."

Turning, she surveyed the small room. "Okay, people. Pack it up. Our boys can't last much longer."

Hefting her pack, Mercy touched the scalpel in her pocket. She wouldn't be taken by the Warriors again. She'd use it on herself before going back to that hellhole and the punishment her Master had waiting for her.

Though strangers, these people treated her kindly enough. Emery ensured the men left her a comfortable boundary. When one overstepped, he immediately moved back, apologizing. Apparently, Emery's first comment about them being safe but stupid was accurate.

She was willing to stay with them. For now.

***

Fresno, CA - Captain

My jaw dropped and long seconds passed as I stared at Moon Moon. He smirked, folding his arms across his chest, leaning one shoulder against the wall.

No wounds, no bruises, nothing.

"You motherfucker!" I lunged against my bonds, snarling at the young man.

He flinched, then straightened. "You really thought I died? Fooled you, didn't I?"

How long had he been spying for Steve? Couldn't be too long—*unless an army attacked as soon as I left,* my brain supplied unhelpfully.

No. No, I couldn't think like that.

We hadn't had a major breach since Spartacus—I shied away from that, and the memories I couldn't handle right now. Dimly, I realized Moon Moon hadn't stopped talking. Unclenching my fingers one at a time took extreme effort, then I looked up at that little shit.

"Why?" I rasped, interrupting his spiel.

He strutted closer, bending to place his hands over mine where I gripped the arms of the chair. "Because you can't win against them. Because you don't understand your natural place in the world..."

I headbutted him, his nose breaking with a satisfying crunch against my forehead. He fell backwards, howling and clutching his face, blood pouring between his fingers.

"Coward," I snarled.

The guards rushed in, thick leather straps swinging. I ducked my head, pulling my shoulders high, clenching my teeth. Thin strips of fire everywhere... Pain, pain, beautiful, physical pain. I welcomed it, let it drive out grief, uncertainty, everything...

In the back of my mind, my inner critic *tsk*ed and took notes. I'd really have to talk to Kestrel when I got back to Oregon.

A foot connected with my shin, and I screeched. As if that was what they'd been waiting for, the guards stepped back, forming a ring around myself and my interrogators.

Slowly, I straightened as much as I could, keeping one eye on the guards, the other on Moon Moon.

"So. Those the only reasons you switched sides, chicken shit?" I croaked.

His face turned red. "Maybe if you treated me like an equal instead of an idiot!"

"You *are* an idiot!"

***

Hours later, after sitting and staring at each other in silence, they hauled me out, taking me to a different building than the one I'd been locked up in yesterday. Guards surrounded me on all sides, two holding my arms to frog-march me through the halls. We walked past cells anywhere from one to packed in each.

Those prisoners stared at us, some curious, others uncaring. Their level of 'give a shit' corresponded with their cleanliness. I could only assume it indicated how long they'd been here. A man wolf whistled, sticking his arm through the bars, trying to reach me.

Lunging, I snapped my teeth, just missing his fingers. He pulled them back hastily, checking them. "I'll remember you, blondie," he shouted, pushing greasy dark hair behind his ears.

"Likewise," I called over my shoulder.

Behind me, Larry snapped to the guards, one of whom slapped me. Raging internally, I laughed in his face.

At the end of the hall, we passed through another pair of doors into an empty cell block. They flung me into the one closest to the doors. Metal bars formed the outer wall, the other three were white painted brick. A tiny window, also barred, gave me my only view of the outside. Late afternoon, from the looks of it. A bucket sat in one corner, and in the opposite, a single folded blanket.

I didn't fight when they chained me to the back wall, mostly because two men stood just out of reach, guns pointed at my head.

Moon Moon leaned close, his hair brushing my arm when he locked the manacle around my wrist. When he straightened, he ran a hand up my thigh, his fingers moving to cup my crotch. I grabbed his pinky, ripping it back. He let go with howl, then I kneed him in the groin hard enough for him to rise onto his tip toes.

With a gurgle, he folded like an accordion, his knees collapsing under him. Larry snapped at the men when one started towards me, fist raised. Grumbling, he backed off, fingering the gun on his hip. After cracking my neck, I looked at Larry—and froze.

"That's *my* jacket," I snarled, lunging for him, only brought up short by the chains.

My jacket. Noah's jacket. The one I'd inherited upon his death. At least it wasn't missing, but how dare this...person...wear it? Growling, I leaned against the wall, watching the distance between us. Waiting for him to make a mistake and step too close.

He grinned, running his hands over it, the leather soft with wear and time, then flicked his fingers, sending the guards out. "It's too fine a jacket for a *mubeopja* like you." He examined one of the antler buttons. "I think it makes an excellent memento of the terrorist known as the Ghost Captain. Look for me tomorrow at your execution. I'll be wearing it."

"Yeah, you hold onto it for me." Glaring at him, I stuffed my hands in my pockets. "I'll be wanting that back."

He laughed, clapping his hands. "There! The American bravado. I haven't seen that since I was here for university."

I waited while he prattled on. Silent before, but once Curly was out, he couldn't stop talking, it seemed. He talked about my execution, watching me expectantly. I snorted. He thought death would scare me?

No, I had too many people waiting for me to fear death. Hell, at this point, I'd welcome him like an old friend.

"Now," he continued, "do you remember my name?"

"I know your name," I said, grinning. He stopped pacing, watching me intently. An unspoken challenge hung in the air. "You're Larry."

His face darkened. "Kam. I am Major Kam Jeong Gwon. I need—*you* need to know the name of the man who brought you down. When you die, call my name."

"Why?" I asked.

He paused, mouth open. "What?"

"Why would I want to call your name? I mean, I'm sure there's *someone* out there who cares enough, but if you think it's me, you're barking up the wrong tree."

"No!" He leaned away, as if I was contagious. "When people know it was I who brought the Ghost Captain low, I will be..." He straightened, adjusting my jacket over his shoulders. *"Famous."*

I laughed. "Bitch, why would bringing me down make anyone famous? I'm an idiot. Just ask my friends. Oh wait. You can't find them."

Larry wrinkled his nose, snarling. I caught a couple words and cocked my head.

"Yeah, why *didn't* you guys torture me?" I asked.

His eyes widened. "You understood?"

I gave him a Look. "Dude. Really? You really think I wouldn't bother learning *any* Korean? Geez."

He looked around the cell for a moment, flustered, unsure, it was hard to tell. Finally, he chose to ignore my knowledge of Korean and focused on the question.

"No one would believe that a broken, tortured creature was the great Ghost Captain." The way he said it made me think they'd tried. Ouch. "They will have a hard time believing you are a woman, already. So, we left you whole..." I cringed inwardly at his choice of words. Whole? But he continued. "We left you whole because otherwise, your forces might say that the person we executed was not Ghost Captain and put another in your place. Arriving cold and hungry to your execution puts you where they are—small, scared. Human." He smiled. "Killable. In one swoop, we eliminate you and your legend. Brilliant, yes?"

I yawned. "Dude, it's not Ghost Captain. It's just Captain. Although Ghost is a fucking awesome name," I finished under my breath.

Larry's lips tightened. "So brave, are you? I think you won't be so much when you see what we have in store for you." Spinning on one heel, he headed for the exit.

"Hey," I shouted after him. "Would you mind closing the door? There's a draft in here."

His back stiffened. Marching out, the solid steel door slammed shut behind him.

I waited a moment, but it seemed I was finally alone. Sliding down the wall, I groaned when I laid flat on the floor. Cuffed to a chair was bad enough. My shoulder screamed at me until I adjusted its position, then stretched my legs, sighing when the cool concrete touched the bare skin of my lower legs.

Ever since moccasins became my main footwear, I ended up cutting off the bottoms of my pants. It meant less fabric bunching, especially since I always got knee highs to keep debris out. I hated having dust, seeds, and pebbles in my shoes. That hadn't changed once I switched footwear. Fortunately, the tanners and makers humored me and my preferences.

Scooting until my head rested on the folded blanket, I gave some attention to my impending death.

Relief swept through me. Relief and...regret?

The relief I understood. Lay down my burdens. Let go of the loneliness, heartache, pain, grief. See all those who'd gone before me. Noah. Sonya, Peter, Mama, and all the fighters whose real names I didn't know.

I turned the regret over, looking at it from different angles. Regret? I would regret not seeing my sons grow up. I'd regret the grief my death would cause.

And I would very much regret never finding out who was really behind this shit show and having the chance to murder the motherfucker responsible.

Oh, that one left me aching.

Pursing my lips, I made a decision. Sitting up, I cracked my neck. Yeah. Nope, not gonna die in the morning. I had a legitimate mystery in my life and a series of murders to solve.

As well as one to commit.

No dying for me. Now, I just needed to figure out how to skip my own execution.

Undoing my pants, I stuck a finger in the tiny slit I'd made in the waistband, fishing out the short, flexible picks I'd tucked in there.

Thrain was right. You never knew when you might need some tools.

CHAPTER 18

Portland, OR – Grace

Grace carefully held the cup to the fighter's mouth. Amber drank deeply, one bandaged hand raised to steady it until she sagged against her pillow, exhausted.

"Thank you," she rasped, smiling up at Grace, who touched her shoulder gently, looking into Amber's single visible brown eye. The other—as well as half her face—was covered in more bandages of varying colors.

She moved through the wounded, dispensing water and musing on the past two weeks. After the explosion, she didn't remember anything until she woke up in a troop transport on her way to Portland. Charlie lay next to her, still and pale.

She'd cried out, but many hands patted and brushed, soothing her.

"It's okay." Seahorse had ridden with them, fresh bandages wrapped around her head. "He's alive, thanks to you."

"To me?" She'd been so confused.

"You saved him. You had a tourniquet on him and were wrapping his wounds with your shirt- You seriously don't remember?"

In the present, Grace shook her head. She still didn't remember, and according to the resident therapist, Kestrel, she might never.

A blessing, maybe?

Ever since arriving in Portland, she'd stayed in the hospital, helping in this ward. The wounded had been brought here, to facilities she'd never have suspected could exist. They had doctors and nurses, as well as dozens of volunteers. Portland had been free for over a year. If this is what they could accomplish with no funds and no outside help, Grace felt pretty good about the future, for the first time in years.

Seattle, she'd been told, was nothing more than a smoking ruin, and more dead were still being found. The Army's dead were buried south of the city, ready to be moved once they were sure none of the surviving men would be court-martialed.

The Irregulars' dead were brought into Oregon. Something about a meadow and a lair, but when she asked for clarification, her questions were met with blank stares. *Keep your secrets*, she thought.

After helping the patient, she straightened, and a hand patted her butt. "Hey there. Come here often?"

Turning, she smiled. Reaching out, she stroked Charlie's hair back, running her fingers over the stubble on his cheeks. "Every day, handsome."

He tugged her hand, pulling her down to sit on his bed next to him. He couldn't speak in anything above a whisper, but the doctors said he would recover his voice with time. Resolutely, she looked down the bed, at the flat spot where his right leg ended abruptly just below the knee. "Finally ready to run away with me?" he rasped

"Mmm." She kissed his forehead, then his lips, lingering. "Name the place and the day. I'll go anywhere you want."

He grinned, closing his eyes. "I'll hold you to that, gorgeous."

"Ah, the O'Connells!" Grace straightened. The doctor—Dr. Simms, marked by a green armband—picked up Charlie's clipboard from its spot at the foot of his bed. She flipped through the pages quickly, nodding once. "How are we today, Charlie?"

"Any day I get to flirt with a beautiful woman is a great day." He exhaled, breath scraping over his throat.

"Wonderful." She made a note on his chart. "So far, everything seems to be healing well, but we still have to watch out for fevers."

Grace nodded. "I've been keeping an eye on his temp. And he just had a shot not too long ago."

"So I see. Now." Hanging his clipboard back on the bed, she rested her hands on her hips, studying them. "Since you're both well enough, let's talk prosthetics."

"You have them?" Grace exclaimed.

Dr. Simms laughed. "Yes. We've got fabricators. They work off a basic design created by Anansi, modifying them to fit the individual. We won't be able to really get into creating one until your stump is fully healed, but I wanted you to know that you will have one. I've asked Goliath to stop by. Goliath!"

She waved, but Grace didn't think it was necessary. The man who entered was so tall he had to duck to get inside the door. The handsome black man walked with a limp, nodding to them all.

Grace studied him. She'd never seen him before, but at the same time... "The river!" she exclaimed, standing to shake his hand.

He tilted his head. "Excuse me?"

Grace blushed. "Sorry. I think I recognize you. You were on the Oregon side of the Columbia when we sent women across, right?"

"Every rescue," he said, bending over to shake Charlie's hand. "Good to meet you, man."

Before they could continue, a group of children raced through, led by a pair of identical twins. The kids were laughing and shrieking, closely followed by two teenaged girls.

"Gabriel! Michael!" one girl shouted. "I know you started it! If you don't stop right now, I swear..." The threat went unfinished when the kids and their pursuers disappeared through the door, patients laughing in their wake.

Dr. Simms rubbed the space between her eyebrows. "They're good for the patients," she muttered. "They're good for the patients." Shaking her head, she looked to each of them. "Okay, if you're all set, I'll continue my rounds."

"Sorry," Goliath said after she left. "The kids really are good for patients, plus a lot of them are the children of volunteers."

"And the others?"

"Orphans."

Grace winced. Charlie met her eyes, then looked to where the kids had disappeared. They'd wanted children but put it off. Maybe now, they could start the family they'd always wanted?

"Anyway," Goliath continued, "prosthetics. We've got some good stuff, but it does take a while before you're healed enough to get one. Then there's learning to use it."

"If it's not rude to ask..." Charlie hesitated, but Goliath nodded encouragingly. "Can we see yours?"

The huge man pulled a metal chair over, folding himself to fit into it, then tugged on his left pants leg. "I lost my knee, too," he explained. "It's why I couldn't go south with Captain. I only just got mobile right before your first rescues happened."

Grace examined his leg from her spot on the bed. Obviously made from scrap metal, it was riveted together, but there didn't appear to be any sharp angles.

"The knee looks really good," she said, leaning closer.

"Yeah." Goliath knocked on his knee, which made a hollow noise. "Getting a knee that moved took some doing, but we've got a mechanical genius on our side. Another, younger, brother."

Grace nodded, distracted from answering by Seahorse and Sarge entering the ward, each of them carrying a kid—the twins from earlier, she realized. The twins, blond-haired, blue-eyed toddlers two or three years old, bounced excitedly.

One babbled away in baby talk. Sarge nodded gravely when he paused to take a breath. The other sucked his thumb, examining Seahorse. The bandage on her head was smaller than before, but still, the little boy studied it, reaching out with his free hand to touch it carefully.

"Owie," he said.

"Yeah, that's right." Seahorse smiled, adjusting the boy in her arms. "It's an owie, but it's a lot better already. How are you both?" she asked them, hooking a chair over with her foot.

"Doc says I'm doing all right." Charlie shifted.

"No, no." Goliath held a hand out to stop him. "Don't you go trying to sit up or anything like that. You've got a ways, still."

Seahorse bounced the toddler on her knees, her eyes troubled. "Even though the Celt should have reached Captain by now, I was hoping to have you two go south, too. Captain'll want to hear about your friend in person."

"Why?" Grace asked.

Sarge laid his palm across his twin's mouth, distracting the boy. "Michael, hush. We'll go out and find some puppies in just a minute, but first, we need to talk. Michael and Gabriel are two of the orphans," he said briefly, nodding to the boys.

Grace held out her arms. "May I?"

Gabriel shied away, but Michael nearly leaped from Sarge's arms, chattering away. Grace cuddled the toddler, nuzzling his soft hair. Laying her cheek on top of his head, she shared a look with Charlie.

Please? She mouthed, pouting.

Charlie huffed a quiet laugh. "Later," he said.

"We'll wait until you're well enough to ride in a car," Seahorse continued, "but if I know Captain, there's some plans in the works, and information is better than gold. So, I'd like you to talk to Captain yourselves, give them everything you've got. Dr. Simms says at least a month, which is good. They haven't won California yet."

"Fuss, fuss, fuss." An older male voice, oddly familiar, caught Grace's attention.

Charlie jerked, trying to peer around Grace, who twisted to find the speaker.

"You need to eat your soup if you want to get better," he continued.

"*You* try eating it, then," a woman replied. "It's got weird things in it."

"No, no," the man hastily said. "This one's all for *you*."

Grace spotted the old man several beds down. White-haired, stooped, and thin, he had a frail look about him. But something in the shape of his hands, the way he held the spoon out to the young woman in the bed...

Tears spilled down her cheeks. Absently, she wiped them away. Charlie's hand found her leg, squeezing tightly. The little boy, Michael, slipped off her lap, gone in an instant. Swearing good-naturedly, Sarge took off after him, but Grace barely noticed.

"Papa?" she croaked. Charlie gasped, his fingers tightening on her leg.

The old man straightened, peering around the room.

"Papa?" she said, louder.

The old man set down the bowl, pulling glasses from the breast pocket of his worn, button-down shirt. "Is that...Grace?"

"Papa?" Grace sobbed. She tried to get up, but her legs wouldn't work. She settled for clutching Charlie's hand

Next to her, Charlie choked, struggling upright. "Pop?" he whispered.

Grace watched her father walk to them through the tears streaming down her face. Another volunteer helped him walk. When he was mere feet from her, she finally remembered how to stand and flung herself into his arm, burying her head against his shoulder.

He swayed, stroking her hair. "My children," he wept. "My children are here!"

***

Fresno, CA – Faith

The sun had long since set, but Faith couldn't sleep. She waited up with Lucas, Carter, and a few of the fighters for reinforcements to arrive.

The knowledge of her cousin's pending execution made it difficult to relax, so they sat up inside the old house. To the side, Lucas exercised, burning off nervous energy.

She admired the play of muscles under his skin as he slowly lowered himself from his handstand, the way he concentrated, every move precise. The number of times she'd watched him doing what he could in the space he had... She licked her lips, distracted by thoughts of what they could do with space to themselves.

He caught her staring at him. Standing in one smooth move, he caught his lip with his teeth, then released it slowly, smiling wickedly. Giving her a wink, he returned to his calisthenics, as if nothing happened.

Burning and unable to do anything about it, she turned her attention to Phoenix, watching her work. Phoenix and Gryphon had disappeared for a while earlier in the evening, but now they focused on their weapons.

What did this woman know about Hope? They'd shared things she would never know, and it galled her. Hope, Faith, and Mercy had been inseparable whenever their families were together, and now...

Faith returned to the present only to find herself the object of the fighter's scrutiny. She flinched at that sharp gaze, and the corner of Phoenix's mouth twitched. Faith grit her teeth. Phoenix had seen the flinch, and it amused her, dammit.

But Phoenix didn't gloat. Instead, she turned her attention back to the small, easily concealable weapons in front of her. Once she finished assembling them, she tugged the pile of Captain's weapons over and began cleaning them.

Bored and aching for something to do, Faith decided to pull the tiger's tail and walked to Phoenix, sitting opposite her, crossing her legs beneath herself. "Aren't you worried about Captain?"

Phoenix shrugged without looking up. "We've been in tight spots before."

"This time she's been captured!"

"Has she?" Phoenix raised an eyebrow and Faith paused, arrested by the look in her green eyes. "If you mean, has she spent significant time in Steve's hands, then no. But this isn't the first time she's operated behind enemy lines. If there's one thing I know about her, it's that she has a mean streak a mile wide."

The fighter reassembled a gun, never breaking eye contact. "But tell me, you seem awfully concerned about Captain's welfare, considering you just met her, and you two've hardly talked."

Faith froze, no prepared lies on her tongue. This was an observation she hadn't expected. "I can't tell you."

Phoenix nodded, as if Faith had told her everything. "You knew her Before. Pretty well, too. By your looks, you're her relative. Sister or cousin. I know she has a couple cousins close to her in age."

Faith glanced at the men, but Phoenix had spoken barely above a whisper and neither of them paid the women any attention. "I...I was told...isn't it dangerous for you to know?"

Phoenix snorted. "I was with her at the beginning. I'm one of the few who knows her real name, and I've kept her secret. Now that I know who you are, I'll be watching you."

"Are you..." Faith swallowed. "Are you going to kill me?"

The sniper rolled her eyes. "God, you people are so dramatic! No. I'll just ensure you're never in a position where you might squeal."

Now Faith rolled her eyes. "They couldn't make me talk."

"You have no idea what they're capable of."

"No, *you* have no idea. I'm not bragging. They couldn't make me talk, and they tried." Phoenix gave her a questioning look. She shook her head. "You have a bunch of lies, piled on top of each other, ready to go. Each layer is a little more believable than the one before, and by the time they pull your nails, they're convinced you can't stop talking and they'll buy whatever you say. Including that you're innocent when you're definitely not."

Phoenix nodded slowly. "And here I thought you were a nice girl. You'll fit right in."

A knock at the door, and Storm poked her head in. "We're baaack!" she sang. The scar running down the side of her face twisted her smile, but Phoenix didn't seem to notice.

Instead, the fighters leaped to their feet, "Wake everyone up," Phoenix ordered. "Please."

"Already done." Satisfaction dripped from each word. "We're almost ready to go."

Quickly, the fighters finished Captain's weapons. Outside, the Irregulars gathered. "We ready to get Captain back?" Phoenix called.

A quiet chant rose from many throats. Faith had a vision of the words ringing off mountains. "All in, all out. No luck, all skill. One shot, one kill!"

***

Hacienda Heights, CA — Mercy

Dawn graced the eastern skies when Mercy straightened, rolling her shoulders and arching her back. Her final patient lay limp on the table, his hand sporting a bandage where his pinky and ring fingers used to be.

"Too many crush injuries," she muttered, wiping her face with a damp cloth before surveying the room.

Despite being here all night, this was her first chance to look around. The group she'd fallen in with had their headquarters at a mansion on a hill. Enough room for everyone, and best of all, according to Emery, it had a wall to protect them. To Mercy, that wall was barely different from the one at the Masters' compound.

Located on the ground floor, the room she currently occupied had a fire ring outside, shelves with a few more bandage rolls on it, and a small, dry herb garden.

Strangely, it vaguely reminded her of her former infirmary.

"What?" Emery looked up, holding a bucket of water.

Mercy shook her head, the corner of her mouth quirked upwards. "Nothing. Just...too many crushing injuries, you know?" Emery's forehead wrinkled, her face scrunched in confusion. Mercy sighed. "Most of the weapons left here are blunt. Even the knives are dulling. And when all the weapons are blunt, I get a lot of crushed bone, which I hate, because all I can do for them is remove the limb. I can't fix a shattered bone and I hate it!"

Setting down the bucket, Emery reached for her, and Mercy shied away, ducking her head.

"Ain't no need for that, miss," a gruff, older man behind her said hoarsely. "Nobody here is gonna hurt you." He hitched himself higher on his pallet. The blanket lay flat where his left leg should have been. "These boys know they owe you their lives."

The other three men in the hospital room nodded. Slowly, carefully, Emery took Mercy's hands.

"Usually, when we get into a fight, we lose people with injuries like these. Even when we remove the crushed limb. We're happy that they're all doing so well, that we still have them with us. *You* did that. Trust me, their families will go to war to keep you safe for what you did here. You're among friends, now."

Mercy looked down at her hands, resting in Emery's. Her fingers, long, slender—her younger brother called them 'spidery'—curled, gripping Emery.

"You could've fooled me with that first meeting. The men..." She shuddered, remembering the way they whooped and stared.

"I said they won't hurt you, not that they're not dumbasses," Emery said dryly. "Most of them are idiots, especially the ones who spend a lot of time running in small groups."

A man strode into the room, his curly brown hair nearly touching the low doorway. Ashton, Mercy remembered, the leader of this group. She watched him warily, ready to move if he proved unpredictable.

"Ladies." He inclined his head to them. "There's food ready in the kitchen for you. And the boys have visitors."

Three women and one older man entered the room, carrying bowls and cups. The man knelt at the gruff bloke's side, tears in his eyes when he saw the missing leg.

"You okay, love?" he asked.

"I will be," Gruff Bloke answered. "Thanks to her." He nodded to me.

The other wounded chimed in, and Mercy found herself surrounded by people. They didn't paw at her, but each one insisted on taking her hand, or reaching to pat her back until Emery and Ashton moved in. She hadn't talked to him yet, but apparently, he'd heard...something.

Safely bracketed by the two, she took each person's hand, letting go as quickly as she could without appearing rude. She resisted the urge to wipe her hand on her pants. *They're not like him*, she reminded herself.

"Go on," Ashton said when the last one had shaken her hand. "Get some food. Emery will show you where to sleep. It's a women's only room," he added.

Nodding, she followed Emery out the door.

"What did you tell him about me?" she asked.

"Well," Emery glanced over her shoulder, "I told him everything about you, but that was before we ever found you. He's...he's my man."

Mercy flicked her eyes over, then back. "Good for you," she said. "Good for you."

Though she didn't think she'd ever be able to stand another person touching her again. A spot warmed on her lower back, and she closed her eyes briefly, gripping the dog tags hanging between her breasts.

Oh, Jonathan.

CHAPTER 19

Scan of phone conversations, DC area – April 13, 2060, 3:43am

Man 1: They're bombs. What do you think they'll do?

Man 2: As long as they don't hit any areas with people who actually matter,

I suppose...

Fresno, CA – Captain

I rubbed my wrists, the manacles finally off, and wandered around my cell, shaking my legs out. Even standing on my tiptoes, I couldn't reach the stupid bars of the window. Flexing my knees, I bounced on my toes until everything warmed up.

"Getting old," I muttered. "Never thought I'd do that."

How old was I, now? In my thirties, for sure. Thirty-four, thirty-five, somewhere in there. Hopping up, I grabbed the bars. Getting my toes on the wall, I pulled myself high enough to see out.

A large expanse of grass finally turning green, some tall buildings. Had a government look to them. Grunting, I got myself closer. Was that...downtown? Bracing my feet, I hauled on the bars, but they didn't even wiggle.

Not that I'd expected them to.

In the middle of the green, men were hard at work, building a platform. Steve guarded the place like it held the crown jewels, soldiers everywhere.

One stood in the middle, calling orders and directing the workers, who looked like civilians. When they set a thick post in the middle of the platform, piling brush underneath, it finally dawned on me exactly how they planned to execute me.

"Fuck. Burning, huh?"

Ditching the window, I moved onto the door, still muttering to myself.

"Thought I'd get a hanging. Which is worse, burning or strangling?"

I examined the door. A normal one, I guess, having never actually seen inside a jail before. I banged on the bars, but no one answered. Had the place to myself. Nice. Although, going by the smell, there'd been plenty in here, and recently, too.

Scratching my ear, I settled cross-legged in front of the door, picks already in hand.

"I mean, if I hang, there's at least the option of breaking my neck. Burning... Will the smoke get me first, or do I have to wait for the flames? Never thought of myself as a smoker. Seems like a miserable way to go. Won't that make me more of a martyr? Fucking hell..."

I twiddled the lock, but nothing happened. Did this thing even have tumblers? Shifting, I tried peering into the lock, but no luck. Oh, well. Not like I had anything else to do until dawn.

Except I couldn't get those fucking doors open.

Hours later, leaning my head against the cold bars, I closed my eyes. I thought maybe I should cry, since I couldn't escape, but I didn't have the energy or any enthusiasm for it. Drawing my knees up, I curled slightly, imagining Noah sitting next to me.

Almost, I could feel the heat radiating from him. Tucking my cheek against my shoulder, some tears finally fell.

"I'm sorry," I mumbled, wiping my cheeks with the backs of my hands. "I know. Don't give up. But sometimes... Sometimes, I can't figure out how to keep going."

A spot on the top of my head heated up, nearly burning. Cautiously, I touched the spot, but nothing felt different. I looked to my right, sniffling.

"What? Is this your way of telling me whatever I choose is okay? Because I know that's what you'd say. I can choose to not fight, lay down, and die, is that it?" I laughed though fresh tears ran down my cheeks. A warm spot appeared at my side. "Dammit, Noah. I'm gonna get marched to that stake tomorrow. They're gonna put my back to that fucking big stake, tie me to it, and burn me."

I paused. "I mean, my hands will probably be behind my back. That's what they did today. I've got my picks—fucking useless things, can't even get me out of this cell," I muttered, "but they work fine on handcuffs. So what? You think I'll pick my cuffs, steal a weapon, and fight my way out?"

What I'd said finally trickled through my brain. The heat at my side increased. I leaned against the door again, curled around the warmth. "Fine. Fine. I won't give up. I said I'd find the fucker behind this. I'll do it and make sure our boys are safe."

When I heard the thump of multiple footsteps beyond the double doors leading out, I finally moved. Stretching one last time, I tucked one pick back into my waistband, keeping the other between my fingers, and cuffed myself back to the wall.

The doors crashed open, and they came through, a whole cadre of soldiers, marching in precision, armed with handguns and batons. I sat up straighter. I could work with this.

Larry entered last, still wearing my jacket. He waited outside with most of the men while four took up position just inside my cell, ready to shoot the moment I twitched. Two more came forward bearing new cuffs. These two, I noted, only carried batons. Interesting.

"Ooh! That's so sweet!" I smiled. "How'd you know silver's my color?"

Roughly, one cuffed my hands behind my back, then undid the manacles, leaving my feet free. The two hauled me upright, one of them stomping my toes. Hissing, I body checked him, knocking us all off kilter. Immediately, I found myself looking down four barrels. Grinning, I straightened, shrugging.

"Worth a shot."

The men gripped my upper arms once more, frog marching me towards the doors. Larry led the way, flanked by the majority of the men. The four in my cell followed me out, forming a pretty little procession.

The prisoners in the other block kicked up a ruckus. Women screamed at Steve, men yelled. Cries of "How dare you?" and "Motherfuckers!" followed us out.

Outside, the chill morning air raised goosebumps on my arms, and I sighed. Finally! Good weather. Some clouds gathered in the south, but all I could smell was dry, dusty. Still... I might get some rain. If I did die today, at least it was the kind of day I liked.

Stretching to my full height, my escorts' hands slid down to my elbows, and I threw my head back, breathing deeply. Either I'd join Noah today, or I wouldn't. I looked forward to finding out which it would be.

I spotted snipers on the rooftops, a number of guards both around the square and creating a corridor to the platform, armed with rifles, and a set of stands that contained quite a few Steve, these ones very dignified. Moon Moon joined Larry in leading our little parade through the hordes of civilians in the square, the little shit now sporting a new red armband.

It was a surprisingly long walk to the platform with its stake stabbing into the sky, but the new grass was velvety under my toes. Even the brown grass had softened with the turning of the season.

People surrounded us on all sides, only held back by Steve. They jostled back and forth, unable to stay still, looking decidedly unhappy. I nodded slowly. From the looks of them, it wouldn't take much to make them spook. Finally, the mob mentality could be useful to me.

Steve marched me across the grass to the platform. From there, Larry and Moon Moon peeled off to go to the stands. Larry climbed them, taking a seat next to a silver-haired soldier, while Moon Moon stayed on the ground in a parade rest, hands behind his back.

The guards followed me onto the platform, taking up position around the edges, facing outward, while I was pulled around, forced to face the stands, my back to the post. From my new height, I spotted several women in the stands. Two were in uniform and obviously Asian, so I assumed they were part of the entourage, but the rest wore civilian clothes in light, form fitting dresses.

Apparently, I rated high enough on the entertainment list that even these women were forced to attend my execution. Or this was just the norm. Fuck if I know.

One Steve detached himself and stood slightly to the side, facing the stands. Producing a paper from his inner pocket, he opened it, reading in English.

"The prisoner, known as Ghost Captain, stands before the governor of this territory..."

Eyes widened around the square, more faces turning towards me. Whispers rushed through the gathering, fingers pointing. Children were lifted high. In the stands, Larry smiled, flicking his fingers in a little wave.

"Captured by Major Kam Jeong Gwon through diligence and hard work, Ghost Captain is accused of—"

"Since when is the Ghost Captain a woman?" one soul, made brave by anonymity, shouted.

Ignoring him, Steve continued, "Resisting the free, fair, and just rule of the Liberated States of America..."

I squinted, sure I heard him wrong. Free and fair? Since when? Because if someone has to tell you they're free and fair, I could point straight to a hypocrite and a liar. The next crime caught my attention.

"Inciting the people to violence." Okay, I had to give them that one. "Kidnapping patrols in the performance of their duties." I never kidnapped anyone!

"Murder of said patrols." Is it murder when my life is on the line?

"Contravening the Geneva Conventions in her treatment of prisoners of war."

I stared at the man, mouth open. The Geneva Convention? *I'm* breaking the Geneva Convention? I didn't know they even knew what that was, considering their behavior. Hell, I barely knew what it was.

"Hey!" a heckler shouted. "Are you sure this chick is the Ghost Captain? She looks kinda lame to me!"

In the stands, Larry looked irritated, shifting in his seat, tugging my jacket down. Sniggering, I looked back at the man reading my crimes in time to hear my sentence.

"She is sentenced to execution by burning at the stake! Let this be—"

"What am I, a witch?" I asked, unable to contain myself any longer. I was proud. I'd managed to hold my tongue for the entire reading.

"Silence!" One of my guards backhanded me across the face, making me stumble.

Straightening slowly, I reached up, wiping away a trickle of blood from my eye. His eyes widened at my hands, the cuffs dangling from one finger.

I grinned and punched him.

It would've been the perfect moment for a snarky retort, I mourned, even as I kicked my other guard's knee. Something crunched against the side of my foot, and he howled, the knee buckling under him. Spinning, I laughed. I'd even had the perfect line picked out but saying it would've ruined the surprise.

Snatching up a baton, I flicked it open, striking three fast blows to the man on my left. Head, belly, knee. He folded like an accordion. From the stands, Larry screamed for them to shoot me, but the Fresnans stirred, incited by the violence before them. Some Steve around the edge of the platform came to deal with me while the rest watched the crowd warily.

Dancing around, I spun, avoiding a grasping hand. Ducking, I came up forehead first. A nose crunched, the man reeled back, squealing and holding his nose. Vaguely, I heard Larry shouting, and more Steve headed in my direction. Across the square, small fights broke out, the civilians pushing back.

Good for them.

Shoving Steve off the platform, I stole his gun, ripping it from his hand as he fell. Spinning on my heel, I locked eyes with a soldier, his rifle already raised. I crouched, ready to charge, but Steve fell, blood spraying. The boom reached me a moment later.

Whipping around, I searched the rooftops. I knew that gun. There! To the east, the rising sun a glow at her back. Phoenix. I whooped. Spinning, I took in the square. Irregulars were seeded throughout the crowd, helping the civilians get a little of their own back. All the snipers on the rooftops were mine.

Taking three fast steps, I leaped, flipping off the platform, landing at a run. Elbowing my way through the crowd, I headed for the stands.

The fighting hadn't reached it yet, the soldiers on the ground enough to fend the mob off for now. As long as Larry and Moon Moon hadn't left yet, that's all I cared about.

Shoot a man, spin around another. I punched a man as I passed, giving his opponents, a middle-aged couple, the chance to close in. Trip this one, flying tackle at that one, and I rolled to a stop at the foot of the stands. Snarling, I scrambled to my feet, the two guards nearest me closing in. I fired point blank at one, but the gun clicked, the slide locking back.

Empty.

I crouched, flicking the baton and circling. One raised his gun, mouth open in a shout lost in the din. Charging, all I could see was the barrel of the gun, yawning wide. Ducking, I knocked the gun away. A palm strike to the chin and he collapsed at my feet. The other man was already down, his chest a mess.

Running, I leaped for the stage, grabbing the railing. A quick scramble and I stood on the stage. Two older men drew weapons. They fell first, by the snipers' hands. Others shouted for guards. The courtesans ran for the back of the stands, as far from me as they could get.

The two women in uniform squared off against me.

"I'm not here for you, or them," I said, waving to the old men. "I just want him." I nodded to Larry. "I'd rather you weren't killed."

"We will not die easily," one woman said, hand on the gun holstered at her side.

"I won't be the one doing it. But if you want to protect someone, protect them." I pointed to the women at the back.

"Them?" She laughed scornfully. "They are nothing, they are whores—"

She broke off, yelping when the other one hit her. "How dare you?" the second woman shouted in Korean. "They had no choice! My brother died trying to protect them, and you act like this?"

The second hit the first again. I edged around them as their fight escalated. It seemed like they had some things to work out.

"Larry!" I sang. "Oh, Larry! Where's my jacket, Larry," I snarled.

He stood, waiting for me. When I closed in, he shrugged my jacket off, tossing it over the back of a chair.

"Is that loser Moon Moon still around, or did he ditch you, too?"

His lip curled. Squaring off, he bent his knees, hands staying loose at his sides. Oh, this one would be a tough fight.

Good.

He closed in, fists, knees, and elbows coming from all directions. He was good. Really good. All I could do was block and deflect, trying not to let him hit me where it would really hurt. All his blows blended into the beating I'd gotten yesterday, disappearing under the adrenaline.

Slowly, I found his rhythm, until a chance blow caught my cheekbone. Shaking my head, blood and sweat flew.

"You are the Ghost Captain everyone is so afraid of?" he sneered, chest heaving with the effort of beating me up. "*You?* How do they even consider you a threat?"

I shrugged, struggling to catch my breath. "To be fair, I did start in Oregon. It's been a long few years. You shoulda seen me when I was fresh."

As if. If I'd met him in my first year, I'd be dead right now, but he didn't need to know that. I didn't need to think of it, either.

With a shout, he rushed in again, but this time, I knew him. Ducking the punch aimed at my head, I grabbed the knee he lifted and *heaved*. He went down with me on top. Scrambling to contain him, I levered myself up.

He thrashed a moment, then fell still, glaring murder at me. "Yeah, you never thought I could win by sitting on you, didja?" A drop of blood fell from my lip, landing on his white shirt. "Surrender now, and you can live. You kept your boys off me. I'll keep mine from killing you."

His lip curled. "I should have let Moon Moon dirty you when he asked."

"I'll take that as a no."

"Captain, you bitch!"

Moon Moon lay on the stairs, only his head and shoulders visible, pointing a gun straight at me. Larry twisted, sending me sprawling. A shot rang out. My free hand slapped my thigh, looking for a gun, but all I found was me.

Above me, Larry froze, his mouth open in a silent scream. He stayed there for long moments before toppling to the side.

Slowly, I rose. The blood drained from Moon Moon's face, and he scrambled to his feet. The fight surged behind him, and he nearly leaped the rest of the steps to land on the platform. I advanced on him, rolling my shoulders. My shirt sagged oddly, catching on my elbow. Without taking my eyes off the traitor, I pulled it off.

His eyes flicked down, over my scars and bruises, then stopped on my chest. Oh, yes, the leather bra. Or the jagged scar over my collarbone. Or the claw marks on my ribs. Baring my teeth, I rushed him. He raised the gun terror plain on his face. I went left in one long leap, then right, coming up against his arm. Knuckles out, I punched him in the throat, twice.

Moon Moon slowly sank to the ground, the gun falling from nerveless fingers, his other hand clutching his neck. Keeping an eye on him, I snagged my jacket off the chair, shrugging it on.

The strange scent on it sent a twisting pain through my heart. Even though I knew Noah's scent couldn't have stayed on the jacket for this long, I could pretend because he always smelled like leather. Now...

Taking a deep, shuddering breath, I grabbed Moon Moon's gun. He still struggled to breathe, but his movements had grown weaker.

"Hey, you!"

I turned when a strange woman shouted. The courtesans stopped well out of reach, watching me warily. One stood at the front, a tall woman with red hair. Most of the old men had fled, but I saw a couple lumps on the ground that I knew weren't by me and suspected weren't from the snipers, either.

"You really this Ghost Captain?" she asked.

I shrugged. "I'm Captain."

The women exchanged a look, then one nodded. The redhead squared her shoulders. "We'd like out of this shithole."

Looking around at the fighting, I shrugged. "I didn't plan this party, but I think you'll get your wish."

"Captain!" I knew that voice. Scanning the crowd, I found him. Gryphon fought his way through the mob, Chaos, Storm, and Sweetpea... Was that the Celt? "Captain!"

I punched the air. "Yo!" They headed in my direction, rolling inexorably over the Steve in their way. "Listen," I said to the women, "find a hiding place, stay there, don't move until this shit is done."

A brunette shook her head, her eyes going to the scars on my ribs. Oh, yeah. The cougar, years ago. "No way. We know how that goes. The men fight, then afterwards, the women are raped. Not doing that again."

The *again* made me cry inside, but I shook my head. "Not in my army. We win, that doesn't happen to women."

"How can you promise that?"

I indicated the fight. "Look at them. Really look."

Long seconds later, "They're *women?*"

Yes, look. Look at the ones who aren't here anymore. Look for those who have fallen... With difficulty, I pulled myself back to the present, spotting two familiar faces in the crush. "Nebula," I bellowed. "Ink! On me!"

The two bashers finished their fight, then made their way through the crush. While they fought, I gathered the women. "Lose anything that's easy to grab," I said. "High heels can go, too. Let's get these boots..."

They were squeamish at first, handling bodies, but soon they all had a good pair of boots on, and there were a lot of barefoot bodies on the stands. The bashers emerged from the morass by the time we were done.

"Captain!" Nebula cried, reaching a hand out. Taking it, I hauled her up, cupping the back of her head briefly. "Good to have you back. We could use you in this fight."

"Getting there," I said, giving Ink a hand. "These ladies need guards and safety. Can you do it?"

The women stared wide-eyed at the fighters. One tentatively touched Ink's weapon of choice, a baseball bat spattered in blood.

She grinned at the woman. "Sure thing. We'll get 'em out."

"Commandeer any fighters you need along the way, then get back in here," I said, examining the fighting below. "It's all hands on deck."

"Captain!" Saluting, Ink spun on the women. "Get your shit. Life just got a whole lot better."

"How would you know?" the redhead asked bitterly.

"Because several years ago, I was where you are, and Captain got me out, too."

"Go," I ordered. "Out now, talk later."

They herded the women towards the back of the stands, still relatively free of people. I hoped the snipers would keep an eye on them. Gryphon and company were stuck about thirty feet away from the stands, deep in a brawl.

I quickly checked the mag. Nearly full. Nearly full but nowhere near enough. *Noah...look for me.* I rubbed my cheek against the jacket, and again, that strange scent hit my nose. Snarling, edgy, I armed myself.

Baton in one hand, gun tucked into my pocket, I leaped over the railing, coming knees first onto a Steve raising his rifle. After whacking him around the head twice, I grabbed his rifle, rolling off.

Moving quickly through the fight, I gave my handgun to a man just throwing his into a soldier's face. Startled, he took it. I handed the rifle to the woman next to him. A group of Steve worked in concert, herding civilians together. They did their best, but unarmed, they were outmatched.

Barreling into one, I spun, ducked, stole a gun, shot a couple more. When I finished, a line of Steve lay in a neat circle around them. Several civvies stared at me. My jacket hung open, giving them plenty to look at.

"You—you're really the Ghost Captain?" A pasty-faced man stared at me, unable to get past the scars.

I squinted. "You're the heckler!" He shrank in on himself. "Don't worry about it. And call me Captain." I waved at Gryphon, who adjusted course.

"Piece of advice? Take all their weapons and keep moving. Get some place safe and stay put!" I shouted, running to reach my friends.

"Well, shit, Captain." Gryph grinned. "You hardly needed any help. I'm not sure why we bothered hurrying."

"Nice bra!" Storm grinned.

"Nice bruises," Sweetpea added, giving me a quick once-over, making me wish I'd kept the damn shirt. It was a tattered mess, not like it covered anything, but still. Chaos grinned but looked resolutely away. Good man.

"Captain." The Celt grabbed my arm. "We need to talk ASAP."

"Good to see you, too. Can it wait?"

"Considering I had orders to talk to no one, I need someone else to know."

"Spill."

"We got intel from DC that Secretary of State Keller was in on the plans. Contacts there are looking to find proof and the full extent of her collaboration."

Fury roared through me, but I only jerked my head, telling her I'd heard. "Okay. New plan. We're taking the city back today."

Gryph nodded. "I like your plans. So simple."

Putting his index and thumb into his mouth, he let out a series of piercing whistles that carried over the fighting. It was repeated around the crowd, the fighters passing it on until I heard the deep boom of a drum.

"What the hell?" I stared around, trying to spot the source. A short beat, three long beats, a short beat... Dot, dash, dash, dash, dot, dash, dash... They were spelling *attack* with the drumbeats.

"It's something new Shrike decided to implement," Gryph said over his shoulder as the fighting increased.

They formed a circle around me, occasionally firing, often engaging in hand to hand. Steve became more erratic, panicked. The ground under us squelched with every step.

"You'll need these." Storm threw her backpack at me. It clanked when it landed. The handle of my machete protruded from the top. "Sorry we didn't bring you any moccasins. Weren't expecting them to take those."

"No worries." Shedding my jacket, I strapped my guns on, hands moving automatically. Red pooled around my knee where it rested on the grass. At the bottom of the bag, I found a knife. Nice.

A scream rent the air. "Mama!"

My head whipped around. "Kid!"

The call was repeated. Grabbing the rest of the gear and my jacket, we raced to find the source. Swinging the bag at random uniformed heads, I stayed on Gryph's tail.

"Kid!" Storm called.

We converged on her and once more, they formed a circle around me and the kid, a little girl around eight. She screamed, blood running from a cut on her head, her hands clasped in front of her. No sign of a woman, either on the ground or on her feet. There was a chance her mom still lived.

"Hey. Hey." Heart pounding, I brushed the girl's hair back from her face, digging through Storm's pack with my other hand. The kid flung herself against me, still crying. "Need a hand! Kid's got a cut."

Storm broke away, kneeling next to us. While I calmed the kid, she grabbed a bandage from a pocket, quickly wrapping the kid's head. The little girl sniffled and moaned, hands pressed to her mouth, eyes rolling, uncontrolled shivers running over her tiny frame.

"Here, little one," I whispered. "It's okay, we'll find your mom." *Maybe.* "You'll be okay, sweetheart, just stay in the middle and we'll take care of you. Keep her in the middle." I shouted to be heard over the fight.

Wrapping my jacket around her, I threaded her hands into the sleeves. It nearly reached the ground, but when she hugged herself, she calmed noticeably. Snot ran down her nose. Fishing a spare cloth out of the pocket, I wiped it away, mesmerized by the simple, maternal gesture.

My heart spasmed. Gasping, I bent over. Brown haired, brown eyed, she could never be mistaken for mine and Noah's, but with his jacket slung over her shoulders... I could clearly see one of the twins wearing it, laughing, Noah ruffling his light hair.

Groaning, I clutched my chest, my heart feeling like I'd taken a knife.

I'd never have that. Never see him play with the boys, never watch him carry them on his shoulders, teach them to climb a tree or drive a car. I'd never have a daughter with him, see him teach her self-defense, how to recognize a good man from a bad one, never...

Never, never, never echoed through my head. All the things I'd never have with the only man I'd ever love.

The drum thrummed in my blood. *Never, never, never. Never see his smile, never hold him in my arms, never taste his kiss... Never, never, never. Betrayal took him from me. Betrayal nearly took me from my children. Never, never, never.*

Above me, they shouted to each other, a jumbled mess of questions. I heard nothing but my own loss welling to the surface again, as fresh as the day I lost him. Pressing my fists to the ground, I screamed into the muddy earth. It ripped from my heart, building since the day I'd buried my lover. Rising, I drew the machete. Stepping between the fighters, I left the safety of the circle.

Chaos shouted, put a hand on my arm, but I shook him off. The Irregulars fell back, surprised. Screaming again, I charged, wielding the machete like the avenging angel he'd once been.

CHAPTER 20

Fresno, CA – Faith

Faith kept a wary eye on her cousin in the aftermath of the battle, and she wasn't the only one. She'd stayed on the edges with the Resistance members less inclined to fight, setting up barricades to keep the NKs contained or assisting with the wounded until they could be seen by a healer, but even they knew what Captain had done.

The four days since the plaza battle hadn't been enough to reassure anyone about her. Those closest to Captain remained on guard. They insulated her from the rest of the forces, relaying orders and only bringing a few people to her at a time. And Eleanor, their den mother, never left Captain's side.

Some of the Resistance muttered resentfully when she was near, and part of Faith couldn't blame them. She'd gone berserk. Faith had gotten one glimpse, and the sight of it would haunt her to her death, she was sure.

Captain, wearing only cut-off cargo pants and a bra, had charged into the melee, teeth bared, hair flying. She slid and spun through the fight, screaming wildly, her companions running to keep up. They weren't even fighting, just shouting and waving at the others. Irregulars scrambled to get out of her way, pulling the civilians and Resistance members with them.

Though none of them lost their lives at her hands, several had been wounded and two would carry the scars with them for the rest of their lives. Everybody knew she'd apologized, but she gave no reason for why she'd lost her mind.

"Faith. Faith!"

Faith jerked, reflexively squeezing the damp cloth in her hands. Her mom walked over, blue eyes worried. "Are you okay, honey?" she asked, brushing Faith's hair back from her face.

Faith nodded, throwing her cloth into the bucket of water. "Yeah, mom. Sorry. I just got...distracted." Better to keep it vague than admit how Captain's mental stability worried her.

The wounded were being moved indoors, and Faith had joined the legions of cleaners. It was dull, thankless work, but it kept her out of her cousin's path while she tried to sort through complicated feelings.

She'd saved their lives, given herself up for their sakes. She'd been her best friend, and the memories wouldn't leave. But she killed people indiscriminately. She had limited remorse for her actions and felt no need to explain herself to others.

And so Faith went, round and round.

"Here." Abigail took the bucket from Faith. "Go outside, get some air. Now," she said sternly when Faith would have protested. "Go find Lucas or something."

Shoulders slumped in defeat, Faith obeyed. It was a big city. What were the chances she'd accidentally run across Captain?

One hundred percent, she thought glumly. She'd gotten twenty steps from the old hospital when Captain emerged from the tents currently containing the wounded. As always, she had Gryphon, Phoenix, Eleanor,

Storm, and Sweetpea with her. Often, she'd be accompanied by Dereva, the beautiful driver, and her little brother, Anansi, though today, the youngsters were absent.

A small cavalcade of vehicles, navigating their way through broken streets and buildings, caught her attention. They pulled up in front of Captain and the first one out was the driver, Dereva. Then, two men emerged, heading straight for Captain.

"Stretch," she said, her hands reaching for him. "It's good to see you." But her lips never smiled. Faith had seen her smile once or twice, but since the battle, nothing.

The fighters pressed their foreheads together, the tall man tilting his head down to meet hers. Faith edged closer, mingling with the growing crowd, pulled in by curiosity.

"What brings you here?" Captain asked.

"Them." He gestured to the vehicles, where a party of four waited to be acknowledged. At their head, an older woman, somewhere in her late forties or early fifties with gray-streaked brown hair, watched their exchange.

She walked with the easy step of a hiker, her back slightly curved as if she frequently carried a heavy pack. Pausing a few steps from Captain, she nodded warily.

Captain examined the woman. Faith wondered what she saw. Did she still see the person, or did she only see a threat assessment?

"I guess I have you to thank for all the supplies them Outsiders kept sending north." The stranger broke the silence first, her voice rough, hard.

Captain nodded once, sharply, as if she'd come to some conclusion. "Guess I have you to thank for those things not reaching the Valley. You from Jefferson?"

The woman raised her eyebrows, nodding slightly. "You know of us?"

"Please. I'm from Oregon, not SoCal. Don't insult me."

The stranger held out her hand, smiling slightly. "Name's Catherine Rose, though if we're not fighting, then folks call me Rosie."

Captain clasped her arm. "Captain."

"Your lot went right through our mountains, never found us. Not that good, are you?"

Captain bared her teeth in a parody of a smile. To give Rosie her due, she almost managed to hide her flinch. "We weren't looking for you. Was looking for Steve. Found plenty of them."

They stared at each other for an interminable time, Rosie clenching her jaw as if to keep something back.

Maybe Captain had pity on her. Maybe she had other things to do, for she broke the silence. "I have no fight with you, nor interest in your home. All we need is to move freely through the mountains."

"We ain't stopped you yet. We don't want no trouble. All we want's to be left alone. Do no harm, take no shit."

The rebel leader nodded. "I respect that. Me and mine will leave yours alone. If any of my people cause you trouble, I will personally rain hellfire down on them. However, if your lot harms or hinders any of mine, or betrays us to the enemy, I will return to your mountains, and this time, I'll be hunting *you*."

Rosie took a long look around at the heavily armed fighters moving casually through the crowds, the wounded being slowly moved into the hospital, and at the vehicles they arrived in.

She swallowed. "Fair enough."

That exchange seemed enough for the stranger, because they left shortly after. Stretch and his husband, Gameboy, took those who wouldn't recover in time for the next fight north.

Faith turned away, but Captain spoke, this time to them. "Listen up," she shouted. "Spread the word. In a week, we're clearing out. Those people who want to join us, talk to them."

Captain pointed. Several people raised their hands, including quite a few Chapter leaders. Eleanor moved to stand with them. "We will be set up in the hospital's lobby every day until we leave. If you ask to join the fighters, be warned you will be physically tested to ensure you're capable."

Faith slid out of the crowd, looking for Lucas. Only a week until they left, and she really needed a new pair of shoes. Hers had given up the ghost.

***

Washington, DC – Constance

"I've got it!" Constance bolted upright, papers flying around her. "I know how we can check!"

"How?" James's tousled head appeared from the far side of the couch. "I've gone over everything a million times, but I can't put either of them at the Keller residence at the time of the recording."

After the initial shock of finding a series of phone taps from the Keller residence, they'd been stumped on how to prove the Secretary of State, Annaliese Keller, was there. And while the second person had never been named, once they had the meat of the recordings, they knew the other person *had* to be her son, Arnold.

Except they couldn't find definitive proof either of them were at their Virginia home at the time.

"I've even checked the charge stations," James continued.

Constance smiled, pushing her hair back. "Not charge stations. *Gas stations.*" He looked confused, so she continued. "A lot of people don't know it, but the government cars are still gas. They're more reliable in case something happens to the infrastructure. What if they were driving gas cars?"

"Hell yes!" James scrambled directly over the back of the couch, arriving at the laptop right before her. Then stopped. "We can't get into CCTV feeds from here."

"They can track it?"

He nodded, then snapped his fingers. "We'll hit up a café. If we keep things down to twenty minutes at a time, we should be able to stay just ahead of anyone hunting us."

***

James shoved her into the doorway, pressing her against the wall, watching the sidewalk. Constance clutched his jacket with trembling fingers, panting. She'd only just accessed the CCTV when James shut the laptop, saying they had to leave.

They ran out the back door as the bell jangled. She caught a glimpse of a dark suit just before the door shut behind her.

"Are they still there?" She tried squirming around to see, but James pinned her to the wall.

"Don't move," he murmured, his lips next to her ear. "I don't think they know it's us checking the footage. Just...don't move." That last came out on a growl, waking her senses up.

Suddenly aware of *him,* Constance's breath hitched, her hands relaxing against him. She splayed her fingers across his chest, flexing her fingertips, feeling his heartbeat thundering under her palms. His hand slid from her arm to her hip, the laptop bag landing gently on the ground.

"We can't," he whispered huskily. "We definitely have people behind us."

"Mmmmm 'kay." She arched her back, pressing herself against him. She loved the unfocused look in his hazel eyes. Normally unflappable, this was the vaguest she'd ever seen him. "What should we do about that?"

"Best thing is to make them not see us."

"Nobody likes looking at PDA." Tipping her head back, her nose brushed his cheek.

"True." His eyes flicked to glance over her shoulder. "They're on their way."

"Then let's disappear."

His mouth captured hers, one hand rising to cup her head. His fingers tangled in her hair, tugging slightly. Moaning, she hooked the fingers of one hand into his belt, tugging, trying to bring him closer. Flicking her tongue against his lip, she smiled when his breath paused.

He kissed her until she didn't know where his breath ended and hers began. The stars could fall from the sky, and she'd only pull him closer. She kissed him until her entire life shifted on its axis, making room for two.

Eventually, he lifted his head slightly, his hot breath washing across her lips. "I think, um, they've gone."

Closing her eyes, Constance leaned her head against the cool bricks. *Calm down. Calm down,* she told herself. *Think cold thoughts. Winter. Snow. Cold breezes. Ice cream.*

Her eyes popped open. "We still need a café," she hissed.

His lips, those oh-so-talented lips, curved. "You remembered?"

She giggled. "Oh, my God. I can't believe I forgot!" He smiled wider, satisfaction oozing off him. She smacked his chest. "Stop being smug! We have to...have to..." She sighed, those kisses still in the forefront of her mind. "Keep going?"

He rested his forehead against hers. "You're right. Of course, you're right. Okay, I can do this," he said to himself.

Taking a deep breath, he straightened. She bit her tongue on a protest. Grabbing his hand before her resolve failed, she pulled him out of the doorway and immediately shivered. Had it been this cold before? Two seconds ago she'd been steaming!

"Come on," she said. "Café. Now. We need that intel."

***

Hacienda Heights, CA – Mercy

Sighing, Mercy shook her head. She finally knew why no one ever really challenged the Masters. These idiots were all too busy arguing over petty shit while the Kingdom Come to bloody Earth continued sending out raids and capturing people.

She sat on the roof of the house Emery's people used, watching Ashton argue with some random bloke about territory. If it involved water, she could understand, but this was literally just about boundaries?

A footstep alerted her to another's presence. Emery's head appeared over the edge of the roof. "There you are. Ashton wants us to prep for that raid next week. See what you need so we know what we have to find and all that."

She continued watching the argument below. All anyone wanted from her was her ability to heal. Better than with the Masters, since no one tried forcing her to bed, but why should she go into danger for these people?

"Mercy?"

"What happens if I don't want to go?" she asked finally. "What if I'm tired of treating people who are injured because of their own stupidity?"

There was a long pause. "Listen," Emery said carefully. "I know you were treated badly by Kozlov. But nobody's bothered you since you've been here, you know? Ashton does that. He makes sure the men don't touch the women. He protects us. All we have to do is help out a little."

"What if I'd rather leave?"

The other woman shook her head, her fingertips white on the roof. "You're a healer. A good one. Do you know how rare that is?"

Silently, Mercy rose to her feet. Implicit in Emery's words was the threat: *Do as you're told or be thrown to the wolves. Do as you're told or else.*

At the edge, she twisted awkwardly to step down onto the railing. Emery held up a hand to help her. Taking it just long enough to get her feet on the ground, she let go.

"You said it's better here," she said when she came level with Emery. "It's not. It's just that it's harder to see the bars."

"We all have to do what's necessary to survive."

Mercy snorted. "What a load of bullshit."

***

Bakersfield, CA – Captain

"Aanisah." I held my hands out to the saboteur. "*Assalamu Alaikum.* Why didn't you stick around after my rescue?"

Leaning down, I pressed my forehead to hers, her headscarf providing some padding. She laughed quietly.

"*Wa Alaikum Assalam.* A truckload of officers was attempting to escape. We caught them before they got anywhere."

I led her to my tent. With augmentations from Fresno, we'd managed to surround nearly half the city. Our camps lay closer to the frontlines, while the Resistance kept a fifty-foot gap between us. The camp was a hive of activity, trucks going in and out, usually returning with boxes that were set up on our southern edges, closest to the Irregulars.

Saboteurs mingled with the fighters, exchanging stories of the last two weeks while the Resistance kept their distance. *As well they should,* I thought darkly, after the shit four of the Chapter leaders just tried to pull.

The coming fight steadied me. Or maybe I'd become addicted to the feeling. I didn't know anymore, and I was afraid of the answer.

At my tent, I gestured for her to sit, settling cross-legged on the ground next to her. We watched the bustling city, tiny figures rushing back and forth. Bakersfield had the best defenses I'd seen so far. They'd dug in, completely cleared and leveled the ground, and now they were arming.

We couldn't see what happened within the outer boundary, but we could see all the fun, oversized weapons they assembled just outside their fence.

"Where are we going next?" Aanisah asked.

"Whoa." I huffed a small laugh. Reaching inside the tent—barely more than two tarps, a couple walking sticks, and some guy lines—I fished out a couple cans of peaches. "Put your feet up, sit a moment." I handed her one of the cans.

"You know we are ready to go," she said, cracking the can open just enough to drink the juice.

"Trust me, where we're heading, you're gonna want a couple days break. Besides, can we not take care of the city in front of us first?"

Shrugging, she reclined on her pack. "Fine. Be that way. Would you like to know the easy way into Bakersfield?"

"Captain!" Eleanor called before I could answer.

I waved.

"Aanisah, my love." Eleanor smiled at the saboteur. "We have some halal meat for you—we found someone to say the prayers over the steer first—so don't go anywhere without stocking up."

Aanisah's face lit up, then she and Eleanor exchanged greetings. "Thank you."

"Now." Eleanor rounded on me, hands on her hips. "What have I told you about being nice?"

"When wasn't I nice?" I protested.

She stared at me levelly. I wracked my brains. I hadn't threatened or shot anyone since the last battle. Except for…

"Oh," I said.

"Yes. *Oh*. They've been harassing me."

"What happened?" Aanisah looked between us, highly entertained.

"They tried to talk battle strategies with her, and she ignored them."

"I didn't ignore them," I protested. "I told them they're fucking idiots and then left."

Eleanor closed her eyes, taking a deep breath through her nose. "Captain—"

"It was justified." Tugging my pack over, I used it as a pillow and laid down. Recounting this would piss me off, and laying down, I'd look like less of a threat to them. "Murray and Weeks wanted to sneak inside and get the civilians out."

"Well, that's good."

"Ah." I held up a hand. "That's not all. While they're being sneaky, they wanted us to drive over there," I pointed to Bakersfield, with its tanks, howitzers, mortars, and more that I couldn't identify, "with guns blazing as both a distraction *and* the main form of attack."

Aanisah stared at me, mouth hanging open.

"Wait." Eleanor shook her head, wiggling a finger in her ear. "They want us to what?"

"Oh, you heard me right." They'd asked to speak to me in private, then took me to a tent filled with the other Chapter leaders. They'd offered me a seat—making me the only person sitting down—and hovered over me. I'm not positive, but I think they were trying to intimidate me physically. Which didn't make any sense. When I said no, Weeks got in my face, yelling.

So, I punched him in the balls.

The memory of it made my hands clench. How many more did they want to die? And it would be us doing the dying, if we followed their plan.

"But that's...that's..." Their plan still hadn't sunk in for Eleanor.

"The stupidest fucking thing I've ever heard, yes. Which is what I told them."

Eleanor sank down, graceful even when stunned, leaning her elbows on her knees. "It's...I mean, I thought we were finally coming together as a whole. Why would they lie about this?"

"Because they don't want to admit they're stupid?" Aanisah suggested.

"It's okay." I patted Eleanor's shoulder. "Aanisah knows how to get in, then we can do things our way."

Phoenix walked past just in time to hear my comment. Grinning, she punched the air. "I love our way! Beats the hell out of what they want to do. Some of the fucking dumbest shit I've ever heard," she added under her breath. "Which buildings are we bringing down first?"

"We'll need some of those Resistance people. Duran and Nixon, plus Faith."

"Ooh." Phoenix winced. "She doesn't like you much these days."

She'd noticed too, huh? Faith wouldn't talk to me, though she'd been ready to go when it was time. "She doesn't have to like me, she just has to point to some things on a map."

"Really?" Aanisah and Phoenix said in unison, devilry in their eyes.

Shaking her head, Eleanor rose to her feet. "If we're planning, I'll get the rest of the table."

"Poor Eleanor." Phoenix watched her walk away. "She so desperately wants us to act like decent human beings."

"Too bad it's so much easier being an asshole."

***

I followed closely behind Duran, one of the two Resistance leaders from Bakersfield. She led a small group of us, fifteen fighters and five insurgents, down narrow alleys towards a major road.

In the distance, flashes lit up the sky, the ground trembling beneath us. We'd been coming and going from Bakersfield for the last week, retrieving civilians. Most of them hid underground, anxious to keep their loved ones as far from the fight as possible. Others, pressed into service, ran supplies and ammunition to the perimeter.

Duran and Nixon had been invaluable, first connecting us to the Bakersfield Chapters, then finding the civilians. The whole time, Gryph, Phoenix, and Anansi dropped enough mortars and shells to keep Steve busy, sure they were dealing with the main attack.

Tonight, we had a double objective: Evacuate the families of the collaborators, held in a protected hotel, and detonate the charges the saboteurs had been setting all week.

There'd been protests about the collaborators' families until Phoenix spoke up. "Captain is easily the biggest asshole here," she began. "I mean, I could tell you all the terrible things she's done, but..."

Whispers raced through the crowd at the speed of sound, and I winced.

"I'm sure you've heard all the stories and then some," she continued. "The acid one is the worst *I've* seen," fucking whispers picked up a notch, damn her, "but if even *she* won't leave people in there, how bad does it make you that you want to?"

Closing my eyes, I'd tipped my face skyward, hoping to hide the tears. Had I gone so far there was no turning back? I clenched my teeth. My only hope was that I'd see Noah again after I died, but the way Phoenix sounded, I'd passed the point of no return.

But people settled, and actually voted in favor of rescuing those particular families, so...yay. It's not like we could retrieve several hundred people all by our onesies. Okay, we probably could, but it would be easier with their cooperation.

The past week had been an exodus of near biblical proportions, the fighters ensuring there were no Steve to raise the alarm while hundreds of people filed through the sewers and into an old, formerly walled-off storm drain to the outside world.

There were undoubtedly small pockets of people still inside, but Shrike said we couldn't wait too much longer. She had reports of Steve mobilizing in San Francisco, preparing to push back.

And why not? This was the longest we'd ever sat still outside the Lair.

My heart clenched at the thought of our mountain home, and for a moment, I hated the lowland air, the warmth, and the mass of humans I now had to deal with. More than that, I hated being so far from Noah.

Tingling heat rushed over me, every hair standing on end, and I relaxed. *I'm right here.* The words whispered over my skin. I closed my eyes, holding onto the sensation, aching for more but afraid what little I had would vanish.

Duran returned from her brief scout. "This is the only way to cross," she whispered. "Even the sewers don't reach where they are."

The ground rocked with the force of a mortar that reached farther than usual. On the street ahead, Steve scurried like ants. From here on out, Phoenix and Gryph would bombard the shit out of the city, using everything we'd brought from Fresno.

My kind of cluster fuck.

"How are we supposed to reach the targets now?" Storm breathed at my back.

I glanced at the sun's position. Just a finger above the horizon and closing fast on the coastal mountains. *I don't even know that range's name.* I'd been here how many times, and I didn't know their official name. Damn.

"All right, gather 'round, children." We huddled against the wall, staying low. "Weapons ready. We're spreading out, taking the clearest routes and meeting up at the hotel. I know we have grenades and fun stuff like that. We need at least one good throwing arm per group. Who knows this city like the back of their hands?" Every Resistance member's hand went up, as well as three of the Irregulars. "Good. We're taking them south. If we get split up, once you're outside, put a few miles between you and the city, then loop around.

"Duran, you've got point." She nodded. "Chaos?" He grinned, blue eyes dancing. "Concentrate on planting charges at every stop. Just...make sure we have enough time to bug out, yeah?"

"Sure, Captain." He opened his duffel, digging through it. "I've got all kinds of goodies." He pulled a small, T-shaped drill thing out of his pack.

I narrowed my eyes suspiciously. It looked familiar. "Is that an auger?" I demanded.

He nodded happily. "You never know when you might need one. Can we go now? I'd like to see my wife by dawn. She worries when she can't see me."

An invisible knife plunged into my heart. Why did the crazy man insist on following me? Because I'd get him out, if it was the last thing I did. "Armbands on, people!"

"Wait!" Duran reached for me, then thought better of it. "What will you be doing?"

Chaos snickered. "She's bait, decoy, whatever we need."

I nodded and continued. "And we'll need a working vehicle. Who can...?"

A Resistance man raised his hand. "I can get you one, Captain."

"Good."

"What do you want? A transport?"

I shook my head. "Something that can make shit go boom."

After tugging my red armband higher, I tucked a stray braid under my beanie and strode out of the alley and into the street, dodging vehicles as I went. *Walk with purpose*, that's what Lucas said to do. Act like you know what you're doing.

Fake it 'til you make it, Kitten's voice whispered in my ear. *Act confident, even when you're not.* I caught glimpses of the others, dashing through traffic and avoiding Steve and Dorothy—the *real* red armbands.

"Hey, you!" Dorothy shouted, pointing in my direction.

Catching Storm's eye, I jerked my head, motioning her on. "Yessir!" I threw a half-hearted salute, turning slightly to keep an eye on my people.

"Aren't you an eager one? You must be new." Trailing off, he looked at me again and whistled. "Where did you get that eye, kid?" He involuntarily raised his hand before dropping it.

"Fight. Sir. You wanted me for something?" I prompted when he kept staring. The last small group was nearly through and...yes! They were free. Time to ditch Dorothy.

"Uh. Yeah." He looked down at the board he carried, flipping through papers. "You're a big motherfucker and you look like someone I wouldn't want to meet in a dark alley." I grinned, which didn't reassure him. "You're with me. We're on guard detail for Colonel Park Soon Jee."

A colonel, huh? That might come in useful to us. My smile widened. He began sweating. "My name's Clemens, and from here on out, you answer..." He cleared his throat. "You answer to me. What's your name, kid?"

I bit back the first name that sprang to mind, Peter, and settled on the second. "Bill." Nice and generic.

"Well, Bill, our boys are watching the perimeter while the soldiers have actual bodyguard duty. You don't have to do anything except shout if those crazy rebels make it through."

"Oh, I can do that. Sir." I struggled to contain my laughter. "Why are we guarding him? Isn't he, like, the guy commanding this place?"

Clemens gave me an odd look. "Don't be ridiculous. And didn't they tell you in training not to ask questions?"

Don't ask questions? They're specifically instructed not to ask questions? I wish I'd known this sooner. The shit we could've caused if we just knew that all you had to do was look authoritative...

"You're armed, right?" Clemens apparently didn't like silence. I motioned to the visible weapons I carried. He stared at me a moment too long. "Odd choice. What were you, guarding farms? Oh, yeah, I bet you got lots of clean pussy out there." He nodded to himself, motioning for me to follow. "Yeah, in here, the gooks get the best women, but we still do okay, especially if you find one a little younger..."

Clenching my hands and breathing deeply, I dropped back a little. To my left, Storm appeared briefly in an alley. I gave her a thumbs up and she disappeared as quietly as she arrived. This colonel got more interesting all the time. Just ahead, Steve and Dorothy milled around each other.

Game time.

***

I gently lowered Dorothy to the trash-covered ground behind a dumpster, panting lightly. After kicking some of it over him, I went hunting for the next one. We were half a mile into this shit show, and this was the third perimeter guard down.

Jogging silently, I headed for my next target. They fell quietly, leaving Clemens for last. They'd been joking, talkative men, but every 'joke' left an increasingly bad taste in my mouth. Now…I slid around the last corner, Clemens's labored breathing drawing nearer.

There were no heroes in this lot, each one jockeying for rearguard, deemed safest because it was closest to a large concentration of Steve. Apparently, they didn't expect us to come from that direction. After we'd been shown the route, Clemens gave me the lead, the position least coveted. I guess they thought we'd walk into trouble.

Clemens reached my position. I hauled him onto a side street and into a recessed doorway before he could squeal. By the time his mouth opened, he was on the ground, and I knelt on his chest. He struggled, but I could tell he only had experience with opponents weaker than himself.

"Who the fuck are you?" he gasped.

Pulling my beanie off, my battle braids fell around my face. Grunting and wheezing, he writhed, but I had him where he couldn't move. Pressing harder against his throat, I watched his eyes bulge.

"Who are you?"

Readjusting to stay centered, I leaned harder. "If you'd just talked like a decent human being, I might've let you live. If you hadn't been so happy talking about little girls, I might've put your presence here down to desperation. But you were just so happy telling me filthy, hurtful 'jokes.'"

His face darkened. "Who…you?"

"They call me Captain."

His eyes widened, realization hitting him, but it was too late. I gave a short, hard push. He jerked, heels drumming on the ground, then lay still. I waited for a minute, fingers against his neck to make sure he was truly dead, then went after the one who really interested me. Park Soon Jee.

I closed in on Steve when the first explosion rocked the ground. To the south, flames lit the sky and a cloud of dust and smoke rose into the air. The small party angled north, the soldiers shouting for their perimeter guard, but no one answered.

They picked up speed. Another explosion, quickly followed by another, only ratcheted their anxiety higher. Park Soon Jee's purpose became ever more interesting. Why were they running away?

I'd learned that a commander stayed with his men to the bitter end. It was the only thing I admired about Steve, so why was this colonel running from a fight? Where were they heading?

Okay, that last question didn't matter too much in the moment. I couldn't guess, so I couldn't ambush them. Fine. Stretching into a full run, I closed in from the rear. A building a block ahead crumbled, the sounds lost in the ruckus.

They slowed and I plowed into the group, bowling two over before they knew what hit them. Spin, stomp, slash, kick... These ones fought with ferocity and skill. I laughed. Maybe tonight would finally be the death of me.

Except... The people truly responsible were still free.

Howling, I kicked a man in the knee. Something crunched and he dropped, screaming. Two soldiers teamed up, attacking me from either side. Frantically, I went back and forth, blocking with no time to strike back. I backed a step, then another, constantly shifting so neither could get through. Until a large shape barreled into the man on my right, carrying him away.

Chaos. I'd know that fighting style anywhere.

Quickly finishing off the remaining man, I spun. The only ones still standing were the three of us. Me, Chaos, and Park Soon Jee. He stared at me, frozen, one hand resting on his weapon. My machete kissed the skin of his neck, a thin line of blood running from the cut.

Chaos relieved him of his weapons, finding a knife in the small of his back and a small gun in an ankle holster. Nice.

"Careful one, aren't you? I like that." No answer. Guess Colonel Park didn't feel like talking.

Chaos zip-tied his hands together, then led him towards the fence. Best to get out now, before the other half of the city fell down. Hopefully the others were out already.

"Hey." I tugged on Park's bound hands. "Do you speak English?"

He remained silent. Fine. Sung Ki could have him.

We broke into a fast walk. "Okay, Chaos. Why are you here instead of helping get those people out of the city like you're supposed to?"

He snorted. "It's my turn. Besides, Storm, Duran, and the other Irregulars are more than competent enough to get them out."

"Your turn for what?" I demanded.

Park Soon Jee slowed. Chaos gave him a little push. "What? My turn? I don't know why I said that. That's ridiculous..."

I glared at him. By this point, we were so used to operating in occupied cities we could avoid patrols and have a full-blown conversation, because without a signal, we stopped at the corner, took a quick peek, and waited for the patrol to run past with hardly a pause.

"Spill."

His mouth worked. Finally, he slumped. "Listen, it was a promise we made, okay? We had to keep it." I punched his arm, hard. "Ow!" He rubbed it.

"Get to the point!"

"Gryphon, Archangel, and I all promised each other we'd look after the other's woman if anything happened, okay?" My heart stuttered at hearing Noah's name like that. Heat flared in the small of my back and I blinked back tears. Chaos didn't seem to notice. "So me and Gryph are just...trying to keep that promise. Though you don't make it fucking easy," he muttered. "And after you got your ass captured in Fresno, well, we decided we couldn't let you out of our sight again, but Gryph's needed on the frontlines, and then you wanted to go off on your own, and..."

"I get it," I said, my voice gone all husky. "I... Let's get out of here so I can yell at you two boneheads."

CHAPTER 21

Bakersfield, CA – Faith

Sitting on top of an old bridge crossing the freeway, Faith and Lucas watched bombs drop on Bakersfield. After a particularly large one, she clutched Lucas's hand, biting her lip.

"Are we sure this is the best way to go?" she asked.

He laced their fingers together, resting them on his leg. "I honestly don't know. Well," he amended, "it's better than what Carter said some of the Chapter leaders wanted to do."

"But...an entire city? Can we even rebuild this?"

He scooted closer, wrapping his arms around her. Resting her head against his shoulder, she tucked her hand inside his jacket, over his heart. His strong heartbeat reassured her. As long as she had moments like this, and those with her parents, life hadn't gotten too bad.

From the camp, a vehicle bounced over uneven roads, heading across country to them. Adjusting her position against Lucas's shoulder, she watched it come. She couldn't even tell what it used to be, it was so patched. Armor plating had been welded to its sides, and there was no reflection on its windows, so the glass was probably gone, too.

At the bottom of the bridge, the vehicle rolled to a stop and a young fighter, Sweetpea, hopped out, leaning her forearms on the roof. "Yo! Captain's back and she's brought a Steve! She wants you back ASAP."

Sighing, she clambered to her feet with Lucas's help. Heaven forbid anyone take too long to answer Captain's call.

"Which of us do you think she wants?" Lucas asked good-naturedly, tucking her hand into the crook of his elbow for the walk down the hill. "Because I doubt it's me. I don't think she likes me much."

Sweetpea practically danced in place, waiting for them. Faith rubbed her mouth to hide a smile. "I don't know what help I can be, either."

Once seated, Sweetpea revved the engine, flipping a U-turn and driving as quickly as was safe. Faith tried questioning the fighter, but either she was remarkably immune to interrogation tactics, or she really didn't know much.

Was this a prisoner? Don't know. A turncoat? She shrugged. Faith sat back, folding her arms across her chest, pouting. Lucas laughed, shoulders shaking, and patted her knee. She glared at him, eyes narrowed, but he only laughed harder.

They stopped in the space between the camps and were immediately met by several Chapter leaders. Four of them looked particularly irate. Her lip curled. She remembered these leaders. Effective enough during the occupation, they didn't take too kindly to the loss of their power and influence since the Irregulars' arrival.

"We *deserve* to know what's happening in that tent!" Weeks shouted before Lucas climbed out.

Turning, he bent, offering his hand to Faith with an exaggerated bow. Smiling, she took it, stepping out of the beat-up, armored vehicle like it was a limousine at a red-carpet event. He played bodyguard, gently moving her away from the aggressive Chapter leader and escorting her to Captain's tent.

He stepped back, holding the tent flap open. Smiling up at him, she lightly ran her fingers across his chest before she bent over, entering the low tent. He followed her, standing in an awkwardly bent position.

Faith half-expected to see an injured NK, or the entire Irregular command structure, but it was just Captain, cross-legged on the ground, facing an older NK, blindfolded, sitting with his back against the central pole.

She looked curiously around. She'd never been in here before. Captain's bedroll leaned against the corner, her backpack next to it, a couple boards were stacked on top of each other to one side, and that was it.

"Sung Ki's updating the maps with better targets for Gryph and Anansi," Captain said without turning. "So I need you to interrogate this fella, Colonel Park Soon Jee."

Faith walked around the NK, studying him. "Well, for a start, he's not a colonel."

"No?" Captain raised her eyebrows.

"He's a general." Faith hesitated. "How do you even know he speaks English? A lot of the higher ups don't."

Captain rose smoothly to her feet. "If he won't talk to you, I'll send Sung Ki in," she said, as if Faith hadn't spoken. "If he won't talk to her, then it's on to me. And I don't know interrogation shit at all. Mostly, once men end up in my hands, I start by cutting off their balls."

Park Soon Jee's thighs tensed, and a drop of sweat ran down his cheek. Captain smiled slowly. Chills ran down Faith's arms. How did someone smile so coldly?

"There." Satisfaction filled Captain's voice. "He does know English. And if you don't talk to her," she addressed him directly, "then you will be talking to me again."

***

Bakersfield, CA – Captain

I strode to the front, where the guns never stopped, Storm and Sweetpea in my wake. They bracketed our general, who walked quietly between them, hands bound in front of him.

"Phoenix!" I bellowed.

Those nearest pointed us south. I followed the line, walking behind a variety of weaponry that I couldn't even name. Bombs, rockets, mortars, whatever could hurl shit that went boom really fucking far away were lined up, keeping a steady rate of fire on Bakersfield. Smoke lay thick on the ground, swirling and eddying in a slight breeze.

Not that it mattered. Steve simply retreated further into the city, out of our reach. Even the destruction we'd caused in there last night hadn't stopped that. In order to root them out, we needed something different, and our general could provide it.

"Phoenix!"

"Yo." A slender figure emerged from the smoke. Phoenix wiped a hand over her cheek, smearing more dirt. "Whatcha got for me? More bombs?"

"Better."

"Bigger rockets?"

"Better." Her eyes narrowed and she folded her arms. Stepping aside, I swept my arm out dramatically. "We've got him."

She shrugged, glancing back, towards the city. "Who's he?"

"The guy who runs this entire shit show."

She froze, then turned slowly to face me. I grinned. So far, he hadn't divulged troop locations, but hopefully, someone would find Sung Ki soon and bring her here. Based on Shrike's intel, though, everyone had been recalled here and to San Francisco.

"Captain." I turned at Sung Ki's voice. "I heard you have captured a..." She stumbled to a halt, her face paling.

The general also turned, and he sank slowly to his knees. "Park Sung Ki?"

Sobbing, she rushed to him, flinging herself against him, wrapping her arms around his neck. I leaned down. "Did he say 'Park'?"

Phoenix nodded. "She's crying. I've never seen her cry like this."

Storm and Sweetpea turned to me. Storm lifted her hands, like *What now?* I shrugged. They were talking too fast for me to follow. Finally tired of standing, I sat cross-legged, waiting for them to finish. The gun crews tossed them curious glances but kept up a steady rate of fire.

"You know," Phoenix sat next to me, "we're gonna run out in a couple days."

"Maybe not. I mean, look at them. They obviously know each other. I was gonna give him the chance to surrender. Maybe this will make it easier?"

We studied the two, who finally moved apart. Ignoring Storm's protests, Sung Ki cut his bonds. When he tried to approach me, the fighters moved to block him, but Sung Ki held a hand out to stop them. I nodded, backing her.

The general knelt in front of me. I leaned back, looking between him and Sung Ki, but she nodded encouragingly and motioned for me to sit straight.

Sitting back on his heels, the general bowed low, touching his forehead to the ground. "I thank you," he said in heavily accented English. "She has told me how your people saved her. How you have always shown her dignity and respect."

"Um…You're welcome?"

Sitting up, he rested his hands on his knees. "She is my niece, my only remaining family. I was disgraced when they banished her. I thought her dead and have prayed for her nightly these last years. Now I know why I have always felt my prayers were unanswered."

"What we did, we would do for anyone in her position. We *have* done it."

"What I want to know," Phoenix butt in, "is did you know what happened to her and why she was banished?"

"Yes. It was the same reason for my disgrace. We protested the treatment of women. All those who did were made to disappear in some way."

"Then how did you become the man in charge?" I asked.

He smiled slightly. "You have killed everyone else."

"Fair. Does this mean you'll answer my questions?"

He studied me. "You are not as I imagined you." I raised my eyebrows. He smiled faintly. "I thought you would be a wild man, frothing at the mouth, killing everything in his path and calling it righteous."

"And what am I?" I regretted it as soon as the words slipped from my mouth.

"I believe you are every bit as bloody, but it is the blood of birth, of creating something from the ashes. You have control. Compassion. You surprise me. Ask your questions."

All thoughts of troop deployment or surrender vanished with that simple word. There was only one thing I wanted to know. "Who in our government helped you invade? We know you had help. The Chimeras—trucks—are too good. It was all too perfect."

"Ah." He nodded. "There were several. I do not know all their names, but my predecessors left papers—"

"No!" A strident voice interrupted us. "I have a right to know! We demand justice!"

Closing my eyes for a moment, I pinched the bridge of my nose. God-damn Resistance. When I finally looked, Weeks and Murray, closely followed by the other two troublemakers, Lindsey and Hatfield, were stopped by a few fighters.

I motioned for them to let the Resistance through. Carter came along after them, waving his hands apologetically.

"We *demand* you hand this man over to us," Murray shouted, gesticulating wildly. "He should be tried and executed for what he did to the citizens of California."

"Nah."

The four kept walking purposefully forward, confident in themselves. I stepped between them and the general, folding my arms. They stopped abruptly an arm's length away.

"I said move!" Murray screamed, spittle flying from his lips.

"No." I examined my nails. Hmm, a lot of dirt under there and...was that some blood?

"What do you mean, 'no'?" Murray asked slowly.

"Ooh." I rubbed my jaw, shaking my head. "If you don't know what 'no' means, you probably shouldn't be around people. Understanding consent is crucial to a healthy society."

The fighters, circled around us, laughed openly at the four of them. Sung Ki pulled her uncle back a little, giving me some room. These four shifted, suddenly aware it was just them against an army.

"Oh, don't worry." I waved my hand. "My people won't interfere in anything. They just want a good view."

Sure enough, Dereva magically appeared in the middle, pad of paper and pen in hand, scribbling away while fighters shifted and swirled around her.

"Still." Hatfield shifted. Her fingers flexed and clenched at her sides. "That man, whoever he is, should be handed over to us. We, the people, will bring him to justice."

My lip curled. "Get fucked."

To my surprise, Lindsey charged first, the woman's fists coming in a rapid combo. Stepping back and sideways, I gave her a little nudge, sending her flying into the dust.

The other three charged together, surrounding me in a brawl. I laughed. This was a basher's paradise. Sidestep, elbow, turn, lunge, stomp, kick… Lindsey regained her feet and ran straight in. I kicked her in the kneecap. I kept this up until I cleared just enough space to palm both thigh guns. I'm sure to the Resistance, it looked like the guns magically appeared in their faces.

Weeks stood directly in front of me, Lindsey on the ground behind him, holding her knee, tears of pain sliding down her face. Hatfield and Murray slowly raised their hands.

Weeks opened his mouth. "I think—"

Wrong. I kicked him in the balls, dropping him where he stood. Murray winced, sagging at the knees, one hand dropping a few inches before he remembered the gun.

General Park stepped into my field of vision. "I think," he said, "that I can resolve this. On behalf of the North Korean Liberation army, I surrender. To her." He pointed at me.

I smiled at Murray and Hatfield. "Game over, bitches."

***

General Park Soon Jee was as good as his word.

We didn't have to fire another shot against the North Korean army. Per his request, he dealt with those rapists we knew of himself, often consulting Sung Ki. I didn't stick around for the sentencing. Instead, I was too busy in meetings.

With Shrike, General Park organized removing Steve from the state, pulling slowly back to San Francisco, where they boarded ships. This time, their departure didn't hurt so much. We hadn't lost anyone in the Bakersfield fight, and the civilian casualties remained low.

For the first time, I had a chance for a good sit-down with the Celt. Park Soon Jee gave us the paperwork he'd mentioned. I took his word it was everything he had. I don't know, I liked the old man. Plus, Sung Ki vouched for him.

The paperwork seemed to confirm what Grace's DC contact said: The Secretary of State, Annaliese Keller, was definitely involved, if not a mastermind behind this whole shit show. But why?

And Grace. I couldn't quite believe my little sister was still alive, healthy, and happily married to Charlie.

"What took you so long to get down here?" I asked the Celt.

She scratched her cheek, glaring. "Listen, Seahorse *told* me not to talk to anyone, and she said to stay low. So, I went through eastern Oregon. And you know those homesteaders?"

I nodded. A lot of the freed people wanted space and to make their own decisions. Some opted to stay in the Willamette Valley and take up farming. Others took animals to the eastern side, where grazing was good. Being remote, Amana and Lavender immediately planned markets in Sisters, where each side could trade goods, food, animals, whatever.

God, it sounded so tranquil compared to this.

"Well, they all wanted to feed me, okay? But then I didn't want to eat all their food, so I helped them with some hunting. And then I twisted my stupid ankle when I was on the PCT somewhere in northern California. So that took a while."

"Fair, Celt, fair. Just so long as the trip was quiet."

"Yeah, no Steve." She fiddled with one of the beads in her hair. "What next? I mean, are we done?"

I shook my head. "No. Spread the word. We still have LA."

And I could give Aanisah orders to move out.

***

Diamond Bar, CA – Mercy

Mercy eyed the man working a short distance away. Emery helped her lift the bucket. The water was high this year, or so she'd been told. And ever since her little conversation with Emery, she'd never been left wholly alone. They didn't try to talk to her, but someone could see her at all times.

Stretching her back, she surveyed the mountains around them, brown now, but soon to get a little bit of green with the coming winter. But here, near the river, tall grasses waved in the breeze.

"Everybody used to fight over this area." Emery moved to stand next to her. "After the third year, they sat down and worked out an agreement that no one group could control it, but they could all use it."

She spoke in such a gentle, coaxing way. *As if she wants me to see the differences between them and the Masters,* Mercy thought sardonically. *Fuck those bastards.*

"I need to look for some herbs and plants," was all she said. Picking up her pack, she headed away from the people, examining the ground. She carried a little digging tool in her belt, made for her by one of her earliest patients. Yes, many of them were very sweet, but that didn't change the fact that she couldn't leave if she wanted to.

Wrapping the roots in a small sack, she stowed it in her bag, and moved on. "Plantain, plantain," she murmured. Catching a glimpse of a man staying twenty feet behind, she snorted, and her litany changed. "Fuck off, go away, disappear, leave me alone... Plantain!"

She found the low-growing plant amongst the grasses near a small gully. Kneeling, she dug through it, taking only a portion of the plants. Crawling along, she stubbornly ignored her tail.

The shrubs just ahead rustled and she froze. Was it an animal? She didn't want to draw attention to it if it was. Those idiots would probably trample all her precious plants if they thought a rabbit or deer hid here.

Until the grasses parted and a pair of dark eyes and a shaved head looked out at her from the shadows. The woman put a finger to her lips, motioning Mercy closer. Mesmerized, she slowly worked her way over. Upon closer inspection, she realized the woman hadn't shaved her head. Instead, she wore a dark hijab.

The woman smiled at her, eyes sparkling. *"Assalamu Alaikum,"* she whispered. "I see you have a tail, and you don't seem happy about it. Want me to take care of that for you?"

"Take care of it?" Mercy put two fingers on her neck, checking her own pulse. Normal. Her hands were steady, no nosebleeds, so probably not high. The woman still watched her. Giving herself over to this unlikely hallucination, Mercy shrugged. "How?"

The woman held up a huge knife, the blade also darkened. "He won't even know what hit him," she promised.

Mercy choked on a laugh. Then, a new idea hit her, and she pinched herself. Nope, it hurt, so she wasn't asleep. "Who are you? Why on earth would you make an offer like that?"

The hijabi woman shrugged. "My name is Aanisah, and once, someone did the same favor for me. Is he hurting you? I can make it stop."

"No!" Startled, Mercy glanced over her shoulder, but her tail didn't seem to notice anything odd. "He's not hurting me. They're...surprisingly okay. They just won't let me leave."

"Why?"

She hesitated, but something about this woman... "I'm a healer, and there's not many of us around who don't kill half our patients."

Why had she told Aanisah that? Now this woman might want to kidnap her. Although something about Aanisah's direct and nonchalant behavior said Mercy would enjoy it more. She might even have...fun?

But Aanisah seemed to have other things on her mind. "Do you want to stay with them?"

"Not forever, that's for bloody sure." Aanisah raised her eyebrows, so Mercy tried to explain. "They really are safer than where I was, and it's okay, but I've had enough of being told where to go and what to do. I want to make my own decisions, but not if it means they'll get hurt. But you'd never be able to take them on by yourself."

Aanisah laughed silently. "Who said I am alone? My Captain follows me and will be here soon. I am merely the scout, *Alhamdulillah*."

Mercy wrapped some plants in a bag, then began filling another with more leaves. "Can you explain? I understood all those words, but not their order."

Aanisah settled down under her bush, resting her chin on her hands. "Yes, the potential for freedom can be terrifying after so long in captivity.

It makes it difficult to imagine any other way of life. I am an advance scout for an army, and they will be here soon to help those who need it. And to punish those who earned it."

"Where is this army from? How have we not heard anything about it?" Even if Ashton wouldn't tell her much, Emery was very open with information. If a new group had formed, maybe they would have the ability to take on the Kingdom.

But Aanisah shook her head. "It's not safe to tell you more. But soon, before the next dark of the moon, they will be here. I would help you in any way I can."

Now Mercy snorted. By the next dark moon? That was...she tapped her fingers on her leg, counting. About a month away. "How could you help me?"

"Tell me your name and where I can find you again. I will bring my Captain and the army, and you can take your freedom."

Mercy chewed her lip. This was, without a doubt, the weirdest conversation she'd had in her entire life, including all the times she'd spouted religious nonsense at the Masters. She'd already been more open with this woman than she'd been with anyone except Jonathan.

Fuck it.

She carefully explained where to find Ashton's compound, assured Aanisah one more time that she was safe, and despite how carefully she watched, she couldn't see how the woman managed to leave the shelter of the bush without alerting everyone to her presence.

By the time she rejoined the rest of the group, she almost thought she'd imagined the entire interaction. Probably nothing would come from it. Pity. She kind of liked the woman.

CHAPTER 22

Grapevine, CA – Captain

The tiny cluster of gas stations and fast food joints lay at the bottom of the hills, behind us. At the base of the hill, I folded my arms.

"Is it just me, or are these roads shittier than usual?"

Chaos stepped up next to me. "Nope. They spent years putting rebar into these so they could withstand tanks, so... This is what roads that are deliberately bombed look like."

"Just checking."

The scouts ran ahead, climbing the uneven, rocky slopes with the agility of mountain goats. Assholes. I wanted to take a nap just looking at it.

"Oh, come on." Doc nudged me. "Don't tell me you're getting old?"

"Shut up. Dereva?"

"Captain?" She looked up at me, her bright blue eyes startling against her dark skin.

"I'd like a few people to camp here. I have no idea how long we'll be, but if we bring people out of there," I nodded to the hills surrounding LA, "I doubt anyone's gonna want to walk all the way to Bakersfield, even if we now have water along the way."

I squinted at the sky. Just last week, we'd had three days of solid rain. Now, it was warm, with clear blue skies. Pushing my sunglasses farther up my nose, I flipped the sun off and turned my attention back to the road.

I sighed. "We might as well get on with it."

Splitting into multiple small groups so we wouldn't overwhelm what water sources were up there, we spread into the hills.

***

"Why did I want to come again?" Shrike asked the air. She leaned on River, panting.

I stacked my hands behind my head, pacing in small circles. That last hill had been no joke. I hadn't realized how little I'd been walking these last months. "Because despite your protests, you're actually as crazy as the rest of us."

"I must be. God! Make it stop." Fanning herself with her wide-brimmed hat, she allowed River to lower her to the ground.

"Make sure you drink plenty of water," Doc ordered, suiting action to words.

"You know," Chaos leaped down from the rock he used as a vantage point, "according to the Californians, this is a cold fall."

"Get the fuck out." River stripped off her long sleeve shirt. "These people have no idea what cold is."

"Yo!" Storm shouted from above. She and Sweetpea raced down the slope, adroitly avoiding thorny bushes. "We found a big-ass fence."

"Not a fence," Sweetpea argued. "It's like...shipping containers, as far as the eye can see."

"Stacked on top of each other," Storm finished. "Like a fucking fence."

"Harder to get through, though."

"Girls," Eleanor reproved. "Fence, barrier, why don't you just tell us about it?"

Breathing hard, they paced, cooling down. Once they could speak without needing to catch their breath, they started again.

"Just over this ridge, there's a big fucking fence," Storm said, pointing. "Sure, maybe they're kind of like shipping containers, but twice as high. Can't tell how thick. The barrier is solid."

"I can't tell how the hell they put them down," Sweetpea added. "Like, maybe helicopters? But that would still be a whole lot, because as far as we could see, it's unbroken."

"It's pointless to speculate how they did it," I pointed out. "But they did have help from our government. Who knows what kind of false orders might have been given? What I'd like to know is, are there any roads up there? Anything that makes it look like it's been or is being patrolled?"

"None," Storm said firmly. Sweetpea confirmed.

"And last we heard, there's electricity there, because they're live streaming the city's cameras," I mused. "I wonder who's keeping that whole thing working?"

"Well..." Chaos shifted. I raised my eyebrows. "The army may have been testing some new equipment. A buddy of mine worked on the city a few years ago. It was just the basics, so that if the power grid ever went out, they could still keep an eye on everything from a central control room. Um, it looks like their experiment worked?"

"What does that matter?" Eleanor interjected.

"I just want to know if we're gonna go against some small army." I paced the narrow space. Above and below, scrubby grass covered the ground, interspersed with bushes. Most everything was dry and dusty, but I vaguely remembered this area being used for cattle.

They had to have water somewhere.

"Could they electrify the fence?" Shrike asked. "If the army set it up so that the cameras never run out, is it possible to add that barrier onto it?"

Chaos shrugged.

"You said you couldn't see how thick the barrier is, right?" I asked the scouts. They nodded. "It touches the ground?" More nods. "It's not electrified, otherwise the whole thing would be shorting out."

Shrike opened her mouth again, but I shook my head. "Trust me. Now, how about we go see the nice fence for ourselves?"

The sun passed its zenith by the time we made it to the barrier. We stood in a row, craning our heads back to see the top. Roughly twenty-five feet tall, the barrier was a boring gray that showed signs of weathering. Small patches of rust bloomed in some areas. I estimated it'd break down in about two hundred years. Yep, not waiting around for that.

Chaos groaned. "I'm on the bottom, aren't I?"

"Yep." I stretched my neck and shoulders. "And I'm next. River, you've got the top."

Eleanor and Shrike watched anxiously as we prepared. Doc grumbled and dug through her pack, pulling out a small pot I suspected contained a muscle ointment. Those who weren't wearing them put on moccasins, and all of us ditched our packs. After knotting every rope together, River coiled it and slung it across her body.

Picking a small rise, Chaos braced his hands against the barrier and set himself, setting one foot on a rock to give us a step. I climbed his body first, making sure my feet were as close to his neck as possible. When Storm stood on my shoulders, she did the same. Sweetpea's chest nearly touched the barrier, we all leaned into it so much.

I could feel the moment River gained the top of the barrier. A weight lifted. Then another, when she gave Sweetpea a hand up. The rope hit my arm, then Storm's weight disappeared as she walked up the wall. I leaped down, tucking and rolling. When I came to a stop, I stayed on my back, shifting just enough to get the rocks out and slowly working everything.

Doc tended Chaos first, rubbing the ointment into his neck and shoulders. Even at this distance, the smell of it made my eyes water. "What is that?" I asked.

"You don't want to know." Grimly, Doc headed for me. "Your turn."

"I think I might prefer to—"

"You don't get a choice."

Wincing, I sat up. Above us, the fighters chattered, excitedly calling information to each other.

"Look at this gully! They don't even need a fence here!"

"Hey! I think I see water over there!"

"Let's see how far the gully goes!"

After that last one, their feet pattered away, the scouts racing in each direction.

"I'm still here," River shouted. "I've got the rope anchored enough to get everyone up."

Doc's hands, firm yet gentle, rubbed the ointment into my back and shoulders, reaching under my bra straps, ensuring no muscles were neglected. "There." Sitting back on her heels, she wiped her hands on a rag. "We can use this to light a fire tonight." She handed it to me.

"You mean to tell me I'm flammable, now?"

"Yes, but you also won't have sore muscles tomorrow. You're welcome, princess."

"If you weren't so damn useful and sarcastic, I'd toss you out on your ass."

She just laughed. By the time the scouts returned, we'd all gained the top of the wall. About ten feet wide, the damn thing sounded hollow, but we weren't breaking into it anytime soon.

"We should go east. There's definitely water," Sweetpea reported.

"I saw Phoenix through my scope," Storm said. "They're all good."

"East it is."

The sun sank quickly below the horizon, but we had a little fire burning merrily in a circle of rocks. Doc was right, that rag worked wonders to get a fire going.

I laid back, using my pack as a pillow. Above me, the sky darkened, but the sun caught on a low-hanging cloud arching across the sky, feathering out at the ends. It looked like an outstretched wing, glowing golden.

The moment hung in the air. The quiet chatter from the others faded away, until it was just me and the golden angel's wing against a deep blue-black sky. My chest tightened and tears rose in my eyes, but I refused to blink. I would watch that cloud until it disappeared. I'd...

The light faded, and with it, the wing vanished, now looking like what it was: a cloud.

The tears spilled over, and even as I wiped them away, I didn't know why I cried. It was just a cloud. So what if it reminded me of an angel's wing? So what if Noah's name had been Archangel? So what...

Curling onto my side, I drew my knees to my chest and pulled the blanket over me, burying my head against my pack. A tiny warmth bloomed in my chest, an inexplicable heat spreading, but tonight, all it did was remind me of what I could no longer hold in my arms.

"Is she alright?" Shrike asked from the fire.

"Are any of us?" Eleanor replied gently. "She'll join us when she's ready."

When I'm ready, hah. I would never be fully ready.

***

Bakersfield, CA – Faith

Faith wandered through Bakersfield, hand in hand with Lucas, staring at the devastation. "Where do we even start?"

A horn blared behind them. She yelped when Lucas pulled her to the side of the street, just in time to see one of the Hummer-style vehicles roll past with a scraper attached to the front, one of the Irregulars in the driver's seat. It pushed bricks and concrete chunks ahead of itself, turning to the side and depositing the load against another broken building.

Pulling her closer, Lucas tucked her hand into the crook of his elbow. "One piece at a time, with what's right in front of us. Sacramento is coming along nicely. No reason we can't get Bakersfield cleared. Come on."

"Where are we going?" Laughing, she ran to keep up with his longer strides as he led her past the destruction to an overgrown parking lot.

Resistance members filled the space, talking quietly until a Chapter leader, Duran, climbed atop a vehicle slowly being swallowed by weeds.

"Can I have your attention!" she shouted, waving her hands. Slowly, people quieted, whispering and pointing to the other leaders. "We've separated the city into sections. We'll start with the least damaged areas with houses, then move to apartment complexes, then to the rest of the city. All those who are physically able are asked to join in the efforts. If not, we need more cooks and people to sort through supplies to see what we have and what we need.

"The Irregulars," people shifted uncomfortably at the mention of the fighters, "have already begun clearing the streets, bringing in livestock, and hunting."

Basically, Faith filled in, they're working their asses off for a place they didn't plan to stay in, so everyone else better step up.

Duran continued, "Come talk to any of us here," she indicated the leadership, "to find out where we're starting and what you can do to assist—"

"How much are those Irregulars gonna demand for helping us?" a man shouted.

Faith snorted softly. As if anyone had a use for money anymore. To the side, she saw a man kneeling, then moving around the group, holding a black box to his face. Her eyes widened. An old camera! She'd wanted one so bad when she was a kid, but her parents convinced her not to try, since finding that photo stuff, film, was impossible.

Except not. While she watched, his thumb moved constantly, pushing a little lever on top of the camera. Nudging Lucas, she pointed to the man. "Camera," she whispered, delighted.

"They haven't asked for anything." Carter climbed on top of the vehicle, standing next to Duran. "All they wanted was to make their home safer and see us free."

"Then why haven't they left yet?" another person yelled.

"Los Angeles." Carter folded his arms. "Have you heard anything from there since the invasion? No? And why do you think that is?"

"Who the hell knows?"

"And that's what Captain and the others have gone to find out!" he shouted. "Their job is fighting, but we're builders. We're trades and crafts-people. It's time we found our lives and purposes again!"

They cheered. Half-heartedly, yes, but still, a cheer.

"Come on." Faith tugged on Lucas. "Let's show them how it's done!"

Weaving through the crowd, they were near the front of the line. Carter greeted them with a smile, writing their names on a paper. "Good you see you two! Seems like I've hardly talked to you for weeks."

Faith smiled. "We've been busy."

"Yes. Oh." He looked up. "Have you seen Jon lately? I thought he'd gone up to Yosemite, but when folks up there came down, they said he hadn't been there."

They exchanged a look. Faith shook her head, Lucas shrugged. "Haven't seen him," he said.

Carter frowned. "I hope he's okay."

Malva nudged him with her elbow, her hands full of a box of gloves. "He's probably holed up in Sacramento with a woman. Remember three winters ago? You were pulling your hair out and he was playing house. Here, you two." She tossed two pairs of gloves at them. "You can follow that group."

Heading in the direction she indicated, Faith pulled on her gloves. "This will be new. I like it."

Tilting his head, Lucas examined her, his hazel eyes warm. "Construction worker looks good on you."

***

Los Angeles – Captain

We spread through the streets of LA while the sun slowly set. The light shone off dusty and broken glass, dead grass, and broken houses. To the south, skyscrapers loomed.

It hadn't been difficult finding everyone. We slowly gathered on our way in, finding two groups climbing on the rollercoasters of Magic Mountain, treating it like a giant playground. Which it was, but never like this.

Now, we were finally in the basin itself, somewhere off the I-5 freeway. I hadn't seen this much concrete in years. Signs were spray painted. Torn billboards fluttered in the breeze. Weeds and thorny plants grew through cracks in the concrete, but at the same time, it all looked...different to what we were used to.

The streets were full of weeds, yes, but they weren't torn up by tanks. There were signs of bullet holes, but they all looked ancient. And it was completely deserted. No people anywhere. There'd been no city this large farther north left unoccupied.

"I wonder if anybody is still alive." Phoenix said what I'd been thinking. Going by the murmurs from those around us, I wasn't the only one.

"They're still here." Shrike spoke confidently. "There may not be many, but there's still some here."

"How do you know?"

"Because people are like cockroaches. We're damn difficult to wipe out." Fair enough. "Now, all we need is to find someone to lead us to the barbarians."

"Aanisah is here with the saboteurs." I looked around at the fighters. Two hundred elected to come to LA, the rest helping with rebuilding or monitoring Steve's final departure. Sung Ki oversaw that lot, working with her uncle. "We just have to cause a little havoc and they'll find us."

"Havoc's already here," Chaos called, pointing to one of the fighters, a tall person who wore their black hair shaved on the sides with a thick braid starting at their crown and ending at their shoulder blades.

They gave me a quick glance. Black eyes. It was the eyes I remembered. Fierce, humorous, and batshit crazy. They wanted to *parachute* from the skyscrapers to ambush Steve in Fresno.

Hell to the fucking *no.*

Phoenix laughed. "We have Chaos, Mayhem, *and* Havoc? I don't know whether I need you to stop this shit or give me more."

Setting off at an easy lope, we headed south. Fighters all around were stopping and starting, readjusting bandoliers and magazines that jiggled as they ran. Phoenix had two crossing her chest, one for the Barrett rifle, one for her handguns.

I chose magazines, as always. Two in my cargo pockets, and a box of bullets in my backpack, on top of the water where it would be easy to reach. Without any idea what to expect, we'd come loaded for mountain lion.

Despite it being evening—and autumn—sweat trickled down my back. No fog here, no rain, no clouds. Hell on earth.

Until we passed a giant cactus, white blooms glowing in the evening light. I slowed, jogging closer for a better look. How any plant so spiny and dangerous produced such a lovely, delicate flower was beyond me. Pink dusted the center of the petals, following the curve around.

"Arch—" I stopped abruptly. The empty space beside me yawned wide, but my heart warmed. Here. He was here. Shaking, I ran to catch up with the others. No time for regrets tonight.

***

"Guys!" Phoenix hissed, waving. "Get a load of this!" She peeked around the corner of a house, laughter in her voice.

We hadn't found anyone the first night, and eventually bedded down around an office complex, but late on our second day, the scouts spotted a small party of roughly twenty-five people walking cautiously. Signposts said Glendale, wherever the hell that was.

We followed the group to a little residential area. By the time we arrived, the sun had set, but we had enough light to see this suburb was entirely stucco houses, the roofs mostly intact. Maybe because of the stucco and tiles, maybe another factor, but the next street over was decimated, while this one looked hardly touched by fire.

Phoenix hissed again, so I went low, crawling to see, while Gryph peered over her head. A small group of people entered a house, leaving two lookouts behind. They spoke too low to make out words, but loud enough I knew they talked.

Careless.

"What are they doing?" Behind us, Storm hovered, practically jumping.

"Looks like stealing." Phoenix shot her a grin.

She snickered. "I like this lot already."

One of the scouts, Legs, hustled over. "Captain," she whispered. "You need to see something."

Leaving the others to watch the small group, I followed Legs down a block. Before we reached the end, she dropped down, crawling on hands and toes behind a wall to where her battle partner, Mayhem, waited. Taking her lead, I did the same until she stopped and indicated I should look.

Raising myself just enough to see, I immediately spotted it. Or them, rather. A large group of men, maybe fifty in all, armed with spears and clubs, plus a few bows and arrows, walked boldly down the street. The route they took would bring them right to the looters.

Maybe LA wouldn't be boring after all.

Leaving the scouts to continue tracking the group, I headed back to our main forces. Whispered orders divided my forces, some encircling the entire area, others prepping for a fight. I had no idea who we might be fighting, but worst came to it, we would just end their skirmish.

I saw the exact moment the lookouts finally noticed the big group, right around the same time they were spotted. Shouting, the lookouts ducked into the house, then came back out again, all the people loaded with huge packs.

Too much to have been sitting here for years. Had this been a storehouse for someone? Meanwhile, the large group began yelling slogans or something, charging forward.

"For God!"

"The righteous will prevail!"

"God is with us!"

"Warriors of Light, attack!"

I scrunched my face at that last one, sticking a finger in my ear and wiggling it around. I had to have misheard them. Except someone shouted that thing about warriors and light again. Who the fuck gives themselves a pretentious name like 'Warriors of Light?'"

I squashed the urge to join the thieves' side on that principle alone.

One of the religious nutcases lit a torch, flinging it into the dead bushes. Apparently, not all the fires had been of natural causes.

The bushes burned, light flaring, revealing the entire scene. The thieves bunched together on the sidewalk, the fastest religious nutcases already engaging them.

My breath caught in my throat.

She was older, her hair hidden under a bandana, but there was no mistaking those cheekbones, or the shape of her face as she desperately turned to face the men, a small knife in one hand.

Mercy. The cousin I'd thought safely home in Australia all these years now stood less than a hundred feet from me.

Unbidden, I charged, bellowing. "Irregulars! On me."

At my shout, people from both sides paused. The slowest men turned to face me, desperately trying to form a line with their spears out, but I went at a dead run, straight for the center of their group.

Knocking the spear aside was laughably easy, and then I was in their midst. A knife came at me. Deflecting the angle with my arm, I followed through with a knee. What it hit, I didn't know and didn't care.

The Irregulars joined the fray moments after. It wasn't even a fight, over almost as soon as it began. Once they realized they were outmatched, the men flung down their weapons. The thieves did too, raising their hands.

"We were taking their things," a woman at the front explained. "We didn't touch any of your stuff, I promise."

"Hey!" A large man gently pushed her behind himself. "Who the fuck are you people? Are you from the south? I told Simmons what would happen if his people stepped foot onto our territory again…"

"I don't know any Simmons, and I couldn't give a fuck about him." Scanning the people, I spotted Mercy, kneeling next to an injured man. She appeared unharmed, but this close, I could see how gaunt she was. "Doc," I called without taking my eyes from her, "how are we?"

"We're fine." She stepped up next to me, Chaos a looming shadow behind her. "Barely a scratch."

"Would you help these folks? Some of them look pretty rough."

Gently touching my arm, she made her way over. The large man reached for her, growling. "I *said*, who the fuck—AH!"

He broke off, howling, when Chaos grabbed his wrist, twisting and spinning the man until he stood behind the stranger, one arm gripping the man's wrist, forcing it between his shoulder blades, the other holding a knife to his neck.

Leaning down slightly, I peered at the stranger's face. "Yeah, don't touch our doctor. Chaos don't like it. We don't, either, but he takes it more personal."

At my nod, Chaos let the man go with a little shove. He faced us, holding his arm and glaring resentfully. His people gathered around him, the woman who'd spoken first laying a hand on his chest. He shrugged her off, his lip curling.

She stiffened, then faced me slowly. "My name is Emery. Who are you, please?"

My eyebrows climbed my forehead. I hadn't heard someone this polite since...well, Eleanor, but if we ignored that...certainly not any of us.

"I mean," she continued, "I'd like to thank you, but it's hard to do when I don't know what to call you."

Behind me, the fighters dumped the bodies of the dead out of sight while others kept the living corralled, keeping the two groups separate. More fighters tried controlling the flames, but without water, it was a losing fight.

"We're the Oregonian Irregulars," I said. "I'm Captain."

Mercy's head shot up and she stared, but no one else flinched. How had she heard of me, and they hadn't?

"Oregon?" Emery asked. "This...you've had this in Oregon, too?"

"No. We've had our issues, but not this particular one. Eleanor!"

Laughing quietly, Eleanor wove through the fighters. "Those on perimeter are upset they missed the fight. Now," she surveyed the small group, "how badly did you do this time?"

"I did really good. No broken bones, and that one guy was Chaos, but he tried to grab Doc, so...let's call it 'self-inflicted.' Now, can you get them ready to move?"

Leaving Eleanor to give the introduction speech and get them walking, I went to Doc and Mercy, who kept giving me quick glances. She worked to sew a gash on the man's arm while Doc examined a man with a chunk of wood sticking out of his shoulder.

"How's it going?" I knelt beside them. "As in, can we go to a different location?"

"He'll be fine," Doc said. "She's good with a needle, and he," indicating her patient, "will need more time and light that isn't about to burn down a neighborhood."

"No problem."

"Captain!" Phoenix jogged up. "We should really move, everything here is kind of dry."

"Working on it. Send some scouts to find a building with most of its walls and ceilings, yeah? And if we find people, even better."

There was a long pause. "You want people we can fight, or people who are safe?"

I pondered that a moment, until Doc poked me. "Oh, people who are, uh, safe. Right?"

The group of thieves gathered their wounded and started off with Chaos at Doc's side. Gryph waved me over, pointing to a blinking red light on a garage, aimed right where our fight had been.

"Do you think they're watching?" Phoenix asked.

"Fucked if I know." I studied the camera and light set right above the garage door. "But if they are, we should say hi."

CHAPTER 23

Scan of phone conversations, DC area – July 8, 2065, 9:02pm
Man 1: There is no information on this Captain character whatsoever! She's
messaged me six times today!
Man 2: You better find something. With a name like Captain, I've heard
rumors he's military.

Washington, DC – Constance

Constance watched James over the paper she held in her hand, struggling to keep her lips together. He hung by his knees from a pull-up bar, hands behind his head, crunching upwards. Biting her lip, she watched the play of muscles across his stomach and chest and vehemently told herself she definitely *wasn't* remembering his kiss and the feel of his hands on her.

They carefully hadn't touched since then. She was afraid if they did, her entire ability to focus would go out the window. Not that she had much left, anyway. Apparently done, James grabbed the bar and unhooked his legs, slowly lowering them to the floor.

"I'm gonna jump in the shower," he called over his shoulder, unhooking the bar.

"Yeah, sure." She raised the paper higher until the door closed and the shower turned on.

Scanning the paper again, she remembered why she held it. Something about it bothered her, but she couldn't sort it out. It was like a logic problem, where you had to spot the one inconsistency in order to unravel the entire solution.

"We've got the first meeting at the Kellers." She ran over the information they did have out loud. It helped her think. "CCTV shows Arnold was in Richmond the night of the recording. But who the hell is this guy?"

She held a transcript of some lobbyist recorded talking to Bryce McKinney, her old boss, and he was deeper in the scheme than McKinney. She just couldn't identify him.

Frustrated, she blew out her breath, sitting back on the couch. Grabbing the remote, she flipped on the screen. Maybe a distraction would help clear her head.

Scrolling through the channels, it landed on a ruined suburb. LA TV never stopped rolling. The government *couldn't* stop it, no matter how hard they tried. Then the sharks controlling the upper echelons realized how much it fascinated their audiences and figured if they put it on every screen, people would watch it. And the money rolled into their pockets.

"Maybe one of them is this asshole," she muttered, glaring at the sheet of paper. "Those bastards have certainly profited from this."

On screen, one group flung a torch into a dry bush, and she shook her head. Another fire? And there were so many more of this lot than the people they were charging. It would be a slaughter. Just as she prepared to change the channel, not wanting to see the carnage, a new group entered their view.

These ones were different, but she couldn't quite put her finger on it.

The bathroom door opened. "James." She gave him a quick glance. He toweled his hair dry, fully dressed, thankfully. She didn't think she could handle more eye-candy today without spontaneously combusting. "There's a new group in the fight..." She trailed off. The fight had already ended.

A large man pointed out the camera, then a woman approached it. Tall and broad-shouldered, she looked moved like...not quite like James, more like the mixed martial artists she'd sometimes seen. Her long, blonde hair was done in a series of braids. The largest ran from her crown down her back, like a mohawk, with smaller ones on the sides. They slid and shifted over her leather jacket as she walked. A scar cut through her left eyebrow, just missing her eye and continued into her cheek. Her grim expression sent a frisson of fear down Constance's spine.

This was not a woman she wanted to meet in a dark alley. *This wasn't a woman you wanted to meet anywhere,* she amended.

The woman looked up, directly into the camera, as if she hadn't seen anything like this before. Then, her forbidding expression broke into an evil grin as she lifted her middle finger to the camera and walked away, like she didn't have a care in the world.

James laughed, startling her from her examination. He sank slowly to the floor, howling with laughter until someone pounded on the wall.

"Shut up!" their neighbor shouted.

Grabbing a pillow, he pulled it over his face, his body shaking. Constance leaned in cautiously, eyes wide. He'd laughed many times over the weeks they'd been living together, but she'd never seen anything like this from him.

"Goddamn it," he gasped, his arms flopping at his sides. "I can't believe that woman is still alive. Holy shit."

He stared at the screen with hungry eyes, still chuckling. This new group crossed in front of the camera, and Constance finally put her finger on it.

They were mostly women, and they all carried guns. The residents of LA stopped carrying firearms years ago, when the ammunition ran out.

The visuals jumped to the next camera, following these people, many of whom disappeared as they walked. Oh, a lot of people had to have tuned into this one, if the powers that controlled the screens were following them. She found herself constantly looking for the tall, scarred woman who walked at the back of the group, her head constantly turning.

"James, who is she?"

But James just kept muttering to himself.

"James!" Finally tearing his eyes from the screen, he sat up, facing her. "James, who is she?"

He shook himself. "That." He took a deep breath. "That is Captain."

***

Glendale, CA – Mercy

Mercy helped support Thomas, the man with a broken spear in his shoulder. Emery walked on his other side, casting baleful looks at Ashton.

"He didn't mean to hurt you," Mercy murmured.

Emery looked away. Ashton had shaken her off after that fighter twisted his arm. Mercy guessed embarrassment. He was used to being the big man around town, brokering deals and peace. Since she tended to like anyone who wouldn't allow a woman to be hurt, she liked the big fighter already.

But it was the name Captain that shook her. She'd put Aanisah out of her mind for, what? A full turning of the moon, half convinced she'd imagined the encounter, but now the very same person Aanisah mentioned rescued them?

And Captain was a woman? Her long hair, turned red by the firelight, cast shadows over her face, but Mercy could see well enough to tell the leader of the fighters was a woman. Aanisah hadn't mentioned that.

Thomas leaned heavily on her, and she cursed silently. He needed rest, she needed to get that spear out of his shoulder, but the fire continued raging behind them, forcing them on.

A broken piece of concrete rolled under Thomas's foot, and he fell into her. She gave a short cry, already crumbling under his weight, when suddenly, Captain was beside them, one hand shoving Thomas upright, the other wrapping around Mercy's upper arm in a hard grip.

As quickly as she appeared, she left, disappearing into the dark. Mercy stared after her, nose wrinkled. "What the bloody hell was that about?" she asked the air. "Why care if we stumble?"

"Because if you fall, you make noise." The voice drifted out of the dark, preceding a woman with blonde curls barely contained by braids and a scar down the entire side of her face.

If it wasn't for the scar, the Masters would have fought over who added her to his harem. Even with the scar, she was arresting, drawing the eye with the contrast between her beauty and obvious violence.

"Best to keep moving," the fighter added.

"Who are you?" Mercy asked.

"Storm."

"Storm? Really?" Emery peeked around Thomas at the woman. "Sorry, it's just...you don't look like a storm, you know?"

Storm nodded. "Yeah, I get that sometimes. Listen, keep walking. We're almost there."

"Where?" Mercy asked, but the fighter had already left.

"How do they do that?" Emery peered around them. "How many more are going to appear out of thin air?"

Ashton waited for them to catch up. "Stay quiet," he ordered. "We're too close to Kingdom territory. You don't want to draw their attention, do you?"

They fell silent. Mercy glared daggers at his back, but if he noticed, it didn't show. How dare he bring that up? She was closer to her worst nightmares than she'd been in weeks, and she couldn't go back again. If they attacked, she'd...

Wait. They were surrounded by fighters who'd handled the Warriors of Light like they were naughty children. Could she...ask them to deal with the Kingdom Come to Earth?

Maybe, but it'd be better if she talked to their leader.

Soon, they crossed a wide highway. On the other side, they were led to a shopping center, long since emptied of anything useful. Inside, they piled into the warehouse at the back. Immediately, the fighters began setting out a perimeter, pulling out cooking stoves, and getting fires lit.

Doc found her. "Let's get this man taken care of."

Working quickly, they boiled water, removed the bulk of the wood, then Doc pulled a magnifying glass from her pack. "Do you want to hold the glass or do the tweezing?"

Mercy elected to hold the glass. "Your knowledge of muscle structure is way better than mine."

"Oh, I don't know about that." Doc spoke absently. Her bodyguard stayed nearby, lighting a stove of his own and putting a pot of water on. "I've had more formal training, yes, but you have worlds of experience. Plus, your herbals and ointments game are as good as our herbalist's, and she also had formal training."

When they were done, the bodyguard offered first Doc, then Mercy, a pouch. She took a handful of what turned out to be dried meat and berries, all mixed together.

"Thank you," she said. "I...thanks."

"What is it?" Doc settled next to the big man, who immediately raised his arm for her to tuck herself against his side. Apparently, he was more than her bodyguard.

Mercy chewed her lip, unsure whether to trust them, but Doc's body language said she was completely at ease with this man. Blowing out a quick breath, she squared her shoulders. "I need to talk to your Captain. Do you know where I can find her?"

The couple exchanged a look before Doc shrugged. "She's watching the front. Just don't try sneaking up on her, okay?"

Odd request. Mercy hustled for the door, nearly running past Emery, who sat with other members of their group, Ashton nowhere in sight.

Poor thing. Ashton was nowhere near as good as Emery hoped.

Putting her friend from her mind, she hurried to the front. "Shit!" She couldn't see the rebel leader. Was it too much to hope she'd stay bloody put and be easy to find?

Walking quickly, she stepped lightly around broken glass. Rounding the corner, a hand seized her jacket, half lifting her off the ground. Snarling, she thrashed, clawing at the hand that held her, kicking wildly.

Slowly, soothing words drifted through her panic. "Easy, easy. You're safe. You're okay." Those hands that had grabbed her so roughly now gentled, setting her back on her feet, and running over her arms. "I didn't mean to scare you. You're okay."

She looked up, into Captain's light eyes, caught in a stray beam of the lowering moon. The light did nothing to soften her features, instead emphasizing the scars running over the left side of her face.

Her fear swiftly transformed into anger. "What the fuck d'you bloody think you're doing, scaring the shit out of innocent people?" she snapped. "Why'd you jump me like that? The fuck is wrong with you?"

The bloody woman huffed, her mouth quirking at the corners. "To be fair, you came sneaking around the corner and I fight constantly to survive, so…" Captain folded her arms. "What was so important you decided to follow me out here, anyway?"

The words tangled in Mercy's throat. How to ask? *I want you to attack the compound where I was enslaved. I want you to kill the men who took away my freedom. I want you to kill the men who've hurt so many. I want the chance to kill the man who raped me.*

What came out was, "I need your help."

Captain waited patiently. Mercy, so used to reading men, found her nearly inscrutable. Nearly. She had the sense the woman waited for something specific, but she didn't know what. Although, this close, with nothing to distract her, she seemed vaguely familiar.

Mercy shook off the feeling. "You protected us without knowing anything about us. Why?"

"Kinda figured the dudes who sounded like a bunch of religious fanatics were the bigger assholes." The leader sounded bored, but her body language was tight, her arms folded.

She narrowed her eyes. Something was definitely going on here, but she'd come too far to stop now. "What if I told you they're worse than you think? That they've enslaved hundreds of people and murdered more? That they've raped, tortured, and mutilated more people than I can remember?"

Captain tilted her head. "I'm listening."

"What if I could tell you where they are, and where they are within their compound?"

A slow, predatory smile spread across her face. "Now you're talking."

***

Mercy knelt with Captain on the roof of a six-story office building, the tallest in the area. Broken concrete had been piled against the walls below, clearing the road. This region, while not within the fences of the compound, was Kingdom territory and regularly patrolled.

She'd been through a few times as a field medic. Not often, but enough to know the compound lay directly north of them, just four blocks away. Overhead, the sun barely warmed her skin, though Captain had shed her leather jacket, leaving her in just a blue t-shirt, showing her impressive weaponry.

"Don't you find all those belt pouches a bit...in the way?" she asked, leaning back to see a canteen, a huge knife, and a smaller knife also attached.

"You get used to it," she replied absently, examining the area through her scope. "There." She handed over a smaller scope. "You can see the fence line."

Ignoring the proffered scope, Mercy studied her profile. The nagging feeling insisted she'd seen this woman before, but where? She hadn't been in LA this whole time. She couldn't picture any of this lot staying under the Masters' radar for this long, but Oregon seemed far-fetched.

The Masters tried sending men out, through the mountains. They always returned with less than they left with, and all of them talked of an unscalable wall.

"Do I know you from somewhere?" she finally asked, then closed her eyes, immediately regretting it.

The silence grew long enough that she reluctantly opened her eyes. Captain faced her fully, her cold gray-blue eyes stern, made harsher by the scars. Gritting her teeth, Mercy met that gaze, filled with sorrow, compassion, and a feral anger.

She'd lied to the Masters' faces. She'd quietly killed some of the worst of humanity, and helped women escape. Meeting this woman's gaze should be easy by comparison.

In broad daylight, she could make out individual features. Thick eyebrows, beautiful eyes, high cheekbones, a small, full mouth.... Captain wasn't pretty, had never been, but something about her...

Captain's lips quirked in a sardonic grin, and all the pieces crashed onto Mercy.

"Holy fuck me. Hope!" Words poured out in a jumble even she couldn't follow, while Hope simply sat there, waiting for her to calm down. Finally, "How the bloody hell are you so bloody chill?"

"Practice."

Mercy froze. "Who else?" she croaked.

"Faith."

Mercy slumped, relief coursing through her like cool water. She and Faith had always been closer. Except Hope wasn't finished.

"Uncle Dan, Aunt Abigail—though they haven't recognized me yet—and a few other people. Now." She shifted, sitting cross-legged. "How did you know my name?"

"Your name—oh. Captain." Mercy's hand went to her bandana, automatically ensuring her hair was covered. "I ran across someone. Aanisah. She mentioned you were coming."

Captain smiled. "I expect we'll see her again soon."

"So, you've...done this before? Planning...whatever this is?" She waved vaguely around.

Her smile broadened. "Oh, yeah. I'm *good* at this.

***

Mercy stared around, her mouth hanging open.

The compound *burned*.

Women and children, including the Mistresses, were brought out of the former hotel in small groups, guarded by fighters. Taken to the side, they were carefully corralled, ensuring the fight stayed well away from them. Amongst them, she saw a tiny girl with huge hazel eyes.

Susannah's daughter, safely held in a woman's arms. Tension flowed out of her. This one promise, then, she'd kept.

Mercy stood with Doc and the other medics, some of whom were also trained fighters. Occasionally, a person was brought to them and quickly treated.

Then there were the fighters, led by Captain. Mercy couldn't mistake her for anything other than a war leader. Certainly not her mischievous cousin who loved mechanics. No, the woman cutting through men like paper looked nothing like her cousin.

And yet, hope filled her chest. She'd finally be free of this place, never to worry about being recaptured, or forced back into slavery. Hope that she might finally heal a little.

Constantly, her attention was drawn back to the fight. Master Leister fell quickly. Mercy snorted. A fate too kind for such a cruel man. One by one, she watched the men who'd hurt, humiliated, and tormented her fall to the fighters.

The Warrior who enjoyed torturing the Bondmaids not in her Master's good graces, dead. The handsy Son of Judea, who loved touching the youngest women, dead. And the list grew. But amongst them, she didn't see her Master.

A man charged through the fight, laying about him with a heavy club. A fighter fell, clutching her arm. Another howled, their knee crumpling under them. It was Macey, the overseer. Who'd beaten, raped, and tortured at the Masters' commands and his own whims.

Following his direction, Mercy realized he made a beeline straight towards Hope.

She clutched Doc's arm. "Someone has to warn Captain! That man making his way to her? He's Macey, and he's the best. When they need a champion, they bring in Macey."

Doc followed her pointing finger. "Oh? He's a good fighter?" She tapped a medic on the shoulder. "Captain might have a live one, there. Spread the word and prep for more wounded." She turned away, grumbling something about snipers being unable to hit a fast-moving target in the melee.

Mercy wiggled a finger in her ear. "Wait. What?"

"Oh," Doc leaned in, "we like betting."

"Are you bloody nuts? Why the hell would you bet on whether she wins?" Mercy stared in horror at the woman. "I thought you people were all right. How can you be so heartless?"

Doc laughed. "We're not betting on whether she wins, we're betting on how fast she takes him down. I think she'll do it in..." She studied Macey, "Twenty moves."

Bets flew thick and fast, one young woman taking notes. More injured were brought in, and Hope faced off against Macey.

Mercy had no words for what happened. They traded blows, Hope slipping around him, narrowly avoiding being completely flattened by the huge man. Except he kept missing. She danced in and out, her blade flashing, leaving behind a red line every time.

"Dammit!" Doc slapped her thigh. "She's playing with him. I didn't even think of that."

Soon, Macey was covered in dozens of red lines. His blows slowed, became clumsy.

"She's bleeding him out," Mercy breathed.

"Did you tell her about that man?" Doc asked.

Numbly, she nodded. "I mentioned lots of men, though. I didn't think she'd remember this one."

Macey raised his club, but he never got a chance to bring it down. Maybe she was tired of the fight, maybe she felt she had more urgent things to do but, spinning her blade faster than Mercy could follow, Captain lopped off his head. The body remained upright for several seconds before slumping to the ground.

"Who the hell is she?"

"Honestly, no idea," Doc replied. Mercy hadn't realized she'd spoken out loud. "She kidnapped me from the hospital I'd been forced to work in, and I haven't looked back. She's clearly insane, has only three emotions, and is one of the best people I've ever met."

Once Macey fell, the fighting wrapped up quickly, the Warriors and Sons losing any heart for the fight. And the aftermath...there was none of the prolonged shouting and posturing, myriad injured, or hasty retreats she usually saw. Counting only ten injured—all of whom would recover, as long as they didn't get an infection—made this the most unusual battle she'd ever seen.

Captain's people were so far beyond the capabilities of anyone she'd seen here, it made Mercy's head spin. The fighters didn't seem to consider it anything more than a skirmish, though Ashton looked pale.

Good.

He wasn't a good man; he just wasn't as bad as the Masters.

"Why did I bring so much ammo?" the petite woman they called Phoenix complained. "I'd planned on having a lighter load for the walk out of here."

"I wouldn't worry about it too much, love." Mercy started at the British accent coming from the large, handsome, black-haired man with her. "I'm sure there's someone here who can give us a proper fight."

"At the very least, there's dealing with *them*." Phoenix pointed at the row of survivors, forced to kneel in the street while behind them, the emptied slave pens burned.

The big blond man, Doc's bodyguard and husband, raced away from the hotel the Masters had converted into their house.

"Get back!" he shouted, waving.

The fighters still within the compound followed him out, several laughing and turning to look at the building. At the far end, Mercy spotted her little herb garden. Making her way to the Bondmaids and Mistresses, she found Mary, her Master's current favorite.

"Mercy!" she gasped. "You're alive?"

"Yes, but my garden—"

"You slut!" Mistress Kozlov slapped her across the face, hard. "You brought these godless degenerates here?" *Slap.* The blow rocked her head. "You, accused of immorality and lewdness, dared come back and—"

Her hand raised again. Mercy clenched her teeth and closed her eyes, but the blow never fell. The women around her grew silent. When she opened them, Captain stood there, holding Mistress's hand.

"I am trying very hard to remember that you were in their grasp for probably a long time," Captain said. Mercy could tell it was definitely Captain by the barely controlled fury in her voice. "But the next time you raise your hand against her, or anyone else here, I will assume that's deliberate and not a result of deep conditioning."

"Bitch!" Mistress screamed.

"You just met me. How did you know?"

The other Mistresses formed behind her, and some of the Bondmaids. Mercy inched closer to her cousin. "What are you planning to do about them?" she whispered.

"Honestly," Captain muttered out of the side of her mouth, "I hadn't thought that far ahead. I also hadn't realized they'd be this brainwashed."

Before Mercy could apologize, a rumble started from the ground.

"Earthquake!" she called, the warning echoed by several others.

"Nope!" shouted the blond man. What had Doc called him? Ah, Chaos. "Not an earthquake! Fire in the hole!"

The fighters already knelt, hands over their ears, many with their eyes shut. Kneeling, she forgot to close her eyes. The hotel slowly caved in on itself, the concrete folding like sand. Dust billowed into the air, mingling with the smoke from the fires, blocking out the sun. The noise of it deafened her, even with her hands over her ears.

She remained kneeling for long moments after it was done, staring at the blank space where the building used to be. "Did you have to do that?"

"No. But it was awesome. Eleanor!"

Her head spinning, she saw the same older woman she'd met last night, who'd spoken so kindly to them as she'd given the barest explanation for all these heavily armed people, weaving through the crowd of fighters.

"Captain?"

"First off, I didn't do this. This," she waved at the women, "is entirely *their* fault." She pointed at the men still kneeling in the middle of the road. Several of them had fallen over from the explosion and were just struggling upright.

"Repent, sisters!" Mistress Kozlov screamed, throwing herself to her knees. "We have sinned against God and the Prophet. We must pray!"

Eleanor surveyed them. "Oh, dear."

Many of the women followed Mistress Kozlov's lead, but more just climbed to their feet, swaying and looking around themselves, blinking like they'd just woken from a deep sleep. Mistress Kozlov prayed loudly, her hands clasped before her, face raised to the sky.

"Yep." Captain folded her arms. "Are we even equipped to deal with this?"

"No."

"Will leaving those men alive help them at all?"

Eleanor looked troubled. Mercy lifted a finger. "Pardon, did you say 'leaving those men alive?' What else were you planning on doing with them?" Captain tapped a finger on the gun strapped to her thigh. Mercy swallowed. "Oh."

The women wailed louder.

"It's what we do with rapists and those who are a threat to the safety of women and children."

Eleanor absently rubbed a finger over her mouth. "There's so many more than usual," she finally said.

"So?"

"We've occasionally left them alive."

"As a warning and minus some parts."

"Exactly." She looked up at Captain while the women continued praying loudly. "What do you think those men would prefer? Dying here as martyrs, or living without the parts they've used to abuse women for years?"

"Captain!"

Mercy spun. She knew that voice! There! Aanisah walked jauntily through the fighters with a crew of hijabi women. Mercy smiled.

"*Assalamu Alaikum!*" Aanisah hailed her. "I told you my Captain would find you, didn't I?" She lightly patted Mercy's shoulder. "What about those assholes who wouldn't let you leave?"

Captain turned slowly to face Mercy, her face cold and forbidding. "Who wouldn't let you leave? Which assholes?"

"Um..." Briefly, Mercy considered staying quiet, but the waves of rage coming off the war leader changed her mind. She waved at Ashton's group. "Them. Because I'm a healer."

Captain's long legs covered the ground between her and Ashton in a heartbeat. With a heave, she pulled him closer, until they were nose to nose. "You kept a woman *prisoner*? Why shouldn't I throw you in with that lot?"

"No, please!" Emery pulled on her arm.

Rounding on Emery, Captain's eyes blazed. "Were you a part of it?"

"It was to keep her safe!" Emery cried. "I've been out, I've seen what people would do to each other. A healer in this world is the difference between life and death. Ashton was the safest choice for her."

Mercy started when Captain looked at her. "Did you feel safe? *Were you safe?*"

Ashton wrenched against her hand, and seemed surprised when Captain rocked but didn't let go. Turning her head slowly, she snarled. "Don't. Fucking. Move."

"Oh, my God," Mercy whispered. "She's gone full feral."

"Don't anybody move too fast," Eleanor said in a low, soothing voice, walking slowly to Captain.

"Eleanor," Captain ground out. "There's no need to try to manage me. I won't slaughter the lot."

"Maybe not," the older woman said in the same tone, "but you're frightening almost everyone."

"I'm not scared," Phoenix volunteered cheerfully, "but then again, *I* didn't imprison any women, so..." She shrugged, grinning.

"Mercy." At her name, Mercy looked into merciless eyes. "You choose the justice here. As the one wronged. What will happen to Ashton?"

"What?"

Ashton snatched at her wrist. "Mercy, tell her—"

"Shut up!" Captain snarled, shaking him.

Mercy saw the female fighters surround Ashton's people, including the psychotic short one, Phoenix. Everything hinged on her word?

Taking a deep breath, she let it out slowly. "They wouldn't let me leave, but I never felt unsafe with them. Actually, for the first time in years, I didn't worry about someone attacking me in my sleep."

Captain contemplated that as she turned to look at Ashton and his people. "*She* saved you." She shoved him away. "But I swear, if you give me or mine any trouble, I will end you."

Goosebumps ran down Mercy's arms. She could easily believe this woman capable of anything. No. Not anything. She'd never allow innocents to be harmed. But outside of that? Oh, yes.

The fighters slowly left, and Mercy shook her head, trying to regain her equilibrium. It'd all gone sideways so quickly.

"The devil is a woman!" shrieked Mistress Kozlov into the silence. "You are led by Satan's mistress!"

She closed her eyes. For a moment, she'd forgotten the woman's religious insanity. She understood it. Mistress had been under her Master's thumb for years before their world collapsed. She might never regain herself.

When she opened them, the Mistresses were being led away. Taking her arm, Captain led her quickly to the prisoners, drawing a knife from the small of her back.

"What's she doing?" she whispered to Aanisah, who followed on her heels.

"Not sure." The saboteur frowned. "Storm?"

The beautiful blonde woman with the scar down the side of her face moved to Mercy's other side. "She's meting out the only justice available to us."

The male fighters backed off, leaving women surrounding the men. Her Master lunged to his feet. Captain held out a hand, preventing a fighter from knocking him back down.

"How *dare* you?" Kozlov raged, spittle flying from his lips. "Demon! God curses you for this! You will be cast into the fire, where you will burn for eternity!"

"I thought I was a demon." Captain tipped her head, her tone casual. "If I go to hell, isn't that home? Seems like I should enjoy hell."

Her Master screamed.

"Oh, my God." Mercy swayed, drawing his attention.

"Bondmaid!" He rounded on her, but Captain stepped in front of him, preventing him from reaching her. Still, he coaxed. "You have returned. I will forgive the charges laid against you because you have come back. Now, come here." He crooked his finger. "Step away from these demons in human flesh and return to the fold, like a good girl."

Mercy stared, frozen, at his hand, extended towards her. Blood rushed from her head and her breath came short. Hands caught her arms, holding her upright.

"Captain," Storm said urgently, "do something."

"No," Mercy said at the same time.

Kozlov focused on her. "What?"

"No," she said, louder. "I'm staying right here."

Captain smiled, the corners of her eyes crinkling. "There you are."

Mercy's eyes cleared, and she looked up at her cousin. "Yes. I...I am." The corners of her lips curved in response.

"Bondmaid!" Kozlov screamed.

"My name is Mercy." Shaking, Storm and Aanisah still holding her arms, Mercy faced him, looking him in the eyes for the first time since she'd met him. "But you can't call me that. You don't get to call me anything."

Slowly, Mercy reached up, pulling her bandana off. She had no more reason to fear her Master.

Shrieking, he rushed her. Captain stuck her arm out, clotheslining him. Kozlov hit the ground hard, wheezing when he tried to catch his breath. The other men, Masters, Warriors, and Sons, shouted, but none made a move to stand in the face of the Irregulars' weapons.

Captain nodded slowly, kneeling next to Kozlov. Gripping his shirt, she hauled him upright. "I wasn't sure, but looks like you're all a bunch of frauds." She shook her head. "Who'd a thunk it. Not a single true believer in the lot."

"What?" Mercy looked at her, still dazed by her own defiance.

"I've met some true believers before. Had to shoot three of them before the rest would cooperate. These guys aren't even struggling." When she mentioned shooting, Kozlov thrashed weakly in her grip. She shook him like a dog holding a rat, drawing one of her guns. "Tell me, asshole. Why shouldn't I put you down like the rabid mouse you are?"

Kozlov's eyes flickered, doubtless remembering the way Captain had just wiped the floor with Macey. He whimpered. "Please don't kill me. I can help you! I could make people follow you. You'd be great! Keep me by your side. I'll help you!"

Captain's lip curled. "Doc!" she bellowed, flinging him back to the ground.

"Why?" he squealed.

Mercy stared, her jaw dropping. Kozlov, her former master, the man who'd been in control of everything from the moment she met him, the terror of her nightmares, the man who'd warped his own wife's mind possibly beyond recall, *squealed*?

When the company doctor arrived, Captain motioned. "We have work to do."

It was bloody, and unpleasant. Mercy helped. She knew exactly what each of these men had done to women who hadn't been able to fight back. In the end, she decided this was worse than the poison she would have used.

Because they would live. Broken men, and they would live.

Before the sun set, the Bondmaids were free.

CHAPTER 24

Bakersfield, CA – Captain

I stepped away from the celebration taking place in a large park inside Bakersfield. It'd been a long two weeks in Los Angeles, my people spreading out throughout the valley, finding those who wanted to leave. Some, unbelievably, had found peace in the south and chose to stay, but most joined us for the long trek out.

The party began in the afternoon, and it showed signs of going all night. Bakersfield produced stores of alcohol. Whether it'd been a lucky find or someone knew about it beforehand, I neither knew nor cared. All I wanted was to ensure no one was harmed.

The Irregulars stayed to the sides, mostly interacting with each other. Storm passed me a flask. Taking a swig, I passed it back. Nowhere near as strong as 'Nansi's Dirt Huggers, so my lot should be fine.

I hope.

Those who'd come with us from LA looked around as if they'd never seen scrubby trees and grass before. Which, considering how dry the LA

Basin is without imported water, they'd probably never expected to see so much greenery again. They also greeted these people like long-lost friends and family. Who knows, some of them probably were.

A cry rose above the noise of the celebration, and I whipped around, wading back in before conscious thought. That was definitely fear.

And rage.

A drunken Ashton faced off against a woman standing with her back towards me. Both were encircled by the mob. Irregulars spread out through the crowd of Resistance and Angelinos, ready for shit to hit the fan.

"Oh, come on!" I recognized Ashton, the asshole from LA. "It was just a little kiss. Don't be so frigid. It's not like I'm trying to grab your pussy."

I cast one glance heavenward. Why were there so many stupid men?

"I told you to keep your bloody hands off me!" the woman screamed, her hands clenched at her sides. Mercy. Fuck, that asshole had to grab Mercy? Even a blind man could see she'd been through hell.

I made to intervene, but Aanisah stepped forward. Slender, shorter than Mercy and a good deal shorter than Ashton, she stood between them, staring boldly at the big man.

"My Captain told you that if you gave hers any trouble, she would end you. But you aren't worth her time or effort. My Captain works hard every day to help us—to help *you*—and this is how you repay her? By attacking a woman?" She *tsk*ed, shaking her head. "It is my duty and pleasure to teach you a lesson because I would not let the healer sully her hands in a fight with you, either."

I'd reached them by now. "Are you sure?" I asked.

She laughed. "Oh, yes. I like this woman. She is like me when you found me. I would do for her what you did for me." She thought a moment. "I would even use the acid on this one, if I had some."

"I could probably find some."

"Acid?" Mercy said at the same time.

"Long story. Not important. Maybe we should skip the acid today," I decided.

"Very well."

"Oh, and Aanisah?"

"Yes?"

"Take him apart."

Ashton thought his size would help him. Instead, Aanisah treated him like a jungle gym, climbing his body and using her entire weight to throw him around. At one point, he barely held his ground, swaying, and she ran at him, going into a baseball slide underneath, kicking straight into his balls at the last second.

He folded like a lawn chair. Hopping to her feet, she got in a couple solid kicks before his girlfriend, Emery, made it through the crowd, screaming.

She turned her wrath on Mercy, who flinched. Stepping in front of her, I shook my head. She backed down, but I still gave silent instructions to the Irregulars present. *Watch them. Stop if they attempt harm.*

Hard eyes and nods all around. Yes, they'd watch this pair. In the ensuing awkward silence, Mayhem and Legs shared a glance, then Mayhem whooped, raised their flask, and the celebration resumed.

When I left the party, Mercy followed me back to my tent, flanked by Aanisah, Sweetpea, and Storm. Set up using walking poles, my tent sat so low it could disappear completely in the dark. We stepped around backpacks set in small circles, those few uninterested in the large celebration acting as guards and having their own little parties.

After all these years, even in a safe zone, we couldn't leave our packs unprotected. Our lives had depended on them too many times. The sounds of the party carried through the late afternoon air, back to full swing. People laughing, singing. I smiled when music drifted over on the cool air.

"Go on in." I pointed to my tent. "I need to have a word with these three." When the tent flap closed, I stepped away with the scouts and the saboteur. "You've heard the news the Celt brought last month?"

"Yes."

"I'm going east." Storm opened her mouth, but I held up a hand. "I don't know how. But I want you both to watch her back. She won't go with the others from that hellhole."

"I'd rather go with you." But Storm nodded. "From what Mom said, they're less likely to accept our help if she's around. Some of them blame her."

"Fuck. Okay. I need you three to keep her safe. Stick to her like glue in the future. But right now, I need you to find some people and bring them here."

Leaving them with their task, I bent low, duck-waddling to the side of the entry. Mercy took a spot in the corner. When I pointed next to her, she nodded. Sighing, I folded my legs beneath me, sitting beside her, and arching my back. Bending like that's a real bitch.

"Getting old?" she asked dryly.

"Go jump off a bridge," I said, grimacing.

She smiled while I lit a tiny lantern, hanging it from the center pole.

"Why do you have a map in here?"

"This is where we plan when it's wet outside."

She nodded, staring around with interest. I looked at it with fresh eyes. What did she see? My blankets were already unrolled on one side, my pack sitting at the foot. Against the back wall, a large board leaned against another pole, our maps tacked to it.

I didn't even want to know what she thought of me.

Soft footsteps sounded outside. "Come in," I called.

A quickly muttered, "How does she *do* that?" preceded the tent flap being pulled back. Faith and Lucas ducked in first, quickly followed by her parents.

Mercy shrank back, into my shadow, so I pointed the four of them to sit on my bedroll. Dan and Abigail shifted, their eyes darting everywhere. Abigail kept glancing at the entrance, then glaring at me like she couldn't decide whether to run or yell.

Until Mercy leaned forward. "Faith?"

The world held its breath while they stared at each other. Faith hadn't changed much, now that her two-tone hair was cut. Her bruises had taken time to heal, and she no longer limped. I could see how well-loved she was, and she thrived on it. She still had hope for the future and faith in people's goodness.

By contrast, Mercy was thin, some faint scars showing on her arms, but the biggest change was her eyes. They were wary, now, weighing everyone on the scale of her life experiences.

Faith squealed, lunging forward. Mercy flinched. I leaned over, blocking Faith. "Not so fast."

"What are you talking about?" Abigail jumped in. "This is our niece! We have a right to see her privately, without strangers."

Faith, Mercy, and I paused, exchanging glances. "They still don't know?" I demanded.

"How do they not know?" Mercy asked simultaneously. "All I had to do was see you in daylight. And actually be able to look at you directly," she added.

Faith held her hands out. "I wasn't sure how to tell them, especially with your...you know. Your reputation."

"Tell us what?" Dan leaned forward. "What?"

I wiggled my fingers in a little wave. "Hi, Uncle Dan. Aunt Abi. Long time, no see."

***

I'm not entirely sure what I expected from them, but it wasn't for Aunt Abigail to gasp, slumping against Dan. Or for him to turn white.

Lucas had the most prosaic response. "Captain is your *cousin?*" he whisper-shouted. "Wait, she's the Oregon one, Hope?"

"Nice to meet you formally." I nodded to him. "Welcome to the family, I suppose."

While my aunt and uncle fell apart at their niece being me, Mercy took a moment to gather herself before crawling forward.

"Hi," she said softly.

She flinched away when Uncle Dan moved to touch her. I shook my head at him. *It's not you,* I mouthed. Which was pointless, because he wouldn't look at me. But when Faith and Abigail met Mercy in the middle, moving slowly to embrace her, she closed her eyes, leaning into them.

For long moments, they were silent. Then, tears ran down Faith's cheeks. Abigail's shoulders shook. Soon, the three of them were sobbing.

Feeling like an outsider with my own family, I slid out of the tent, gaining my feet just in time to see a large group approaching. More and more Irregulars appeared out of the growing shadows, joining them. Laughter, greetings...

Growing shadows? I glanced at the sun. It would be sunset in an hour. But for now, Seahorse, Sarge at her side, grinned at me. Walking slowly, I met them, hope, disbelief, and grief warring in my chest. The others slowed down so Seahorse met me first.

Tilting my head, I pressed my forehead to hers. We stayed that way for long moments. Her presence here could only mean one thing.

"You did it?"

She nodded, her forehead rubbing almost painfully against mine. "We did."

The sob caught me by surprise. It was done? We'd cleared the entire West Coast? I sank to my knees, wracked with sobs. Grief surged to the surface, and I huddled there, hugging myself and wishing for a different set of arms.

People gathered around, their voices a babble over my head until Gryph knelt in front of me, resting a hand on the ground to look into my eyes.

"What is it?" he asked gently.

"It wasn't in vain. I swore it wouldn't be. I wish he could see this."

He hauled me up, hugging me tight. "Me, too," he whispered against my hair. "Me, too."

***

Finally reassured I wasn't dying, most of the fighters left to tell everyone we'd won. Seahorse, Sarge, Phoenix, and Gryph stayed close. Eleanor came over at a run, anxiety and joy in her voice. Seahorse answered her questions, the men stood guard, and Phoenix sat shoulder to shoulder with me, wiping her eyes occasionally, until I calmed.

I mopped the last of the tears away with the hem of my shirt, accepting the canteen Eleanor offered. "Captain," she said gently, "you need to address your people. Tonight, while they're all gathered and almost sober. Letting them get all the information second and third hand is..."

"A fucking terrible idea," Phoenix finished.

"You're right," I croaked. "You're both right. Let's go back to that party." Gryph helped us both to our feet, wrapping an arm around each of us. "Hot Fuzz's family is having a reunion in my tent." I jerked my head. "They'll want to hear this, too."

"Oh, shit!" Seahorse stared at me, her eyes wide. "I almost forgot! Fuzz's sister and brother-in-law are here, too..."

I froze, causing Gryph to jerk to a halt. "They're...they're here?"

"Yeah. I told them how Fuzz died. They're...well, they grieved again after we took them to his grave, but they seem more at peace now."

I cleared my throat. "Bring them, too."

"Babe?" She looked at Sarge, who loped off.

Eleanor exited my tent, followed by most of my remaining family. They looked at me, surrounded by my found family, and only Mercy seemed comfortable enough to approach.

"Eleanor says it's done? Can I go home now?"

"We don't have flights yet," I said hoarsely, drawing a startled laugh from Gryph, "and we have no idea how the outside will react to us. Last time we reached out, it...wasn't good. Besides, there's some stuff we have to do before it's done."

Eleanor cocked her head, listening. "We should go." She took my arm. "They're getting rowdy."

The low rumble of an engine interrupted her, and Dereva drove up at the wheel of my old pickup. "I've got some guests. Need a ride?"

A couple already sat on the toolbox, their backs against the cab. It'd been years, but of us all, she'd changed the least. Her plump, unscarred cheeks told me she'd lived well, but Charlie...I inhaled sharply. His pant leg ended abruptly below the knee.

"That happened in Seattle," Seahorse whispered. "I'll fill you in on our way over."

Sarge gave up the passenger's seat to Uncle Dan. Aunt Abi managed to crawl in there with him, though I think it was mostly to avoid me. I vaulted into the back of the pickup, straddling the tailgate box, facing Seahorse.

I barely managed to give my sister a nod before the rest of my family piled in. Faith squealed when she saw them, lunging. She finally got the enthusiastic greeting she'd been craving when Grace shrieked, hugging her tightly.

She and Lucas hemmed in my sister and brother-in-law, the girls both talking at once while the boys started slow, giving each other nods. The fighters filled in the space between, Gryph taking the machine gun out of habit while the others found guard spots.

"Wait!" Storm, Sweetpea, and Aanisah ran over, waving. They clambered onto the running boards, grinning. "You told us to stick to her," Storm shouted over the rumbling engine, pointing to Mercy.

Dereva stuck her head out the window. "Do we have everyone, or should I wait for the other half of the Irregulars?"

I looked around. We'd definitely had more people in here in the past, but never with such a demarcation. Lucas, Faith, Mercy, Grace, and Charlie sat a little apart from us. The fighters worked to give Mercy room. We knew the best way to help someone in her position was space.

Gryph, Phoenix, Doc, Chaos, and Eleanor had the middle, and Sarge, Seahorse, and I occupied the tail box. I shook my head. We fit, but at the same time, it all seemed so...crowded. Maybe it was all the emotions riding high.

"Go," I shouted. "Anybody else who wants to come can walk."

I'd prefer to walk, too, but Eleanor was right. I needed to talk to my people before things got out of hand. While we drove, Seahorse filled me in on their fight, and its aftermath.

"We honestly thought we'd get down here sooner," she finished. "But finding enough boats to get rid of Steve took some time. Then, Charlie got a fever and Grace refused to leave him," she said approvingly. "After all that, we had to stop by the Lair. It only seemed fair she got a chance for closure with her brother. And then there was her dad and other brother."

Papa and Sean had seen Grace? Good, that was good. I glanced frequently at her, but she was caught up in talking to Faith. Mercy listened, a small smile on her mouth. The first I'd seen from her, I realized. She smiled less than I did, these days.

"What else about her husband?" I jerked my head towards his leg.

"Fabricators have got his measurements, finally. It took a while for the swelling to go down. Then, it's just the usual: fittings, physio, and relearning how to walk. He's lucky, though. Still has his knee."

I nodded. That was a better end than many got.

***

Bakersfield, CA – Grace

As happy as she was to see Faith glowing and healthy, as much as her heart ached for the pain she could see in Mercy, Grace couldn't help but focus on the woman sitting sideways on a toolbox set in front of the tailgate, directly opposite her.

There'd been precious little information about Captain on their journey south. All the Irregulars were remarkably closed-mouthed about their leader, to the point where she hadn't even realized Captain was a woman.

She only knew who she was because one of the fighters called her by name, and now, all she wanted was a clear look at the woman's face. She currently sat in profile, and Grace kept one surreptitious eye on her.

The setting sun glinted off blonde braids sliding over her shoulders, streaked with gray around her forehead and temples. Her eyes were constantly drawn to the terrible scar running through the leader's left eyebrow and down her cheek, barely missing the eye.

"Are you alright?" Charlie murmured under Faith's excited chatter.

She nodded, leaning into him. "Look at her," she breathed. "Would you ever guess?" He shook his head.

But at the same time... She seemed so removed from the people around her, yet she had such presence. Everything about her clearly said she'd wade through enemies like other people waded through water.

The boogeyman and the liberator, all rolled into one. They'd heard her name on the outside. She and Charlie had carried news of her in the past, though her name was already known.

Captain glanced over, sunlight shining in her one visible eye, making it glow a vibrant gray, the other cast in shadow.

Grace frowned. Why did this woman seem so familiar?

The corner of Captain's mouth twitched. Reaching down, she banged on the side of the pickup. "Get me into the middle, Dereva!" she shouted.

Lifting her head, Grace saw they'd reached the celebration. She'd heard them partying when they arrived in camp. Now, the driver slowed to a crawl, honking the horn. When people saw who sat tall in the back, they made way. Some threw salutes, others glared. Still more stared at her in awe.

The pickup rolled to a halt and Captain rose to stand on the toolbox. A sea of people crowded around the pickup and Mercy tensed.

The three women who'd been hanging onto the running boards gathered around Mercy. Grace gave them a quick glance. They were an unusual trio. A hijabi Muslim woman, a beautiful woman with strawberry-blonde hair and a scar running from temple to jaw, and a slight, younger black woman.

"It's all right," the blonde murmured. "Just listen. We'll keep you safe."

Captain stood tall, a fierce war leader in front of her troops. "All in, all out!" she bellowed.

"One shot, one kill. No luck, all skill!" the fighters roared.

Throwing her head back, Captain screamed at the sky. Rage, joy, and a grief so deep it brought tears to Grace's eyes echoed off the tall buildings around them.

When she looked down, her teeth bared, the shouts and cheers slowly dissipated. "We have won back our homes," she announced, her voice rough. "But it doesn't end here!"

Grace perked up. She'd heard the news about the Secretary, then? What would she do about it?

"North Korea didn't do this alone. We've had intel that people within our own government not only gave aid but were a part of the planning!"

Boos and hisses filled the air. "What do you want us to do, Captain?" a bold woman shouted. She pushed her way to the front, and Grace recognized the Celt.

Captain paused. "I want you to rest," she said eventually. "I want you to find your families, make love, and create a life for yourselves. I want you to take up your real names again."

"But what about that fucking Secretary?"

"I want you to build homes, find peace. Take your names back. But I'll be keeping my name a while longer," she replied. Her voice deepened, her feet shifted, and Grace thought she looked ready to fight. "There's some things back east that need fixing, and I aim to see that it's done."

"Yeah!" The Irregulars cheered.

The pickup rocked, the big man at the gun and the petite woman with a huge rifle rising to their feet. "We're going with you," the woman said, folding her arms. "The rest of you lot need to get fat and sassy for us and make sure we've got some place to run to," she shouted. "Because if I know our Captain, we're gonna really piss some people off!"

They laughed. Captain jumped off the pickup, rocking the whole thing, walking amongst her people. Grace narrowed her eyes. Leaning into Charlie, she murmured, "Is it just me, or does she seem familiar?"

"Yeah."

Mercy and Faith shared a look. "What will you do next, now that it's over?" Faith asked brightly.

"Find myself a leg," Charlie said, smiling faintly. They laughed, but Grace could see his puzzlement, and he followed Captain's progress through the crowd.

The truck rocked again when Abigail and Dan clambered out of the cab. When Dan saw Grace, his mouth dropped open. "I didn't know you were here!"

Faith interceded, explaining their presence. Grace sighed, relieved. She loved him, she really did, but Uncle Dan had a habit of asking questions like an interrogation.

"Uncle Dan doesn't look like he's changed at all," Charlie whispered, laughing silently as they watched Faith gesture. It looked like she was telling her father to back off.

"Well, he's skinnier."

Soon, Captain returned to the truck, smiling faintly, and leaped into the bed again. *How the hell did she do that?* Grace wondered. She looked older than Grace, yet moved like a woman several years younger. A dark-eyed brunette woman with a messenger bag slung over her shoulder shifted, a direct contrast to the blond-haired, blue-eyed man she sat with.

"We're coming with you," she said bluntly. "And there's not a damn thing you can do about it."

Captain smiled, though Grace only caught part of the expression. "I guess having Chaos and someone to patch us up is a good idea. You might as well join the party."

Mercy straightened. "I'll walk back to the camp. I need to think."

When she hopped out of the pickup, three women followed. The hijabi woman, the strawberry-blonde, and the black woman. Grace watched them curiously. Hopefully, she'd have a chance to talk to Mercy later and find out what that was all about.

Slowly, Lucas and the remaining fighters left, leaving Grace and Charlie alone in the back with Captain, who thumped the side of the pickup.

"Dereva, take us back, please," she called. "I need to talk with these two."

Dread settled in Grace's stomach, and she took Charlie's hand, squeezing it. He squeezed back, bumping her with his shoulder. Except Captain didn't speak, watching the people celebrate. Grace's nerves screamed. This was worse than being called into the principal's office.

"Do you want to know more about the letter telling us about the Secretary?" Grace finally asked, unable to take the silence any longer.

Captain waited until they were well away from the crowd, then lit a small lantern, carefully placing the glass back to protect the flame. Grace frowned. There was still some sunlight left. Not enough to make out the details of Captain's face, but enough to see her. So why...?

Then the rebel leader raised the lantern, illuminating her whole face for the first time this evening. The light played over the fine scars and faint lines around her eyes, the grim set of her small, full lips. The blunt nose and high cheekbones.

Grace gasped. "Hope!"

CHAPTER 25

Scan of phone conversations, DC area – July 8, 2065, 9:02pm

Man 1: Except there's nobody missing. Those soldiers we sent in are the only ones we haven't got bodies for, but that sergeant was dishonorably discharged for the whole thing, so we know for sure they're dead. Besides, news of Captain predated them going into Oregon. Idiot.

Mono County, CA – Captain

I stood at the machine gun in the back of my old GMC, knees bent to absorb the shock of a bad road. Dereva kept the pace slow to avoid accidental damage. To my left, the snow-covered mountains rose tall. A small convoy of vehicles followed us, far more than necessary, but these assholes—*my* assholes—refused to let me sneak off alone to deal with Keller and whoever else was behind the Invasion.

Down here, so close to Nevada and the desert, I was glad for my leather jacket, and tugged my beanie a bit closer over my forehead. We finally had actual winter weather. The ground had a light dusting of snow, but nothing too bad.

Phoenix, Gryph, Grace, and Sheba rode in the back with me while Anansi sat in front with his sister, maps open in front of him. He'd been giving me unhappy looks for days, ever since we left the San Joaquin Valley.

"You know," Sheba looked up at the mountains. "Crossing is a lot easier when you have access to cars."

Phoenix laughed. "And a road that happens to start where you are and go all the way to your destination."

"And not have to dodge an army that wants to kill you," Gryph added. From habit, he and Phoenix watched the sides and rear. From habit, I stood at the gun.

Never mind that the highway had broken in places, and we'd been forced to go cross-country. But Phoenix was right, being able to drive had given us so much time and safety.

'Nansi tapped on the roof. "Hey," he called. "We're almost to Mono City. You said you have to go the rest of the way on foot, right?"

We parked outside an old grocery store on the outskirts of town, the mountains rising high in the west. Sunset would come early today. Anansi clambered from the pickup, pouting at being left behind. Sighing, I hauled him away.

"Hah." I cupped the young man's face. I had to reach up to do it. He'd gotten so tall in the last few years. "If you go to the fence, you'll try to leave with me."

His mouth twitched in a little smile. "Listen," he looked at me earnestly, "you need a guy like me. You know I'm smart, adaptable—"

"And a genius," I finished, stroking my thumbs over his cheeks. "Which is why I need you to stay here. I know you've been organizing the non-coms," I interrupted when he opened his mouth, "creating plows from random shit, ensuring people are fed. You've been designing fencing that can be built with a minimum of fuss."

He shrugged. "I needed something to keep me busy."

"And you've been keeping those people alive. But it's winter and they're not prepared for it. A lot burned. You're the perfect man to help with the rebuild. Oregon can probably use your insight on things, too. Basically, you're too important to everyone here for me to risk your life."

He compressed his lips, his jaw tightening under my fingers.

"Besides," I added, "you mom will kill me." Giving in, he laughed, leaning down to hug me. I rested against his lean frame, holding him, and used my final weapon. "TK would worry."

"Oh, that's low," he protested, drawing away.

"I know." I smiled. "But you know I'm right." He stuck his tongue out. Reaching up, I ruffled his kinky black hair. "Look after my kids while I'm gone, alright? Tell them stories about me that aren't scary. Please?"

His mouth trembled. "Why do you have to do shit like that?"

"Because I'm a horrible person."

And because I was ninety percent sure I wouldn't make it out of this alive. I didn't want the others to come, either, but I figured Phoenix and Gryph would somehow show up anyway with Eleanor, Doc, and Chaos in tow.

When I'd asked Eleanor why she wanted to come, she said, "Because," and refused to say more. Mercy wouldn't be left behind, either. Despite her freedom, it worried me how thin she stayed. Something ate away at her, and this might be the most therapeutic thing for her.

Which meant I also had Storm, Aanisah, and Sweetpea. "You *ordered* us to stick by her," Storm said, folding her arms. "We're only following your orders."

"Which would make this the first fucking time you've ever obeyed me," I grumbled.

And before we left, every Irregular and quite a few others tried begging, wheedling, and outright bribery to be allowed to come. I put my foot down when Seahorse, Sarge, Stretch, and Gameboy showed up outside my tent.

"You people are integral to this place running smoothly. If you all go, shit will hit the fan."

"What about you?" Seahorse demanded, hands on her hips. "You're not important?"

"I'm a basher," I snapped back. "All I'm good for is fighting. Sure, I could take over defense, create a police force type thing, but you guys can do that as well as me. Better, even. You're not going."

"You're letting Grace go!"

"Only to contact her informant, then she's heading right back here."

"Fine." Seahorse folded her arms. "Then we'll go with you and escort her back."

Eventually realizing I wouldn't win that one, I backed down. Which is why we now had a whole convoy. The fighters would help us make contact, then escort Grace back. We hardly needed twenty extra people for it, but they were a bunch of stubborn assholes.

I trained them well.

The only reason I didn't have the whole lot is because I hadn't had time do any repairs. Over half our vehicles were beyond use until they saw a competent mechanic and had a shit ton of repairs and more modifications. Which meant they couldn't come.

Thank God.

Those of us going all the way to DC grabbed packs loaded with ammunition and food.

"Remind me why we had to come so far north, again?" Phoenix asked, studying the horizon through her scope.

"Because I know this area," Sheba replied. "I know this place has the communications that Grace said she needs, and an airstrip. If you really think her people have pull, then you'll want an airstrip."

I found Dereva mucking about under the pickup's hood. "How's everything here?" I asked.

"Hoses are great, I'm just checking this one connector here, but it's holding." Straightening, she wiped her hands on a grimy old t-shirt. "But I really wish you'd let me come with you."

Putting my hands on her shoulders, I leaned down, pressing my forehead to hers. "No. This isn't up for debate."

"Why?"

"There's something I need to tell you before I leave. There's something I need to ask you to do. Please."

Something in my tone caught her attention, and she froze, wide blue eyes so close to mine. "What? Why are you talking like you're not coming back?"

I ignored that. "I've asked 'Nansi, but I'm asking you, too. Look after my kids for me. Tell them stories that won't make them..." I swallowed back tears. "Stories that will make them less scared of me."

A fat tear rolled down her cheek. "Okay."

"Second, I know you've been talking to Goliath. Like, seriously talking. Stop holding him at arm's length. Fuzz would want you to be happy, to live a full life."

"What about you?" Her breath hitched, more tears filling her eyes. Her fingers dug into my arms, nails biting through the leather. "You're still...still..."

"I was happily single before I met him. And while I'm not happy anymore, I still prefer this over trying to get along with another man. Now shut up. I need to get this out." Swallowing again, I blinked rapidly. "You've met Fuzz's other family. You know that Grace is his sister." She nodded. "He has two sisters."

"How did you know? He mentioned one, but never said her name. You knew him Before, didn't you?"

I nodded, the corners of my mouth turning down. "He was my baby brother."

She gasped, sinking to her knees. I knelt with her, holding her while she cried. "Why didn't you tell me sooner?" She slapped my arm. Hard. "You went through it alone, you idiot."

"I wasn't alone. Archangel knew. Amana, too." She'd seen his page in The Book, the written record every fighter filled out. It contained our real names, Social Security numbers, and all our family members. If we fell, she recorded the manner of death. At the end—now, I guess—she would use it to find them and let them know what happened to us. "And I want you to know that I've considered you a sister for a long time now. You're the twins' aunt. I need you to be there for them. Please?"

"You asshole!" She hit me again. "You complete and utter bitch! How dare you spring this on me?"

"Because I need you to tell Grace when she comes back. I don't dare tell her about the kids while we're out there, and I can't risk her accidentally blurting something out. It's bad enough she knows who I am. She's already in enough danger."

"From who? Steve's gone."

I clenched my jaw, speaking through gritted teeth. "Remember when Sirius went to Idaho? We're all under threat. Right now, she's innocent. I need her to stay that way. So tell her about her nephews, will you?"

Dereva stared up at me, her cheeks wet, furious even in her grief. "I could almost hate you right now." I simply looked at her, my heart in my throat. I needed her to agree. Finally, her shoulders slumped. "Oh, all right, you bitch. I'll tell her. Only when she gets back."

I hugged her carefully, her lean, wiry arms gripping me tight. "Thank you."

"Yo, Captain!" Goliath stood twenty feet away. "You good? We're about to leave."

"You're coming, too?"

"Damn straight. Don't worry, not all the way. I heard you loud and clear last time. Besides, I promised Charlie I'd make sure his wife made it back to him, safe and sound."

Yes, last time, when he tried to bribe me to allow him to come. "Good. I'm glad she's got a bodyguard."

***

Mono City, CA – Grace

Grace glanced furtively over her shoulder, looking for the last person in line, her sister. Who also happened to be the Ghost Captain, the rebel of living legend from Oregon. She breathed out slowly, struggling to contain her emotions.

It'd only been a few days, nowhere near long enough to fully grasp all the implications. But her sister's vibes had changed drastically over the years. Hope had once been sassy, always smiling, ready with a joke.

Now, the overall feeling she got was of heaviness, which didn't even touch on the physical changes. Graying hair, she would expect. But the scars... By the darkness in her sister's eyes, Grace suspected the emotional scars were by far the worst.

They walked through trees that reminded her of the alpine forests in Yosemite, not the huge trees of the Willamette Valley. Despite the snow, the air remained dry, and she tugged her scarf higher. Occasionally, she glimpsed open spaces, but Sheba took them on a route that stayed well away from them.

It's what she'd do, too.

To the south, light gray clouds filled the sky, pushing north, partially covering the lowering sun. Most of the fighters were elsewhere. She'd seen a bunch leave with them, but they disappeared into the trees, occasionally returning to confer quickly with their leader.

"Let's pick up the pace," Captain called. "I smell snow."

At the front, the strawberry-blonde with the fearsome scar, Storm, moved into a lope, Sheba right on her heels. The oldest woman, Eleanor, kept up easily. Turned out, it was Mercy who struggled with the pace the most.

"Sorry," she gasped. "I haven't gone this fast this long in...ever."

Grace slowed with her, breathing heavily. "You've got this."

Sheba hissed, holding up her hand. "Someone's coming."

Phoenix stepped out of a thicket. "Not bad. Cap, fence is half a mile away. Goliath, Seahorse, and Sarge are on different sections, looking to see which has the best ground for crossing."

Captain walked over to them, resting a hand on Mercy's back, peering at her face. "Let's take five," she called. "Phoenix."

The petite woman threw a sloppy salute, making Captain scowl. "My Captain?"

"Get fucked."

"Right away!" She spun on her heel. "Where's my husband?"

"Get back here, smartass." Captain snagged her pack, hauling the smaller woman back. "I want to go check out the fence and the army's routine. We need a guard set up here."

"Hmph. Civilians," Phoenix grumbled, but she smiled slightly.

"Find Chaos while I sort them out. He's in charge here. I want you and your giant rifle so we don't have to get too close."

The petite woman snorted. "Find me a tree tall enough, I can see clearly from here."

"You don't need that," Grace broke in. "It's a four man patrol every ten minutes."

"Maybe." Captain didn't sound convinced. "But different sections, different commanders. I want to see if anyone here is a slacker."

Grace glared at her sister. Why did she always have to sound like Captain? Never Hope. She hadn't sounded happy to see Grace since the night she'd revealed herself to them. A pang shot through Grace. She missed Charlie. Missed his level head and his strong arms. She didn't sleep well without him nearby.

When the big blond man, Chaos, strolled through, Captain broke away to speak to him quietly, then vanished into the trees, followed by Phoenix.

"Get some rest," he said kindly. "You won't get much sleep tonight."

***

Washington, DC – Constance

Constance stared at her phone, willing it to ring, but it remained stubbornly silent.

"You know you can't force it," James said. "Come on, it's late. You've got the bed tonight."

Sighing, she planted her hands on the floor, rising and stretching along the way. She paused a moment, hands flat on the floor, feeling her spine loosen. When she straightened, James wiped a grin off his face.

"I still don't know how you think that's nice." Shaking his head, he picked up two folded blankets and a pillow.

They'd been trading off on who got the bed and who slept on the couch since she'd arrived. It ensured that every other night, they got a good night's rest. That was the plan, anyway. Ever since they'd been followed, she didn't sleep as well, too aware of the man across the room, and afraid that those men had let them go and were simply tracking them, ready to arrest them later.

She stubbornly shook her head. "No. You take it. She's going to call tonight. She has to."

They'd taken a risk and gone to another café, this time to send an encrypted email to Senator Baser. They could only send one thing, so she'd chosen an audio file of Secretary Keller and her son. Then, she'd left the phone number she'd only given to one other person, Grace O'Connell.

Sighing, James came to her. "Listen." He scooped her up. Closing her eyes, she wrapped her arms around his neck and buried her face against him, inhaling his warm scent. "We need sleep. We can't keep burning the candle at both ends."

Reaching the bed, he laid her down. Stubbornly, she refused to let go. "What's the point? I can't sleep anyway."

He relaxed onto the bed next to her. "Why?" Biting her lip, she shook her head. He smoothed her hair back from her face. "You think they let us go."

"You said it," she mumbled against his shoulder. When he shifted, she curled tighter against him. "Who can sleep when you don't know when your world will explode?"

The bed moved again, and his other arm wrapped around her. "I won't let anything happen to you," he whispered against her hair. "What will make you feel better?"

"Can we just...stay like this? For a little while."

***

The phone buzzed against her neck. Grumbling, she swiped at it, but her fingers encountered a stubbled cheek instead. Frowning, her eyes still closed, she assessed. Warmth, a heavy weight over her waist... Shooting upright, she stared down at James, his eyes already open.

"Aren't you going to answer that?" he asked.

Grabbing the phone, she fumbled to answer it. "Hello?"

"Hello." The voice was smooth, feminine, with a hint of an accent. It was a voice filled with hard-won authority. "Who are you, and how did you get that file?"

"Senator Baser." Her legs still tangled with James's, Constance met his eyes. "How good of you to personally call."

***

Fresno, CA – Faith

Groaning, Faith arched her back, stretching. "Since when did junky couches get so heavy?"

"Since we had to carry it two blocks to a recycling plant." Lucas reached overhead, the movement lifting his shirt just enough to reveal a narrow strip of skin right above his belt. "Still," he added, "it's good to see people working jobs *not* about war."

Looking around, she nodded. He was right. Everyone was involved in restoration efforts. People emerged practically from the woodwork, offering their former hobbies as skills that could revive the state. This couch would be dismantled, the wood going to build something new, and they'd see where they could use the fabric and stuffing.

More and more people left the city, seeking their fortune on the land. Those who'd done well with their tiny gardens now looked to grow larger ones. Others took the animals the Irregulars had gathered and tended their herds on rocky ground.

"I want to see all of it," Faith said, turning in a circle. "I want to work on a farm for a while, then help with the animals. After that, I want to go to Oregon. I'm tired of being cooped up in a city."

His arms slid around her waist. Smiling, she leaned back against him. "I'd like that." His voice vibrated pleasantly in his chest. "No more walls. What about your parents?"

"Oh, Mom's already gathering seeds. Her and Dad have been allocated a small plot not too far from the city. She's even got some chickens. She said she'll keep a room for us."

A gong sounded.

Together, they walked towards the park, slowly joined by more. "I really hope they keep these communal kitchens," Faith said, swinging their linked hands. "I don't mind cooking, but I really prefer doing it with other people."

Joining the line, they grabbed plates.

"Did you say you don't mind cooking?" One of the cooks paused in setting down a pot. "We could always use more help here. Oh! I know you. You're Abigail's girl. I'm Emma."

"You know my mom?"

"Oh, yeah, she's been bringing us fruit from those trees in your old apartment. She's been telling us all about it and bringing us what she has. Although I'd like to see some spinach. There's a salad I want to make, but I can't find anyone with it."

Faith selected a bread roll, setting it in her stew. "The Woodward Park kitchen has some. I can go and trade. What do you have too much of?"

Emma brightened, strolling down the line with them. "Would you mind? You know, everyone's all over the place. Because each kitchen is supplied by the local residents, we've got a weird mix of supplies. Which usually means good stew and oddball salads. But when they have more than they can use, it's a shame if food goes to waste."

Lucas nudged her. "Go on, you know you want to. And you'd be very good at negotiating."

"Oh?" Emma raised her eyebrows.

Faith shrugged. "I worked for the Resistance in the office." Emma's mouth dropped open. "I had to deal with a lot of people and not get caught. Turned out, I'm good at it."

"Good. You're hired. You help ensure nothing goes to waste and we all get a balanced diet." Recovering quickly, Emma beamed. "Wait until I tell my husband Abigail's girl was really active Resistance all these years." Leaning in, she lowered her voice. "Most people hated you for collaborating."

Faith reared back slightly, her breath coming too fast. Lucas put a protective hand on her back. "I didn't—"

"She was part of the North Fresno Chapter," Lucas said in a hard voice. "I can vouch for her, as can Carter, Hackett, Varro, Duran, Nixon, Captain, if she was here, and—"

"Shut the door!" Emma's eyes widened and she lowered her voice. "You met Captain?"

Faith bit her tongue, wanting to blurt out her relationship to the infamous war leader. Since when did she have a hard time keeping secrets? Oh, yes. Since the war was done and she didn't want to hide anymore.

"I went on a couple missions with her. We both did."

"Oh! Oh, Harvey will be green! After you've eaten, tell me everything about her. What's she like? Is she really as terrifying as they say? What about her scars? I saw her at the Freeing of Fresno..."

Emma continued chattering while Faith and Lucas found spots on the grass. *Well, if people hated me before, by the end of the day, everyone should love me because I worked with the 'infamous Captain.'*

CHAPTER 26

Border Fence, Bridgeport, CA – Captain

Through thick snowfall, bouncing lights heralded the next US patrol. Lowering my head, I let the snow bury me in a shallow gully, not that I needed it. These boys relied entirely on tech, leaving them completely night blind.

As soon as the lights passed, I waved. Eleanor and Storm crossed the distance at a run, Storm sliding in like a batter on a home run, snow spraying around her.

Gryph cut the last few wires, allowing those gathered to squeeze under. Following the gully, they were soon lost to sight. It took three patrols passing before we got everyone across. I really should have thought harder about this. Ten of us planning to go east, twenty to get us to the army base? Way too fucking many people.

But with Grace and Mercy here, I was glad for all the extra eyes.

Pulling my scarf firmly around my mouth and nose, Sheba and I booked it, the last through. Gryph yanked the fence down while I zip-tied, numbed fingers fumbling with the fiddly little shits. Another set of lights emerged on this side, and we flattened down. Working nearly blind, I yanked the tails tight, cutting them with a single swipe each.

I wanted to leave the tails, let them know we'd crossed, but I had to think about my people going back. Can't leave any evidence that we'd come through...

Exploding from the snow, we high-tailed it across the path and into the trees on the other side, snow quickly filling our tracks.

"Do we have a heading?" I asked as soon as we rejoined the main group.

Storm looked up from her compass, breath puffing in the cold air. "Due east from here. Roughly five miles."

"Like walking in the park, kids. Let's move."

"Wait!" Sheba held up a hand. "Be careful. There are some crazy militia wannabes in these woods. I've seen them through my binocs sometimes."

As soon as those words left her mouth, over half my forces disappeared into the woods. "Next time, lead with that, yeah?" I said. "*Before* we cross the fucking fence."

"Where did they all go?" Grace whispered.

"We have to go in smaller groups to avoid leaving too large a trail," I said. "Move out."

***

Border Fence, Bridgeport, CA – Mercy

Mercy stayed in the middle of the remaining group, hanging onto Doc's pack while Grace held onto hers. Eleanor followed behind, occasionally whispering words of encouragement. The big blond fighter, Chaos, led the way with Sheba, though he constantly reached back, taking Doc's hand, whispering to her, smiling.

Maybe there was some hope left in this world.

Miserably hunching her shoulders inside the large coat she'd been given, Mercy chafed her hands. For the first couple of hours in the snow, she'd been delighted. Now, she just wanted to be warm. Her toes were freezing, even inside the combat boots and wool socks.

How much longer until they were finally at the bloody base, and she could be inside?

She abruptly crashed into Doc, who'd frozen when Chaos raised a clenched fist, looking to their left. He signaled *hide.* Mercy felt her way to the base of a tree, crouching and holding onto the trunk, the rough bark catching on her mittens.

The others disappeared, though she never saw them leave.

Footsteps, clearly audible as they crunched through the snow, made her shrink back, hoping to blend into the trees. Gripping the trunk, she followed the sounds, struggling to see them through the dark and snow.

Light burst through the night, shining right into her eyes. Throwing up a hand, she turned her face away. A man spoke. "Well, well, boys. Look what we have here. A little girl, all alone in the woods. Are you lost, little girl?"

Little girl. The words echoed through her mind, joining all the other derogatory names. *Bondmaid. Whore. Slut. Cunt.* Snarling, she lunged, but the man slapped her down, laughing.

More male laughter, all around her. Her breath came short, but she curled her lip. She'd be damned if she let them hurt her like that again.

"Hey!" Sheba burst out of her hiding spot. "Leave her alone." She attacked, knife in hand, but two men caught her, a third wresting the knife from her hand, slapping her across the face.

Gasping, Sheba was thrown to her knees next to Mercy. The stocky woman's face, red from the cold, showed a white handprint across her cheek, but it didn't stop her from spitting curses at the men.

From her position on the ground, the lights no longer blinding her, Mercy counted nine men in camouflage uniforms, night vision goggles pushed up on their heads. Except...their uniforms weren't very uniform. One had a bulkier Kevlar vest. The one near her feet sported a large hunting knife with an antler handle.

She thought furiously, hoping Doc, Grace, and Eleanor had the sense to stay hidden. Actual army people were supposed to have regulations about their clothing, right? Because the more she looked, the more differences she found.

The man with the hunting knife hauled her up with rough hands. Spitting, she twisted in his grip, but he shook her until she stopped, her head spinning. "Well, boys. What should we do with all this fine booty?" He slid one hand down, fingers hooked into claws, reaching for her crotch.

Screeching, she swiped at his face and hell broke loose, Grace erupting from her spot, shouting. She swung her rifle like a club, hitting a man in the arm, but more of them overwhelmed her.

"Search the bushes!" Hunting Knife ordered, spinning Mercy around, wrapping one thick arm around her throat, the other around her arms and waist. Two of them hauled a struggling Doc from the bushes near a bend in the trail.

"Get your hands off me," she snarled. "You have no idea what you're dealing with..."

She cut off abruptly when Bandana Man struck her across the face. "Shut up, cunt!"

"Enough!" Her voice ringing with authority, Eleanor pushed through the men. "You should be ashamed of yourselves!"

For a moment, Mercy thought the force of Eleanor would end this, until the tallest wrapped a beefy arm around her throat, sneering, his free hand sliding down her front.

"Guys!" The only man who hadn't moved yet, the one with the heavy duty Kevlar vest, stepped forward. "We should call Sergeant Pierce, tell him we've found intruders."

"Shut up, Simms," Hunting Knife snapped, his breath brushing Mercy's cheek. "We have time. It's not like we have to follow every rule. I mean, we volunteered. Seems like we're due some compensation."

The rest of the men laughed, boasting about what they'd do. Grace stubbornly struggled against her captors, mindless in her efforts to free herself. Mercy wanted to shout *Stop it! They enjoy emotion. Don't give it to them.* But that, too, would be emotion and they'd enjoy themselves even more.

Doc merely looked at them like they were less than the dirt on her boots, her head lifted, a knowing little smile on her lips.

"Hey." Bandana Man poked her chest. "Why are you smiling, bitch? Looking forward to what I'm going to do to you?" He grabbed his crotch.

"Where's your friend?" she asked innocently.

"What?"

Mercy did a quick count. American Flag was missing. Even as she turned, something flickered in the corner of her eye. By the time she turned her head, another disappeared into the bushes with barely a rustle.

While their captors shouted, guns waving, Hope glided out of the night, pack gone, snow dusting her leathers and battle braids.

"Surprise, fuckers."

Mercy shrieked in defiance, her pulse pounding. Excitement drowned fear and trepidation. Clenching her hands, she renewed her struggle, twisting, teeth bared, catching Hunting Knife by surprise. He'd been goggling at

Hope—no, Captain—who flowed into motion, whipping out her machete from where it'd been hidden by her leg.

Mercy suddenly found herself freed and surrounded by her protectors, Storm, Sweetpea, and Aanisah. Once they were assured of her safety, Storm and Sweetpea rushed the next man. Working in concert, they took him down, Storm going high, Sweetpea aiming low.

Chaos dropped Bandana Man, whose head flopped at an angle Mercy recognized. Broken neck. Doc's other captor already lay dead at her feet.

More Irregulars flooded the trail until the only uniformed man left was the Kevlar vest, Simms. He faced Captain, wide-eyed. His hands raised, he slowly sank to his knees while the Irregulars dragged the other dead away, burying them under the snow.

Doc leaned against Chaos, her hand resting on his chest. Mercy examined them. This was why Doc had been so fearless. She knew these people would be here, that Chaos would save her. Even as envy struck her, she shied away from it. There was only one man she'd trusted, and in the end, the weight of numbers and surprise had taken him from her.

A gentle hand touched her shoulder. "It's okay," Aanisah whispered. "Living will get easier, *Alhamdulillah*."

Mercy's lips twisted, angry words bubbling to the surface.

"I know," the saboteur continued. "Many of us do. We see it in others like us. You're not alone here."

Her anger deflating, Mercy relaxed slightly, examining Aanisah with fresh eyes. *Many of us.* The fighters? They were mostly women. Unwillingly, her eyes were drawn to Storm, with her strawberry-blonde curls, terrible scars, and stern demeanor.

"You okay?" Turning, Mercy found Captain behind her, her face grim. "You have a lot of people here you can talk to, who understand where you've been. You're not alone."

"Aanisah just said that," Mercy said through numbed lips. "What now?"

The corner of Captain's mouth twitched. "Well. Simms here has agreed to take us to the communications bunker thing."

He leaned back as far as he could, held securely by Sarge. "I have?"

Captain nodded firmly. "Damn straight you have."

"Uh...and if I don't?"

The war leader looked pointedly around, where even the signs of blood had disappeared. Simms gulped. "Get moving, boy."

***

Using Simms's comms and the earpieces from the dead to track the patrols, they evaded the rest of the pursuit. Some of the Irregulars disappeared again. Storm muttered something about leaving false trails, but Mercy wasn't quite sure how that worked.

Chaos touched the tiny unit in his ear. "I've missed tech," he said, grinning down at Doc.

Simms watched the bigger man morosely. With dawn, the sky lightened just enough for Mercy to see his expressions, and she noted envy when he looked at the soldier. For what? His fighting abilities or his relationship with Doc?

"The airstrip is just through there." Simms pointed to a thick line of trees and brush. "The main base is to the north, the communications bunker, I've heard, is more south. I don't know any more than that. Security is really tight."

"Spit it out," Captain said absently, map already out.

"What?"

"You've been moping all night. Spit it out."

"You killed my friends!"

Captain made a non-committal sound. "Friends? Seemed like you didn't agree with them being a bunch of rapists. Was I wrong?" She finally looked up, her expression neutral.

Simms flinched, then straightened slightly. But he wouldn't meet her eyes. Mercy studied her cousin, trying to figure out how the bloody woman managed to intimidate without resorting to threats or violence.

Eleanor came up beside Mercy, knee bent while she stretched her foot. "She's not even angry," Eleanor murmured, amusement rich in her voice.

Mercy slid the older woman a sidelong glance. She hadn't had a mother figure, so comforting and strong, since... Since she left her own mother in Australia and boarded a plane to go to Grace's wedding. Her breath hitched at the thought of her mom. Unconsciously, she leaned towards Eleanor, focusing on their conversation.

"I thought you were supposed to be the voice of reason," she whispered.

"That's what they think. So, you can't tell anyone how much I enjoy all of this. It would only encourage them." Eleanor smiled and warmth bloomed in Mercy's chest. When Eleanor wrapped an arm around her waist, she hesitantly did the same. "You'll be alright, my love. We are the Irregulars, and we have you."

Mercy wiped the tears away before they could fall, sniffling. She was only distracted by Captain, rising to her feet and folding her map.

"Okay, children. Fuck shit up, don't get caught."

"All in, all out. One shot, one kill. No luck, all skill!"

***

Bridgeport, CA – Captain

Sliding through the scrubby bushes, I angled for a little shed away from the main hangars. After watching it all day, it had the most suss activity. Twice, once in the early morning, once in the evening, a four-man team switched out.

To my left, bushes rustled vigorously. Phoenix found another victim—I mean, apprehended another soldier on patrol.

The US base and its airstrip were obviously built after the Invasion. Everything had a temporary look that was forced to go permanent. Three hangars sat grouped together on the northern side of the airstrip. Beyond them squatted a square building slapped together in a hurry. Barracks and offices, maybe. Then, *all* the way down here, on the southern end, a little shed, that, according to all information, contained their backup comms.

"The main stuff is there." Simms sullenly pointed to the north. "But scuttlebutt is this is the backup."

"Scuttlebutt?" Seahorse gave him a disgusted look. "This ain't the Navy."

Monitoring the shed, we slept in shifts, more Irregulars slowly trickling in. Nebula and Ink came in shortly before dawn, stopping by my position.

"We left them thinking we'd gone straight east." Ink snickered. "Good thing the snow melted today."

Yes, melted and frozen again. I looked up at the clear sky. The crescent moon hung low in the west, ready to set. For the first time in years, I couldn't see some of the constellations. Lights to the north irritated me. They were too bright. If we even got close to them, they could night blind us.

When the Big Dipper stood in the correct position, I walked through camp, nudging people with my foot. Mercy slept next to Grace, the two of them in the center of our cold camp. As safe as I could make them. They were the last I touched.

"Remember," I said quietly, making eye contact with every fighter, "your job is to stay hidden. Let us take the heat. I need you invisible to escort Fuzz's sister back to safety."

Those who would be returning, led by Seahorse and Sarge, nodded grimly. Seahorse spared a moment to glare at me, still pissed she had to stay behind.

Keeping one eye on the sky, monitoring time, the fighters spread out. We had to hit the shed at the shift change, in... Next to me, Chaos tensed, three fingers raised. Shift change in three...two...one.

Four men drove up and parked their Jeep, marching smartly to the shed, rifles in hand, their boots hitting the ground in near perfect time. One knocked, a sharp staccato, different to their last two. The door opened, salutes happened, and the shift switched mere feet from us.

The formalities done, they chatted quietly. Ignoring them, I extended a hand to crawl forward when Chaos barred my way. Silent, he pointed to a tiny nubbin attached to a tree, a pinpoint smooth spot the only indication it wasn't gnarl.

Motion sensor, yes. He'd spent time the last day showing us these. We had a lot to learn, being inside a tech zone for the first time in years.

We'd also spent time talking about pitfalls and gaps. I indicated a narrow track crossing the invisible barrier. Deer trail. Animals didn't give a shit about motion sensors, so trails meant constant alarms and bored guards.

Chaos smiled slightly, nodding.

This entire exchange took bare seconds, and the soldiers were still at the door. The previous shift headed to the Jeep, dragged along by one tired soldier. As they left, the new shift entered a code into the keypad.

Raising my hand, fist clenched, I opened it, pointing forward. *Go.*

All we had to do was cross ten feet before they could raise an alarm or shoot us.

Easy.

***

Exploding from sparse grass and bushes, still lightly coated with snow and ice, we charged straight for the soldier at the door. He spun, rifle rising, aiming. He gave a quick shout before Gryph leaped from the roof, landing on the poor bastard.

I hit a man in a tackle, rolling to my feet. A random fist caught my cheek, rocking me. His mouth dropped open in surprise when I stayed on my feet.

Or maybe it was the hair. Our battle braids drew eyes wherever we went.

So, I punched him, then kneed his groin while he was distracted.

It was probably the hair.

Storm and Sweetpea stayed on either side of Mercy and Grace. Aanisah spearheaded their little group right through our desperately quiet fight, straight into the shed.

One man on the edges made it to his feet, grabbing frantically at the comm device dangling from his ear. I snatched it, catching his collar, and yanked. Roughly my height, the soldier recovered quickly, flowing into a smooth combination of kicks and punches.

I wanted to laugh, then cry. This is *exactly* how our soldiers—how *Noah*—fought. Strong. Precise. Determined. But they all lacked a certain...viciousness that came from fighting not just for your life, but for your right to exist *as you were.*

If they lost, they risked death at worst. We risked slavery, rape, forced impregnation, and birth. Compared to that, death was nothing. We risked having everything we were torn from us.

Unfortunately for him, I was also intimately familiar with these moves.

Sidestep, duck, block, breathe. Never forget to breathe. Take hits, keep moving. I kicked him in the stomach, this soldier with a Second Lieutenant's gold bar on his shoulder. The man doubled over. I brought my knee up, aiming six inches above his head.

He toppled over, unconscious. Well, I hoped he was just unconscious.

I swayed and Chaos's heavy hand landed on my shoulder. "He was a tough son of a bitch, that one."

"Makes sense he'd go down, then." Phoenix looped zip-ties around feet and wrists, hog-tying the men as fast as she could. Gryph raised an eyebrow elegantly. She grinned. "He went up against the OG Bitch. Of course he lost." She sat back, surveying her work. "God *damn* I'm good. Beat my own time."

Chaos muffled his laughter, he and Gryph dragging the tied men into the shed.

"Yes, yes, you're wonderful." I followed them in after giving the trees a quick wave.

Grace already sat at a computer thing in the back, typing complicated sequences of commands. Her eyes were narrowed, focused. At times like this, when she did something completely different to how I remembered her, I superficially recognized her as my sister—same eyes, same color hair, same features—but her *expression.*

A sudden thought struck me. What did she see when she looked at me?

She muttered to herself while Mercy peered over her shoulder. I stopped by Phoenix. "I thought she said she needed an encrypted phone?"

She shrugged. "I dunno. I lost track of all this shit a long time ago. I'm just along for the ride."

Wandering over, I stepped over bound and gagged men. The shed itself contained control boards, screens everywhere, and cables snaked all over the floor. I examined the images, listening to Grace's muttering. Things like *mime, smokescreen,* and *tap cross* mixed with other phrases even stranger.

Suddenly, Grace sat straight, a smile lighting her face.

"Constance!"

***

Washington, DC – Constance

Constance paced the studio apartment. Fifteen steps from one wall to the other. Ever since they'd seen Captain on LA TV and heard from Senator Baser, she itched for action.

"I can hear you pacing," James called from the bathroom. The shower turned on.

"Bullshit." But she laughed.

"If you can't sit still, find something that will hold up in court."

That was the essence of Baser's call. Without something that could be presented in court, they were stuck. Illegal wiretaps were useless. Even if they managed to place Secretary Keller at her residence on four of the dates, there were still three where they couldn't do it.

"It's not enough," Baser said. "I would take it with what you have here, but she will go free. Then all of this becomes useless. We won't be able to present this to court again."

Constance ran her hands through her hair, studying the wall. Photographs—actual, *printed* photographs—were stuck to it. Red yarn stretched from photos to transcript notes. They'd followed the trails told by wire taps, bank statements, wire transfers, and more, all of it gained illegally, damn it.

They had the names of Senators, including her old boss, Bryce McKinney, Congress people, lobbyists, and others from the top tiers of government. All of them had planned or funded North Korea.

A loud, electronic chirp jerked her from her musing. Spinning, she sought the source. Her eyes widened.

"The phone!"

The phone, whose number she'd only given to two people, rang. Diving to the desk, then the bedside table, she shoved aside papers, a couple dishes, and a napkin from the diner down the street. Dropping the phone in her rush, she snatched it up, fumbling to answer it.

"Dammit, dammit, dammit," she muttered, swiping hastily. Finally, it caught, and a face she hadn't seen in months appeared on her screen.

Grace O'Connell smiled at her. A thin woman with light brown hair looked over her shoulder. Grace looked tired, bags under her eyes, dirt smeared on her face, but she smiled.

"Constance!"

"You're alive!" Constance sank to the floor. "You're okay. Oh, thank God. But where's Charlie?" Her heart sank.

"Charlie's fine." Grace waved her concern away. "He was injured and he's still healing, but he'll be fine."

"Where have you been? Where are you now?"

Grace glanced nervously off camera, then hunkered down. In the background, Constance heard thumping noises.

"No time," Grace said hastily. "I need your help. We need a flight to DC as fast as you can get one. Ten people, from the Bridgeport, California military airstrip. Soonest. I won't be going, I'm heading back to Charlie right after this."

"Time's running out," a woman called. "We need to go."

The bathroom door opened, and James stepped out, toweling off his hair. "Constance? Who are you talking to?" He fell silent when he saw the phone, his body tensing.

On the screen, Grace half stood. "Wait!" Constance gripped the phone tighter, as if that would stop the other woman. "What's happening? Why are you in such a hurry? Where are you?"

"No time to explain." Grace smiled desperately. "We're not supposed to be using this equipment, so... Hurry, please! Bridgeport, California, military airstrip, plane, ten people."

The screen went dark.

"Who was that?" James sat next to her, and she immediately leaned against him, staring at the phone.

"I told you about that couple from Oregon, remember?" He nodded. "They've been going into Washington state and getting people out a couple times a year for a while now."

"And?" he prompted when she fell silent.

"They need a plane for ten people, to an airstrip I've never heard of. And I don't have a way to help them with that!" she burst out.

He shifted her so that she sat between his spread thighs, her back against his chest. Slowly, he drew the details out from her. When she finished, he rested his chin on her shoulder, staring at the wall. Finally, he nodded.

"Got it. I've got a contact who owes me a huge favor *and* he does contract work for the military sometimes. Pack your things. We need to move." She gaped at him. "What?" he asked. "Don't you want to meet them?"

"Yes!"

***

Mono County, CA – Grace

To Grace, it seemed like they ran south for hours, until she was stumbling, tripping on clumps of grass. Every time she did, the huge black man behind her would boost her up, muttering words of encouragement. In the distance, she heard men shouting. And somewhere back there, her sister worked to distract the soldiers and give her time to escape.

It was hard to be afraid *for* the tall, scarred woman who appeared and disappeared like smoke, and much easier to be afraid *of* her. Then, Grace would remember Hope as she had been, and worry for her safety.

The sun settled against the horizon before they turned west, ensuring they didn't arrive at the fence until dark. Through the entire day, none of them spoke. All communication was through hand gestures. She couldn't even be sure how many fighters there were. They kept coming and going.

Stopping only when they reached the cleared ground leading to the fence, everyone, even Sarge, needed a break. Grace looked up at Goliath. "Thanks for your help. But, umm... Why are you helping me like this?"

He looked away. "I didn't know who you were until recently." Grace cocked her head. "You're Fuzz's sister. I didn't put it together because of your married name. You're a Wilkins."

"You...you knew his name?" she said faintly.

"Served with him, ma'am. We were good friends right until the end."

"When we're out of here, will you tell me some stories?"

Biting his lip, he nodded, blinking furiously. "It would be an honor, ma'am."

"Thank you." She touched his arm gently, then, her eyes swimming with tears, made her way to where Seahorse sat on the ground, leaning against a downed tree, watching the fence through her scope and chewing on some jerky. She wanted a distraction.

"How are we getting back across?" she asked, groaning quietly as she sank down next to the commander.

"They haven't stepped up their patrols. I'm guessing they don't have the manpower to run more." Seahorse spoke without lowering the scope. "Which is good for us. But they're a hell of a lot more alert now. What we need is a distraction that goes off when the next patrol shows up."

"What do you have in mind?"

"Oh, usually something that explodes. Though the timers are unreliable."

Grace rubbed her thumb over the smooth gold of her wedding band. "Can I...offer an alternative? It's something Charlie and I would use to draw attention from where we wanted to go."

"Shoot."

***

Sarge stepped back, folding his arms. She stood next to him, Seahorse on his other side, the three of them surrounded by the fighters not keeping watch. Together, they surveyed the falling tree they'd repositioned, delicately balanced on a slender branch.

A separate branch had been pulled back, held now with just a strip of leather. Once the leather broke, it would hit the tree, knocking it from its precarious perch.

"How long will that leather hold?" Sarge asked, eyeing the leather dubiously. "It looks pretty strong to me."

Grace drew her knife, sawing carefully. "Not for long."

Seahorse and several of the other fighters broke into muffled laughter. "Yeah, you're definitely Fuzz's sister." Seahorse shook her head.

"Okay." Grace stepped back. "We really want to get moving. This should give us enough time to get to the fence and whatnot, but..."

It tore a little.

"Faster than slow is good." Seahorse nodded. "Move out, people."

Their whole run back to the fence, Grace feared she'd hear the tree topple. Not only would it falling too soon prolong their danger, she really wanted to look good in front of these people. They were her sister's people, and well...she wanted to impress them.

At the edge of the trees, they donned their packs and waited. The moment the patrol was out of sight, they raced as a group to the fence. Sarge and Dionysius pulled wire cutters as they ran. They'd barely stopped before they began clipping, Sarge starting from the top, Dionysius down low.

Grace hissed. She could hear an engine in the distance. Now would be a good time for that tree... Except there was no sound.

"Go!" Seahorse shoved people through the gap.

Grace squeaked when the commander unceremoniously grabbed her collar, pushing her through the narrow gap Sarge made.

Lights were visible and they were still only halfway through... The Celt yanked Grace's arm. "Run!"

She'd gotten five feet when a loud crash drowned the sounds of the engine. Men shouted, the lights turned seconds before they would have flashed over the fighters gathered around the hole. Grace squealed, then bolted after the Celt as fast as her tired legs could carry her.

Seahorse caught up to her easily, breathing hard. "How far until we reach the no tech area?"

"Down here?" Grace gasped. "No idea."

"We don't stop," Seahorse called.

The shouting changed. A searchlight tracked over the ground. It didn't take long before the soldiers spotted them running.

"The trees!" the Celt cried, veering left.

They followed her. Above, the buzzing whine of a drone grew closer. "Those things have guns!" Grace screamed, leaping over a small bush.

"Spread out," Sarge bellowed hoarsely.

Bullets peppered the ground. Clenching her teeth, her breath puffing her cheeks with every exhale, Grace strained for a bit more speed. Couldn't...die...here. Wouldn't!

The drone fell silent. Risking a quick glance, Grace laughed breathlessly. The drone fell in irregular loops, its tech destroyed by whatever the North Koreans had done.

"Don't stop," Seahorse shouted. "Some of those bastards are coming through the fence, and they can shoot."

"One mile," Sarge bellowed. "One. More. Mile."

She thought she'd die, but she made it.

Chapter 27

Bridgeport, CA - Constance

Clutching the straps crossing her chest, Constance clenched her teeth as the cargo plane bounced roughly on landing. Next to her, James blinked, yawning and stretching. She huffed while the plane rolled to a stop.

"Seriously?" She glared at him.

He grinned. "Gotta sleep when you can."

Mumbling curses under her breath, she fumbled with the fastenings, unable to undo them quickly enough to suit herself. James, finished with his own, bent his head over hers. She smiled at the swirl of hair sticking up on the back of his head.

The copilot exited the cockpit. "Alright, folks! We've got cargo to unload first, then we can collect the passengers."

Following him to the back of the plane, past loaded pallets, Constance covered her ears when he lowered the ramp, but the loud gears wouldn't be drowned so easily. A cold wash of air ruffled her hair, and she shivered. As soon as the door touched the runway, soldiers poured in.

Methodically, they searched the aircraft while a lieutenant stopped in front of them. Constance stepped back, bumping into James, her heart pounding. Placing his hand on her arm, he moved around her, half hiding her from the soldier's view.

"What's going on?" the copilot, Addams, asked irritably, watching the soldiers. "Why all the security?"

"New precautions," he said shortly. "What's with the passengers?"

Addams handed over the shipping manifests and paperwork, including their travel papers. In this, at least, Baser could help them. They hadn't told her *why* they needed to go, but she produced identification and the correct paperwork for them to inspect the base and report back to the Senate.

Crossing her fingers behind her back, Constance bit the inside of her cheek. She hadn't thought the base would have so much security, especially since it was several miles from the fence itself.

James' warm hand closed around hers, reminding her she wasn't alone. She didn't know what they could possibly do if they were found out, but she was sure he'd think of something.

The lieutenant grunted, flipping through the paperwork. "Great. Inspection." He looked at them like they were mud on his boots. "Confine yourselves to the base grounds. It's not safe in the forest. You can leave in the morning," he said to Addams. "We need to inspect your plane thoroughly."

"Captain Benz won't like that," Addams warned. "He expected to leave today."

"He better get used to disappointment," the lieutenant said carelessly. "Unless he'd like to stop working for us."

Addams's lips thinned. Constance sympathized. When Benz left the cockpit, swearing at the soldiers who ordered him out, guns drawn, he stood close to James. Constance studied the captain. Tall, over six feet, and fit, he had thick brown hair that fell in waves to his collar, a luxurious mustache, and deep blue eyes. *Expensive haircut for a cargo pilot,* she noted.

"The fuck have you gotten me into?" he muttered from the corner of his mouth, glaring at the soldiers bringing dogs and equipment onto his plane.

"Honestly?" James shook his head infinitesimally. "You don't want to know. I don't entirely know, but I can guarantee it'll be the ride of your life."

"You fucker. After this, we're even. And you better fucking tell me what the hell you've gotten me into or I'm out of here. You can find your own fucking way back to DC."

James nodded, pulling Constance after him when a soldier ordered them out. Leading them to the edge of the airstrip, halfway to the hangars, he glanced around. Once he was sure they couldn't be overheard, he motioned them to gather around.

"Yesterday morning, Ms. West heard from a contact of hers who's been moving freely in the Occupied Zone, smuggling people out."

"Fuck!" Benz reassessed her, his eyebrows raised. "Didn't think you were the type to know people like that."

"Yesterday morning, we received a call from that contact, asking for a flight out."

Benz folded his arms, not satisfied with the minimal explanation. She nudged James. "Better tell him the rest."

James clenched his jaw, then relaxed slightly. "If you tell anyone what I'm about to tell you, I will skin you and stake you out under the sun," he said grimly. Benz and Addams nodded. "We suspect Captain is here."

Benz's swift intake of breath was hidden under the breeze. "Why the fuck would you think that?"

"Because I know them. I was sent in shortly after the Occupation. Met Captain then. And if Captain needs a ride, I will damn well get one, even if I have to shoot you and figure out how to fly the plane myself. I owe them."

Benz nodded, smoothing his mustache with his thumb and forefinger. "Are you *shitting me?* How the fuck did you never mention you knew the most notorious bastard in the world?"

James stared at him levelly. Benz nodded abruptly, seemingly satisfied. Constance looked from one to the other, thoroughly confused. Was this some strange male ritual, or did it have to do with their mysterious past?

"James." Elbowing him, she nodded to the soldiers glancing at them. "I think it's time we went and inspected this place. Maybe we'll find out how we're supposed to meet up with our passengers."

"You mean you don't even have a way to communicate with this guy?"

"They're from the Occupied Zone," James reminded him. "They had to borrow tech. I'll bet you a hundred bucks that's what's got these boys so worked up. I'll see you this evening. Meanwhile, we have an inspection to conduct."

***

Constance started awake, her heart pounding as she stared wildly around at the unfamiliar shapes around her. Slowly, she settled back. That's right, she was in a base in eastern California, right next to the Occupied Zone.

After their 'inspection,' she'd been given a tiny guest room near the barracks while James and the other men billeted with the soldiers. Smaller than James's apartment, it seemed huge with just her in it. It'd taken her forever to fall asleep.

As her heart slowed, she settled back against her hard little pillow. A shadow detached itself from the door and she squeaked, scrabbling upright.

"Shh..." She relaxed slightly at James's familiar voice. "It's just me."

"What on earth?" Unconsciously, she followed his example, keeping her voice low.

"Well, soldiers gossip, and it seems your ID isn't quite as bulletproof as Baser thinks. Or she has a mole in her office. They know you're wanted. We have to go. Now."

She gasped, clambering off the bed. Her nightgown fell to mid-thigh, and she had no intention of running around a base dressed like that, but when she went to her bag, James got it first, zipping it closed.

"What about Captain?"

"I'll come back later. Did you put everything in here?" he asked, already hefting it.

"I need to get dressed!"

"No time, they're already on their way. Leave your shoes off, they're too noisy."

When he eased the door open, checking the hallway, she saw *he* had boots on. Frowning, she tugged on his sleeve, pointing to his feet. He merely grinned, teeth flashing white in the dim light. Taking her hand, he led her quickly down the hallway. She grudgingly admitted that he was far quieter than she'd have managed in her shoes, but that didn't mean she had to be happy about running barefoot through the place.

Opening her mouth to ask the whereabouts of their pilot and copilot, James pulled her into a side room with a large conference table in the center. Pressing her against the wall, he left the door partially open. The cadenced footsteps of soldiers on a mission grew steadily closer.

Pressing her mouth against James's jacket to muffle her breathing, she bit the fabric, her fingers digging into his sides. Four soldiers marched past their hiding spot, one glancing quickly into the room before moving down the hall, heading to her room.

James' heart pounded steadily against her cheek. His calm slowly seeped into her until she rested against him, waiting for the signal to move. When their footsteps faded, he peeked into the hall, then tugged her after him.

Constance moved into a slow jog to keep up with his rapid pace.

An explosion rocked the building, shattering the small windows lining the hallway. Alarms wailed and people shouted. Footsteps echoed through the building as people, jarred from sleep, poured into the hallways.

"Fuck!" James snarled, holding her still.

Glass littered the floor, but she was already pulling ballet flats from the outer pocket of her little duffel. "I'm almost ready. I'm almost ready."

"You're good," he muttered, but as soon as she tugged on the second shoe, he immediately pulled her down the hallway, glass crunching underfoot as they ran. He paused near the doorway and Constance leaned against his back, gasping.

"I swear I'll go to a gym when this is over," she whispered to herself. "I'll get in shape this time."

Behind them, soldiers shouted, their words piling on top of each other. "Halt! Raise your hands slowly. Get down on your knees! Put your hands behind your back!"

"Which is it?" Constance snapped without thinking. "I can't do all of them at once!"

She broke off when she really looked at them. Five soldiers clustered in the hallway, guns pointed straight at them. The barrels yawned wide, filling her vision. Her hands shook, her grip tightening on James's belt.

He stepped in front of her, nudging her back. Shaking her head even though he couldn't see it, she moved to his side. He couldn't protect her from this.

Before anyone could move, another explosion flung everyone to the ground. Constance struggled to her elbows half a second before James. "Won't...die...lying down," she gasped.

A pair of moccasined feet appeared in her view. Gaping, she followed them up a pair of cargo pants, over a leather jacket, past more weapons than she'd ever seen outside of...of...today, to a woman's face. Firelight flickered on the scars around her left eye, turning the small braids falling around her face and shoulders to burnished gold.

"Goddamn right, sister," the woman said, extending a hand down to her.

Stunned, she took the hand as more people appeared silently from the dark, wearing a variety of clothing styles. Four waded into the soldiers, hands and feet flying. The woman hauled Constance up effortlessly just as the last soldier hit the ground. Constance was shocked to see three of the fighters were women.

James gained his feet a moment later, automatically putting himself between her and the biggest threat—the scarred woman. Only after she was safe did he stop and pay attention, Constance noted with a spurt of hysteria.

On finally looking up, James froze.

"Well, well, well," the woman said loudly, to be heard over the sounds of unchecked fires and collapsing rubble. "Look what the cat dragged in. Sergeant Perry."

Constance's breath caught in her throat. The woman from LA TV.

Captain, herself.

James choked, then laughed. "What the fuck are you doing in the middle of hostile territory? I would have found you."

She laughed shortly, her eyes grim. "I live in hostile territory. This is nothing. No, we heard the soldiers were planning to arrest her." She nodded to Constance. "Figured anyone on the military's shit list was someone worth meeting."

She started for the landing strip. Constance automatically followed, without conscious decision. She marveled at Captain's strength of character and assurance to draw everyone after her without hesitation.

Ahead, a plane—Constance recognized it as the one they'd arrived on—started its engines, rolling slowly forward. Behind them, a commotion drowned out everything except the plane.

"Time to go," Captain shouted. "Don't forget, try not to kill these ones."

A loud report broke the air and gravel flew nearby. James grabbed Constance, putting her in front of him, urging her to run. "Fuck them," he yelled. "That's our ride, and we don't want to miss it."

"Okay. *Move!*" Captain bellowed.

They broke into a run. Captain dropped back, putting Constance at the front. She heard more loud *pops*, gunfire or something, but all her attention was on running. She risked a glance over her shoulder. Those behind would run a few steps, fire, then run again.

She couldn't gain on the plane. Captain shouted, and a large, black-haired man appeared next to her. Before she could ask, he scooped her up, flinging her over his shoulder, and accelerated. She gasped and grunted with every step, her stomach bouncing painfully on his shoulder, knocking the breath from her.

From her new position, she watched the fighters abandon their strategy of run and shoot in favor of bolting after them. They reminded her of a vid she'd seen of wolves chasing down their prey, swift and deadly, intent on reaching their target, all feral grace and speed.

Her breath exploded out of her when the big man jumped. He immediately staggered forward a few steps, then dropped her unceremoniously to her feet. He bent over, gasping for breath as the last fighters leaped into the plane.

A slender woman with strawberry-blonde hair pressed the button, closing the back of the aircraft. Constance realized she wasn't the only new person here. Besides the blonde, there was a short black woman, a dark-complexioned woman wearing a hijab, and a curvy brunette.

"Nice," the blonde said when it shut firmly, putting the controller down carefully. "I could get used to this again."

"Don't say anything," James said loudly. "We've had visitors in and out all day and there might be extra ears."

"Extra...?" Captain's forehead wrinkled, then smoothed out. She nodded. "Fine. Where's Chaos?"

Chaos? Constance was fairly sure they'd left chaos behind them, but apparently, the word had another meaning to these people.

"Making sure the captain doesn't talk to anyone we don't want to meet," the brunette said.

Captain turned to James, resting a hand on his shoulder and stepping close. "It's good to see you," she said, tipping her head down. James leaned in, and they pressed their foreheads together, eyes closed.

Constance watched them, expecting a pang of jealousy, surprised when it didn't come. There was nothing about this that spoke of sex or lust. Captain stepped away from him and approached her.

"Thanks for the pickup," the rebel leader said softly, cupping her neck, her palm rough against Constance's skin, and dropped her head to press their foreheads together.

Constance closed her eyes, dizzy at having another face so close to her own. Captain's warm breath, smelling of herbs, washed over her face. There was no meeting of minds, no magical telepathy, but peace washed over Constance, peace and the surety that here, she was safe. No harm would come to her, she was welcome, and wanted as a friend.

When Captain raised her head, Constance looked dazedly around the plane. A petite blonde stepped up, repeating the move. The feelings changed slightly, but with every woman who greeted her like this, Constance felt she recognized them in some way, though she'd never met any of them in her life.

When the last one left, Constance found James at her side. "What was that?" she murmured, still stunned.

"That's their greeting for people they know and trust," he said softly. "They're welcoming you like they would their own."

"Why?"

As quietly as they spoke, Captain heard. She said, "You came for us, even though it was dangerous to you. And you basically told those soldiers to fuck themselves. I admire that in a person. Now, how long to get back to wherever the fuck it is we're going?"

Constance's head spun. This was the closest thing she'd ever had to a spiritual experience, and they all acted like it was another Sunday.

"Five hours, give or take," James replied.

"Guess we have time for a nap, then."

Constance's mouth dropped open when the leader of the uprising that encompassed the entire West Coast unbuckled a blanket from her pack, spread it on the ground, and settled down, her back to the wall, using her pack as a pillow.

"Wake me up when we get there," she said, closing her eyes.

Shaking her head, Constance slowly lowered herself to a seat, struggling with the straps and buckles. "I need some yoga," she muttered, her legs still trembling from...everything. She shivered, just realizing she still wore only her nightgown.

"Here." Constance looked up into serious, clear blue eyes. The woman held out a blanket, pushing light brown hair back under her hat with her other hand. "I'm wearing enough to stay warm, and I don't think I could sleep just yet."

Constance felt a shock of recognition. She knew this face, but not looking like this. Where had...? Oh, God. LA TV. "Mercy," she whispered.

Fortunately, Mercy didn't hear her. Gingerly, she took the seat next to Constance. The strawberry-blonde sat on Mercy's other side. Around them, the rest of the fighters followed Captain's lead, stretching out. The large, black-haired man curled around a petite woman. Two of the others slept back-to-back, sharing their warmth.

"I've got first watch," the blonde said, nodding to Constance. "I'm Storm."

"I'm—"

"Best not introduce yourself," Storm said cheerfully. "This isn't my legal name, so anyone listening won't get much from it, but you shouldn't just yet."

"You sound very...used to this," Constance said carefully.

Storm looked around. "Never been on a plane before. It's all kind of new. Exciting."

"*This* is unusual? Not..." Constance waved behind them.

Storm laughed. "That's our typical Tuesday. Well, if we knew when Tuesday was. When is this, anyway?"

CHAPTER 28

Fresno, CA – Faith

Groaning, Faith set down her basket and stretched her arms overhead. Lucas, she noted, wasn't even breathing hard, and his basket was heavier.

Sexy.

Laughing, she leaned against him while they took a break. Her basket overflowed with lettuces. She'd forgotten there were so many types. Greens, reds, frilly, straight edged... Lucas carried the winter potatoes her mom found at the farm they'd taken over.

Shouting in the distance caught her attention. "What's that? Can you see?"

Lucas shook his head. "But it's near the kitchen, so..." He shrugged.

After helping her shrug back into the basket's shoulder straps, he hefted his own load easily, following her down the road.

Fresno had changed so much in the short time since the NK's were removed. Rubble had been cleared, the fences torn down, and people left the city in droves. The Irregulars were kept busy. No longer fighting an enemy, they now found themselves policing civilians.

The two in charge, Stretch and Gameboy, were less than pleased, mostly because, as Carter said, "They want us to have some rules in place. Otherwise, they said they'll run it military style, whether we like it or not." But even with that, things were so much better. Life was *good*.

Ahead, a crowd gathered. She couldn't be sure, but she thought she saw some beat-up vehicles, similar to what the fighters drove.

"I can't see!" she complained.

"Kitchen's there. We can stand on the benches."

She grinned. "Brilliant! Last one there has to give the other a shoulder massage."

Laughing, they fast-walked, and she *knew* Lucas let her win. He stayed even with her until the last few feet, letting her get to the common kitchen a few steps ahead of him. It made her love him even more.

"Ah, damn." He shook his head, his hair flopping into his eyes. "I guess I owe you a massage." He leered, the expression made all the better when he laughed. "Come on. Table."

He lifted her onto the bench, then stepped onto the table next to her. Shading her eyes, she peered over their heads at... "Grace! It's Grace! She's back. They've got Charlie. Let's go!"

Without waiting for him to reply, she grabbed his hand, yanking him off the benches after her. At the crowd, she stepped back, letting him go first, shouting and elbowing his way through. Holding onto his shirt, she followed in his wake.

Near the center, Lucas stepped aside.

"Grace!" she screamed.

"Faith!" Grace shrieked back.

Colliding together, she wrapped her arms around her cousin. Rocking, they stayed like that for long moments.

"I feel like we didn't really get a chance to talk before you were off with...with Captain," Faith said, her voice muffled against Grace's hair. "Did that all go okay?"

Grace shuddered in her arms. Around them, the noise of greetings faded. "I don't know. There was so much shouting. But Seahorse isn't worried, and she knows Captain better than I do."

"Hey, Grace—oh! Sorry."

Turning, Faith saw a black woman a bit shorter than herself. It took a moment before she remembered. "You're Captain's driver. I'm sorry, I don't remember your name."

"Dereva," Grace said. "What's up?"

Dereva studied the two women, her blue eyes sharp, assessing. "How well do you know each other?"

"We're cousins," Grace said.

She paused for a long moment, her face still. "You also grew up with Peter, then?" Faith nodded. "Perfect. I need you both to come with me."

"I'm not going anywhere without Charlie," Grace said firmly.

Faith finally noticed Charlie, popping wheelies in a rusty wheelchair with a few bits polished to a shine. Lucas cheered him on, then, on noticing the women, coughed and nodded in their direction.

"Subtle," Faith said dryly.

"Listen," Dereva said. "I've got some things that need to be said, and it's not going to be easy for any of us. So, I'd like to get it done as soon as possible. Everybody who was a relative of Fuzz's. Please?"

"Who?" Faith asked.

"Peter." Grace swiped away a tear. "They called him Hot Fuzz."

Faith choked, then laughed, her own eyes wet. "I heard of Fuzz. I didn't... Oh, that suits him so much."

"Please?" Dereva clenched her hands.

"Is it alright if Lucas comes, too?" Faith asked, following the younger woman through the crowd. "He never met Peter, but he and I... Well, he would have been related to him."

Dereva nodded once, jerkily. "Fine. Where can we go?"

"Park," Faith and Lucas said at once. "It's got lots of open spaces," Faith continued. "We'll have privacy there."

And no troubles with the wheelchair. Grace kept her hand on Charlie's shoulder as he wheeled himself down the paths. Taking the lead, Lucas led them away from the kitchens to a small group of trees. Grace seated herself on Charlie's lap. Faith chose to stand. The ground was either full of sharp things or wet, with nothing in between.

Once alone, Dereva chewed her lip, unsure where to start.

"Who asked you to speak to Grace?" Faith asked to get the conversation rolling.

"Captain." Dereva said the name automatically, then paused. "Hope."

Faith's eyebrows climbed her forehead. "You know her real name? Both you and Phoenix?"

"We've been with her since the beginning," Dereva admitted. "But I'm not talking about that. I'm not. God." She groaned. "Okay, blunt is the easiest way. Like ripping off a Band-Aid. All I'm asking is that you save your questions or comments until I'm done, okay?"

Faith's stomach sank. Nothing good ever came when those words were uttered, but they all agreed, even though she could see the same trepidation on their faces that she felt.

Taking a deep breath, she squared her shoulders. "I was engaged to Peter. We were due to be married when he...when he died." Her voice shook. "Hope is like a sister to me. But that's not everything. She has...I don't know if you know this, but she was married. For a while."

The news about Peter and this beautiful young woman being engaged rocked Faith's world. But Hope...married? She'd never talked about getting married when the rest of them were dreaming. She'd just smile, shrug when they asked what kind of man she wanted to marry and stare out the window.

Turning, she bent, hand over her mouth. Warm arms caught her. Lucas held her tight, whispering against her hair. Twisting until her back was against his chest, she watched Dereva, wiping the tears that continued to fall unchecked.

"They were...really good together. Really, really good. I don't know his real name. I only knew him as Archangel." Dereva exhaled, hard. "But he died. It wasn't...it was hard on everyone. Especially her. She doesn't talk about him much. I think it's too painful."

Grace's mouth worked. "How long since...?"

Dereva shrugged. "Three years? I think? I don't know. It's..." Tears pooled in her crystal blue eyes. "This isn't even what she wanted me to tell you. Your dad and brother don't even know, Grace."

"Know what?" she whispered. Faith was sure it was only Charlie's grip on her that kept her from breaking.

"She and Archangel had kids. Twin boys." Dereva swallowed. "She wanted you to know so that you could be there for them. They're in Oregon right now. As far as they know, they're orphans, but they're well cared for."

"What are their names?" Charlie asked when his wife couldn't. She buried her head against his, weeping softly.

"Michael and Gabriel." The couple on the wheelchair started.

"We saw them," Charlie said thickly. "They were running. Grace held Michael for an instant."

Dereva smiled through her tears. "He likes you, then. I've seen him bite someone when he didn't want them to touch him."

"How could she?" Grace finally spoke, fury and grief quavering in her voice. "How could she leave and not tell me? How could she leave them?"

Dereva nodded slowly. "I can see why you'd say that. She left without telling you because it's too hard for her to say it. When she told me, it was more like..." She pressed her lips together, more tears gathering. "It was like she was telling me goodbye. Like she doesn't know if she's coming back. And considering what she's planning, she might not."

"Why wouldn't she?" Faith burst out.

"Because she might just be executed for treason. Or murder. Hard to say exactly what will happen."

Everyone fell silent at that.

CHAPTER 29

Wiretap, Keller Residence – December 10, 2065, 6:38pm
Man: Difficult? You should know better than anyone that's the understate-
ment of the century, Mother. Half the world looks down on us!

Savage, MD – Captain

When I stepped off the plane in...somewhere, back east, the sun barely crested the horizon, not that you could see it. We stood on a tiny, private airstrip, and all around, lights blazed. Not just the floodlights overhead, but smaller ones in the distance. Towns, houses, streetlights...

"Electricity," I muttered.

Doc wandered over, tapping a small screen. "Perry! Where's the search engine on this thing? I want to see books, dammit."

Laughing and shaking his head, Perry poked something. Squealing, she typed awkwardly away. Phoenix looked more like me, watching every small light and blip like it might suddenly jump up and bite her.

The pilot left the plane, closely followed by another young man. Copilot, I suppose. The older man immediately nodded to Gryph, an odd light in his eyes. "Captain?" He gestured to a small hangar. "This way."

Gryph raised an eyebrow, glancing at me. Sighing, I nodded, motioning him to go first. Chaos snagged Doc when she didn't notice us moving, gently urging her along.

"Why is everything so expensive?" she grumbled. "Fucking inflation."

Eleanor had Mercy under her wing, the two of them protected by Mercy's new bodyguards. The three of them looked like they were having fun, glaring at the copilot. Aanisah narrowed her eyes, shaking her head, the poor guy looked bewildered before scurrying off after the other men.

"You coming, Captain?" Eleanor called.

At that, the pilots whipped around, searching behind them, trying to figure out who she addressed.

"I'm coming, Eleanor," I replied.

The pilot stayed by the door. When I reached him, he stuck his arm out, barring the way. "You said you're Captain?" he challenged.

"Lots of other people say it, too."

"Prove it."

"Yo, Perry!" I shouted. He turned. "Do I have to leave this guy in one piece? As in, is he useful? Do we need him?"

"He's got a plane." Perry shrugged. The small woman traveling with Perry watched me over his shoulder, eyes wide. "I mean, I'd trust him with my life, if not my wallet, but if he's dumb enough to go there, do what you have to, Captain."

The pilot looked suspiciously between me and Perry. "Wait. You're serious? She's...Captain? A chick?"

While he was distracted, I ducked under his arm, entering the hangar. "Hey!" he shouted.

Phoenix sniggered. "Come on, Captain. Why so nice?"

"He has a plane. I might want to borrow it later."

A heavy hand landed on my shoulder. Without thinking, I grabbed his pinky, spinning under his arm. When I finished, I had his arm twisted behind his back, forcing his hand between his shoulder blades.

He howled.

"You still want to act like a dick?" I asked. He shook his head. "Good. Because I don't have time for your petty 'but she's a girl!' bullshit. I owe someone over here for a lot of shit, and I aim to deliver."

***

"I just can't find good proof, I'm sorry." The small woman with enough gumption to face down a bunch of armed men shook her head. Constance. Old fashioned name for a modern woman. "All the evidence we have was gained illegally, which makes it useless in court."

We all sat around a table, just like we'd done at the Lair, but there were too many missing faces. Sirius and Archangel, yes, but all those still back home, too.

Phoenix tapped the table, then raised her eyebrow, tilting her head towards my pack. I shrugged. The two pilots had long since crashed in the back rooms. I liked what I'd seen of Constance, so...

"There are several senators, lobbyists..."

"The head of the NRA, Schmidt," Perry added.

"And of course, Secretary Keller and her son." Constance curled her lip. "Not that we can find the evidence necessary to make them pay for it. Senator Baser refused to hear the rest of what we've got, because it's all from the same anonymous source."

While they spoke, I dug in my pack, shuffling past basic camping gear, extra bullets, and a first-aid kit to get to the back. The light shone directly on my hands, distracting me. I hadn't seen them under such bright lighting in…years. Scars crisscrossed them. Some were small nicks and dings, others longer, the result of scratches and minor cuts that didn't heal cleanly.

Shaking my head, I fished out an envelope that used to be white. "What about this?" I tossed it into the center of the table.

Constance eyed me but took it hesitantly. I watched her face while she read the letters, the first signed by the president, ordering the evacuation of all the hidden bunkers out west, like our Lair, the other, a letter promising to cooperate with the North Koreans with the Secretary of State's seal at the top. On her face, I saw surprise. Anger. A hint of fear.

"That woman was smart, not signing it." Sighing, Constance set down the letter with her seal. Then she smiled. "But combined with what we have, it might be enough."

I shook my head. "We didn't come here for 'might.' That woman will pay, one way or another."

The fighters smiled with predatory delight. Constance looked disturbed. "It's not easy getting close to her."

"It's not just getting close to her." Phoenix leaned forward, resting her elbows on the table. "People need to hear what she did. What all of them did."

"They will," I promised, barely holding back a snarl. "None of this will be in vain. It's not worth the cost, but dammit, I will see them pay."

***

Savage, MD – Mercy

Finding a quiet corner, Mercy huddled with her back to the wall, burying her head against her knees. Before he'd gone to bed, the copilot, Addams, told her he "always cheered her on." But she'd never met this man before.

And on the plane, Constance had whispered her name. She hadn't reacted, but she couldn't sleep for the entire flight, trying to figure out how she knew.

Her three bodyguards watched her from a distance, trying to be unobtrusive. When they'd sent Aanisah over, she'd rebuffed her. She didn't know what to say. How could she explain that something felt off, without knowing what it was?

"Mercy, dear?"

Mercy hunched tighter. Even Eleanor couldn't help right now. The older woman stopped well away from her, though.

"May I sit next to you?"

At that, Mercy looked up, unused to anyone asking her for permission. Eleanor stood with her hands behind her back, incongruous in her cargo pants and boots. Mercy thought she'd look more natural in a dress or skirt. Something that flowed when she walked.

"Okay," she said hoarsely.

Eleanor sat comfortably, crossing her legs, just close enough for her knee to press against Mercy's leg. Pulling her satchel around, she fished some knitting out, working on it in companionable silence. Muttering under her breath, she undid several stitches, frowning at her knitting.

"What are you working on?" Mercy eventually asked.

"Socks. I think." Huffing, Eleanor set the item down. "I can't seem to get it, and I've been trying for literal years."

Smiling slightly, her first real smile in days, Mercy shook her head. "Sorry. I don't know how to knit. I could stitch you up, but not that." Shifting, she slid all the way down, stretching her legs out in front of her.

"Ah, that's all right." Eleanor leaned against the wall. "We all have our strengths. There must be someone out there who's terrific with socks. It's just not me. I only try because when the girls come to me for advice, I'm so happy to be able to put this down."

Mercy digested that. "You mean, you do it so that you're happy for a distraction, and they can tell you're always happy to see them?"

Eleanor pointed at her, then tapped her own head. "You've got it in one."

"That's...devious." Mercy evaluated her with fresh eyes. First, she admitted she enjoyed watching Captain work, now she spilled another secret... Mercy watched her through narrowed eyes. "You're spilling secrets so I'll feel safe enough to talk to you," she accused, barely holding back another smile.

Eleanor laughed lightly. "Please don't tell anyone. I don't need them to be able to read me as well as you do." She hesitated a moment, then touched Mercy's knee lightly. "But...will you? Tell me what's bothering you. The girls are getting agitated. They will literally break down walls and blow up buildings to make you happy, you know."

She nodded to Aanisah, Storm, and Sweetpea, who'd given up trying to be inconspicuous and now sat in a row, watching the two of them.

Licking her lips, Mercy leaned closer to Eleanor. "That guy, Addams, he said...he said he'd always cheered for me. But I don't know what he means by that! And Constance. She knew my name, but we hadn't been introduced. How did she know my name?"

Eleanor gasped, covering her mouth. "Oh, I know. I can't believe nobody mentioned it. But why would we? We're so used to not having tech..."

"What?"

"We were told all the cameras in Los Angeles were working." Swiftly, Eleanor told her everything she knew about LA TV. It wasn't much, but enough. By the time she finished, Mercy pressed her back against the wall once more, her knees drawn tightly to her chest.

"They saw...everything?" she whispered. Every rape? Every humiliation she'd ever dealt with?

Suddenly, she was surrounded by women. The other three hurried over the moment Eleanor waved. They sat down, scootching over the floor until they encircled her. Storm took her hand gently.

"Let us help you," she said softly, her terrible scar pulling at her mouth. "We know."

"You don't!" Mercy hissed, yanking her hand away. "How could you? How could any of you know?"

"I was held in a brothel for months," Storm said softly.

"I was not freed until the end of the Oregon war," Aanisah whispered. "Captain found me on the night of the last battle, when she killed my rapist."

"I was held in a 'recreation' area." Sweetpea made air quotes. "Most of us fighters were imprisoned like that. The only thing we didn't have to deal with was religious lunatics."

Mercy laughed shortly. Bitterly. "'Lunatics' is a good way to describe those mingin' bastards."

But she looked at them with fresh eyes. All this time, she thought she was alone. Having company didn't remove any of her pain, but being understood... Sighing, she relaxed. Slowly, they moved closer, until she was surrounded, the pressure of their bodies reassuring, instead of demanding.

Like the human equivalent of a pile of puppies, sleeping together.

***

Hyattsville, MD – Constance

Firmly gripping James's belt, Constance followed him down the dark alley. Captain wouldn't let them go anywhere during the day, which was probably reasonable, but now she couldn't see anything. The streetlights didn't reach this far down the alley, but her nose told her they were surrounded by trash.

At a darker piece of shadow, James stopped, fishing keys from his pocket. He fumbled at the door for a moment, but Captain stopped him before he opened it.

"How long since you've been here?" she asked in a low voice.

"Years."

Something rustled and clanked, then Captain moved past him, spraying something. "WD-40," she said with a hint of humor. "Never leave home without it."

Once inside, they felt their way through the room to the back, where the kitchen was located. "It's my parents'," James said over his shoulder. "They're in Florida right now, so we have to keep a low profile, but no one will look for us here."

"No?" The large, blond man, Chaos, opened and closed cupboards. "Why not?"

"They disowned me after Oregon. The government decided they needed a scapegoat, so I was branded a coward," James said in an even tone.

Constance struggled to contain her shock, and a little hurt, that he hadn't told her. "Why?" she whispered.

"I'll tell you later," he murmured in her ear. To everyone else, "There are enough rooms for everyone, but we can't have lights. But the bills are paid, the water is running, and nobody looks in the alley, as you noticed, so we can use that to go in and out. It's a good place to—"

"Hold it!" Phoenix held up a hand. The petite woman wore her personality on the outside, Constance noted, holding nothing back. She liked her, because you always knew where you stood with her. *If she didn't like someone, she'd probably just punch them*, Constance mused. "You have a shower?"

James nodded.

"Babe." She grabbed the tall, British man's hand, towing him towards the door. "Come on. Don't look for us before tomorrow," she said over her shoulder.

The Brit laughed, waving, as his tiny wife towed him out.

"Do you have more than one shower, and the hot water to handle it?" Chaos demanded.

James nodded. "Instant hot water, heated in the pipes. Have fun," he called when Chaos hefted the small brunette, Doc, over his shoulder, and left even more abruptly than Phoenix, Doc laughingly protesting the whole way.

After they left, Eleanor pulled the kitchen curtains closed and Storm lit a candle, setting it on the table. The candle lent everyone an air of mystery, concealing more than it revealed. With nothing else to do, Constance sat at the table with the fighters.

"So, what are your plans?" she asked.

The fighters laughed quietly, including Captain. "Honestly?" she said. "I'm still surprised we made it this far. But before we can really get into it, we need intel, especially on whether we can expect all our suspects to be in one place at the same time or if we need to hunt them down separately."

James nodded to Constance. "She'll know more about that than me. She worked in there for years."

Captain considered her. Constance found she couldn't meet the woman's eyes for more than a couple seconds. The emotions there... Rage, determination, and so much sorrow it nearly made her weep.

"I only lasted as long as I did because I needed access," Constance told the table. "It took me forever to get my hands on the files." She blinked. Captain wore a simple, engraved band on her ring finger. "Are you married?"

"No," Captain said shortly, curling her fingers into a fist.

"Really?" James smiled. "Because I figured Archangel would have put that there. Where is he, anyway?"

Captain shut down hard. Her entire body tightened. "He died."

James flinched. "How...? I'm sorry, I can see it's painful," he said thickly, "but he was a friend. We served together."

Standing abruptly, Captain left. After a moment, the side door opened and closed quietly, barely audible in the silent kitchen.

Constance looked around, but no one went after the tall, scary woman.

"It's alright." Eleanor gently laid a hand on Constance's. "She'll come back when she's able."

"Please," James whispered. Constance leaned against him, taking his hand. He held onto it like a lifeline. "Tell me."

Eleanor sighed. "I wasn't there."

"I was." Storm straightened. "As you guessed, they got married. They were disgustingly sweet together, too," she said wistfully. "We'd had intel that Steve was massing down the mountains, planning to burn us out. We also heard that Kwan Jae, the colonel of the Salem lot, was leading them.

"It was an opportunity we couldn't miss. We planned an ambush, but they were ready for us. We figured we'd gotten unlucky until Captain comes racing down the mountain, shouting about an ambush and how we'd been led into a trap."

Her hands tightened, tears glittering in her eyes. "Gryph was down by the road when a grenade bounced over. Archangel threw him out of the way, leaving himself in the blast path. Gryph got his body out, but it was too late. We barely got out of there."

James shuddered, dropping his head down, still holding her hand tightly. A hot tear splashed onto the back of her hand. Shifting, Constance pulled James to her, holding him as he cried.

Tears stung her eyes in sympathy for his pain, his body shaking in her arms. Eleanor wiped tears from her eyes, while Storm and Sweetpea wrapped their arms around each other. Mercy looked visibly shaken. Perhaps she hadn't heard the full story before. Of those sitting around the table, only Aanisah seemed untouched.

Stroking his hair, she whispered soothing nonsense in his ear, just wanting his pain to stop. Finally, he sat up, wiping his eyes. "Hail the victorious dead," he rasped.

"Hail," the Irregulars replied solemnly.

"He's gone." They all turned at the hoarse voice to see Captain in the doorway, her fingers white where she clutched the frame. "But he didn't die in vain. None of them did. The coast is freed, and I will fucking make sure it stays that way."

Chills ran up Constance's arms. She believed this woman could do whatever she set her mind to, no matter how impossible. Walking closer, Constance thought she looked too calm. Her eyes were clear, no signs of weeping.

Yet, she didn't doubt the rebel leader's love for her husband. It was in her eyes, the lost look there, as if, after so long, she still didn't quite know how to breathe without him.

"And, if you don't mind me asking, you said you'd been led into a trap. You were betrayed?"

"Yes." Captain sat down, her large, bony hands resting lightly on the table in front of her.

"What happened?"

"I got him," Storm said, satisfaction dripping from every word. "I'd shoot him again if I had the chance."

"I...see. And, with that in mind, how do you intend to make Keller pay for what she's done?"

"Oh, not just the secretary," Captain said. "I owe the whole fucking family. It's personal."

"What do you mean?"

"Her husband commanded the base where four of my people were held and tortured. He'd planned to have them tried for war crimes, terrorism, or some shit." She contemplated her hands, turning them over, flexing her fingers. "And her son committed some crimes himself, blamed Archangel for them, had him court martialed, then sent into Oregon.

"I'm a bit torn about that one," she admitted, surprising Constance with her candor. "On the one hand, I'd never have met him. On the other, he would be alive and well."

"And in prison for the rest of his life," James put in. "Arnold Keller didn't have anything good planned for him."

"You know what?" Constance leaned forward. "I'm surprisingly okay with anything you have planned for them, as long as they see justice. Make sure their crimes can't stay hidden. I'd like to see my old boss amongst those who are exposed, too."

Captain nodded. "I knew I liked you. You've got the nastiness of one of us. You just look sweet."

Constance blushed. That was...once of the nicest compliments anyone had ever given her. "So, how do you intend to do this?"

"Like I said, we need intel. Where we can find each of them. How to send your intel across the net. What the buildings look like. What kind of security we'll have to deal with."

"Facial recognition," Storm added.

"Ah!" Constance smiled. "That's the easiest one. After the bombings here, we lost so many servers and so much information. Even if they get your photo, they don't have anything to tie it back to. As in, they can't match you to something like your driver's license. It's been a serious problem, but it's nice to get some good from it.

"As for the suspects..." Constance tapped her chin. "A lot of them are at the Capitol building frequently. I know the basic layout, but..."

"Is there any way you can draw it for us?"

Constance glanced at James, an idea rolling through her mind, but he looked puzzled. Finally, sighing, she threw up one hand. "The tours?"

***

Hyattsville, MD – Captain

I stood under the spray of water, my eyes closed, years of grime sluicing off. Once the others had enjoyed the showers and were sound asleep, I took my turn.

I hadn't had a hot bath in a while. Nobody had seen a hot shower since Before, but the novelty of hot running water couldn't compete with the emotions roiling in my chest. Between the heat and the water, my tears were completely hidden, even from me.

Having to say that Noah was gone broke something in me. He was *gone*.

And no matter how hard I tried, I wouldn't be getting him back.

Opening my eyes, I thumped the cold tiles, once, then again, the pain of it grounding me. He was gone, Peter was gone, Sonya was gone.

Some motherfucker would pay.

***

Hyattsville, MD – Constance

Constance closed the door, leaning against it. The remainder of the night had been spent assuring the fighters they were safe to shower, finding beds and bedding, and watching people who hadn't had any sort of softness for years look at their humble surroundings and squeal in delight at the luxury.

It was sobering, but she didn't have time to think about it and come to some lofty conclusion. No. Right now, she wanted answers.

This bedroom was nearly empty, just a bed in the corner, a simple blue and white plaid comforter neatly laid across it. No pictures, no art, not even a set of drawers. Just plain white walls and the single bed.

"This was my room," James said abruptly, turning to face her. "Looks like my parents decided to clean it out. No surprise there," he added under his breath.

"Tell me."

Nodding once, he sat on the bed, suddenly exhausted. They'd gotten some sleep on the flight back, but since then, he'd been on an adrenaline rush.

"You know part of it already, since you were looking for me. We went into Oregon, and I walked out with only seven men, no CO, no second-in-command, and less than the full number of people we were supposed to rescue."

He'd been debriefed, and his superiors were angry that he couldn't tell them more about the small band inside the Occupied Zone.

"I mean, I knew more than I said, but they wanted to know exactly who those people were." He glanced up once, wryly. "That's part of why they chose to only use code names, you know. So that no one could endanger them or their families."

Going back to staring at his hands, he outlined how the military branded him a coward who'd gotten his superior officers killed through insubordination, making it so that no one would listen to his story.

Hot words rose to her lips, but she held them back. He needed to talk, but how *dare* anyone suggest he wouldn't do everything in his power to protect the people around him? She'd only known him a few months, but she'd known by the end of the first day that she was safe with him.

"They were thorough, I'll give them that. I did find one journalist who'd talk to me, but he disappeared after a single meeting. I didn't dare contact anyone else."

His father, third-generation Army, couldn't deal with a son who'd disgraced himself. His mother cried, but after talking with a military liaison, she told him they couldn't have anything to do with him anymore.

"Your brother died for this country," she said, "and here you ran away, leaving more men just like him to die? How could you?"

A tiny growl left her throat. If she ever met his mother... James glanced at her, surprised. Her jaw set, Constance met his gaze. He grinned slightly, unclenching his fists. Seeing the chance, she took it, lacing their fingers together. He gripped it tightly, as if afraid she'd reject him too.

Like his mother.

She growled again. She'd never wanted to hurt someone like this before. Maybe the Irregulars were rubbing off on her. But that woman hurt her own son, the man Constance loved, and if she ever met his mother, she'd be getting an earful and then some.

With their fingers entwined, he continued. The rest of the soldiers who'd come back with him died, one by one. "Every single one was listed as accidental or a suicide. But I knew all those men. Not one of them would do that. I think the only reason I wasn't the first one dead is that I'd been drifting, taking buses and trains to new places after my parents disowned me."

"Why didn't you tell me this sooner?" she asked when he finished.

He shrugged, some of the tension returning. "It was hard to think you'd believe me when my own parents didn't."

"James." She smiled lovingly at him, brushing his hair back. "You absolute *spoon*. The first time I met you, you saved a stranger's life, all because she was in trouble." He laughed. She looked around the room again. "And I just realized that there was another bed I could have gone to. I'm just so used to sleeping next to you now, I came in here as a matter of course."

"Because you belong here," he said gruffly, love shining in his eyes. "With me."

She leaned against him. "With you. And you belong with me."

"Yes. I do."

Laying back on the narrow bed, he tugged her down with him.

CHAPTER 30

Hyattsville, MD – Mercy

"No," Constance said firmly. "You absolutely *cannot* go out like that."

"What's wrong with it?" Phoenix demanded, looking down at herself.

Mercy chuckled. The others stared. "What?" she asked, crossing her arms.

"I just...haven't heard you laugh," Storm said. "It's good. Real good."

The others nodded. The women were all back around the kitchen table. Phoenix, per Constance's instructions, stood on a chair. Right now, she turned in a slow circle, her arms held out from her sides.

She wore combat boots, which were good in snow, Mercy now knew, camouflage fatigues, a heavy sweatshirt, and probably a t-shirt or two underneath, if Mercy's own wardrobe was anything to go by.

"But these are my *clothes*," Phoenix protested. "They're good. I've had them for months. They're finally worn in."

"And they look like you've had them for decades." Constance sat back in her chair. "You need new clothes. All of you."

Everyone except Eleanor, Captain, and Mercy protested, their words unintelligible as they piled on top of each other.

"We can't buy anything," Captain said quietly, overriding the protests.

Constance shrugged. "I've got some money set aside. I haven't had to pay my rent for the last few months. My treat. For all our government has put you through."

Though her words were light, Mercy felt so much more going on under the surface. Unfortunately, it didn't look like she was in any mood to explain.

While the fighters grumbled, Mercy looked down at her clothes. She'd be happy to get rid of them, remnants as they were of her time in the compound.

"Wait." Constance looked around them, hand to her mouth. "I can't believe I forgot! Do any of you need to see a dentist or anything?"

"I saw one last spring," Phoenix said, hopping down and sitting in her chair again. The other fighters nodded in agreement.

Constance looked from one to another. "How?"

Doc leaned her elbows on the table. "We're only missing tech. We've still got the skills."

"And Anansi's steam powered stuff." Phoenix grinned. "How much did you swear, Captain, while you guys were building that?"

Groaning, Captain buried her face in her hands. "Don't talk to me about it."

"What about Mercy?" Constance looked between them, still confused, but determined to help.

"Storm took me to one right before we left." Mercy's lips twitched. "We didn't have lollies or treats, and I brushed with what I could—"

"Chewed-up twigs!" the fighters chorused, high-fiving around Captain.

Mercy nodded. "And that seemed to work pretty well, because the dentist said my teeth are good."

Constance's mouth dropped open. "Chewed-up…? Nope. No. I don't want to know any more. Just tell me how you are for period stuff, then, and we can go online and order clothes for you all."

***

Washington, DC – Captain

I adjusted the bill of my brand-new baseball cap, catching Phoenix's eye before turning away. The room I studied had windows everywhere. All of them clean and clear. Only a slight reflection kept me from walking through the damn things. I couldn't remember the last time I'd seen so much glass, not to mention *clean* glass. In the windows, I saw Phoenix touch the brim of her touristy cowboy hat.

Once Constance found us clothing she felt would help us blend in, she and Perry released us into the wild. I'd even left my leather jacket behind today, instead wearing a sweatshirt with some image of a yellow flag with a mountain on it.

"It's very popular," Constance assured me, barely holding back her laughter.

We'd entered the Capitol in ones and twos, trickling in with the normal people, who all looked weird. All soft and smooth, with brightly colored hair and makeup. They talked too loud. Their clothes were lightweight compared to our normal stuff. Most of them huddled against the cold breeze, and no wonder. The sweatshirt I wore was definitely made for warmer weather.

And it seemed Constance was right. I saw the flag emblem on hats, pins, even backpacks. I'd have to ask her what it was from.

Constance and Eleanor spent ages on those of us with facial scars, hiding the wounds under layers of makeup and sunglasses. Now, Gryph, Storm, and I wandered through the center of the government.

Ahead, Eleanor and Mercy walked together, listening to the tour guide. "Once upon a time, we had a few Secret Service agents and the rest were contracted security," the guide was saying. "After that fateful September and its aftermath, the decision was made to utilize the only people our government could truly trust, the brave men and women of the mightiest military in the world!" She spread her arms.

Up and down the hall, uniformed soldiers were stationed, rifles in hand, stock still, staring straight ahead.

"Which is why the Senate and House of Representatives changed the laws governing US soldiers' ability to operate on US soil. Because DC is not a state, they have been allowed to operate here just like they would on any base around the world. They have also..."

I tuned her out, studying the place. What few entrances there were all had extra guards, metal detectors, and some type of scanner thorough enough you had to take everything out of your pockets. Basically, a frontal assault would never work.

Not that I planned on doing that anyway. I wanted hostages and visibility, not a bloodbath. Well, not right away.

These poor bastards were only doing what they were commanded. Though I had to wonder, at what point did you have to take responsibility for your actions? Because there was more than enough hinky shit going on to make a person reconsider.

Torturing people, or those volunteers trying to rape strangers, them leaving us to deal with everything on our own... The list could go on if I had a better memory.

"...Lt Colonel Arnold Keller!" The tour guide's gushing, and the name, pulled me from my thoughts. "He's just returned from a stint at the border, and the stories are just chilling!"

Arnold Keller. Noah's old CO. Handsome, somewhere in his forties, with thick, sandy hair, the man wearing a pristine dress uniform smiled at the tourists.

The man who tried to have Noah killed the legal way and accomplished it by accident stood mere feet from me. Or should I blame myself for his death? Because he'd only stayed in the Valley because of me. No, not just because of me. If I didn't exist, he'd have stayed to help, he would...

Memories swamped me. Blinded to the present, I touched the wall, staring out a window. Gratitude, sorrow, joy, rage...they flowed through me, an unstoppable force bringing memories with them.

His arms wrapped around me, the fire hot on my face, his chest against my back. Laughing as he kissed me, all heat and tongue and need...

His still face, eyes closed forever when Gryphon pulled the cloth over his face for the last time...

Clenching my teeth against a scream, I bowed my head, waiting for it to pass.

When I finally straightened, the tourists had gathered around Keller, many of them wanting to shake his hand. Eleanor and Mercy were in the line, trying to blend in. He lingered over Mercy's hand, oblivious or uncaring of her obvious discomfort.

She ended up pulling her hand away, taking two steps to the side. The crush of people prevented her from escaping too far. When he kept trying to engage her, I straightened. Time for a rescue, civilization style.

I slid through the crush, surreptitiously using my elbows to get them out of my way. On nearing Keller, I pressed my wedding ring against my finger hard enough to leave marks. *Stay cool, stay cool.*

"Come, now," he pressed Mercy. "What's your name? Please?" he wheedled.

Barely keeping my lip from curling, I smiled brightly. "Lt Colonel Keller?" I chirped. "I heard you just came back from the border? Please, what was it like?"

Reluctantly, he turned away from Mercy, who shot me a relieved look before disappearing into the group.

Keller straightened, folding his hands together behind his back as if he were about to report. "It's dangerous, ma'am," he intoned. "We're constantly on guard to prevent the North Korean scourge from encroaching further into America.

"As a matter of fact, right before I returned, we had an attempted breach." Gasps all around. One woman fanned herself, leaning against the thin man next to her. "Yes, we deal with hardships and danger daily."

"Oh, what happened with those horrible people?" The fanning woman leaned forward, her unnaturally tanned skin flushed darker.

"A band attempted to cross less than two weeks ago." He gestured widely. "The patrol startled them just as they were cutting the fence. Our men and women were badly outnumbered, but they held those animals off until my men and I could arrive. We killed three of theirs in the fight, but fortunately, we didn't lose a single one of ours."

My heart stuttered. The only people who could've been around lately was us. Who had they killed?

"Ooooohhhh." The collective sigh moved through the group, and in that moment, I hated them. It didn't matter that they didn't know we'd won free. It was like they didn't remember or didn't care that we were trapped in there, too.

"We got three of those North Korean bastards," Keller finished, "three less to deal with when this bill passes."

And as quickly as that, I wanted to laugh. North Koreans? Oh, this man was telling his superiors so many lies! The last North Korean left our shores over a month ago. Which meant Seahorse and the rest had gotten away clean. But what about this bill?

With the story told, however, he moved through the group again, smiling and shaking hands, accepting thanks and accolades for nothing, looking for Mercy. I intercepted him, forcing him to look at me.

His lip curled. "You support those...those savages?"

"What?" I didn't have to fake ignorance. On its own, my hand rose to my eye. Forcing it down, I shoved my hands in my pockets.

"Your sweatshirt," he snapped. "That's the flag that represents those savages, the Americans who have given themselves over to lawlessness in the Occupied Zone, who nearly killed my father years ago, when they crossed the border. The same ones who participated in the deaths of the soldiers sent over to rescue them."

I clenched my teeth, starting forward to punch his smug face when a teenager piped up. "That's not it at all! Sir," she added. Blood rose to her cheeks, but she stood her ground. This sweet looking child faced off against a uniform. Fuck me sideways. First Constance, then her. I liked these people, after all. "Captain's a freedom fighter! A hero. Sir. That mountain, green, and yellow is all the hope some people have. Sir."

His lips thinned, but even I could see telling this kid off wouldn't win him any points. I bit my lip, trying not to laugh. This sweet-faced child used 'sir' like an insult. If she'd been from Oregon, I'd recruit her into the Irregulars based on that alone.

Frustrated, Arnold nodded shortly to her before pushing through the group to Mercy. This time, she managed a strained smile for him. I slid through the crowd, lurking nearby in case she needed a rescue.

When he offered his arm to show her around more, she licked her lips and took it, only a near-imperceptible tremor showing her nervousness.

"Can my mom come, too?" I heard her clearly over the tour guide. "I got my interest in the architecture here from her, and I know she'd love to see this."

Hiding my smile, I watched them from under the brim of my cap. Smart. And he was clearly out to impress, because he turned immediately to where she pointed and waved Eleanor over. Yeah, the man wouldn't try anything here, especially not with Eleanor.

Mercy on her own might not be willing to scream if the man got handsy, but Eleanor wouldn't hesitate. She knew how to make a scene when necessary.

They left and I followed my tour group to the Senate meeting room in the north wing, passing by the original smaller Senate room along the way. I half listened to the tour guide talk, pointing out the age of the building, and the artistry of it, neither of which I cared a damn about. I only wanted the layout.

At the far end, a large, raised desk sat with a single chair behind it and two lower ones on either side. A narrow, filigreed table that reminded me of a kitchen bar sat in front of it, more chairs there, so those people would sit with their backs to whoever had the big desk.

I caught the last bit of the guide's spiel. The vice president sat there. Good. The bastard should see what he supported, if he didn't already know.

Facing the fancy desk were four rows of individual desks set in a series of tiered semicircles where the senators sat. Above all this, a viewing gallery went around all four sides. The room had numerous doors, enough that I didn't bother counting.

We'd be better off catching them individually than trying to take them here. The room was a disaster...

"Only the Vice President's Secret Service agents are allowed within the chamber when they're in session," she finished.

Okay. Maybe there were still possibilities. Less guards in here.

The tour ended back at the entrance, Mercy and Eleanor nowhere in sight. When the others would have paused and waited with me, I shook my head. Storm stood nearby, pretending to admire the white dome topping the big building.

"You sure?" she muttered. "You made us her guards."

"I've got her back," I said softly. "She's one of ours."

Storm gave a short, sharp nod and disappeared with the others. Perry and Constance waited for them at his parent's townhouse, hopefully ready to show us everything they'd compiled.

***

Washington, DC – Mercy

Stepping carefully on the intricate tilework, Mercy gaped at the opulence around her. That man, Keller (*"Arnold, please!"*), patted her hand where it rested on his arm. Resisting the urge to snatch it back, she could only hope he'd say something useful, and soon.

"There are several basements, with tunnels and subways connecting the Capitol to the Congressional office buildings and of course the Capitol Complex, too," he continued, leading them down.

Eleanor walked on her other side, examining the windows. "Oh, Mercy, dear, come look at this." She waved, pointing to the detailed cornices. "This is just like that art you made in high school. Oh, your father was so proud of how well you did with that..."

Mercy gave Keller a tight smile and retrieved her hand. "Excuse me."

When Mercy obediently looked at the window, Eleanor lowered her voice. "How are you doing, dear?"

"I can't decide whether to puke or scream."

Patting her arm, the older woman leaned in. "That's why I'm here."

"What? You'll fight him off?"

Eleanor snorted softly. "Of course not. I'm here to show you the correct procedure: scream until one of them rescues us."

"Is that really what you do?" Startled, Mercy looked up at her.

Now Eleanor smiled. Mercy marveled at her grace and humor. The woman had to be in her fifties, yet she easily kept up with the hard pace the Irregulars set. Even here, she didn't slow down. "I've never had to. Captain keeps a weather eye on her people. I know you don't feel safe yet, and it may be a while until you do, but we do not leave people behind."

Mercy glanced back at Keller. He smiled when he saw her. Stretching her lips into a semblance of a smile for him, she turned back, pointing to the plant nearby. "Has anyone ever been captured?"

Eleanor's mouth turned down, and she nodded. "It rarely ends happily, but we do get them back. Captain let herself be captured, once."

"What happened?"

"Fresno fell. Now, we should return to your admirer."

Mulling over this, Mercy let Keller continue leading them down, into the basement, where he showed them the tunnels.

When he leaned in, she snapped back to the present. He lowered his voice. "Rumor has it there's a secret tunnel here."

"Really?" She widened her eyes, all her painful training with Kozlov finally useful. "Only a rumor?"

"After the unrest in the 2020s and 30s, a tunnel was built from each chamber, or so the stories go, so that if there was ever another attempt to take over the Capitol, Congress could leave secretly and safely. But if there really is one, only the Vice President and the President know about it."

Mercy laughed lightly. "That sounds so fantastical! How could that possibly be kept a secret? It would have taken so many people to build it."

He laughed with her. "I know, but it does make this whole place a little more interesting, doesn't it?" Slowly, he escorted them back to the entrance. "I'd love to see you again, Mercy." He said her name as if they were already intimate, and she struggled to keep her composure. "Tell me I will."

Mercy stared up, into his murky blue eyes, remembering Constance's words: he *knew* about the invasion. His mother orchestrated it just for him. "Oh, I have a feeling you will."

"May I have your number?"

Mercy gave him a demure smile. "I think we should leave this one up to God." This answer, delivered so sincerely, would have pleased her Master, once.

His eyes lit up. "You're a Christian! Mother will be pleased. You won't have to convert."

Strangling her desire to knee this man, she held his gaze. "No, I won't have to convert. I'm sure God will make everything happen as it should."

"Must I let you go?" he said, hand to his heart theatrically, a move most women would find charming.

"I'm afraid my mother needs to rest," she said gently taking Eleanor's arm. "I need to be a good daughter, too, you know."

"Of course." Bending, he pressed his lips to her hand. "I will see you again," he promised.

Through sheer force of will, she left it there. Around them, women and older girls sighed, giving her envious glances. Gritting her teeth behind the smile, she took her hand back.

"Thank you," she said. "You made this day so much more...interesting."

"I'll be counting the minutes until I see you again," he murmured, then turned to shake Eleanor's hand. "It was a pleasure, ma'am."

"Lieutenant Colonel," she replied, managing to look tired.

"Should I call a car for you?" he asked.

"Oh, no, thank you. It's only a short distance to our hotel, and if I walk, then I'll be perfectly ready for a nap when we get there. Thank you," Eleanor said again.

"Au revoir!" He waved as they started down the steps.

Mercy spotted Captain lurking near the trees at the bottom. The knot in her chest released. Her cousin stayed for her. Eleanor was right. Captain did keep an eye on her own.

CHAPTER 31

Wiretap, Keller Residence – December 10, 2065, 6:38pm
Woman: That just means that when you become president, you'll go down in
world history for how well you bring the country back, sweetheart.

Portland, OR – Grace

When Dereva pulled the truck up to the community center established next to the hospital, Grace nearly leaped from the pickup. Then, slightly guilty, she turned back to help Charlie, only to find Goliath already had his chair out and was assisting him from the pickup.

"How long you guys going to keep the gun in the back?" Charlie asked. "Isn't it a little pointless, now?"

Grunting, Goliath took his weight when Charlie hopped down from the back. "Guess a part of us still doesn't believe Steve won't come back, you know? You go ahead," he told Grace and Dereva. "We'll follow at our own pace."

"Don't act like you're slow." Grace shook her head. "You kept up with everybody at the border."

"I switched to my lighter leg for that," he admitted. "Now, go on."

"I'm fine, Grace." Charlie settled into the wheelchair. "By the time you find this Amana, we'll be there."

Nodding, she followed Dereva into the community center. "She used to run everything in the Lair," Dereva said over her shoulder. "But because the fight moved into Washington, Portland became the new hub of activity. I hope there's still people at the Lair," she added, more to herself.

"There are." Grace glanced at her from the corner of her eye. It'd been almost two weeks since she'd learned this young woman had nearly become her sister-in-law, and that Hope had children, which still left her stunned. "We stopped by on our way to California. It's where your wounded fighters are going to recover. One woman, Otter, said they rest better when they're in the mountains."

Dereva nodded. "The mountains are home."

Inside, people excitedly gathered around Dereva, demanding news. It seemed word of their victory had already spread to Oregon. Now, they wanted details. When did it happen, who still lived, how had Captain managed to get them out so quickly.

Their level of confidence in Hope astonished Grace. Until she realized she'd begun thinking of her as the mechanic from before the invasion, not the woman she'd last seen punching a soldier in the face and running away, drawing more after her.

Dereva raised her hands. "It's because of Sung Ki," she announced into the quiet. "Her uncle had just become the leader down south." People booed and hissed. "I said he'd *just* become the leader! He didn't have anything to do with their orders to hurt women. He'd been busted down to nothing because like Sung Ki, he protested the abuse! He'd only gotten power because, as he said, we'd killed everyone else."

Several laughed. Quickly, Dereva sketched out the remainder of their time, including that Captain had gone back east to confront the architects of the invasion, and her injunction for people to take up their own names and rebuild their lives.

"But in the meantime," Dereva finished, "I need to talk to Amana."

"Hey, who are you?" a woman, her dark brown hair tied up in a bun, asked Grace.

"I'm...uh..."

"She's Fuzz's sister." Grabbing her arm, Dereva towed her away.

"Who's Fuzz?" the woman called after them.

"She's new. I don't know her." Continuing down a hallway abuzz with the news of the end of the war, Dereva headed straight for the back.

"If she runs this place, shouldn't we look for offices?" Grace asked.

"Hah! I've never been here, but I know her. She's made the kitchens the heart and soul of this place. A militia runs on its stomach, and she'll bring that here, too."

Delicious smells wafted past Grace's nose, leading them straight to the kitchen. There, they found a hive of activity, people chopping, stirring pots, checking things in the ovens.

"Dereva!" The woman who hailed them walked out to greet them, preceded by her burgeoning belly.

"Oh, my God! You're pregnant?" Dereva squealed. "How far along? Why didn't you tell anyone you were pregnant before we left?"

"Come, sit." Going back to the kitchen, she returned with a tray filled with bowls of soup, fresh bread, and steaming mugs. "I don't say anything so you won't be distracted. *Capitán* knows, *Madre* knows, that is all."

Dereva's eyes widened. "You didn't even tell Storm? Oh, she's going to kill you!"

Amana looked around. "Where is *mi hermana?*"

Dereva opened her mouth, and Grace could see the moment she realized she might get in trouble for her next words.

"She went back east with Captain," Grace said impatiently, pushing aside her bowl. "Listen, I'm looking for some people—"

"No." Amana set the bowl back in front of her. "First, you eat. Two bites, then we might talk."

Dereva spooned her soup. "Listen to her," she muttered urgently. "This woman controls everything here. She knows all, sees all, and hears all. Plus, if you don't, she'll take your food away."

Amana stared at her from implacable black eyes. Biting back her impatience, Grace took two bites. "Please, I need your help. It's something Captain asked me to do," she added.

At Captain's name, the Latina softened. "Very well. What is it?"

Resting her elbows on the table, she whispered, "Captain asked me to look after her boys. The twins, Michael and Gabriel."

Amana narrowed her eyes, suddenly fierce. A chill crossed Grace's spine with the sudden realization, *this woman is dangerous.* "Who told you?"

"I did." Dereva leaned in. "Captain told me to do it. This," she tipped her head to Grace, "is Captain's sister."

The Latina's eyes widened as she studied Grace. "So you are, Grace O'Connell. Very well. But you will have to handle the boys gently. For their safety, we told them they are orphans."

Grace started. She hadn't introduced herself. Dereva wasn't joking when she said Amana knew everything. Then the last thing Amana said registered. "Why would you tell the boys they're orphans?"

"Because some *pendejos* tried to kidnap them when they were babies and give them to Steve."

The blood drained from Grace's face, and she slumped against the table.

"Grace! Grace!" Charlie and Goliath entered the dining area, and Charlie wheeled over, pulling her off the bench and onto his lap. "What did you say?" he demanded over her head. "Grace, baby..."

"Some people tried to kidnap the twins when they were babies," she whispered through numb lips. "They tried to give them to Steve?"

Swearing, he held her tightly. "It's okay. Steve's gone, and we won't tell anyone about it. We'll adopt them, tell them stories about their mom, and just...not mention who she is."

"Hey!" A tall, thin, young black man walked in, his hair an afro around his head. "Why didn't you wait for us? Driving like a bat out of hell..." He slowed, eyes darting from one to another. "Aw, you already told Amana, didn't you?"

"My brother, Anansi. Forgive him, he's an idiot." Dereva waved. "Have a nice time with TK?" she asked sweetly.

Flushing, the young man muttered under his breath. Recovering during this family banter, Grace sat up but didn't leave Charlie's lap. "Can we meet the boys?"

Amana studied them for long moments before nodding. "*Sí*. I will—"

"Sit down," Dereva said firmly. "I'll find the kids."

"I'll help," Goliath rumbled. "You'll never catch them both on your own. They're worse than rabbits."

"I was planning to bribe them," Dereva said as they walked away.

He snorted. "Won't work. They can smell a trap. And right now, on straight stretches, they're the fastest thing on two legs."

Grace paced between the tables, all thoughts of food forgotten. Charlie watched from his chair. "You know," he said eventually. "This is totally unfair. I'm usually the pacer."

"Oh!" Grace looked up, stricken. "Babe, I'm sorry, I didn't—"

"Grace," he chided. "I didn't say it to make you feel bad. I'll just be happy when I get my leg."

"About that," Amana interrupted. "Your leg is ready. I'll let the doctors know. Prime!" she called.

A teenaged girl with blonde hair and black eyes came out of a side room. Through the door, Grace glimpsed copper pipes and glass spheres. She couldn't fathom what they were for, and the door shut before she could see more.

"...fabricators know Charlie O'Connell is back," Amana finished. "Also, tell them they've got enough time for fittings and physio. These two aren't going anywhere. You still have to see your father and brother," she said to the O'Connells.

"Right!" The girl spun and darted from the room, only the patter of feet lingering in the air.

How on earth did she remember who Grace's family...Oh. Grace watched Amana with fresh eyes. This woman was as dangerous as the fighters, in her own way.

As soon as the girl left, one of the men in the kitchen brought another bowl for Charlie. Amana smiled and nodded. "She sets the first appointment and tells you when to be there. Now. Eat." She waved them to the table. "It will take them time to find the boys and catch them."

"You talk about them as if they're feral." Grace frowned but sat.

Amana laughed. "Have you met three-year-olds? They are wild. They have grown up in the mountains, and here, they have supervision, but still, they run and play with the other orphans. It is a good life. My own baby will run wild, too." She smoothed her hands over her belly.

Charlie picked up his spoon and nudged Grace, then began eating. Sighing, she followed suit. Obeying her sister's last wish was more nerve wracking than she'd thought. And she still had to tell Papa that he had grandchildren.

Most of her soup was gone when children's happy babble filled the air. Panicked, she looked at Charlie. "What do we tell them?"

"That we're their aunt and uncle," he said firmly, taking her hand. "We'll tell them that you're their mom's sister."

"People will think what they want," Amana added. "As long as you don't say it is Captain, you are fine."

Goliath entered, bending low so the little blond-haired boy sitting on his shoulders could safely make it into the room. He screamed with laughter, arms wrapped around the big man's head. Dereva followed, carrying the other one on her back, bouncing with every step. He chortled, bouncing harder.

Grace straightened. These were her nephews. She could do this.

CHAPTER 32

Washington, DC – Captain

I stayed near Eleanor and Mercy, keeping an eye on them without being obvious. I still drew eyes to me, but with my hair normal and scars covered, I couldn't figure out why. All things considered, keeping my distance made sense. No need to draw attention to them, too.

I paused at a window, continually amazed at all the reflections visible in it. And the lack of trees. How did these people not go insane with all this brick and concrete? Okay, better get used to it. If I ever made it back home, Portland should be inhabited again. I'd probably live there for a while, too.

I shied at the thought of living anywhere but high in the mountains. Mountains were safe. I could let my guard down.

My eyes widened. I recognized that man. I'd seen him two blocks ago. Wearing a black jacket, jeans, and baseball cap over dark brown hair, he stood out amongst the brightly colored people around us.

He passed me with a cursory glance. He had a lean face, sharp angles, and a droopy lower lip. After letting him get a building ahead of me, I started after him. When Eleanor and Mercy turned left, he waited a beat, then followed.

Well, fuck me. They had a tail. I know what I'd normally do with a tail, but killing a man didn't seem like a great idea in the middle of a city. Scratching my head under the edge of the baseball cap, I contemplated the situation.

What I needed was somewhere no one would think twice about a bit of violence. Where...

On a computer screen, Constance pointed to an area across from a railyard or railway station. "Stay away from this area. There are several ways to get back here without going near there."

"Why?" Phoenix asked.

"It's full of refugees from Georgia, Maine, and even some from the West Coast. It's pretty lawless and very dangerous. Just...stay away."

Smirking, I darted left, then took the first alley right. Running full speed for a couple blocks, I dodged back to the road I'd last seen the women on. Leaning against the corner, I tugged my brim down. I'd been there less than a minute when I spotted Eleanor's auburn hair.

Jerking my head to catch her eye, she brought Mercy closer, then pressed Mercy's shoulder. "Pretend to tie your shoes," she whispered.

Obliging but confused, Mercy knelt.

"You've got a tail," I said softly, barely loud enough for her to hear. Mercy started, but Eleanor pressed harder against her shoulder. "Remember where Constance said not to go?" Eleanor nodded once. "Go there. We shouldn't be noticed there."

"What will you do?"

"It's either dump or pump, and I'd prefer information."

Without a word, she tugged Mercy up. Her spine straight, Eleanor never looked back, heading straight for the ghetto.

***

Trailing their tail once more, I watched people on their phones, ear buds in, ignoring the world around them, and had a sudden thought. What if he had some kind of subcutaneous tracker or some shit? Or maybe they had smaller trackers now. What then?

I shrugged. Whatever. I could pump him for information and *then* dump him. Yeah, that was a good plan. Well, not *good,* but it was a plan. An idea. Fuck. Technology would be the death of me at this rate.

As they neared the ghetto, their tail slowly tensed. I could see why. Made up of tarp and pallet shelters, some tents, and a whole lot of trash, the ghetto surrounded a brick building, spilling into a former parking lot. Craning my head, I saw more tents, more shelters...*Holy shit.*

It covered several city blocks, looking worse than Salem's Poor Town before we took the city back.

When Eleanor darted sideways, into the ghetto, holding Mercy's hand, he swore. Unzipping his jacket, his hand went to the small of his back, then he followed them in. Barely holding back a snigger, I closed on him.

He might as well be walking into my own back yard.

***

Hyattsville, MD – Constance

The alley door opened slowly. Constance started, looking instinctively to James, who picked up a gun, gliding to the door. Holding a finger to his lips, he motioned her to stay to the side.

"We're back," Storm called softly before poking her head through the door. She nodded, smiling, when she saw the gun. "Good call. Anyone else back?"

Sweetpea followed her in.

"You're the first," Constance said, sagging with relief.

"Fuck. I hate waiting."

"Fighting is mostly waiting," James said, returning to the wall.

Constance frowned at it, holding a tack. While the others went to the Capitol, they'd gone to his apartment to retrieve all their information. They'd been recreating it from photos while also going over the intel again to see if they missed anything.

Storm studied the wall intently. "I know. That's why I'm a scout. When things are boring, I get to run around and look for trouble."

The fighters sat down, shuffling through papers. Phoenix and Gryphon were next to return, and Phoenix looked just as disgruntled as Storm at having to wait.

Constance shook her head. Something about Gryphon nagged at her. "Why do you look so familiar?" she finally asked. James chuckled. "What?" She rounded on him, her hands on her hips. "You know something, don't you?"

"Well..." He drew the word out, teasing.

She narrowed her eyes. "If you don't spill in the next two seconds, I'll...I'll...I'll never make you coffee again."

Laughing, James hugged her. "I'll give you a hint. He was one of the people who was supposed to leave Oregon."

She tapped her chin. The fighters all seemed highly entertained by this, Phoenix sitting on her husband's lap, watching Constance with lively green eyes. Gryphon watched his wife, lovingly. *He might be more recognizable without that scar*, she thought. *Without the scar...*

Her eyes widened and she gasped. "Tom Carrington?"

The hottest action star of the fifties and early sixties, who'd disappeared when the invasion happened? She couldn't wrap her head around the polished, handsome man who spent as much screen time shirtless as not with this handsome, rough, scarred man who now preferred combat boots over dress shoes.

He grinned. "It's been a while since anyone but my wife called me Tom."

Aanisah opened the door next. About an hour later, Chaos and Doc entered. Doc hurriedly stuffed something in her mouth, crunching loudly.

When everyone stared, she paused, her cheeks bulging. "What? You can't tell me we're the only ones who stopped for ice cream?"

"Who are we waiting for?" Chaos looked around the room, cursing under his breath. "Eleanor and Mercy?"

Solemn nods all around, and Storm glanced at the window again.

"Is no one worried about Captain?" Constance asked.

"Meh."

They laughed, immediately dismissing her concern. Storm passed more papers to Phoenix, who passed a strawberry back. Sweetpea curled on the couch where she could see the windows, and the men huddled in a corner. Doc glared ferociously at a printed transcript, as if trying to decipher its secrets by willpower alone.

Constance looked from one to another. "Why not?" She put her hands on her hips.

"She got caught by Steve once," Phoenix said around a mouthful of strawberry.

Out of season, Constance wouldn't have eaten them, but the fighters continually asked for more fruit. "What happened?" The comment seemed random when the fighter rarely was.

Phoenix shrugged. "We got Fresno back."

***

The Ghetto, Washington, DC – Captain

The man moved fast, snarling at anyone unfortunate enough to get in his way. One woman was too slow, and he kicked her feet out from under her. She went down with a cry, landing hard on her elbow. Grimacing, I risked a quick glance over my shoulder.

We should be far enough from the road.

The slums had their own series of narrow alleys snaking between shelters. Some shelters had their front flaps pulled back, revealing dirty faces, horrific scars, and old injuries. A man sat on the ground in front of a ring of bricks, a tiny fire burning inside it. His left leg ended in a stump, twisting scars disappearing under his ragged pant leg.

A little girl played with her doll. When she looked up, a patch covered where her eye should have been, revealing a swath of missing hair, her scalp also covered in scars. But amongst the hurt, there was life.

The little girl sang softly as she played with her doll. A group of kids kicked a bundle of rags, shouting and laughing. A woman hunched over a fire, tasting her soup, her eyes closed while she licked her lips.

Until the man in black walked through, snarling and spreading more hurt. Fine.

I could play that game, too.

Dashing down a side alley, I took the next left, running past inhabitants who'd long since learned not to care about weird people in their midst. Another left, and I paused, crouching, listening to the squawking complaints, following the tail's progress.

Close enough. Driving forward as hard as I could, I barreled down the narrow alley. Speed up just a bit, and...I slammed into his side, lifting as I ran. He shouted, but we smashed into a brick wall before he could do anything.

Rebounding off him, I hit the ground rolling. The man fell to his knees, arm across his belly.

"What the fuck?" he snarled. "I'm gonna fuck you up, asshole."

Rising to my feet, hat gone, I grinned, beckoning him forward. Groaning, he rose, his hand going to the small of his back. Grinning wider, I held up a plastic gun, dangling it between two fingers. His eyes bulged.

"What...?" His eyes flicked over me. "You're a chick. Who do you work for? Do I know you?"

Without looking, I worked the slide, sending a cartridge flying, then ejected the mag, throwing everything in different directions. With a muttered curse, he charged.

Whooping, I braced, shoulder down. At the last second, I sidestepped, sticking my foot out. He barely managed to avoid it, stumbling but still on his feet. I launched into a series of blows, driving him slowly back. Blocking and ducking, he managed to catch my foot, curling his arm around it.

Instead of turning and rolling—the usual escape—I launched up, catching him in a scissor grip, taking us both down. It became a dirty, hardscrabble fight on the ground, both of us grunting and straining. His punch landed solidly in my middle. Doubling over, I gasped for air.

He closed in. Rising, I slammed my elbow against his face. His jaw flopped oddly and he screamed, thin and high pitched. His right hand rose to his left shoulder.

Gun! I lunged, taking his wild punch, rolling around it to ram into him, lifting him bodily before slamming him into the ground. Rearing, I raised my fist, but he stayed down. Poking him cautiously, he still didn't move.

Breathing hard, I fumbled around his ear and jaw, looking for any sort of comms. How tiny would they be now? My questing fingers found a curly wire running from his collar, up, around his ear.

My jaw dropped. No way. This shit was old tech. I vaguely remembered it from movies. As I searched, a small pile of weapons grew. EM, belt knife, ankle gun, brass knuckles—I pocketed those—knife through the pocket of his pants, thick wire with wooden dowels—*ooh! For strangulation!*—he carried plenty of weapons, but only that curled wire going to a small box for comms.

Couldn't be. Grabbing the larger knife, I cut away his clothing.

"What are you *doing?*"

Looking up, I saw I'd attracted a small crowd of locals. The woman who'd spoken was middle-aged. Frizzy brown hair streaked with gray covered half her head. The other half, including that side of her face, looked like the skin had melted and cooled. Fire scars.

"Are you crazy?" she continued. "Stupid? Definitely stupid."

"What are you talking about?" I asked irritably. I'd seen an old TV show where they had comms in their mouths. Could he? "You think I should have done this in front of the police station?"

"So, you take him down *here*? Do you know what people will do to us if he goes missing here?"

I squinted up at her, my fingers in the unconscious man's mouth. "What?"

"Where have you been, girl?" she snapped, folding her arms.

"Not here. Obviously. Hah!" Triumphant, I yanked a false tooth out of his mouth. Setting it down, I brought a brick down on it, pebbles skittering away from the blow. A screeching whistle tore through the air. Inside, tiny little components littered the asphalt. "Relax. I'll take his tracker out of here before I destroy it. Once I find the fucking thing."

The woman bent, examining me, her eyebrow climbing when she saw my face. "You're not bothered by this at all, are you?"

A little boy leaned forward, barely held back by his father's grip on his ragged sweatshirt. "Who are you? You fight *good*. Can you do more?"

Glancing around, all I saw were more people, all of them hungry, cold, and looking for anything to alleviate their boredom and misery. "I, uh…fuck!" Hopping to my feet, the crowd edged back slightly, pressing against those behind them. "Eleanor! You in there? I could use a hand."

Eleanor edged through the crowd. "Really? You were doing so well. I thought you might have grown a little and finally learned a little empathy. Maybe how to talk to people?"

"I'm sorry. Have you met me?"

Mercy entered the tiny clearing around me, eyebrows raised when she saw me tugging on an unconscious man's clothing. Pulling it off his shoulders, I froze.

On his shoulder blade sat a familiar mark. Eleanor, and every woman who'd been kept in a brothel, had the same mark branded on her hip. Dorothy—the Corps, made up of Americans who collaborated with Steve—wore this as a tattoo, just like this man. The stylized letter K let the world know he was a part of Steve's army.

I swore under my breath. Eleanor glanced down, then paled, one hand coming to rest on her hip. Dropping it with some effort, she turned back to the people.

"We aren't here to hurt you." She began with her usual. "This man was following us, whether it was to harm or spy, we don't know, but I can assure you, we'll do our best to ensure no one here suffers as a result of our actions."

"Who are you?"

Ah, yes, the Question. The first question everyone asked. Eleanor might lead with this, except that she found it best to reassure people before getting into who we were.

"We are the Oregonian Irregulars, a militia created for Oregon's defense and freedom."

The burned woman snorted. "Oh, very impressive. You three are an entire militia? Hah! Oregon might be freed sometime in the next century."

"Oregon's already freed!" Mercy said hotly. I winced. Maybe we should have talked first about how much to tell them. "They've freed the entire West Coast!"

"Mercy." I nudged her. "It's okay. If they want to think we're lame, it's okay. I like it when people underestimate me. Now, help me find that tracker."

Settling down, she glared at the woman one more time before turning to the man in front of us. "How do you know he has a tracker?"

"There's tech," I said dryly. "I'm gonna assume there's tech in everything for the near future. How do we recognize one?"

She tugged her lower lip. "It's not like there's a course in pre-med titled *How to Locate and Identify Subcutaneous Trackers*. But unless they've gotten microscopic, it's probably in a fleshy part of his body. Butt, upper arms, or thighs."

I listened with half an ear as Eleanor fielded questions about Oregon, more people showing up, some of whom were fellow Oregonians. Until one bugger asked, "Do you know Captain? Is he real? Have you met him?"

There was a long pause where Eleanor very carefully didn't look at me. "I know Captain. They're very real. I've worked closely with them several times."

"Hey." A pair of dirty shoes appeared in my field of vision.

Following them up baggy, patched jeans to a teenager with shaggy hair and an impish grin, I squinted. The kid wore nondescript clothing, all of it raggedy. "Yeah?"

The kid held out a phone. "Here."

I laughed quietly. "I hate to break it to you, kid, but I don't remember any phone numbers."

"No." The kid held it out insistently, a look in their eyes I'd seen too often. Desperation, hope, a desire to belong. "Not to make calls. Look."

I shrugged. "I don't know what I'm supposed to be looking at. I haven't held a phone in…I don't know how long."

"Oh." Sheepishly, the kid lowered their phone. "It's a scanner. If that guy's got a tracker on him, it's putting off a signal. Without knowing the frequency, I can't track it, but my scanner can find the signal on him."

"*Your* scanner?"

They nodded, pride glowing on their dirty face. "I made it. Full native dev, custom tech specs, the works."

Sitting back on my heels, I motioned the kid forward. "Sounds good to me. Have at it."

Kneeling next to Mercy, the kid ran their phone over the man's body. The phone kept up a single, low tone until the kid reached his legs. In the back of his left knee, the tone rose to a whistle.

"Here." The kid pointed. "It might vary by a couple inches, but it's in here."

I nodded. "Nice. What's your name, kid?"

After testing the blades, Mercy chose the belt knife, cleaning it as best she could. Shifting around to his head, I sat on the man's back.

The kid shrugged, watching everything with lively interest. "What's it matter? My parents threw me out anyway."

Anger burned low in my gut, but I kept my voice even. "What for?"

"I'm…" The kid swept their hand over themselves. "Broken. I don't follow what they said a girl should. But I don't like heels, dresses, or makeup! I feel better like…like this."

I snorted. "More the idiots them. What do you call yourself?"

The kid looked at me cautiously. "Duck."

"Awesome. Hi, Duck. I'm Captain." My code name slipped out before I thought, and the reaction was instantaneous. Immediate interest, people who'd been here just for the show suddenly had a vested interest in everything. Phones were produced, all of them trained on my face. When would I remember I'm notorious?

"Fuck."

"Don't worry about it." The acerbic burned woman snorted. "It's not like anyone here can afford data to upload anything."

"Hey!" Mercy glared at me, her fingers bloody. "Hold him still, would you? I'm trying to do minor surgery, here."

Shifting, I punched the man across the face, knocking him back out, then rose. Some people gasped, staring at me with horror. One woman pressed her hand to her chest.

"Where you going?" Duck asked.

"I can't let my photo get out," I said grimly.

"No problem." Duck tapped their phone, then snapped a photo of me. "I've got this. By the time I'm done, every photo of you—even your social media—will be wiped out. And..." They turned, pointing their phone at the crowd, "no phone is safe."

Multiple people shouted, angry and surprised. Cries of "Where'd my vid go?" and "I just took that photo!" rose into the air.

Rubbing my chin, I leaned towards Eleanor. "Can we keep them? Please?"

Eleanor laughed. Duck glowed.

***

Hyattsville, MD – Constance

"Okay." Phoenix set down her stack of papers. It'd grown dark outside while they worked. "I'm starting to get worried. Even if Captain's not back, where are Eleanor and Mercy?"

Constance stretched, arching her back. Near the door, Gryphon and Chaos huddled together. She caught snatches of their hushed conversation.

"...could we have stopped her...going alone?"

"We promised, and now..."

"Archangel will never forgive us."

She frowned. She was fairly sure Archangel was the name of Captain's husband who'd died. Gryphon ran his fingers through his shaggy hair, then scrubbed his hands over his face.

"We need to look for them," he announced. "It's been too long."

Storm immediately stood, scooping up her rifle. "I'm down. Captain told us to watch out for Mercy. Let's go."

Sweetpea rose, grabbing a short club from under the couch—*when had she put that there?*—twirling it between her fingers.

"Whoa! No. Bad plan, bad plan." James blocked the doorway. "You said drawing attention to yourselves was not on the agenda, right?" Sweetpea swished her club harder. "Do you *really* think DC has anything that could possibly hurt that woman? She's a tank."

"No," Gryphon growled. Constance's heart jumped. She remembered that exact sound from one of his movies. She *loved* that sound. He continued, "She's a bloody basher, and we don't leave anyone behind."

"All in, all out," the others chanted.

The hair on Constance's arms rose. They'd said this often. There was no mistaking the automatic response from the fighters. She edged closer to them, drawn by an invisible rope. This camaraderie, the responsibility, and the willingness to put themselves on the line for each other...

She'd never known it could exist like this.

James still argued with Gryphon, barring the way to the door. Chaos hefted a huge rifle, tossing it to Phoenix, who caught it easily.

She stood next to Aanisah. "Why aren't you trying to break down the door?"

Smiling, Aanisah held up a colored block. "I will make a new door, if necessary, *Alhamdullilah*."

Squeaking, Constance bolted to James's side, clutching his arm. "What?" he asked, holding her close. "What happened?"

Shaking, she pointed to Aanisah, who giggled. "It's okay." Aanisah jiggled the block, making James blanche. "It doesn't have a detonator in it. Yet."

Chaos sighed. "Aanisah. We don't have a lot of this. We should save it for later."

Rolling her eyes, Aanisah tucked the block back into one of her belt pouches. "Fine. I was only going to make a new door, since the soldier will not move. But unless my Captain opens that door in the next ten minutes, I will be leaving."

In the hallway, the doorknob rattled. Constance found herself pushed to the floor, James covering her. From under his protective body, she watched Phoenix kneel behind a chair, resting the barrel of her rifle on the arm, aiming straight at the door.

The others quickly dispersed. Chaos pressed Doc against the brick wall. Gryphon stood so he'd be behind the door when it opened. Sweetpea and Storm stood with their backs to the wall, ready to round the doorway, weapons in hand. Aanisah disappeared.

The door swung open, revealing Eleanor, holding the arm of a dirty, ragged teenager. Mercy stood next to them, her hood up, hands tucked into her pockets, and behind them all, Captain loomed with a bulky thing over her shoulders.

"Move, please," Captain grunted. "This is heavy."

James let her up as Eleanor led the way in, seeming not to notice the number of heavily armed people around her, popping out of the woodwork.

"This is Gryphon," she pointed to the large Brit. "The small, angry one is Phoenix. Don't let her bad temper stop you, she's one of the most loving people I know. This is my daughter, Storm." She hugged Storm tightly.

Constance's eyebrows rose. She'd never have figured them for mother and daughter. Unless Storm was adopted?

Phoenix got in Captain's face. "Where the hell have you been?" she demanded. Captain dumped her burden on the ground. The blanket fell away, revealing a man's face. "Oh, and you went hunting without me?"

Constance gaped at the tall woman. She'd been hauling a grown man around on her shoulders? What was she made of? *She was now part of a kidnapping.* Constance leaned weakly against the wall, fanning herself.

"Not hunting." Captain shook herself, rolling her head around. "Trapping. This one was hunting one of them." She nodded to Eleanor and Mercy.

Ignoring them all, Doc immediately ordered Captain to kneel. Producing a bottle from her ever-present bag, she dug her elbow into the war leader's shoulder. Both of them grunted, though Constance suspected it wasn't for the same reasons.

"Oh, I doubt very much it was me." Eleanor looked up from the young newcomer. "Mercy, here, caught someone's eye."

Mercy looked up in the middle of pulling a throw blanket over her shoulders, a panicked, deer-in-the-headlights look in her eyes.

Phoenix grunted. "Whatever. Who's the kid?"

"I'm Duck—"

"No, you definitely want to know who it was," Eleanor said at the same time. "Oh, I'm so sorry, dear. Everyone, this is Duck. They're very good at tech, and they don't have a home because their parents are terrible, rigid people who give Christianity a bad name."

"Hi Duck." Doc turned to Eleanor, hands on her hips. "Why do we want to know?"

Eleanor smiled, stroking Storm's strawberry blonde curls. "Because it was Lt Colonel Arnold Keller. Secretary of State Keller's son."

Muttered curses from the fighters filled the room, then Phoenix squatted next to the stranger, poking him. "Wakey, wakey." His eyes opened slowly, and he blinked at them, reaching up to rub his eyes. He paused when he realized they were tied together. Phoenix grinned nastily. "We have some questions for you," she said.

Done with the massage, Doc unscrewed the lid from the small bottle, the pungent scent reaching Constance from across the room.

"Oh, no." Captain twisted slightly. "I'm gonna be flammable again, aren't I?"

"Suck it up, buttercup."

CHAPTER 33

Letter found in Sacramento, CA

Let this letter stand as an agreement between us, to show the cooperation of our great governments...

As a sign of good faith, and to further the our mutual aims, a messenger will be sent to you regarding the information you've requested. Use it wisely.

Fresno, CA - Faith

Faith washed her hands in the bucket, then helped Lucas clean his. When they were done, he toted it to the garden they'd just weeded, pouring it carefully around young winter plants.

"It looks so good, Mom." Faith hugged her mother with one arm. Together, they watched the sun sink towards the mountains.

Her parents had a small plot of land just outside Fresno. It used to be part of a large, commercial farm. Now, it'd been broken into smaller lots. Most people came out from the city daily to work their land, but Dan and Abigail, partly in thanks to their work behind the scenes, were granted the section with a small house on it.

"It does, doesn't it?" Abigail sighed. "Come on in, you two. Dinner's ready."

"My girls!" Dave walked up from the small shed they used as a barn and chicken coop. "All of us in one place, on the land. Lucas! Come on. Thanks for your help with the planting. It would have taken us forever."

"You know there's tons of people in Fresno willing and able to help, Dad." Faith took his arm, walking next to him towards the house.

They'd come out to help her parents plant the seedlings they'd started as soon as Fresno had been freed. Abigail had left them with her friend, Emma, and collected the seedlings when they returned from Bakersfield.

There'd been so much work, in and outside the city, that she'd hardly had a moment to talk to her parents. So, she and Lucas had been invited to stay the night. Her mom hinted that they had some things to talk about. Faith wondered if it was about her and Lucas and marriage.

Abigail went ahead while Lucas grabbed some logs for the fireplace. Faith slowed a little, enjoying the moment alone with her father. They'd always been close, but lately, with the sudden arrival of the Irregulars and freeing the state, she'd hardly seen him.

After dinner, they sat around the tiny fireplace. Faith watched the flames flickering, staring into the red heart of the coals.

"All right, dears." Her mother stirred. "We need to talk."

Faith glanced at Lucas, who stared innocently at the ceiling. "What about, Mom?" she asked.

"We need to decide what to do about Captain. Hope. Whatever she's calling herself these days."

Faith paused, mouth open, suddenly needing to discard what she'd been about to say. "What?"

"Your cousin!" Abigail sat back in her hair, folding her arms. "She's dangerous. And the way she's been ordering everyone around. Or how she didn't tell me or her own uncle that she was here! She looked us in the face and never said a word!"

And you didn't recognize her, Faith thought. *You looked her right in the face, and you didn't know who she was.*

She had to wonder which part of this upset her mom the most. That Hope never announced who she was to her aunt and uncle, or that she'd dared to order them around.

Lucas licked his lips, then went for it. "Mrs. Wilkins..."

"Abigail, dear. Or mom. You choose."

"Um...Abigail, then. At least until we get more...settled. What do you expect us to be able to decide? She's her own person, and frankly..." Faith nodded for him to continue. Her mother might hear it better from Lucas than her. "She isn't trying to hurt anyone here. If you'd known who she was, that could have put you in danger, since the NKs would've used anyone to get leverage on her."

"Nonsense!" Abigail waved that away. "The way she's been treating her elders is simply disrespectful! Did you know she threatened Carter?"

"Yes, Mom." Faith grimaced when her mother looked away. How did the woman swing from incredibly practical when needed to offended by everything the moment they were safe? "And Carter is the first one to say she was right to do what she did. And you haven't answered Lucas's question. What do you expect us to do? You couldn't stop her when she *was* a kid."

"My love." Dan leaned over, putting his hand on her arm. "We can't ground her. We don't even know where she is, other than somewhere back east. And if you really thought we could do something about her, you'd have said it while Grace and Charlie were here."

"About that." Abigail shifted track. "Why did they leave so soon?"

Faith locked eyes with Lucas. Infinitesimally, she shook her head. No way should they tell her mom about the twins. Not yet, not until they could convince her Hope wasn't a national disaster.

"Uncle Oliver and Sean are up there. Although I didn't learn that until right before she left," Faith admitted.

As she'd hoped, the news of Dan's brother derailed both her parents. Exhaling quietly, she exchanged a look with Lucas. While she didn't like a lot of how Hope handled people, she had to admit, as Captain, Hope had been extremely effective.

After all, they were sitting comfortably in her parents' new home, a fire burning merrily, good stew in their bellies. The garden had been planted, and when it ripened, they'd trade with their neighbors instead of having it stolen or needing to use it as bribes to be left alone.

Life was good.

CHAPTER 34

Hyattsville, MD – Mercy

Mercy hovered to the side with Eleanor while Gryphon and Chaos hauled the prisoner into a chair, holding him so Phoenix could zip-tie him down. She gave each tie an extra yank.

"You like following women, huh?" she muttered. "Do you like scaring them?"

Once he was tied tight, Captain squatted in front of him. Drawing a knife from her back, she cleaned her nails. His eyes followed every motion of the knife tip, though his expression never changed.

"What's your name?" she asked.

"Fuck you, bitch!"

She nodded slowly. "That's your first chance. I'll give you a couple more before we really start having fun. Who sent you?"

"Suck my dick."

"Oooh." She tipped her head, pulling her baseball cap off and holding it over her heart. "You almost hurt my feelings. You get one more chance after this."

"Hang on." The prisoner looked up at Gryphon's accent. His eyes widened. "Perhaps it'd make a difference if he knew you proper?"

"Like?"

The big Brit knelt next to Captain. Mercy detected a hint of worry in the prisoner's face. "Allow me to introduce you to your host this evening. Meet Captain. The rumors? Believe them."

The prisoner's eyes flew to Captain's face. He twitched, thrashed briefly, then fell still.

"Really?" Captain murmured. "What did you hear about me?"

"That you eat babies." Gryphon grinned down at Captain, who laughed shortly.

"Close enough. And you." She tapped the prisoner on the knee with the knife. "Stalling won't get you anywhere. We found your tracker."

"Excuse me?" Duck smiled nervously, shifting their feet. "Um. Your phones. They could look at what phones were in the area when the tracker turned off and follow those."

Everyone laughed, including Mercy. "We don't have phones," Captain explained. "But it should make for interesting times for them."

"Where were you when you broke the tracker?"

"In a grocery store."

"Damn." Gryphon shook his head. "Looks like you're shit out of luck, mate."

Leaning closer to the prisoner, Captain smiled. A bead of sweat ran down the prisoner's face. "I can't tell you how often people have told me I'd catch more flies with honey," she said softly, raising goosebumps on Mercy's arms with her gentle tone. "But here's what I'm thinking: you don't want to talk, I can just start here," she pressed the knife into his groin, "and end here." Lightly, she ran the knife up his body to his throat. "Then, I'll dump your carcass where people can find it, and see what happens next. It's all the same to me."

"Fuck! Fuck!" His eyes flashed white around the edges as he struggled in earnest against the ties. Chaos pressed on his shoulders to keep him still. "No one told me I'd be dealing with Captain. Nobody said you were *Captain!*"

Mercy's mouth dropped open. *That actually worked? Bloody hell.*

***

Once he started, they couldn't shut him up. His name was Aaron Smith (*"At least it's not John," Phoenix muttered)*, and he worked for Arnold Keller.

"Keller wanted me to follow her." Smith nodded to Mercy. "He wanted more information on her. Likes his women fragile."

Storm snorted. "I kind of wish he would mess with her." Captain shot her a sharp look. Storm grinned. "Poison is her preferred method, which is fair. She's been dealing with men who have all the power."

"And what were his plans for her?" Captain folded her arms.

Smith shrugged as best he could, striving for indifference and failing miserably. "Breaking her. Like I said, he likes them fragile. I know he's been looking for a wife. Maybe he wanted her for that?"

Mercy shuddered. As quickly as that, she was surrounded by fighters, the women forming a barrier between her and the prisoner.

Smith nodded slowly. "Oh, yeah. He would have liked you. I think it's creepy," he hurriedly added. "Keller's a sicko."

Liar. He liked working for Keller. She could see it on his face.

"A sicko you work for." Captain set the tip of the knife against his leg. "Is that it? You were just sent to follow a woman for a creep?"

He shrugged again. A bead of sweat ran down his face. "Basically. Can I go now?"

She gave him a scornful look. "Keller mentioned a bill earlier. What's that about?"

Constance wriggled through the fighters, leaning against Sergeant Perry. The only other non-fighter—Eleanor didn't count, she'd spent too many years running with this lot—Mercy often found herself gravitating towards the smaller woman. Her interest in the question piqued Mercy's.

Smith's eyes flicked around the room. Looking for an escape? Mercy snorted. He couldn't hide his emotions for anything. He telegraphed everything he felt.

"What bill?"

"Don't lie to me." Captain pressed harder. "Tell me about the bill."

His mouth worked. "It's the Military Mobilization and Action Act. It's—"

"No!" Constance gasped, the blood draining from her face. Sergeant Perry caught her when she swayed.

Mercy hurried over, helping settle her onto a chair. "Bend over and breathe," she said, pressing a hand between Constance's shoulder blades. "Just stay like that for a moment."

Captain turned back to the prisoner. Mercy noted her knife never moved from its spot against his leg. "Keep talking, dude."

He licked his lips. "It gives the military the authorization to invade the Occupied Zone, damn the consequences."

Constance mumbled something. Captain jerked her head, indicating they should let her up. "Schmidt, the head of the NRA, has been lobbying for this act for the last three years." Constance had a bit more color in her cheeks, so Mercy decided to let her remain up. "He's one of the conspirators."

"He's also the part owner of a weapons manufacturer," Sergeant Perry said grimly.

"You're telling us he's got a reason to want this bill to pass," Captain said slowly, digesting everything.

"About ten *billion* reasons." Constance clenched her hands into fists.

Captain's only reaction was to raise her eyebrows. "A huge fucking reason, then."

She nodded slowly, her eyes flickering. At her side, her right hand twitched slightly. Mercy remembered that habit from their childhood. She did it when nervous or thinking.

"What's Keller's stake in all this?" she asked suddenly.

"Um." Smith gulped. "He's a soldier, of course he's interested."

"Liar." Mercy glared at him. All the fighters looked from her to the prisoner. "You're lying. You know why."

"I'm not lying!" he protested.

"Hah! You lied when you said you think Keller's creepy. You get off on that shit."

He paled. Captain nodded slowly. "Nice catch. I thought he was just in it for the money. Come on, Smith," she coaxed. "Don't tell me. You've pissed me off enough, I wouldn't mind an excuse to hurt you. So, go ahead. Keep your secrets. I'd rather dump your body and see what kind of shit rises to the surface."

It was her casual tone, Mercy decided. Most people would be trying too hard to convince him they were a badass. Captain just *was* and didn't need to convince anyone of anything. When she said she'd do something, she had so much assurance that everyone around her believed it, too.

"Wait!" Smith cried. "Okay. Okay." Perry's attention sharpened, narrowing on Smith's face, who said, "Keller wants to be president. If this bill passes, he's in a good spot to command the attack. He does that, he becomes the war hero who reunited the nation. President's a sure deal."

"*I knew it.*" Constance thumped her leg. Perry nodded once, sharply.

Captain raised her eyebrow. "You did?"

"It's one of the transcripts without names. I was sure it was Secretary Keller talking about making her son president. This piece of trash just confirmed it."

"I got a vid of the confession!" Duck, forgotten off to the side, piped up, holding their phone. "We can use that, too."

"I don't know how it'll go with the threats." Perry shook his head slowly.

Captain snorted. "Please. We know for a fact that the US government does so much worse. Those bastards can't throw any stones. If they try, I'll fuck them over."

The fighters called their agreement. Smith looked ready to break down. "Listen," he cried. "I'm not a part of that. I just do what they pay me to do. That whole torture thing isn't me."

"For someone who worked so hard to look like a killer, you're sure coming off as a creep and a soft touch," Phoenix observed.

"That's because compared to you maniacs, I am!"

Captain looked at Perry. "Any place here where we can hold him but don't have to babysit?"

Perry nodded. "Basement. There's a windowless room that's perfect. We just need to move the food out first."

Storm, Sweetpea, Phoenix, and Gryphon headed downstairs with Perry. Soon, quiet thuds carried up the stairs.

"All right." Captain returned her attention to the hapless prisoner. "Keep talking. When is the bill going to be voted on? What's security like in the Capitol? Cameras? Give me all of it."

"I don't know about security outside of what you can see!"

Mercy nodded. "He's actually telling the truth, there."

"But the bill is being voted on in two and a half weeks. If it passes, they'll be ready to invade by spring."

With Smith safely locked in the basement with a bucket, water, and food, they settled onto the benches or the floor. Captain walked slowly around the room, thinking out loud.

"We need to find out what extra security the building has, how many guards, what electronic shit we have to watch out for, figure out an escape route..."

"Oh!" Mercy raised her hand. "Keller mentioned earlier that there are secret tunnels built from each of the chamber things. Ehm." She frowned, rubbing the space between her eyes. When had thinking gotten so difficult? Oh, wait. It'd been a long bloody day. "Something about trouble a few decades ago. They keep the entrances hidden, but they should end somewhere outside the building. If we can find blueprints..."

"Already on it," Duck said, thumbs working busily over their screen. "I can have most of what you need by the end of the week, as long as I've got wifi."

"What about tracking?" Constance sat up. "They can track what you do—"

"They can't track me." Duck looked up briefly. "I built this phone. They'll need better hackers than they have to find me."

"How do you know?"

"Because I hacked the DOD last month."

There was dead silence in the room. Finally, Constance moved. "Why?" she asked cautiously.

Duck shrugged. "I was curious what they were up to. And my friend wanted to know if there'd ever be relief for her. She was one of the people affected by radiation," they explained.

"Duck and Anansi should *never* meet," Phoenix finally said. Captain nodded.

"Who is Anansi?"

"No!"

Mercy jumped when every Irregular in the room shouted. "Well." She stood up, rubbing her hands. "That's nice. While you all do your planning thing, tomorrow, I'm going back to the ghetto. Those people need help."

Doc perked up. "I'll go, too. We can stop by a park first. I could use more herbs. And if they've got any dandelions, we can pick a bunch of those, too."

***

Hyattsville, MD – Captain

I walked through the silent streets of this city. Everywhere I looked, there were lights, so bright I couldn't see the stars. I could barely tell that it wasn't cloudy. Constance and Perry walked with me, Constance between us. She'd look around, shiver, and lean towards Perry.

"Are you cold?" Perry asked, wrapping his arm around her shoulders. "My mom has a thicker coat somewhere in the house."

We headed towards a meeting with a senator Constance swore we could trust, Aashna Baser. Constance hoped we could come to some agreement and avoid a confrontation with the Kellers altogether. I hadn't yet told her that no matter what, I'd be seeing that family, especially since Arnold sent a man to follow my cousin.

"No." She smiled up at him. "When I was looking for that drive, I had to go a lot of places alone at night. It was terrifying. This just...reminds me of that. Dark alleys, sketchy people."

I nodded. "As long as you know you're safe here. Perry won't let anyone get to you."

She smiled up at him, her face illuminated by another streetlight. I stayed to the edges, as close to the shadows as I could get, though they were few and far between. After an hour, Perry pointed to an all-night diner.

"That's the one."

"You two go in first. I want to check around, see whether she's as good as her word."

She'd promised to only bring her usual security, no cops. Baser didn't know about me. Constance just told her they had more information, new proof against the secretary. I was a bonus, and we still might not tell her who I was.

While they walked towards the diner, I circled the block. Five guys that I could see. She could have a sniper somewhere, but—I turned in a slow circle, head tipped back. No good vantage points, but that didn't mean she didn't have more men stashed in a van somewhere, waiting for a call.

Oh, well. Might as well go in anyway.

Baser's face when I slid into the booth next to her as good as asked what piece of shit she'd just found stuck to her shoe. The senator was an elegant woman in her forties, wearing a business suit with a contrasting, rose colored hijab. An excellent meeting of cultures and styles, right down to the gold stud in her nostril. Constance watched us expectantly, her eyes flicking back and forth between us.

"The senator said she's willing to see this piece of evidence," she said, eyes sparkling.

Baser whipped around to look at me again. "You brought the evidence?" she demanded. "Where did you get it? What is its provenance?"

"Can I get it out, first?"

Impatiently, she watched me reach into my jacket. When I handed her the envelope, she gingerly removed the papers. At the first one, about removing the army from their bunkers, she looked up, her brow furrowed.

"Why is this one important? I mean, other than that President Trembly signed it?"

"There are a series of hidden bunkers up and down the West Coast," I explained. "Look at the date. With them gone, there was no military to fight off the invaders. We were left undefended."

At the second one, she read it carefully, paling with each new paragraph. At the seal, her lips thinned. "I wish I had a way to authenticate this," she muttered, flipping it over to look at the back. Then she looked up, brown eyes staring straight into mine. "Who are you? How did you get this? Because from the looks of it, this was in North Korean hands."

I raised my eyebrows, looking at Perry. He nodded. "She's solid. This isn't the first time we've met her."

"Maybe, but she's got at least five guys outside, plus that dude further down the bar. He's been talking to his buddies the whole time."

Baser's lips tightened. "How do you know that? Are you military? CIA? FBI?"

"None of the above."

"Go ahead, tell her," Perry said quietly. "She won't trust anything until she knows. It's standard procedure."

"I should've brought Eleanor," I grumbled. Constance nearly vibrated when I sighed and turned to Baser. "I got those papers from Sacramento." Baser's mouth dropped open. "The North Koreans had a facility where they stored important papers and shit."

I glanced at her guy inside one more time. If she reacted badly, he might call in the cavalry, and then life would get interesting.

Okay. *More* interesting.

Taking a deep breath, I let it out slowly. "And my name is Captain."

Her jaw tightened, but other than that, she gave no sign. My respect for her skyrocketed. Either that, or I wasn't as well known here as I'd thought. Except her next words told me otherwise.

"I wasn't sure you were real. I've read all the reports, including the ones from Sergeant Perry, and where Lt Colonel Keller, the elder, held several people captive."

I laid my hands on the table, fingers curled slightly. "And did that report go over what they did to those people?"

"What? Just standard interrogation. I know they held them in lighted rooms and wouldn't let them sleep, which isn't great, but..." She shrugged. "It does get information."

I half snarled, half chuckled. Perry eyed me warily. "That wasn't what they did. Those were *my* people they held. One was waterboarded. Another tied to a chair and not allowed to move for hours. Two others were experimented on with truth drugs."

Baser narrowed her eyes. "Can you prove that?"

"I have one who could testify."

She made a face. "One person's word against a war hero's? Who is the Secretary of State's husband?"

My lip curled. "If one man's testimony isn't enough, what makes you think four would do the job?"

She opened her mouth, then closed it again. Her guy at the bar watched her closely. I didn't see any signal, but he spoke to his cup of coffee again.

"This," she placed her hand on the documents, "doesn't look like enough. I'd need to authenticate them first. And I'd like you to come with me."

"Mmmm." I shook my head, anger rising. Why couldn't any of these people be useful and do more than talk and prevaricate? "No can do." I snagged the document from under her fingers, ignoring her protests.

"These are mine until I say otherwise. And I'm leaving here tonight, with them."

I stood. The guy at the bar got to his feet, blocking the door. Until it swung open. Chaos leaned in, yanking him out, into the night. I caught a glimpse of Gryph out there with him.

"What are you people doing?" Baser cried. "Don't hurt him!"

Resting my fists on the table, I leaned forward. "There are some things I came here for. One, to make the people responsible for the invasion face justice. Two, to ensure my people's safety. Keller Senior threatened my people with war crimes and prison. They don't deserve that. We were just surviving."

"Whose justice?" Baser shot back. "Are you suddenly judge, jury, and executioner?"

I jerked my head. Perry hauled Constance to the door where Chaos waited, no sign of the black suit guy. "I have been, but only when there's no one around to see justice done properly. Ball's in your court, Senator."

I followed the others out, pausing at the door.

"See you around, Aashna."

CHAPTER 35

Military Mobilization and Action Act

Military Mobilization and Action Act gives the US Military full access to operate on United States soil for the sole purpose of retaking the West Coast. Residents therein are to be assumed hostile, particularly those of Oregon and Southern California. While the potential loss of life is regrettable, stern measure must be taken to bring law and order back to the lawless states in order for them to reincorporate with these great United States.

God Bless America.

Portland, OR – Grace

Sighing, Grace pushed her hair off her face, flopping onto the couch. "I know we said we wanted to raise the boys, but right now, I'm so *thrilled* they're playing with the other kids."

Charlie didn't even lift his head from the table. "Who would have thought they'd keep going and going? It shouldn't be possible."

They'd taken up temporary residence in Portland. Two days ago, a woman named Lavender assigned them to a two-bedroom apartment near downtown. Most people lived centrally at the moment, she'd noticed, but through discussions with others in the community center, she'd learned that more people were heading out, basically homesteading the land.

The next batch would head out in the spring, when they could plant. In the meantime, everyone was encouraged to grow a small crop in their homes, something they could trade with others or contribute to the communal pot.

Near the sliding glass doors, on top of a tarp and board combo, two sets of three tires were piled on top of each other. Tiny green shoots sprouted out of the top of each. They'd chosen potatoes and carrots, and both were doing well.

On top of all that, they had the twins. The boys had taken to them quickly, something Grace was thankful for daily. She straightened.

"We have to get ready," she said. Her dad and Sean knew they'd adopted kids, but they didn't yet know *why*. Now that they were settled, they decided to have the family over for lunch. It was a talk Grace both dreaded and longed for.

Charlie whimpered. "Maybe I should go down to the furnaces today." He'd begun working with the building's heat, helping adjust the furnaces so that every apartment had warmth. Not enough to go around in a t-shirt, but enough for plants to grow.

"Not a chance, buddy." Crawling off the couch, Grace locked the door. "For better or worse, remember? Though this is definitely worse."

Cursing, Charlie rose, limping on his new leg, and began picking up toys and clothing. Only two days in the place, but the twins made it look like they'd been there for a month.

"Feral little guys." He smiled. "Babe. You think our kids will be like this?"

"Nope! We are so much better behaved than Hope. Our kids will be angels." They stared at each other a moment, then burst into laughter.

***

Grace dried her hands on her pants. She'd run down to the kitchens to grab stew for all of them. Now they just had to wait for Papa and Sean. Oh, God. How was she supposed to tell them?

When the knock sounded at the door, she jumped, then laughed at herself. She'd been expecting it, but still…

"I'll get it," Charlie called, limping to the door.

She set the last bowl on the table, the pot of stew in the middle. Papa asked Charlie about his leg, then gave her a kiss and a hug. Sean waited right behind him. She made sure she was careful. Even after three years, they were frail.

The small talk over lunch nearly made her scream, and she was sure her responses were wooden. She probably should have told them before eating, but at the time, after seemed like a good idea. What an idiot.

When they moved to the worn-out couch, she brought tea, though when she got it, Amana primly informed her it was an 'herbal infusion.' Why the distinction, Grace had no idea, but the other woman laughed herself silly after she said it.

"All right, Gracie." Her father took her hand. "Tell us what's got you so nervous." She jumped, and he smiled knowingly. "I'm your father. I can still read you."

She shared a look with Charlie. He shrugged, then gave her an encouraging nod. "It's about the boys," she began.

"The ones you've adopted? Yes, I was wondering why you decided to do that. Not that I'm judging," he hastily added. "It's admirable that you're helping give the orphans homes, but I'd thought you'd be ready to start your own family."

Papa looked wistfully at them. She could practically see grandbabies in his eyes. Smiling weakly, she glanced at Charlie again. *Go on,* he motioned. Licking her lips, she gathered up her courage.

"Well, that's kind of what we wanted to talk to you about. The boys, um... The boys are family, you see," she blurted in a rush.

Her dad looked confused. "What? Are you saying you and Charlie somehow had kids...? But no," he muttered to himself. "I saw the boys arrive at Home. What?"

Grace closed her eyes. Well, she'd fucked that one up. "No, I mean...Hope. They're Hope's kids."

"What?!"

CHAPTER 36

Hyattsville, MD – Constance

James sat on the narrow bed, toeing his shoes off. Grace watched him sitting, head hanging, forearms resting on his knees.

"Are you okay?" she asked, hanging up her sweater.

Resting one knee on the bed next to him, she touched his hair. He wrapped his arms around her hips, burying his face against her belly. Concerned, she wrapped her arms around him, running her fingers through his hair, waiting for him to speak.

"Will you stay here, tomorrow?" He shifted so the side of his face rested against her. "It'll be dangerous. I need you to be safe."

"No," she said immediately. "No. I'm going with you."

Tomorrow, the bill would go to the Senate and they'd seal their fates. She'd watched the Irregulars prepare, helped as best she could, but now, everything was as done as they could get it. She nearly vibrated with adrenaline, thinking about the coming day.

In her mind, the worst scenario wasn't that one of them died. She knew if it became bad enough that James fell, she'd soon follow. No, her worst fear was that, in their run for the airplane and freedom, they either couldn't come get her, leaving her behind, or they did and they were all caught.

Living alone in a jail cell—because she couldn't stay under the radar by herself forever—sounded like a much worse option.

His arms tightened around her. "The safest place for me to be is with you," she said before he could protest. "We both know it. Besides, tomorrow is going to go down in history books, and I want to be there to see it."

Pulling her down to straddle his hips, he gently put a finger under her chin, turning her face. Obliging him, she fluttered her eyelashes, giving him her best coquettish look.

Laughing, he kissed her, open mouthed. "All right," he said against her lips. "Looks like you're determined."

"I am," she purred.

"And if I tried to keep you here, Captain and company would only release you, then give me Disappointed Looks."

"Instead of you worrying," she took his face between her hands, "I have a better idea. I'm never going to sleep tonight, even with the yoga we all did downstairs. So, why don't you take me to bed."

Wrapping one arm around her, he shifted until her back landed on the soft bed, his arm braced beside her head. He settled his hips between her legs. "Deal."

***

Constance woke to a cold spot in the bed beside her, and a haunting tune. Rising, she saw James already stood at the door, holding it open a few inches. The lyrics drifted through the townhouse.

Rest my angel

Sleep my precious one

I will hold you

Until the night is done

Downstairs, they found Captain standing in the kitchen doorway. Inside, Mercy rocked, holding something metal in her hands.

Sleep my beloved

Rest my sweetest one

I will protect you

Until the night is done

Goosebumps rose on her arms. She remembered this song. It haunted her dreams for weeks after she first heard it on LA TV. She also knew what Mercy cradled.

Dog tags.

The man she'd been with when she'd been captured by the Kingdom Come to Earth fanatics had worn these.

Close your eyes, my love

Rest your weary head

I will shelter you

Until the night is done

Cautiously, Captain approached her. When the song finished, she gently touched one finger to Mercy's cupped hands.

"Will you tell us about him?"

***

Hyattsville, MD – Captain

Brushing my hair, I separated it into three sections, tying each loosely with a leather thong. Eleanor sat in a chair in the kitchen, braiding Doc's hair. When Doc rose, I took her place.

"How do you want it?" Eleanor rested a hand on top of my head.

"Make her look like a statement piece," Phoenix called, running a comb through Gryph's shaggy mop, stroking his hair back from his face. "She needs to wow those assholes today."

Yes. Today, in a few hours, the Senate would vote on the bill to invade the West Coast. Today, we'd join the other people heading to the Capitol to observe the session. Today, all our experiences planning and throwing the plan out the window would be put to the test.

"But it has to stay in place," I hastily added.

Nodding, Eleanor ran her fingers through a section, then she got out her largest needle and some thick thread. I settled my back against her knees. Occasionally, she'd sew a fighter's hair back. She'd done it on mine a few times, and I liked those the best. I could leave it in for days. I didn't usually have it done because I couldn't do it myself.

My head bobbed as she tugged and brushed, but eventually, she was done. "Thank you, Eleanor." I rose.

Phoenix assessed me quickly, grinning wickedly, then took my place. "Make me a beautiful badass, please."

"You're already one." Gryph smiled at her, love shining in his eyes.

I waited, but the expected pang of loss was muted today. Or maybe lessening. When I closed my eyes, I saw him standing by the windows, watching us, a small smile on his face, blue eyes full of laughter. I still wished he were here with me, but I also knew that if I sent anyone to meet their Maker today, he'd be first in line to raise some hell.

Why did that cheer me up?

Mercy and Constance watched us getting our battle braids. I thought they looked a little...longing. "Would you like them?" I gestured to my hair.

They shook their heads, then Mercy pulled her bandana from her pocket. "I thought I'd wear this today." Then she pulled her sleeves over her hands, covering them completely.

"You're not enslaved anymore," I said, a little sharply. "Why wear it?"

She shrugged. "Mostly to see if any of them look uncomfortable at what they left us in. They *saw* me. Enough to know my name. Why wouldn't they rescue me?" She sounded like a lost little girl for the first time since we'd connected in LA.

Tears prickled my eyes. Hastily, I wiped them away, but Mercy and Phoenix saw. "If you want," I jerked my head towards the Capitol, "you can ask them while we're there."

Duck sat on the couch, typing away. They'd taken Constance's laptop last week, and now I didn't recognize it. It'd become bulkier, and I thought I saw a phone incorporated into it. I was a little afraid to ask what they'd done to it. All I knew is that anytime someone asked whether security at the Capitol would be a problem, Duck just stared them down.

"Have you no faith?" they'd ask and leave it at that.

"Okay, some last minute stuff," Duck announced into the silence. "Once I'm on site, I'll be able to take control of everything. Closed circuit freaks," they muttered. "Sergeant Perry, you have my number?"

He nodded. When it was time, he'd text Duck to lock the doors.

"Quick reminder, those doors have bolts that shoot from the door into the frame, like a safe. Once they're locked, nothing is getting in or out, so make sure you use the toilet first." I stifled a laugh. "That room doesn't allow signal to get in or out, so Sergeant, you'll need to go into the hallway real quick. If I manage to find anything more concrete on that tunnel, I'll text you, but no guarantees."

I grimaced. This was the only real hitch. We didn't have a foolproof way out of that damn room. Duck managed to track down anecdotal evidence that said where to find the door inside the Senate chambers, and three of the accounts matched, but we still didn't know where we'd end up outside.

"Perry." I took up where Duck left off. "How's your pilot friend?"

"Anxious to do you a favor."

I nodded. After two more meetings, he was okay. Once he got over being pissy about me being a woman, anyway. "Eleanor, you've got the route memorized, right?"

She nodded, her expression as serene as a pond on a midsummer morning. She should be. She'd driven several routes from the Capitol to the hangar, and studied the maps daily, prepping for when shit hit the fan.

"Duck."

"Yo!"

"You've got the backups of our backups?" Duck had been entrusted with everything we'd put together. After the doors locked, their job was to upload it to every site they could. One way or another, this information would get out.

They grinned, patting one of the pieces attached to the laptop. "Right here. And here." They patted their pocket.

I nodded, then checked the sky. A little bit longer, then Duck and I would leave.

"Are you sure we can't take weapons in?" Storm asked plaintively.

"Definitely not!" Constance said, looking sharply at her. "The fastest way to get caught is to try."

"It's okay," I said. "According to our guide, there'll be a few guards in there, and they'll be armed. Just make sure to look as innocent as possible before you kick them in the nuts."

None of us liked going unarmed into what we knew would be a combat situation, but Constance and Perry had been adamant: No weapons could be brought in. I wondered briefly if anyone had ever taken people hostage before without weapons.

"What are we missing?" I looked around the room.

Perry waved. "I'll leave all the doors open, so that someone can find our friend in the basement?"

"Ah! Right. Yes. Him." I'd totally forgotten about him once we had all the information we needed. "Good. Anything else?"

"Captain?" Eleanor stood. "May I have a word in private?"

I followed her into the kitchen, already tense. Though Eleanor never yelled, her silent disapproval was worse. Too often, when she wanted to talk to me in private, it was because she felt I needed correction. Sure, she was right, but that didn't mean I wanted to hear it right now.

As soon as the door swung shut, she hugged me. Surprised, I wrapped my arms around her. "Are you okay?" I asked.

"I should be asking you that." Lifting her head, she studied me. "How are you feeling? You've been on edge since... Well, you know. Today will be hard."

"Every day is hard," I said wryly. Every day, I wondered about my babies. Not a moment passed when Noah wasn't at the back of my mind—and my heart. But every day, I got up and did this shit again. Soon, we'd finish it, ensuring their sacrifice wasn't in vain.

"But this time we'll be facing that Keller woman, and everyone else who let us down."

I nodded slowly, digesting that. "Yeah, but I have my family with me. I'll be backed by a whole bunch of people who've never let me down."

***

Hyattsville, MD – Constance

Twisting her hands together so hard her fingers cracked, Constance watched Captain and Duck leave. Captain gave them all a debonair smile, as if she looked forward to the coming day.

If she were honest with herself, Constance couldn't wait to see what would happen either. Danger, yes, which she didn't look forward to, but to see the perpetrators face some kind of justice? Oh, yes.

James took her hand, lacing their fingers together. "I'll be next to you the whole time," he murmured.

She leaned against him. Captain and Duck swiftly disappeared down the road, causing a chill to run down Constance's spine. What if something happened to him today? It was possible. Captain lost her own husband. What if she lost James?

Reading the lost look on her face, Eleanor took her free hand. "I can't guarantee everyone will get out in one piece," she said quietly. "But I can tell you this: Captain will move heaven and earth with her bare hands before she'll let anything happen to any of you."

Chaos, Doc, Phoenix, and Gryphon nodded, anecdotes of her resolve spilling out.

Tears sprang to her eyes. James handed her a tissue, concern sharp on his face. "I'm okay," she said with a watery laugh. "It's just nerves making me think the worst will happen. It's...I'm..." The sob caught her unexpectedly. "I'm sorry," she cried. "I guess I'm scared."

The women crowded around them. Even Chaos came, reaching over heads to rest his warm, large hand on her back. James wrapped his arms around her, rocking her within the circle of fighters.

Everything had been so much for so long, and now it was nearly done. How would it end?

***

Washington, DC – Captain

I paused next to a large monument. A plaque at the base called it the Garfield Monument. I shrugged. Probably not the orange cat. Duck stopped with me, their loaded backpack on their shoulders.

I hadn't taken the time to notice before, but the expanse in front of the Capitol was lovely. A meadowland dotted with trees, ending at the sidewalk in front of the Capitol steps.

"How close do you have to be?" I asked, heading across the grass, finally comfortable in my usual clothes—moccasins, cut-off cargo pants, a t-shirt, and my leather jacket. Everything still felt too light. We wore the bare minimum of weapons in the townhouse, and now, Eleanor had everything loaded into the van.

Duck stumbled over a clump of grass. "As long as I'm within a hundred feet, I'm good."

"Front or back?"

"Back. Security rooms are in the back. Lower level. Just above the tunnel entrances."

I nodded, falling silent when we walked past an early tour group. "...push in the late twenties to be more eco-friendly," the guide said, "which is when paving stones and concrete were replaced with plants and grasses native to the area..."

Which explained the meadow look. I hadn't gotten an outdoor portion of the tour. The fresh air made Duck shiver, and I saw heavy coats and warm hats everywhere. "You gonna be warm enough, kid?"

They nodded, unable to answer because of another group. "Both the Senate and House of Representatives will meet today regarding the Military Mobilization and Action Act. If it passes, it will launch an unprecedented military action on US soil to free the West Coast of foreign control…"

Across the meadow, I spotted Doc and Chaos, holding hands, walking purposefully towards the stairs.

Duck's eyebrows climbed their forehead. "They got here fast."

"Yeah." I didn't have the heart to tell them the reason we left so early was because they moved slower than my people. Without the ID necessary for public transport, we walked, and Duck walked…normal speeds, I suppose, which in our terms meant slow. "Let's get you situated."

Going wide, we headed around to the back. Park benches and chess tables dotted the meadows back here, offering visitors places to rest and relax.

"What will you do if you can't stop them today?" Duck asked. "Will you fight them, too?"

I shrugged. "We're used to operating without tech. They're not. We've seen how long it takes them to acclimate, too."

"Aren't you worried they'll come for your family, though?"

My twins flashed across my mind as I'd last seen them, almost a year ago. Blond, dark blue eyes like their father, Michael and Gabriel were happy children. My father, and brother, so weak and frail after years of malnutrition and forced labor.

Grace and Charlie, hopefully with my boys. Faith, happy with a young man in her life. My aunt and uncle. Will, helping with the restoration of Oregon, Dereva, Anansi, and all the fighters who'd become family to me… The thought of any of them coming to harm or dying after surviving this long, after suffering so much…

I clenched my teeth. "If they try…" I breathed deep, searching for calm. "I will *burn* their lives to the ground."

Approval and peace washed through me, bringing with it the scent of warm man, leather, and dirt—the scents I associated with Noah.

Duck's eyes widened. They licked their lips. "Any chance I could...go back with you? I want to get in on that whole..." they indicated all of me, "...'nobody messes with you' thing you've got going, here."

I laughed, startled by the statement. "Yeah. Kinda figured you would. It's about to get real hot over here. Though you'll have to forget your toys for now. It might be a while before we're willing to turn off the no tech shield back home."

Duck gulped, clutching their bag. "Um..." A uniformed soldier made her way over to us. "You know what? Sounds like a great deal."

"Hi!" The soldier waved, rifle slung over her shoulder. "What are you up to, today?"

"Homework." Duck set their bag on a chess table. "My sister's dropping me off out here."

The soldier looked me up and down, pausing on my hair and scar. "I'm going inside to watch the session." I saw no reason to lie to the soldier.

"Where are you from?" she asked.

"Portland." I made no mention of which one, but sympathy flooded the soldier's face.

"Is that where you got..." She pointed to her eye.

"Yeah. I'm taking the day off work. I just feel like this Act is really important to the future of the country." I got into the story. Every word the truth, but none of it quite accurate. Is this how most people lied? "But my sibling has homework, and home isn't a great place for concentration, so..."

The soldier smiled, reaching for my hand. Surprised, I let her take it. "Good for you, being interested in how our country is run. Maybe you'll run for office someday and make some big changes."

I looked at her, puzzled. She spoke to me as if I were...young. For fuck's sake, I had some gray in my hair! Sure, it blended with the blonde, but still.

"I'll keep an eye on your sibling," the soldier continued after releasing my hand. "Don't worry about that."

"It won't be the whole time," I said. "Our aunt will be swinging by later to pick them up. Not sure what time she'll be here, but if you turn around and Duck's gone, I don't want you to worry."

The soldier smiled. "That's sweet of you. Sure. And honey," she said to Duck, "if you see me on your way out, just wave so I know you're good, okay?"

When she left, I sagged, but Duck just opened their laptop, booting it up. "You're awfully chill about having a soldier check in on you," I said.

Duck snorted. "Are you kidding me? This is perfect! They'll never suspect anything now. All I have to do is make up a class. No, this is great." Their eyes never left their screen.

"Hey," I said. They didn't look up. "Hey," I said a little more sharply. Finally, Duck looked up. "Don't forget: Don't upload anything about Trembly unless we get caught." They pouted. I pointed a finger at them. "I mean it. That's our blackmail."

"Fine." Duck stuck their tongue out. "Isn't there somewhere you're supposed to be?"

I held up my hands, backing away. "I'm gone. Just make sure you are, too, as soon as you lock the doors and upload everything."

"Yeah, yeah. Have fun storming the Capitol," they said absently, fluttering their fingers in my general direction.

CHAPTER 37

ANZ News:

Today, the Military Mobilization and Action Act is being voted on in the Senate. Considering recent action at the border earlier this month, this vote can't come too soon. It seems there's little doubt as to the outcome of the vote today, but with the recent traitor found within Senator Bryce McKinney's office and the guard who was found unconscious within the Capitol Building, it's obvious there are people who are attempting to overturn our fair democracy...

US Capitol Building, DC – Constance

Settling into a seat next to James, Constance gripped his hand, watching the Irregulars spread themselves throughout the gallery. Her breath coming short, she squeezed tighter. She couldn't believe they were actually doing it. They'd really take a roomful of some of the most important people in the world hostage—completely unarmed.

James squeezed back. "It's okay," he murmured. "You look completely different like this."

She turned wide eyes to him. He thought she was anxious about being at her old workplace when she had warrants out for her arrest? Actually, that was a very good thing to worry about. Too bad she hadn't thought of it until he brought it up.

"We're insane," she murmured, as serious as those around her. "We're stark, raving mad."

More people entered. James watched with lively interest. "All the best people are crazy," he replied.

On the ground floor, the senators entered, first in a trickle, then a flood. Across the gallery, in the seats above the VP, Secretary Keller and her family entered, the men flanking her. Several other cabinet members took seats around them. And there, a few rows behind the Kellers, sat her father. Turning her face away, she ignored him.

Then Bryce McKinney entered. She tensed, ready to duck behind the person in front of her, but he didn't look up. When she saw the man at his side, the breath left her body.

Albrecht. She'd pushed him from her mind for weeks now, too busy with unraveling a conspiracy and discovering more to life, but the sight of his lean face drained the blood from her cheeks. She swayed.

"Constance? Hon!" James caught her, patting her cheeks.

Several people around looked at them with concern, but before anyone left to get help, Mercy appeared from nowhere, unslinging her new messenger bag. Constance focused on the dark blue nylon. Mercy admired it online, and Constance couldn't resist getting it for her. It'd come in last night. Mercy's smile lit up the room...

She snorted, then gagged at the stench as Mercy wafted a small bottle under her nose. Coming out of her funk, she blinked, eyes watering. "What is that?" she gasped.

Smiling, Mercy stowed it back in her bag. "Just a little plant stuff I learned. You good?"

Constance nodded, her heart still pounding. James wrapped his arm around her shoulders, and she focused on the weight and warmth of it while Mercy went back to her seat.

Leaning so close his warm breath brushed the hair of her wig, James whispered, "If shit hits the fan, he's mine."

She smiled, resting her head against his. "I thought the plan *was* for shit to hit the fan?"

"Then I won't be disappointed, will I?"

After the formalities, the doors closed, and the session began. The Vice President took his seat in front of the US flag hanging on the wall, nodding for them to begin. Speakers took turns, bringing all their eloquence to subjects like the situation out west, how this stalemate was hurting the economy, and the worldwide political ramifications of it.

She listened, rapt, until James yawned at her side, barely covering his mouth in time. Pinching his leg, she giggled silently when he glared, unable to retaliate.

"Why do we have to wait until they make a decision?" he mumbled.

"Technically, we don't, but seeing who's for it will make it easier to figure out who's a part of the conspiracy," she told him. Again.

***

US Capitol Building, DC – Captain

As the proceedings dragged into the afternoon, I stewed in my impatience. No wonder these guys hardly ever did anything useful. It was damn near impossible for them to agree on *anything*. At one point, I spotted Senator Baser, carefully looking around the gallery. I slouched lower in my seat.

On the floor, a woman stood, shouting, "Whose side are you on?" at the current speaker, whoever the fuck that was. All he'd said was that they needed to think about the American citizens still inside the Occupied Territory and determine whether military action would benefit or harm them.

"Because our track record with the ghetto is deplorable," he said without pausing for the woman's tirade.

"These people are crazy," I said, just loud enough for the woman next to me to hear and give me a dirty look that turned to alarm when she really looked at me.

One row ahead, Mercy rubbed her arms. Poor thing was cold again, even with her jacket and between Storm and Aanisah. I shifted. It was sweltering in here. I could've left my jacket with Eleanor and been fine.

Taking the opportunity, I studied the people around us. I'd barely been outside in daylight these last couple weeks. Perry and Constance deemed it too dangerous, worried that we'd stand out. Now, I finally had a chance to people watch.

Brightly colored hair, interesting tattoos, and impractical clothing seemed the style of the season. I quite liked the hair and tattoos, but why would anyone want to squish their feet into these ridiculous shoes? They clicked and clacked on the floors, didn't have any grip, and worst of all, they all came into sharp points.

The better to kick your opponent with, I guess, but how were you supposed to stay on your feet after that?

These people were well-fed to the point of being overfed, directly opposite to what I'd seen in the ghettos and what Doc had said after every free clinic she and Mercy had done. *"Those people are starving so slowly they don't even realize it. And they're too ignorant to eat dandelions,"* she grumped after returning the first time.

To my left, seated in some fancy wooden area, the Kellers sat, surrounded by what I suspected were allies or sycophants. Across the stairs from them, Gryph and Phoenix alternated between watching the proceedings and dozing with their eyes open.

"...Military Mobilization and Action Act has passed!"

I snapped out of my thoughts when the people around me cheered. On the floor, the senators congratulated each other, slapping backs and shaking hands. Bastards hadn't even bothered sending a scouting party in to see if we needed their help.

Perry slipped out the door, entering again almost immediately. With my back to the wall, I felt the bolts slide home. Message received, we were on our own.

Getting up, I stopped next to Mercy, taking my jacket and draping it over her. "Hold onto this for me, will you?"

Then, I strode through the celebratory crowd to the railing. Resting one hand on the waist high barrier, I hopped over the edge, dropping lightly onto the desk below, landing with a hollow bang, which was immediately drowned out by a high-pitched scream.

Nodding to the chubby old man who'd screamed, I leaped to the next row, ran a few desks down, then jumped again. All around, people screamed. Tablets and phones hit the floor, the senators scrambling to get away from the madwoman in their midst. At the high table, the VP banged his gavel.

"Who do you think you are?" he shouted. "You will leave here at once! Security!"

But security was already on its way. From the corners of the room, people in sharp black suits with pristine white shirts leaped into action, running for me. One had his wrist to his mouth. Ancient comms again. Duck assured us that when the doors were bolted shut, nothing could get in or out.

I guess we were about to find out.

Another whipped his EM out, taking aim. Leaping from desk to desk, zigzagging back and forth between levels, I reached him faster than he thought. I jumped high, landing on his shoulders. Punching him twice in the head, I rolled away right before an EM pulse hit the man.

"Sorry," I shouted, laughing and scrambling to my feet, tucking his EM into my waistband. Finally, I was in a room with the people responsible.

I did feel sorry for the poor security bastards. Well, maybe not. They chose to work as Secret Service, regardless of what kind of assholes were in charge. They could go and find other work if they really didn't agree. Especially since Trembly was *still* in office.

A woman came at me, focused and intent on disabling me. I flung myself over a desk, nearly taking out the senator still scrambling to escape. Catching her arm, I jerked. The *pop* of her shoulder dislocating was lost in the uproar, as was her shout.

All around, people banged on the door, screaming to be let out, but I had no attention to spare for them. The last two security agents came for me. Splitting up, they approached from two sides, a pincher move. They rushed.

I struck, left, right, left... The one on my right grabbed my arm, wrenching it. Exhaling, I went with the move, flinging myself over in a tight flip. Elbow to his face, knee to the groin, then face again, and he toppled over. I ran for the last agent, who came at me in a flying tackle.

Only years of running over unpredictable trails let me sidestep at the last minute. The poor bastard plowed right into a desk. I kicked him once for good measure. Above, a woman screamed a warning.

"Captain!"

Spinning, I came face to face with a lean man, his hollow cheeks made hollower by a leer. Licking his lips, he looked me up and down, feeling safe because of the gun he pointed at me, mere inches from my face.

There's one problem. Guns are meant to be long range weapons. Once you start using them up close, you're better off with a knife.

Almost of their own accord, my hands rose. Stepping forward and to the side, I grabbed the barrel of the gun, yanking it up and back, breaking at least one of his fingers in the process. He screamed, so I kicked him in the knee for good measure.

"Yeah!" Above, Constance leaned over the railing, screaming, the most undignified I'd ever seen her. "Get him!"

I raised my eyebrows, surprised. When he reached for his clothing, I kicked his hands away, then flipped him over. Using his belt, I tied his hands together, then to a desk leg.

When I examined his gun, I nearly laughed again. I had a Glock just like this in the van with Eleanor. "Thanks."

Grinning, I ran for the front, where the VP sat, his mouth opening and closing like a fish. Vaulting over the first narrow desk-like thing, people scattered. Two stayed huddled behind it, watching me with wide, terrified eyes.

"It's okay," I said softly. "I won't hurt you." I looked up at the VP. "I might hurt *you*." Putting both hands on the tall desk, I jumped, pulling myself up. "Good afternoon, assholes," I bellowed, flinging my arms wide. "I see the Oregon Senators over there. Hello, Judas! Who the fuck voted for you, since everyone's been dealing with the Invasion?"

The two Senators gaped at me. "Who are you?" the one with a D before her name recovered first. "How dare you interrupt—"

At an impact on my leg, and a spot of pain, I looked down. The VP had hit me with his gavel, and he had it raised to strike again. "Here..." I snatched it from his hand. "Gimme that before you hurt yourself."

In the galleries, I noticed people hanging over the railing, lanyards around their necks, devices pointed in my direction. Some I recognized as cameras, others, I didn't have a clue.

Meanwhile, people continued shouting. Above all, they asked, "Who are you?"

So, I decided to answer that one first. I stomped on the desk, the wood booming and creating a small island of quiet. "Good afternoon, assholes! Before I was so rudely interrupted..." (Eleanor would be so proud of me, being polite!) "Let me introduce myself. My name is Captain, and I'm here to represent the West Coast."

***

US Capitol Building, DC – Mercy

Mercy hung over the railing, laughing and crying. Hope just walked all over the Capitol's security. Now, she stood on top of their precious high table, weight on one leg, waiting for the furor to die down. Looking every inch the feral war leader she was, her hair woven through with thin cording, knee high moccasins, cargo pants, and t-shirt, she was as different from the people surrounding her as night from day.

Had any of them noticed she'd pocketed at least two weapons?

When they finally grew quiet, several of them gulping water, Captain continued, "I represent the West Coast as it is now, and right now—"

"It's occupied!" shouted an older man. All Mercy could see of him was his dark hair, silvering at the temples. "How could you possibly—"

"That's McKinney, my old boss," Constance whispered.

"NOT ANYMORE," Captain roared. "It's freed now! *We* fought for ourselves while you lot sat on your sorry asses, collecting oversized paychecks!"

"We've had bombings," a balding man protested weakly.

"Yes," Captain sneered. "And we've seen how well you take care of them. My healers have been with them for two weeks. Never once have we seen anyone sent by you, nor have they mentioned any help from your lot."

Mercy shared a look with Doc, across the room. They'd done what they could. Constance had been horrified when they went to the parks and woodlands, gathering plants illegally, but between the two of them, they had decent herbal knowledge. Enough to relieve some of those poor people's misery and pain.

The Vice President straightened, rising to his feet in some attempt to regain his authority. "We only have your word that the Occupied Zone is freed. Our commanders on the border say they've just repelled an attack by the North Koreans earlier this month!"

Captain threw back her head and laughed, sending her hair flying. "Yeah, I heard that too. You wanna know how I know that's bullshit? Steve left over a month ago, and we busted through the fence around that time. Keller saw my people leaving. And I know they didn't kill anyone."

"Bah!" The VP had a death wish, because apparently, he couldn't stand being contradicted. *Was it being contradicted in general, or contradicted by a woman?* Mercy wondered. "We have every right to enforce the law there! Even if it's free as you say, lawlessness still abounds! We've run the models, and all the experts agree. We've seen the vids from LA..."

Mercy shuddered, gripping Jonathan's dog tags through her shirt. Constance put a gentle hand on her arm. On her other side, Storm gripped the railing until her fingers turned white.

"...you people are animals! Worse than animals."

Kneeling, Captain grabbed a double handful of his jacket and shirt and *heaved*, lean muscles bunching under her thin, gray t-shirt, hauling him onto the desk with her. Mercy gasped, a sound echoed around the chamber. Who would have thought she could be so strong?

Twisting, Captain held him so his heels dangled over the edge, his toes scrabbling for purchase. Only her grip kept him from falling. "You call *us* animals? What society do you think formed us? How do you think your behavior is better than ours? You were threatened for mere minutes before you hit me."

She looked around the room. Even from this distance, Mercy found her gaze piercing. "*Minutes.* From that, a body would think you'd understand just how we could defend ourselves. Since, you know, you weren't too eager to rush in to save us."

Shaking visibly in her grip, the VP gulped. "And how...how did you know to be here at this time? If you really were in the Occupied Zone as you claim?"

"A happy coincidence, don't you think?" Her eyes swept the room again. Mercy didn't know how she could be so cool, standing with her back to the people they *knew* to be the architects of everything. "But that's not the only reason we came."

This time, people didn't start screaming, the chatter filling the room but not overflowing it. Mercy shook her head, admiring. Captain had already trained them to speak quieter and calm faster by simply...not giving them what they wanted the moment they demanded it.

Yanking the VP back onto the desktop, Captain released him. "Nope," she continued, "we came to deal with the *real* brains behind the invasion."

Constance elbowed her. "Watch the crowd," she commanded.

Sure enough, several people had tiny reactions. One was the woman across the gallery, Secretary Keller. Her lips compressed, and she squeezed the railing in front of her.

Below, Captain fished a flash drive from her pocket, holding it high. "We have evidence!" she shouted. "Get me a TV, computer screen, whatever will take this."

One of the people huddling against the narrow bar/table/thing got shakily to her feet. Middle-aged, thin to the point of starvation, the woman patted her hair back into place. Bending, Captain passed it to her. The aide fumbled with the flash drive, plugged it in, the whole room watching while she clicked through things. On the screen, a series of folders popped up. A second later, the aide cried out and the whole thing disappeared.

"I don't know what happened." She held up her hands, backing slowly away from the screen. She glanced up at Captain, then Mercy saw her head shift slightly.

"She's looking at Keller," she muttered, her fingers tightening.

Below, Captain laughed humorlessly. "Yes, I'm sure 'something' did happen. Fortunately," reaching into her pocket, she pulled out another drive, "I've got another one! Constance!"

Constance jumped when her name was called. Across the gallery, seated behind the Kellers, her father's head shot up. Constance flinched when his eyes found them, hot anger on his face. Mercy put a hand on her arm. On her other side, Perry shifted in front of her protectively.

"Is that...?"

"My father," she whispered through stiff lips.

Mercy's mouth formed a small 'o.' Yes, running across your father while helping hostage takers wouldn't be good. At the front of that small section, Arnold Keller finally noticed her. His face turned white with fury.

In that instance, Mercy decided she was going down, too. No way would she stay up here, easier for Keller to grab. Yes, there were still fighters blending into the crowd, but below seemed so much safer.

Captain looked up at them. "Constance," she said, softer now. "Please."

I don't know how to work this. Mercy knew what her cousin thought, because if she had to figure out how to run the flash drive on that thing, they'd be here until next week.

Firming her lips, Constance nodded. "Okay. How do I get down?"

Storm leaped lightly over the railing, Sweetpea a second behind her. "Lower her down," Storm said. "We've got her."

Perry lifted her over the railing. She gripped his shoulders with white fingers, only relaxing when the fighters had her feet.

"Okay," Storm coaxed. "Now, just walk down my body. We've got you."

"I want to go down, too," Mercy said.

Aanisah nodded. "I've got your hands."

Between the saboteur and Sergeant Perry, she climbed over the railing, going slowly down. "Is this why you all insisted on pants?" she asked when she reached the bottom.

Sweetpea grinned. "Well, that, and skirts in a fight are fucking stupid."

Aanisah scrambled over by herself, but Perry accepted help from the fighters, which surprised Mercy, though she didn't know why. Jonathan had been willing to accept her help when she was able to offer it.

By the time they were down, every senator had moved well away, leaving them in their own space. Mercy nodded. This, she liked.

Offering Constance his arm, Perry escorted Constance to the front. When she passed by the man with the gun who'd threatened Captain, she paused to give him a little kick.

"There!" she snapped. "That's for attempted rape."

McKinney, who turned out to be quite handsome, with his silvering hair and fit figure, stepped out of the clump of people he'd been hiding with. "I should have suspected this is where you've been hiding," he sneered. "With traitors and war criminals. You can't come back from this, do you hear! You'll spend the rest of your life—"

He sounded just like the Masters. Put a woman down, make her doubt herself, tell her she couldn't be anything without a man...

"Shut your bloody mouth!" Mercy stopped, hand pressed to her lips, amazed that had come from her. Removing it, more poured out. "Don't talk to her that way! Don't fuckin' talk to anyone like that! You're not all powerful, you don't know everything! You hardly know anything, but you use your position to bully everyone else and get away with it!"

In the gallery, she heard whispers that congealed into one word: "Mercy." Her three bodyguards flanked her, hands empty of weapons but ready to fight. Her left hand found the dog tags again. Squaring her shoulders, she raised her chin. She'd be damned if she was ashamed of what those men did to her. They'd hurt her, but she survived, dammit.

Hell, she brought the very people who'd freed the compound. That was something to be proud of.

McKinney gaped at her, his face turning red. "How dare you, you whore! You can't talk to *me* like that! I'm the American government—"

Turning her back on him, chin held high, she walked slowly away. Her guards closed in around her. Captain hopped off the desk, handing Constance the second drive. "Who's the loudmouth?" she asked, her voice pitched so the entire room heard. Giggles ran through the crowd.

"My old boss," Constance said grimly, plugging the drive into the computer, her fingers moving swiftly over the keys. "The Bryce in the files."

"Ah." Captain nodded, rubbing the scar over her eye, then turned to Perry. "You want him, or should I?"

Perry laughed. "A second ago, I would've said me, but you know what? A woman would be a lot more damaging to his ego."

"I can get him!" Aanisah bounced.

Captain gave her a level stare. "You managed to get explosives in here, didn't you?"

She grinned. "They're too old for them to detect," she said, shrugging.

Mercy buried her face in her hands. "Oh, my God."

"Wonderful. Stay put, keep those." Captain put a hand on her shoulder. "In case we need to make a door later."

"Of course."

With nothing more to say about explosives, Captain strode towards the middle of the room, where McKinney went to meet her. He squared up, his fists raised. Mercy recognized the boxing stance. Captain just took apart Secret Service agents less than half an hour ago, and he thought he'd win with *boxing?*

Well, it wouldn't be much of a show, but it would be fun for the short time it lasted.

McKinney puffed his chest out. "You don't scare me."

Captain didn't slow. "The only people I ever heard say that were shitting their pants."

***

US Capitol Building, DC – Captain

A man ran up from my left, swinging wildly. Ducking, I lifted him briefly, dropping him over my shoulder. "Is this the plan? Distract me and have your buddies try to ambush me?"

A hand clamped down on my arm. Slapping my free hand over it, I put my trapped hand on his forearm, exerted nearly no pressure, and dropped him to his knees. A quick kick knocked him back and out of the fight. After tripping the third one, I reached McKinney.

"How dare you show your face here, bitch," he snarled. "We are a Christian nation, and God will punish you for your treachery."

To the side, Baser frantically shook her head, but I ignored her. We'd left them to do things their way for *years*. Their turn was done.

I cocked my head. "Really? That the best you've got? Dude, I've got like, files of you committing honest to God treason, and your best comeback is a bit of name calling and an empty threat? Fuck. I could've sent the kids to deal with you."

He struck, slapping me across the face. Above, it was a mixed response. Rolling my head, I shrugged. "Okay. According to the Bible, it says if a man slaps you on one cheek, you gotta give him the other." I turned my head. "Go on. Don't be shy."

He turned white, then red.

"Come on!" I shouted, spreading my arms. "Isn't this what you're good at? Hitting people who aren't trying to fight back? Last time any of my people were in your hands, a guy named Keller used them for experiments and general torture. You telling me you never heard about that? Don't li—"

He struck mid-sentence. I clapped slowly, but when he stepped forward, fist swinging, I blocked it. "Ah, ah." I shook my head. "Bible only says you get two shots. Now, it's my turn."

I loved competition fighters and bullies. It was so much fun to make them cry. *Did that make me a bad person?* I danced around him, dealing open-handed blows like he'd done. Spinning, I kicked his knee. Something crunched under my foot. He fell, screaming.

Yeah, it probably does.

"I've got it!" Constance called. On the screen, the files appeared. "The sound is all lined up, too."

"Excellent." By this time, I'd nearly gotten used to the camera flashes, and the people hanging over the edges of the railing, determined to capture every moment of this. I wanted them to record everything. Even though Duck should have put it all on the internet by now, I wanted this seen, too.

I paused a moment. Hopefully, Duck was safely ensconced with Eleanor. All we could do now was ride this rollercoaster until it stopped.

The agents I'd taken down were beginning to move. Raising my hand, I signaled Chaos to bring Doc. No point in remaining up top anymore, and

I'd rather have the agents checked to make sure they didn't have any serious damage.

Storm and Sweetpea went to help Doc down, and I nodded to Gryph and Phoenix. *Make sure the Kellers stay put.*

CHAPTER 38

US Capitol Building, DC – Constance

"Dim the lights," Constance called. She expected the fighters to do it, but apparently, the spectators were more than interested in the proceedings—enough to dim the lights for her.

Ignoring the whispers and speculation running through the crowd, and Senator Baser's urgent head shake, she brought up one file after another. Certain parts were highlighted, and where there was audio, it played as an accompaniment.

It took over an hour for the whole thing to cross the screen. Everyone seemed to have forgotten they were locked in a room with 'dangerous criminals.' She'd be willing to bet if the doors opened right this second, they'd all stay put.

When the Secretary's clear tones rang through the audio, there were gasps of shock from the crowd. Above, the Secretary's face twisted with fury before smoothing into a serene mask. Yes, she knew this wouldn't hold up.

While her son's name was never mentioned, her obvious helicopter parenting drew disgusted looks. Gasps rang out when she mentioned her son becoming president. To the side, Captain consulted quietly with Doc, who'd finished tending the injured. Captain nodded,

"You're playing them like a violin." James leaned down, his breath puffing warm against her ear.

She smiled. "You have no idea how much I'm enjoying this."

"Come now." During the show, the VP slowly clambered off the desk. With the display finished, he struggled to look down his nose at a woman taller than himself. "That's hardly admissible in court."

"Good thing we're not in court, then." Captain's voice was hard. "Whose peers would make up the jury? Yours? Or mine? But if you're still in doubt... Mercy."

Mercy looked up at Captain like a deer caught in the headlights. Moving slowly, the war leader reached inside the leather jacket the healer wore, retrieving a battered envelope.

"Perhaps Secretary Keller and her family would like to join us on the floor." While Captain couched it in the form of a request, only an idiot would think it anything other than a command.

Phoenix and Gryphon, the only two Irregulars who hadn't revealed themselves, now moved to the Kellers. Her father rose to his feet, red-faced. She couldn't hear him from this distance, but she knew him well enough to imagine the protest.

"Sit down!" Captain's voice rang through the chamber. Constance's mouth dropped open when her father just...sat. "When I want your input, I'll fucking tell you. Until then, stay."

Constance covered her mouth with her hands, struggling between laughter and tears. He stayed. He didn't rage, protest, insist he was right. No, he just...sat, and didn't move.

"How does she *do* that?" she whispered. "Is she older than she looks?"

Storm, close enough to hear, shrugged. "She's been commanding people for years. I think it's habit, now. How old does she look?"

"Twenty-eight, thirty. Hard to tell. Her face looks young, but that gray..."

Mercy snorted. "She's more like thirty-four to thirty-six."

Despite being right next to them, Captain did an amazing job of pretending they weren't there. Though her shoulders quivered briefly, and Constance had to wonder if they'd hurt her feelings, until the rebel leader gave them a quick glance and she saw laughter in Captain's eyes for the first time.

Above, the Keller men protested coming down. They watched Phoenix's patience slowly slip away. But when Keller Senior said, "Now, now. I'm sure those braids make you look very intimidating, but girls shouldn't—"

She slapped him, knocking him back in his seat, and everything happened at once. Arnold Keller leaped to his feet, fists up. Gryphon shouldered through to deal with Keller Junior. Secretary Keller slipped past them, making her way to the aisle. Several senators, seeing their chance, rushed Chaos. Phoenix drove back two of the spectators in the box seats who thought to make a move.

"She's getting away!" Constance cried.

Thrusting the envelope into Mercy's hands, Captain leaped first to the VP's desk, then onto the wall, grabbing decorations, hauling herself up so swiftly she practically ran up the wall. James moved to help Chaos subdue the senators without causing too much bodily damage, putting down the minor revolt seconds after Captain vaulted the railing, landing lightly behind the Secretary, putting a hand on her shoulder before she'd climbed two steps.

As quickly as everything exploded, it settled down. Turning, she found herself and Doc also protected by the three female fighters. Storm stomped a hand, giving it a little twist before she took her boot off his fingers. Sweetpea stood amidst the remains of a chair, hiding the last pieces she still held behind her back, smiling innocently, her teeth white against her dark skin. At her feet, one of the younger senators groaned.

"You see? Do you see?" the Vice President shouted. "Look at these animals! Why should we listen to these people?"

"Oh, get fucked!" a woman screamed from the gallery. "We literally just saw and heard evidence that you lot planned and funded all of this!"

More shouts rained down, some against the fighters, but most for. The calls continued while they got the Kellers onto the floor, the fighters handling them more roughly than they had her earlier. By the time they made it down, Captain was there to greet them. Constance hadn't even seen her jump.

The Kellers struggled to regain their dignity, straightening their clothing. Secretary Keller raised her chin, staring haughtily around. Keller Senior stepped closer to Mercy. Storm straightened, moving a step forward.

"Really, girl?" He looked at her sternly. "My son told us you were a woman of taste and dignity. He would have given you the world."

"Your son can go fuck himself," Mercy said clearly, before he could continue. "With his handsy attitude, and your controlling behavior...do you think I can't recognize a creeper and a predator when I see one?"

Old Man Keller's nostrils flared. "And look. When a nice man tries to give you a better life, this is how you—"

He jerked once, then fell to the floor, twitching slightly. Women in the gallery screamed in delight, cheering. Aanisah examined the EM she held. *When had she picked that up?* Constance wondered.

"I like this," she announced. "It is the only thing about this I like. My Captain, these people have begun to bore me. This man cannot do anything except spout the most ridiculous bullshit. May we leave soon?"

Captain spun on one heel. "Senator Baser!"

The people around her drew back, leaving her in a small, open space. Folding her hands in front of her, she raised her chin. "Yes?"

"Do you have a way to authenticate this paper, yet?"

***

US Capitol Building, DC – Captain

I really hadn't thought through all the ramifications of taking a roomful of people hostage. Particularly when many of them were used to *making* laws instead of obeying them. I'd thought the most difficult part of today would be either entering or exiting the damn building, not convincing these assholes we had the goods and they should do something about it.

Senator Baser made her way to the front with admirable calm, carefully stepping over the occasional unconscious body or broken piece of furniture. She paused near Chaos.

"My security agent still hasn't forgiven you, you know."

He grinned.

Baser stopped about five feet away. "I need at least two people down here as witnesses."

I shrugged. "Call them."

"Edmund," she decided, pointing to a Hispanic man. "And...Deloris." She pointed to the Oregon Senator who'd shouted at me earlier.

I jerked my chin. Chaos and Perry waded into the lot, guiding them out to protests from all the senators. Well, not the one named Edmund.

"No, you don't have a choice," Perry said to Deloris. "That's okay. Your constituents haven't had much choice here lately, either."

She flushed.

"Now, now, Perry," I chided him. "I'm the rude one, you're the voice of reason."

"I've gotten out of the habit." He grinned. "Constance has been the reasonable one lately, so I've had to pick up the slack."

I gently laid the envelope on the table. "Do not damage it."

Baser nodded, just touching it with her fingertips. The three examined the papers, compared them to documents in the room. Then, reaching into her pocket, Baser withdrew a small bottle, unscrewing the dropper top.

"Hey!" I said sharply. "I said not to damage the papers!"

Baser held the bottle out. "It's Brightseal."

Constance pushed forward. "Holy cow," she breathed, taking the bottle carefully. "It's the newest, and best, way to detect counterfeiting. Anything that comes from a government printer will stay the same. If it comes from another one, the print should turn bright pink."

"Test it."

Handing the bottle to Constance, Baser held her hands up, relinquishing control. Constance selected two papers, one with the president's signature, one she said definitely didn't come from this building. Sure enough, the one from outside turned pink.

The noise settled into a dull roar when Baser squeezed several drops onto the documents, including on the Secretary's seal. The room collectively held its breath, waiting...

"Finally," I muttered to Phoenix. "A moment of quiet."

She cracked up, shattering the silence.

The Oregon Senator looked up. "It's *real*," she cried.

"*Thank you*," I growled when the crowd finally calmed. "Now, what conclusions would you draw from all those wire taps *plus* this?"

Senator Edmund looked around the room. "I would conclude that people within this room had a hand in the misery and deaths of millions of

American citizens. And, if we checked their bank records, including their offshore accounts, we would probably discover they've made even more."

Gryph sagged slightly in relief. Phoenix closed her eyes, unable to contain a single tear tracking down her cheek.

"We have bank statements, too," Constance offered.

Arnold Keller pushed away from his parents, his father barely awake after his shock. "Why am I down here?" he demanded. "I'm not a government official! I chose to serve my country, putting my life on the line every time I'm deployed."

Constance opened a new file. The audio sounded clearly through the room.

Woman: You will be a hero, honey. Mother's taken care of everything.

Man: We were supposed to be rescuing them by now.

Though his name was never mentioned in the recording, you'd have to be deaf not to hear the similarities between this voice and Arnold Keller's man-baby whine a moment ago. And Constance wasn't done, yet.

Woman: I know. You are the bravest man I know, wanting to run into danger like this, but we must make it obvious you're the hero.

Man: What's stopping us from moving? First, you wanted to clear out those...people. But I'm sure the Mexicans are finished with now.

Woman: There's some pesky little rebellion that's happening in Oregon. Someone calling themselves Captain. It's a disgrace to the uniform. We're sending in soldiers. When they don't come back, it will totally discredit this...this...person.

Perry listened with his jaw clenched. They'd been sent to die to make me look bad. The impact left me stunned. I staggered to a table, sitting abruptly.

They'd been sent to die to discredit our efforts.

Arnold Keller tried explaining himself, excuse after excuse pouring out. I heard none of it through the rushing in my ears. The room swayed, and for a moment, I thought I'd faint. Phoenix grabbed my arm, bringing me back into the present.

Standing, I gently set her hand aside to face Keller. "Shut up!" I snarled. My fingers trailed over the Glock tucked into my waistband, but I left it there. This one would be more fun to whip. A pulse beat in his temple, but he obeyed. "You *knew!* You knew they were being sent to die, and you let them go, but you want to claim you're a soldier?"

I stalked closer. "My *brother* was a soldier! He died over there, because *you* wanted to be a hero!" I ignored the starts of surprise from those who'd known me longest.

His mouth twisted, something ugly in his eyes. "You just couldn't stay out of things, could you?" he hissed. "We had a plan! I'd rescue your sad, pathetic, dirty state—"

"Shut up, Arnold," his mother hissed.

Oh, but her pride and joy was on a roll.

"Once those filthy vermin were cleared out, those states would finally be suitable for good, honest, *white* Americans to live in again! All we had to do was wait for you to be desperate enough! But nooo! Instead, we kept hearing about some jumped-up wannabe named Captain. Everywhere, it's how much of a hero he is, how he was *saving* people. Those were *my* people to rescue!" He thumped his chest, making the medals jump. "*I* was supposed to be their hero! Not you! Me! Just ask anyone!"

Shaking my head slowly, I said, "Oh, I did hear about you in there, Arnold. Do you want to know what I heard?" His lips compressed. "I heard you organized an op that went sideways. Badly. When you tried to convince a soldier that every death was a necessary sacrifice, he punched you so hard you needed surgery to fix your widdle face.

"And then," I shouted, over the noise from above, "you tried to have him court martialed. Because he wouldn't go along with your bullshit about 'acceptable losses.'"

"That man is a liar!" he shouted, jabbing a finger at me.

"My husband didn't lie!"

Keller froze, then, flinging his head back, he laughed. "'Didn't?' Then Sanders is dead? This is a good day, after all."

The fighters skittered back, taking the civilians with them. From the corner of my eye, I saw Doc sigh, pull out a bandage, look between us, and put it away again.

"Noah was twenty times the man you imagine you are," I snarled, choking back a sob. "And thanks. You just let all those people and cameras know what I said is true."

Startled, he looked up, like he'd forgotten they were there. "You bitch!"

"Damn straight," I said, swiping tears from my eyes right before he charged.

He knocked me down to cries of outrage. I got to my hands and knees. Rushing in, he kicked me in the ribs, knocking the breath from me. Wheezing, I got a hand on a chair. People were screaming, shouting.

"Finish her!"

"You monster!"

Watching him from the corner of my eye, I got a better grip on the chair. This time, when he charged, I spun on my knees, grabbing a chair leg in each hand. He went down with a crash and a scream, ripping the chair from my hands.

Climbing to my feet, I faced him. "Get up! Get up and fight like a girl!"

When he rose, he favored one leg. I curled my lip. Probably a fake. I hadn't hit him that hard. Shouting, he lunged, fingers curled to grab anything he could. Spinning, I slammed my elbow into his face, closely followed by my other fist.

Keller hit the ground hard, eyes rolled back in his head.

"You *bitch*! You've killed him! I'll have you executed for this!"

Screeching, Annaliese Keller rushed me, her fingers crooked into claws, reaching for my face. My lips pulled back from my teeth, I caught her throat and arm, lifting and twisting to slam her onto a desk. The boom silenced the room, but I didn't care.

"What?" she gasped, her face turned red. "Hate...you." I didn't let up, and her anger faded into fear. "Don't kill me."

Leaning over her, I pressed harder. "Why not?" I whispered. "You've killed plenty."

"I'll do...I'll do anything you want. Give you anything. Please!"

My fingers tightened. "I want my family back!"

Gradually, I became aware of people pulling at my shoulders, shouting my name. "Captain!" Phoenix shouted, hanging on my arm. "Let the crazy bitch go!"

Gryph pried at my fingers. "If you kill her here, you'll be executed," he said quietly.

"I don't care!"

His hands gentled on mine. "They'll think we were part of this. Which we are. But you have people waiting for you." He held a hand low, around hip height.

My babies. My twins. The last physical link I had to Noah. Closing my eyes, I let them pull me off the secretary. It was worth my life, but not everyone else's.

As soon as she was freed, she rushed to her son, spitting threats once more.

"Ooh, yes. We're so afraid." Phoenix rolled her eyes. "Fuck off. He's just unconscious."

"Besides," Storm leaned down, examining him like she would a bug, "he attacked her."

"She *provoked* him!"

New documents popped up on screen. Police reports from various women. "I'm sure," Constance said. "Like these twenty-five women, who have no criminal records whatsoever, must have provoked him?"

"They're sluts. Whores! They led him on!"

"Yes, they 'led him on,' which is why none of these reports have ever been properly investigated. Despite twenty-five women filing reports against him, he's still walking around, scot-free."

Phoenix edged over to her. "Where'd you get that list?" she asked from the corner of her mouth.

"I had Duck hack the police and FBI on a hunch," she whispered back.

"Nice!"

Ignoring their chatter, I took two steps away, needing a moment.

"You! Captain person! What did you do to him?" I look around for the source of the screech. To my left, a woman leaned precariously over the railing, pointing and screaming. "*What did you do to my son?*"

I frowned up at her, my stomach sinking though I didn't know why. "Lady, how the fuck would I know? Where did you leave him?"

The man with her spat in my direction. "You just mentioned him! Our son is Noah Sanders."

My legs turned to rubber. Wobbling, I took two steps towards a chair when Gryph slid across a desk on his hip, catching my arm. "I've got you," he murmured. "Who'd have thought his parents would be here?"

Not me. Not fucking me. They were supposed to be in Michigan, not DC.

"Answer me!" his mother screamed, tears streaming down her face. "Where is my son? The last we heard, he went to Oregon. That man," she pointed at Perry, "made it sound like everyone died, but how? What did you do to him?"

"She saved him," Gryph said sharply, helping me to sit.

"He married her," Phoenix added. "That's your daughter-in-law."

"Technically, none of us are married," Doc offered. "Legally, I mean."

Closing my eyes, I held back the tears, grateful to them for their distractions. Here and now, it wasn't safe to cry. Gryph wrapped me in his arms. "It's okay if you do," he whispered.

"No." Shaking my head, I put my hands on his shoulders. "It's okay. I'll cry when we're safely in Oregon. They deserve answers. *Some* answers."

Pushing to my feet I made to go to them when Phoenix caught my arm. "It's not safe," she whispered. "I heard thumping on the door. We need to finish this. It's blackmail time."

"Fine. Tell Constance to run the stuff on Trembly while I talk to them." *Who knows when I'll have another chance. Or if they'll even see me again.*

Phoenix strode back to the screen. "Constance! Play the Trembly tapes."

Gryph already had his back to the wall, fingers laced together to make a stirrup. He nodded. I gave him a jerky nod, then ran at him, stepping lightly into his cupped hands. He flung me up, braced enough for me to use his shoulder as another steppingstone. Gripping the railing, I hauled myself over, coming face to face with Noah's parents for the first time.

His mother's face was red with weeping, her hair grayer than he'd told me. His father looked eighty, though he should only be in his early sixties. I glared at the people edging closer and they moved away, but the galleries were so packed there wasn't a lot of space to move.

Below, an audio file played. Something where two men talked about making the president do whatever they wanted.

"Why would my son marry a scarred, ugly woman like you?" I rocked. Mrs. Sanders didn't hold back. "He has a type, and you definitely aren't it."

Biting back the flippant, angry retort on the tip of my tongue, I tried to find a way to get through to them in the next minute. Inhaling, I ignored the angry words pouring from her, giving her the only truth I could.

"Your son is the love of my life," I said softly. "And I am his, though he's no longer on this earth."

"How?" She reached for my arm, stopping an inch away.

I bit my lip, struggling for a calm I didn't feel. "He...died...three autumns ago. Saving that man's life." I tipped my head towards Gryphon. "They were like brothers."

"My son has a brother!"

"I know." Speaking quietly when I wanted to scream nearly tore my throat out. "He talked about him, and his sister. His nieces and nephews."

"Oh, he told you, did he?" she sneered. "What did you do to my son? Why didn't he come home like he was supposed to?"

Survivor's guilt weighed heavily on my heart, but at least I'd learned by now that I wasn't responsible for his death. Steve invaded our shores, and Noah was too good, too honorable, to leave while people needed his help. Even if I hadn't been there, I believe he would have stayed.

"I loved him." Running my hand over my hair, I steadied. Eleanor put love into every braid she did. I think that's why she liked to braid our hair, so we carried reminders with us that someone loved us and wanted us to come home safely. "The summer after we met, we were married."

The golden air lit the meadow with an otherworldly hue. Noah waited for me next to Shepherd, wearing a dark gray, button-down shirt, the sleeves rolled up to his elbows, heat and love and lust in his cobalt eyes.

"...I pledge to you my living and my dying, each equally into your care.

I shall be a shield for your back, and you for mine.

You are my friend, my lover.

Grow old with me, as I will do with you..."

"We promised to grow old together," I said, with only the slightest tremor in my voice. "But life has a way of fucking with plans, doesn't it?"

Her lips twisted, but Noah's father put a hand on her arm. "Annie, dearest." She glared at him but didn't shake him off. "Look at her. She's barely holding it together."

"She shouldn't be holding it together at all!" she rasped, rage in her eyes. "Why isn't she falling apart? If she loved him so much, she shouldn't be able to stand."

Something in me broke. "Is that what you want?" I snarled, bending to get right in her face. "You want to see me screaming and tearing my hair out? You think I should fall apart and wither away because he died? Fuck you! I *had* to get up every fucking day. I have responsibilities. They gave me as much grace as they could, they let me mourn, but there's only so long I could lay in bed."

I straightened, glaring at the woman, my throat tight. "If I'd stayed in bed forever, he would be ashamed of me. If I'd passed on my responsibilities, he would have died in vain. And I will be *damned* if he died for nothing. If you want to see someone falling apart on the daily, don't look here. I live my life to make him proud, and to remind myself what he lived for."

Mr. Sanders watched me with tears in his eyes. "I think my wife was wrong. You're exactly his type. I would...I'd like to sit down with you, someday."

My lips twisted in a semblance of a smile. "If I don't get executed for terrorism, I'd be happy to. Though you might have to wait a little while."

"Anthony!" she tugged on his arm. "Why are you being nice to her, Anthony? If it wasn't for her, our boy would still be alive!"

"Hush, woman." He patted her hand. "She's right. We have to live to make Noah proud. And she needs to get back to taking these politicians to task for the terrible things they've done."

Nodding to the old couple, I hopped over the railing for the third time today. Gryph met me halfway between the gallery and our people.

"Are you okay?" he asked quietly.

I nodded. "I don't know for how much longer, but for now...yes."

"Put on that Captain face we love so much, then, and end this."

Pandemonium reigned by the computer, the VP and several senators trying again to get through to Constance.

"Stop that!" he cried, waving his hands. "No one needs to see any of this!"

"I'll take a copy!" a journalist cried, the sentiment quickly echoed by a dozen more.

"No! No!" The VP stared wildly around the room until his eyes landed on me. "You can't do this! This information was illegally obtained, which means if you distribute it, you're committing a criminal act!"

I shrugged carelessly. "Last I heard, I was down for war crimes and life in prison. What would you be up for if this information got out?"

He wrung his hands, then smoothed them out on his pants, leaving a smear of sweat. "What will it take to keep this quiet?" He licked his lips, a drop of sweat running down his face.

"Okay." I nodded. He was right where I wanted him. "Trembly is no longer in office. You step down as VP. No retirement payments for either of you. Get rid of this unlimited time in office bullshit, get medical attention and food to the people in the ghetto. All the senators, lobbyists, and sundry other people, the Kellers included, actually get prison time and huge fines. I want them broke. I want you broke, too. Donate it to charity, one that you can't touch.

"Finally, you don't come after *any* of us. You did what you did for greed and power. We did what we did to survive. We get amnesty. Moreover, you write a paper right the fuck now stating that, and every motherfucker in here is gonna sign it in the next ten minutes."

Chaos walked around the room, his ear to the wall. He waved, then shook his head. They were coming through, ready or not. Fuck.

Catching Storm's eye, I tilted my head, asking a question. She waggled a hand. *Not yet.* Aanisah studied a panel, leaning in and sniffing. I hoped like hell they were getting close.

"Get writing," I snarled, grabbing a book and tearing out a blank piece of paper. "Make it quick but thorough."

In two minutes, he had a nice, general amnesty written out. *I hereby declare that all persons on the West Coast, from Washington, Oregon, and California, are given amnesty for anything and everything they have done in order to survive and regain their freedom.*

Signed,

I read it over. "Get signing. You lot!" I waved to the senators. "Line up, bitches! You've got to put your signature on this piece of paper. If you choose not to, that's okay. It just means that Baser has more people to look into."

"Me?" Baser looked up, her hazel eyes wide.

"Yeah, you. Rumor has it you're the only one with anything remotely resembling a moral compass. So, you're the only one I can trust to actually make shit happen."

She glanced quickly around the room. "Fine, but later. I'm going back with you."

I snorted. "The hell you are!"

She snorted back. "The hell I am! If I'm going to properly investigate, I need information from the source. I need to see Oregon, what you've done, and talk to the people, especially the ones held captive by Lt Colonel Keller."

"I'm going, too." Senator Edmund looked up from signing the amnesty. "I don't know what my constituents need anymore. It's time to reconnect."

"I'll go as well." Deloris from Oregon folded her arms, glaring stoutly around the room. "And if you try to stop me, I'll...I'll...I won't sign your paper!"

I'd barely begun arguing when Perry appeared from the edges of the room. He drew a finger across his throat repeatedly.

"Fine," I snapped. "But don't fall behind."

"What?" Deloris looked around. "All we have to do is open the doors."

I half laughed. "Are you crazy? As far as those guys are concerned, we're dangerous and insane. Okay, they're not wrong, but they'll come in shooting. I'll have to get violent to protect my people, and the next thing you know, we're all in prison for the rest of our lives. Not happening. We're busting out of this joint. You just need to keep up."

The senators weren't moving fast enough. "Pick up the pace, people!"

The banging noises were clearly audible now. Senators scribbled what I could only hope were their real names on the piece of paper. Movement from the base of the VP's desk caught my eye. A panel sat open. Storm led the way in, closely followed by Mercy—still wearing my leather jacket—Constance, and James.

"That's enough!" I shouted, grabbing the amnesty document from the table. "Senator Baser will bring it back with her."

"Wait!" The other Oregon representative pulled out their phone. "Let me just..."

He snapped a photo of the document. Flipping it over, I held it so he could take a picture of the back. "I've got this," he said, giving me a firm nod. "I'll start things over here. There's people we can trust."

I nodded back. "Give the bastards hell."

Other senators were still confused as to what was going on.

"Back? Where's she going?"

"What are you people doing?"

"No time for chit-chat, folks." Shoving the three senators in front of me, I handed them off to Gryph and Phoenix. "Go! Move!"

A section of wall burst inward. Snatching the EM from my pocket, I flung it at the face peering through. He pulled back with a shout.

"Captain!"

Spinning, I went through the low door in a baseball slide. Phoenix slid the panel home, wedging two books behind it. A bright light pierced the dark. Hissing, I averted my eyes. The light shone on the gold lettering of one of the books Phoenix used to stop the door.

The Bible.

"Sorry!" Constance averted the flashlight on her phone. "Just thought this would be easier if we could see."

"Eleanor's gonna be pissed if she finds out you used a Bible," I said.

"What do we do now?" Baser looked around at all of us, crouched or laying in the low tunnel.

"We go the only direction available to us." Storm wriggled around. After a few feet, she gave a tiny, "Yay. The tunnel opens up here," she said, louder.

"Go, go, go." I pushed against Phoenix's feet.

From the sounds, pandemonium still reigned, but it was only a matter of time before they tried that door.

"We're gone." Phoenix cackled. "Holy shit! I can't believe we actually made it into the tunnel."

"Phoenix?"

"Yes?"

"Shut up and walk. Fast."

CHAPTER 39

Portland, OR – Captain

Dereva drove through quiet streets in the late afternoon. Some people were visible in parks, enjoying the unseasonably warm late winter afternoon.

Coming back, we skipped the border gate, cutting the fence, just like we always did, to intense eastern disapproval.

We'd gotten a couple days into Oregon when Dereva and Wilder found us. Only too happy to take the ride, we didn't waste any time. The senators weren't equipped for a long walk, and we didn't have enough food for a long journey, anyway.

We stayed at a homestead along the way, the kids staring wide-eyed at obvious strangers, but the adults were welcoming, offering us a dry place to sleep in the barn.

It'd only been a week since that day at the Capitol, and I still couldn't quite believe we made it safely into Oregon. Or that I could refer to Oregon and the Pacific Northwest as 'safe.'

The senators, bundled up to their eyebrows, stared around Portland. Baser pulled her scarf down. "Where are all the people? I thought you said..."

I pointed. Ahead of us, a crowd waited in front of two large buildings. The senators, gripping the cab, stood on unsteady legs to look. Rolling my shoulders, I took three deep breaths.

Too many people, when I looked for only six.

At the front of the crowd, a heavily pregnant Amana waited. Leaping from the pickup before it rolled to a stop, I went to her.

"I brought some more mouths to feed," I said, the scene both reassuringly familiar and oddly strange, topped as it was by wild cheers. "Sorry."

"Humph." But her mouth curled into a smile as she stretched her hands out to me. "Welcome home."

Bending my head, I pressed my forehead to hers, eyes closed, taking a moment to realize *I was home.* Now, I just had to figure out how to live in it. What did I do now? Go back to being a mechanic? I was also a mother, but I'd only had a couple months' experience at that job.

Shoving it back, I firmly resolved to take it day by day. *I can do this. But it'd be so much easier and more fun with you.*

Under cover of the cheers, in this relative privacy, she whispered, "Your family is here, safe, and healthy. All is well."

I nodded, our foreheads rubbing painfully. "Thank you."

A conversation went on just behind us.

"How did they know we were coming?"

"Amana knows all."

"What?"

"You get used to it."

The rest of it was drowned out by a shriek. "Amana!" Storm ran over. I pulled away, and she got her first good look at her sister. "*Why didn't you tell me you were pregnant?!*"

Leaving them to their reunion, I moved through the crowd, looking for my family. People I didn't recognize kept getting in my way, then hurriedly moving out of it. Vaguely, I heard Phoenix and Gryph introducing the easterners to the locals, but all that died away when I spotted my sister, standing next to Charlie.

In front of them, two blond little boys danced around, barely kept close by the adults' grips on their tiny little hands. My knees went weak, and I sank slowly to the ground right as Grace spotted me.

Tears filled my eyes. My little babies weren't so little anymore.

They led my boys over. "Look!" Grace pointed at me. "That's your mama."

The little boy's face scrunched. "'at's not mama! 'at's Cap'n!"

The tears flowed freely, now. "Can I be both?"

But they held back. Not shy, not these ones. They were their father's sons. But wary of me, of Captain. I could only hope time would fix that, but until then...

"Captain!"

Turning slightly, still on my knees, I barely caught the girl who flung herself into my arms. Pulling back slightly, I recognized Cub's growing features. Her downy hair now grew thick and long, several shades darker than when she'd been a toddler herself. I reckoned her to be around ten by now, though no one knew for certain. But that didn't matter, not with those wiry arms wrapped tight around my neck.

"You came back! I knew you would. And you got Steve gone, too. I knew you'd do that. I told the other kids you would."

Seeing me with Cub made Michael and Gabriel bold. The boys stood just within arm's reach, watching us.

"I want a hug," one boy announced.

It caused a fresh wave of tears, but I freed an arm, pulling him in. Looking at the other one, I asked, "Would you like a hug, too?"

He nodded, walking forward with his father's confident attitude. "Yes."

Epilogue - The Present

H ope stared into the blazing lights, her eyes unseeing, still lost in the past. "It's amazing how people forget. Aashna did her best, and for a while, the big, sweeping changes we needed did happen." She shook herself, the corners of her mouth quirking. "But we don't need to get into that. We know about Aashna Baser."

She paced down the length of the stage. In the crowd, the tension slowly eased. They hadn't been freed from her spell, not yet, but the strength of it waned. "I do have one request for all of you."

"What?" a random voice from the crowd shouted.

There was a smattering of laughter, and the hint of a smile on the rebel leader's face blossomed. "I need you all to remember this day, this story. Old man Keller is dead now," she paused at the cheers through the small stadium, "but Annaliese and good old Arnold have never faced consequences like they should."

She paused, considering her next words carefully, then shrugged. "Fuck it. We did terrible things, and experienced wonderful moments. We did the impossible. Now, it's your turn. You are the new generation. Be uncivilly disobedient until they make the changes we need to continue having a better world. Don't let them roll back what we accomplished here.

"I never planned on talking about the past. In truth, if it hadn't been for my boys, I wouldn't have. So my request to you is this: Don't forget the former Vice President, Darwen Plummer. Make him afraid of the consequences of his actions. Through his greed, and a shitty mother's desperation, they spawned a war that slaughtered hundreds of thousands."

"We sacrificed everything!" she shouted to be heard over the crowd's cheering and screaming. "Our actions from the past are meaningless without you. Tonight, I'm officially passing the torch to you. Anyone who hears or sees this, you are now part of the Oregonian Irregulars.

"We are family. Your sorrows are our sorrows, your joys, our joys. We rise or fall together. Like the Phoenix," she pointed to the front row, where Alexandra Carrington sat, "let us rise!"

The crowd roared, but to the reporters and journalists who missed nothing, she seemed strangely limp, as if she'd released a huge weight and didn't know how to stand anymore. Tipping her face to the star-studded sky, a close observer could see a tear run down her cheek.

Still, the crowd continued to celebrate. Below the roar of the crowd, tinny voices in earpieces demanded more information, uncaring that she'd laid bare her most glorious days and her worst nightmares for the consumption of strangers, in the hopes of leading them to a better way of being.

Hope watched them curiously, numb after plumbing the depths of her every emotion. She hadn't expected such jubilation, though she didn't know what, exactly, she had expected. Maybe for them to file out solemnly, weighed down by the knowledge of all those deaths. Or perhaps, they could be angry that their own government had perpetrated the greatest calamity to ever take place on American soil and demand radical reform.

"What about the files?" one journalist, braver than the rest, shouted to the war leader. "Can we have those?"

Her fingers went to her neck, fishing out a fine cord. The bright lights flashed across an old scar over her collarbone before she drew out a small pendant. Pulling the cord over her head, she knelt at the edge of the stage.

"Take it," she said wearily. "Make copies. Put it everywhere. Because it seems that the first time we did it, they managed to erase it. Don't let them erase us again."

Walking to the center front of the stage, she found her family, sitting in the front row. The twins looked like they'd been through the war themselves. Then, Gabriel untangled himself from the Carringtons and their children.

The stage stood barely two strides from the front row. He crossed them in one, reaching up to grasp her ankle.

"It's not in vain, Mom. I swear it's not."

Slowly, she reached out, resting her hand on his bright gold hair, looking into eyes almost as deep a blue as his father's. "Thank you."

Post Script - 5 Years Later

Washington, DC

ANZ News: Today, Ms Hope Sanders has been formally acquitted of all charges relating to her last, explosive, visit to Washington DC, and of the events surrounding her...ahem, taking the entire Senate hostage on February 12, 2071.

The court was packed with her former followers, the self-named Oregonian Irregulars. They proceeded to intimidate everyone around them, to no one's amusement except their own. How Judge Chalmers found the former rebel leader innocent is beyond the comprehension of this journalist and all those who seek justice for the terrified people in the Senate House that day. When Ms Sanders herself took the stand, Judge Chalmers nearly had to empty the courthouse, due to the wild behavior of these Irregulars, led by two young men we have recently discovered are the children of Ms Sanders...

Hope lay in darkness, water slowly seeping into her clothes.

Where...?

She fought to breathe around the pain in her stomach.

What...?

She'd been walking after the after-acquittal party. Yes. Then... An alley. A woman. Screaming. Two men. One hand scrabbled weakly, found the barrel of a pistol. Still warm. The scent of gunpowder. Her other hand finally climbed the tortuous distance to her stomach, fluttering around the oblong hole there.

A knife.

Yes. One of the men got in a lucky shot. The angle...the angle said she didn't have long.

Warmth flowed steadily over her still fingers.

Her head lolled. There. A man-shaped lump. Just beyond her feet lay another, arms outstretched. Hah. She wouldn't be going alone, then.

Hope sighed, remembering that day five years ago, when she'd stood on a stage and told the world her darkest secrets and greatest joys.

A good day. The day she'd finally repaired her relationship with her children. The day their lives started anew. They'd been a real family again.

Her eyes slid closed, a tiny smile curling her lips as a tear trickled down her cheek. People remembered him. Even after all these years, people remembered him. Would they remember her as fondly?

She wanted Noah. She needed to feel his arms around her again, see his smile, taste his kiss. Would she finally join him? If it meant seeing him again, she'd welcome death as the old friend he was.

Die for a cause. Die for a reason. Was dying to see a loved one a reason? A young woman's frightened face danced at the edge of her vision. Yes. There'd been a woman. She was safe. She'd run towards the street, screaming for help. So, she'd been stabbed doing something good.

Good enough to get her into heaven? Because surely, Noah would be there.

Her sight darkened, the shouting at the alley's entrance growing more distant by the second. Golden light, purple and cobalt at the edges, grew, filled her entire vision. A shadow slowly coalesced in the light, forming into the wavering figure of a man.

So dark, this man. Had he come to drag her to hell? She knew, with every fiber of her being, she hadn't been good enough to see her family again.

To see her heart again.

Except...

As the man approached, her vision cleared, cobwebs dropping from her eyes. Bright blond hair... Deep blue eyes... Her own filled with tears, spilling hotly down her cold cheeks. It'd been so long.

"Noah," she breathed.

"You got here a bit sooner than I would have hoped." Noah smiled, reaching down for her hand. His fingers closed around hers, warm and *real*.

How...?

"Was...wasn't trying to rush."

He knelt, cupping her cheek, pressing his forehead to hers as her breathing slowed. She smiled, truly at peace for the first time in years.

"It's okay, babe. It's time."

"Hail the victorious dead," she whispered, sagging against the wall.

When the first responders arrived, her pale, gray blue eyes stared sightlessly into the night, a faint smile still on her lips, her breathing stilled.

Author's Note

T hank you so much for joining me on this journey!

It was such a privilege to bring the Oregonian Irregulars and **The Northwest Uprising** to you.

If you're not ready to say goodbye to strong, multidimensional leading women and you want to keep in touch, you can subscribe to my newsletter at the QR code below AND download the first 2 completed chapters of my newest book *The Stillness Within the Storm,* book 1 of The Dragon Queen Cycle.

If you enjoyed the books, I would love it if you would let your friends know and bring them into this budding family!

And, as always, please leave a review! Every review helps more readers find great books :)

Again, thank you so much for coming with me on this adventure!

What's Next?

As I mentioned in the Note, I'm working on a new series, The Dragon Queen Cycle. Here's a raw Sneak Peek into Chapter 1 of Book 1, *The Stillness Within the Storm*

FYI: This is a wholly unedited first draft. Even though it's complete, I thought it'd be fun* for you to see how much it changes.

*I'm surprisingly nervous about showing you a piece of the first draft. NO ONE has ever seen anything first draft before.

Chapter 1

Jennifer shifted in her seat, trapped between a sleeping soldier and the window. Peering over his sprawled form, she caught the eye of the sergeant in the aisle seat.

"I have to go," she whispered, barely audible over the airplane's white noise. He nodded. "I can just...climb over him."

At that, the sergeant frowned. "Absolutely not," he said in a normal voice. The young soldier next to her snorted in his sleep, sagging further into her space. The sergeant seized the young man's ear, squeezing until his fingers turned white. The soldier shot up with a yelp, waking the passengers closest to them. "Wakey wakey," the sergeant said with an evil grin. "It's time for you to be a hero."

"Wha-? Sir!" The soldier squirmed in his seat, pulling his arms and legs in.

Jen covered her face in embarrassment when the sergeant pulled the soldier out. "My name's Sergeant Owen Jeffries, miss. If you need anything—including making obnoxious soldiers move—you just send for me."

Jen edged into the aisle. "Um, thank you. I wouldn't want to put you out."

Sergeant Jeffries laughed. Jen couldn't help but smile at his infectious laughter. The sergeant, older than the young soldier he held, looked between thirty and thirty-five, with thick, light brown hair cut severely short, and hazel eyes. Jeffries shook the soldier to the amusement of the other passengers.

"Apologize to the lady for taking up so much space she had to ask me for help, pup."

"Sorry, ma'am."

"And give her your name, in case she wants to complain!"

"Private Gavin Novak, ma'am, assigned to the 116th. Ma'am." Gavin straightened as much as he could with his ear held firmly by the sergeant. With his chocolaty brown eyes and dark brown hair, curling where the Army barbers left it a little longer, he certainly looked like the puppy Sergeant Jeffries called him.

"Oh, I won't be making any complaints." Jen squeezed her legs together, desperate for this to end so she could use the toilet one more time. They had to be landing soon, didn't they? "I'm sorry, I just..."

"You go on, miss." Sergeant Jeffries shook Gavin again. "We'll be right here, having a little talk about politeness and not taking up more than your fair share of space, won't we, puppy?"

Gavin squeaked in the sergeant's grip. Unable to wait any longer, Jen hurried down the single aisle. On her way, she looked around the cabin, hoping to see another white jacket like hers, with a red cross over the heart and another on the arm, but it was a sea of camouflage.

The pilot's voice rang out over the intercom while she was in the toilet. "Ladies and gentlemen, please return to your seats, as the seatbelt sign is now turned on. We will be landing in about twenty minutes. Local time is five pm, London time. We here at UN Airlines would like to thank you for your service.

"Cabin crew, prepare the plane for landing."

Jen hurriedly squeezed back into her seat, much more comfortable now that she didn't have the pressure on her bladder or a sprawling man next to her. Peering out the window, she watched the coastline grow rapidly.

Biting her lip, she devoured everything she could see. At twenty-five years old, she finally had her first time on a plane, and she went straight to dream destination, England!

The plane bounced lightly on landing, wind roaring around the wings as they decelerated. Jen clutched the arms of her seat with white fingers, eyes wide as she watched the ground race past her window. As soon as the seatbelt sign turned off, everyone stood up, even though they had nowhere to go.

She wrinkled her nose at them. It didn't make sense.

Gavin opened the overhead locker. "Which bag is yours, ma'am?"

"You don't have to call me 'ma'am,'" she said, reaching under the seat in front of her. "I'm Jen. And my bag is right here."

She pulled a backpack out, hauling it onto her lap.

"I can help you get your other bag from the baggage claim." Gavin pulled a small bag out, setting it on the seat next to her.

Sergeant Jeffries already stood in the aisle, the plane slowly taxiing to a stop. Men filled the aisle, waiting with varying degrees of patience for the doors to open.

"It's okay." Jen hugged her bag. She had a few books, some socks and underwear, a spare sweatshirt, jeans, and three t-shirts, as well as her toiletries in the full backpack. "This is everything."

Jeffries glanced at her sharply. Catching his look, Jen turned back to the window, the silence around her suddenly painful.

"Well, Jen," Gavin said heartily, "looks like you're perfect for England, then, all things considered."

"Miss," Jeffries broke in, "where are you headed? Or is Bristol your final stop?"

"London." She finally looked at him again. So much concern, and from a stranger...

"And if I want to check in on you, make sure none of these puppies are being insufferable? Name, rank, serial number!"

"Jennifer Banprionse, nurse, serial number one-eight-zero-four-seven-en-seven, sir!" She straightened, throwing her shoulders back.

"Banprionse, huh?" Jeffries shifted, the line finally moving. "I'll see you there, kid."

Jen offered him a timid smile, responding to the warmth the sergeant offered, when the world exploded.

***

Incoherent screaming filled her ears. Groaning, Jen tried to move, but her arms wouldn't work. Panicking, she thrashed, opening her eyes. The seat sat three inches from her eyes. Blinking and squinting, she followed it up. She lay on the floor, in the narrow space where her feet had been resting for hours.

Twisting, she looked up at clouds lit red and orange. Staring at it for long moments, she pondered this. Hadn't there just been an airplane? Yes, because the seats were around her, still in their neat rows.

"Miss! Jen. Jen!" A rough hand grabbed hers, and Sergeant Jeffries's worried face appeared in her view. "Are you alright, girl? Does anything hurt?"

Struggling upright, Jen shook her head. "No, I'm...I'm fine." She looked down at her arms. Yes, everything was here. Ten fingers, two legs, two feet. She'd have to take it for granted she had all her toes, since her old work boots were still in one piece.

"What about you?" She surveyed him, then gasped. "Your shoulder!"

"Never mind me, woman. I'm upright."

"Never *mind?* You have a chunk of metal sticking out of you!"

A slightly curved, white piece of metal protruded from his left shoulder, just below his clavicle. Roughly four inches visible, she calculated, but there was no way of knowing how much was embedded. The thoughts popped into her head, and she finally remembered the red cross on her white jacket.

She'd been training as a medic for the last year for just such a situation as this.

Galvanized, she grabbed the back of the seat, hauling herself out. Wind ruffled her hair, and she stopped, shock of the impact giving way before the impossible scene surrounding her.

The entire top half of the plane was gone. Completely. The lowering clouds were lit by multiple fires. The terminal burned, the fires swiftly spreading. People rushed about, but most of those on the plane were injured. All around her, men cried, or worse, were silent.

She stared at the destruction, her heart beating like a mad thing. Clenching her shaking hands into fists, she bit her lip, using the minor pain to draw herself back. *Begin with what's in front of you,* Nurse Haskell always said. *Help those you can see first, worry about the rest later.*

What was right in front of her? Sergeant Jeffries.

"Don't touch that," she snapped when he probed the metal shard. "Do you want to bleed to death? You have arteries near there, and I don't know how close that is to them."

"I can't help with this in me," he complained, sitting only when she pushed him down.

"You'll help even less if you're dead."

Ripping open her backpack, she pulled out her small, personal first-aid kit and a t-shirt. She took a moment to read the slogan one last time—*Not all those who wander are lost*—then ripped it along a seam. Rolling it, she wrapped it around the shard, then used a bandage to hold it in place.

"If you really want to help," she said, taping the pieces in place, "I need you to triage the wounded." Training had gone over triage many times. Hopefully, she'd remember everything. Right now, one step at a time. "Do you know how to triage?"

Jeffries snorted. "I've been on a couple of battlefields in my time. Oi! Anybody here capable of standing?"

"I can stand." Gavin Novak struggled up from the seat across the aisle.

Stepping over a still body, Jen examined him briefly. "Just let me get this leg taken care of first."

He had a deep gash on his thigh, but nothing spurted. *Thank God.* Another t-shirt, another bandage. She should have brought more clothes. Oh, wait, she'd left without permission, carrying only what she could fit in her backpack.

"We need to get out of the plane." Jeffries stepped carefully over men crying and groaning. "You'll have more space to work out there," he said when she opened her mouth to protest.

"While you get the doors open, I'm going to see if there's any gushers." It'd been strange, during training, when her teachers would call a wound by a casual name, but here, on the ground, it made sense. Like this, everyone knew what kind of an injury she referred to, rather than only trained medical staff.

They'd been adamant that treating gushers—open wounds with blood pouring out of them, it didn't matter where it was located—first saved the most lives.

"All right!" Gavin waved. "We've got the door open and the stairs are in place."

"Take these men outside first." Jen pointed to the ones she'd already bandaged. "They should be stable enough for now. But I can't wait for you to bring them out to me."

Begin with what's in front of you. Fine. Squaring her shoulders, Jen sorted through the people on the plane.

Acknowledgements

Thank you to Tatiana Baghdanov, Olia Baghdanov, and Judy Sullivan. You guys are the best beta readers an author can hope for!

Thank you to my editor, Dave Pasquantonio. Your insights, comments, and questions always lead to a better book. And of course, your encouragement keeps me going.

A special shout-out to Chrystal Zaplishny, who won the drawing, for naming the leader of Jefferson County, Catherine Rose, or Rosie to her friends.

Finally, a huge Thank You to everyone who participated in my Kickstarter campaign! Without you, we wouldn't have these gorgeous maps!

To my Backers:

Olia Baghdanov, Alexandra Corrsin, Judy Sullivan, Cynthia Coffman, Kendell Macomber, Mania Siapin, Jessica, Hillary Stone, Tatiana Baghdanov, Hanya, Katy, Suzanna Kudryashov, Brittany Tilley, Raya Siapin, Aingeal Wroth, LJ Shubin, Megan Kell, Danae, Sven Lugar, Angela, Chrystal, Joanna Siapin, Rachel, Paul

Thank you!

About Author

Nadya Siapin is the author of The Northwest Uprising trilogy and is now moving into Arthurian myths with The Dragon Queen Cycle.

An avid traveler and story lover, she mixes what she knows with what she imagines and is always on the lookout for slightly insane, definitely chaotic quotes for some characters 2 series into the future. (Sometimes, she manages to plan ahead.)

A dual citizen of the United States and Australia, Nadya uses her travel and backpacking experience extensively in her writing. She splits her time between the US and Australia. She can (occasionally)be persuaded to wear shoes. You can check out her other work or follow her on social media here.

instagram.com/nadya_siapin/

facebook.com/nadya.siapin.author/

tiktok.com/@nadyasiapin.author